I0634716

CHINA STAR

A Novel

Copyright © 2024 Maurice Medland

All rights reserved. No portion of this book may be reproduced in any fashion, print, facsimile, or electronic, or by any method yet to be developed, without the express written permission of the publisher.

ISBN: 978-0-7953-0107-0

Published in 2024 by RosettaBooks

RosettaBooks is a registered trademark licensed to RB Content, LLC

www.rosettabooks.com

CHINA STAR

A Novel

by

MAURICE MEDLAND

RosettaBooks®

For my family

Acknowledgements

Sincere thanks go to:

Lieutenant Commander David Randall, Director of Training for the Naval Diving and Salvage Training Center in Panama City, Florida, for reading and correcting the passages on marine salvage operations;

My son, Lieutenant Commander Steve Medland, formerly of USS *Tunny* (SSN 682), for his comments and corrections on submarine operations;

The talented staff at The Editorial Department—Ross Browne, Renni Browne, and Peter Gelfan—for helping take this book to the next level;

My agent, Bob Diforio, for his always wise counsel and unflagging efforts on my behalf;

And finally, to my wonderful family—my wife, Karen, my daughter Melissa and her husband Rick, my son Steve and his wife Kim, and the most beautiful grandchildren imaginable, Lauren, Kristen, and Blake. Thanks, guys, for your love, support and friendship. I love you all very much.

Any errors are mine alone.

The weak have one weapon:
the errors of those who think they are strong.
—*Georges Bidault*
French Journalist and Politician

Chapter One

"**S**uits on the quarterdeck, Skipper."

Matt Connor cursed under his breath. Through the dark glass of the welder's mask, he focused on the bead forming up around the patch. There was no need to look. Suits could only mean Kaohsiung port officials, American IRS agents, or Gray Wolf's enforcers. Whichever they were, they were trouble, the kind that could shut him down. *Lousy timing.* In a few hours he'd have been under way.

"Not now, Sam. Get rid of them."

"One of 'em's wearing a skirt."

"I don't care what they're wearing, get rid of them. If they're from Gray Wolf, tell them the check's in the mail."

Sam laughed and said in his rich baritone, "I think he's heard that one before." He squinted into the late afternoon sun glimmering across Kaohsiung Harbor. "Anyway, they don't look much like Gray Wolf's boys."

Matt blew out a long breath. That left Kaohsiung port officials and American IRS agents. They could cause him a lot of trouble, but at least they couldn't kill him.

He dialed the feed down, and the acetylene torch flickered out with a pop. He tilted the mask up, leaned back against a capstan, and wiped his forehead with the back of his hand. He wasn't worried about being seen. Dressed in his grubbies, there was nothing that would distinguish him from a dozen other crewmen swarming over the ship, making preparations to get under way. He shielded his eyes and focused on the pair.

The man was black, early forties, close-cropped hair graying at the temples, dark suit. The woman was white, late twenties or early thirties, short brown hair, cream-colored business suit with a short skirt. Damn. He'd thrown enough IRS agents off his ship to know them when he saw them. They looked as if they'd been plucked out of their offices in Washington, D.C., and set down in the Taiwan seaport without a hair out of place.

The IRS sent out a new team of agents to harass him every few months, and they had a talent for showing up at the worst possible time. The pair stood awkwardly on the quarterdeck, clutching briefcases, flinching at the chaos around them.

Matt couldn't blame them. *CoMar Explorer* appeared to be in a state of total confusion. Cranes swung pallets of supplies aboard as crewmen scrambled to secure topside equipment and make last-minute repairs. On the dock below, a chain of longshoremen shouted commands in Mandarin, passing crates of provisions into the ship's hold, while engineers in blue jumpsuits pumped acrid-smelling diesel fuel into her tanks. He smiled at the anxious look on the agents' faces. Bureaucrats out in the real world.

The bastards never gave up. If you want to be Public Enemy Number One in America, just start your own business. Every federal, state, and local agency in existence will come swooping down on you, trying to bleed you dry with one hand and close you down with the other. After a year of trying to comply with countless idiotic government regulations, he'd moved his ocean-salvage business out of the U.S. to the Republic of China—more commonly known as Taiwan—and established new headquarters in Kaohsiung, a bustling seaport on the South China Sea.

He'd thought that would solve the problem, but he couldn't bring himself to give up his U.S. citizenship—which convinced the Internal Revenue Service that part of the money he made was theirs, no matter where in the world he made it. Neither Matt nor his lawyer saw it that way, but the IRS had more lawyers than he did and slapped a $2,800,000 lien on his ship. He didn't have the time or money to fight them, but it didn't matter; as long as he stayed out of the U.S., they couldn't touch *CoMar Explorer*.

His first instinct was to throw the agents off his ship, but something about the woman—a kind of aura around her—made him hesitate. At first he thought it was the sun behind her that gave her that radiant quality, but her companion had the same sun behind him and he didn't glow. He stared at her. A gentle breeze lifted her hair, pressed her skirt against her thighs. He told himself there'd be no harm in seeing them; they were on his turf now and couldn't do anything to hurt him. The truth was that he hadn't talked to a woman—especially an American woman—in a very long time.

"Take them to the crew's lounge," he said. "Have Francisco get them some coffee. I need to change my shirt."

"Aye aye, Skipper."

He ducked down through the after hatch and paused on the ladder with his head above deck. "Make sure the fuel tanks are topped off, Sam. We've got a long way to go."

"Go where, Skipper?"

Matt suppressed a laugh. He hadn't told anyone where they were headed, not even his first mate. No one was going to scoop him on this job. It was too big and too important to the survival of Connor Marine. He flashed an exaggerated grin.

"You'll find out along with everyone else once we're at sea."

He slid down the ladder to the second deck and wound his way forward to his sea cabin, checking along the way to see that everything belowdecks was secured, dodging questions from crew members. They'd be under way by midnight, and he'd announce their destination and answer all their questions once they were far at sea. He was sure they'd like what they heard. Unlike the crews of most ocean-salvage companies, Matt's shared in the profits, like pirates of old, and this job promised to be the biggest in the company's history.

"Hey, Traveller." Matt tousled the fur of the scrawny yellow dog sprawled across the deck in his sea cabin. "You're about to live up to your name, old buddy. We're fixing to make tracks." The dog put its head down and went back to sleep, paws crossed, while Matt rummaged in his locker for a shirt. He found a blue one, faded but clean, and pulled it on while he glanced around the room. He liked this small cabin, used it exclusively for his quarters whether in port or at sea. Unlike the captain's stateroom, which was luxurious and isolated, the sea cabin was spartan, just a bunk, a desk, and a locker. But it was located near the bridge, where he could see what was going on.

Fumbling with the buttons on his shirt, he looked out the porthole at the black nuclear sub moored across the way. The USS *Salt Lake*

City, a Los Angeles-class attack boat, had come in early that morning. In all the time he'd spent in Kaohsiung, he'd never seen a U.S. attack boat in the harbor before, and the damned thing had parked right across from him. He probably knew some of the senior officers aboard. He had no doubt that they knew of him.

Like the IRS agents, the sub had shown up at the worst possible time. Seeing it brought back memories he'd been struggling with for years, and right now he needed to stay focused. As he watched, a young officer in khakis came aboard, saluted the colors, and dropped down the after hatch. The thought of a hatch screwing down over his head made him suck air into his lungs. He wiped sweat from his forehead and saw his hand tremble. *Christ*. Nothing had changed. He closed the porthole and turned away.

That part of his life was over, but just seeing the sub reminded him how much he missed the Navy. He could never go down in one of those steel coffins again, yet in his most private fantasies he saw himself having his commission restored. There wasn't much chance of that. No chance, in fact, now that he was persona non grata in the U.S.

Matt let out a sigh and sat down at his desk, grateful for what he did have. Starting with one beat-up tugboat in San Diego, he'd built Connor Marine & Salvage into a small but respected company. It was a boom or bust business that demanded eighteen-hour days and seven-day weeks, but he couldn't stay away from the sea. He'd managed to keep afloat during the busts by borrowing on his ocean-going tug to keep his crew intact. It had been a gamble, but his crew had never missed a paycheck, even in the leanest of times, and the gamble had paid off. He now had a bulldog-loyal crew of the best divers and salvors in the industry.

But even the best crew would take you only so far without the right equipment. After years of scrimping, a couple of lucrative jobs, and a four-million-dollar loan from Gray Wolf, he'd finally been able to buy a decommissioned salvage ship from a broker in Amsterdam. She was a 1930s vintage ship the Dutch Navy had declared surplus, and he felt a certain kinship with the cast-off vessel. She'd been through several owners and was a sad spectacle by the time he brought her limping into Kaohsiung Harbor.

He'd put his heart into her restoration, feeling somehow that in proving the old ship was worth another lease on life, he was proving the same thing about himself. After months of hard work she still looked rough on the outside, but her main systems were functional and Matt was convinced that he was now in a position to compete for the major salvage contracts. Mortgaged to the hilt, he'd re-christened her with the lofty name *CoMar Explorer*, in honor of a ship he'd always admired, and waited for the phone to ring. It was another huge gamble, but all he needed was one big job to stay alive, and it looked like he had it.

He unlocked the center drawer of his desk and retrieved the fax from his agent. A U.S. flag freighter with a load of manganese had run aground on an island off Macau. A job like this could be worth 25 percent of the value of the ship and cargo—maybe five or six million dollars—depending on the weather conditions and the difficulty of the job.

He glanced at his watch. June 10. Big jobs didn't come along often, and with a payment on *CoMar Explorer* in arrears, this one had come along just in time. Gray Wolf wasn't known for his patience.

The phone on his desk buzzed. He swiveled around and hit the speakerphone button.

"Captain."

"Hey, Boss-man. When you come?"

Matt sighed. "'Captain,' Francisco, not 'Boss-man.' You're a sailor now."

"Francisco chef, no sailor."

"Everyone on my ship is a sailor."

"Not me, Boss-man."

"What do you want, Francisco?"

"Man in suit 'bout to bust. He say why you not come?"

Matt felt a knot form in his stomach. He looked at his watch, sorry now that he'd agreed to see the two IRS agents.

"I'm on my way."

He switched off the speakerphone, locked the dispatch away in his desk drawer, retrieved his tax attorney's card from his card file, and walked aft to the crew's lounge with Traveller close at his heels. He paused at the door. The woman sat on a leather couch drumming her fingers on her briefcase, while the man stood behind her, pacing.

"Welcome to Kaohsiung," Matt said, stepping over the coaming. "I hope you've had a pleasant trip, but I think you've wasted your time. We've been all through this before."

"All through what?" the black man said.

"Two-point-eight million in back taxes and penalties. You say I owe it. I say I don't." He took the dog-eared business card from his shirt pocket. "Here's my tax attorney in San Diego. Talk to him."

The man walked around from behind the couch. Smiled. Full of himself. "We're not from the IRS." He extended his hand. "Cliff Howard, U.S. State Department." He nodded to the woman on the couch. "This is Susan Elliott, Central Intelligence Agency."

Matt blinked. What the hell could the State Department and the CIA want with him? He made an attempt at a smile.

"Sorry. You government types all look alike."

The woman's eyes made the trip up and down his too-lean frame, his faded blue shirt, grease-stained khakis, and scuffed boots.

"You're Matthew Connor?"

Matt felt his ears tingle. He'd had about four hours sleep and knew he looked like hell, but it galled him to have some manicured bureaucrat—even one with an aura—look at him as though he'd crawled out of a cardboard box.

"Some of us have to work for a living."

"I'm sorry, I didn't mean—"

"Forget it."

Matt glanced at their ID's and took a seat on the couch opposite her. There wasn't that much difference in their ages, maybe ten years, but she made him feel old. Traveller sat beside him, sphinx-like, staring up at the pair. A low growl emitted from his throat.

"Nice doggy," Susan Elliott said.

"Don't patronize him," Matt said. "He's had a hard life."

"Why's he growling?"

"You survive on the docks by knowing trouble when you see it." Matt reached down and stroked the dog's ragged ears. "Cool it, Trav."

"Don't tell me, let me guess. I bet his name is Travis, like Travis McGee, because you live on a boat."

"I live on a ship and his name is Traveller."

"After an insurance company?"

"Two L's. A horse."

Susan Elliott's eyes widened. "Oh, I get it. Robert E. Lee's famous horse. Are you a southerner?"

Matt gave her a dip of the head. So she was well-read. "Just a student of military history."

Cliff Howard twisted in his seat. "Can we get down to business here?"

"Sure," Matt said. He glanced over their perfect hair, across Kaohsiung Harbor at the container ships moored at Chichin Island. He'd always prided himself on being able to size people up in about three seconds, and these two were no challenge. Howard was square-jawed and aristocratic-looking, older than he'd first thought, a bureaucrat used to waving his government credentials around. Susan Elliott was maybe in her late twenties, not yet experienced enough to know how to throw hers around. Or maybe she had a different weapon, an athletic body poured into a short-skirted business suit that exposed an unbusinesslike amount of thigh when she crossed her legs. Now that he'd met her, he was sorry he'd let his libido talk him into this. She was pretty, no doubt about that, but she seemed to have all the maturity of a teenager. He glanced at his watch, eager to be rid of them and under way. "What can I do for you?"

"We're looking for someone for a special assignment," Cliff Howard said. "When we asked around, your name came up. When we found out you were Admiral Jacobs's brother-in-law—"

"Ex brother-in-law."

"He said you'd be quick to point that out," Susan Elliott said, tugging at her skirt.

Cliff Howard glanced at her. "When we found out you were related, we went to see him."

7

"How is he?" Matt said.

"Fine," Susan Elliott said. "He was just appointed CNO."

"*Jake*?" Chief of Naval Operations. He'd had no idea. But he shouldn't have been surprised to learn that his old mentor had the number one job in the Navy. Jake had a gift for politics, knew how to use people to get what he wanted. Not bad. Four stars on his collar, a corner office on the E-ring, and a four-striper for a secretary. His ex brother-in-law had gone as far up as Matt had gone down, and at about the same speed. He managed a smile. "Good for him."

"He had good things to say about you," Susan Elliott said.

"I'll bet."

"No, really. He said you'd someday have been sitting in his chair as CNO if you hadn't been so hardheaded."

"Let's cut the crap," Matt said. "I'm sure you know I left the Navy under a very big cloud."

"We've gone over your record," Cliff Howard said. "What we were hearing from everyone didn't jibe with what we were seeing in your file. That's why we went to see Admiral Jacobs."

"Great guy," Susan Elliott said. "Old Navy family. He said you'd have gone all the way if you hadn't resigned over some fire aboard a nuclear submarine. He said his sister, Barbara, wanted to be married to an admiral. She walked out when you resigned your commission. You pretty much lost everything overnight. Is that about right?"

Matt glared at her. Jake must have left out the part about his father disowning him. "You tell me. You've got all the answers."

"Not all. Why did you resign?"

"That's none of your business."

"He said you'd say that, but he did his own private investigation of the fire. He told us you were executive officer of the USS *Phoenix*, a nuclear-powered attack submarine. At thirty-two, the youngest in the Navy. Fire broke out under way, running deep off the Marianas. A man died before you brought it under control. You and the skipper were automatically relieved.

"The skipper's career was finished, but the Navy's a little more forgiving for an exec, especially a rising star. Admiral Jacobs tried to convince you to stay and rebuild your career, but you refused. He said you'd have had to expose someone else—a chief named Flemons—for the delay in reporting the fire, and you wouldn't do it. He couldn't figure out why you covered for him, but when he went poking around he found out the chief had a kid who was autistic, needed care for life, and you wouldn't do anything that would cost him his pension."

Matt folded his arms across his chest. So that's what his old mentor had come up with. Let Jake believe what he wanted. He'd die before he'd tell him—or anyone else—what really happened down there.

"He doesn't know what he's talking about."

"He said you wouldn't defend yourself during the Court of Inquiry. The chief could have helped, but he didn't say a word. You accepted full responsibility and resigned. The chief got to finish up his career. He's kicking back in Florida now while you're running a tramp ocean-salvage ship out of Taiwan."

"What do you mean, tramp ship?"

"Isn't that what you call a ship that can't return to the U.S. without being seized for nonpayment of taxes?" she said.

Matt stared at the pair of bureaucrats.

"If there's a point to this, I'd like to know what the hell it is."

"Sorry if this seems intrusive," Cliff Howard said. "The record doesn't always reveal the true story. We just had to find out what happened."

"Why? What do you want from me?"

Cliff Howard nodded to the CIA agent. She opened her briefcase and pulled out a sheaf of papers. On top was an eight-by-ten color photo she slid across the table.

Without picking it up, Matt cocked his head and looked at the picture. Headshot of a young woman. Black dress, short string of pearls, short brown hair, exotic eyes, not much makeup.

"What's this?"

"Her name is Elizabeth Grayson," Susan Elliott said. "She's the only daughter—only child, in fact—of Senator John Grayson."

Matt glanced at the picture again. "She looks Asian."

"Eurasian, actually, her mother is Chinese. One of the famous Tang sisters."

Matt shrugged.

"Prominent Han Chinese family known for, shall we say, marrying well. The eldest sister married the top general in Beijing, the second married a billionaire real estate developer in Hong Kong. The youngest, Elizabeth's mother, emigrated to the U.S. and married a wealthy politician."

Something about the young woman's countenance pulled Matt into the photo. He picked it up. A senator's daughter. It figured. The look on Elizabeth Grayson's face reminded him of his ex-wife. Haughty, disdainful of anyone less intelligent, determined to get what she wanted. Like Barb, she was beautiful, but the look in her eyes said it all. Trouble. *Someone I wouldn't want to know*. He tossed the picture back on the table.

"So?"

"She's a scientist," Howard said, "an expert in microlaser technology. That picture was taken while she was a grad student at MIT. After a teaching stint at UC Berkeley, her cousin, who heads up the largest tech company in China, invited her to do medical research at a lab in Canton—or Guangzhou, as it's now called."

Matt's head came up. Guangzhou was near Macau. He studied the two for a moment, then told himself to stop being paranoid. No one knew he was on his way to Macau, not even Sam.

Howard said, "He convinced her they were on the verge of a breakthrough and that she could help—something to do with killing cancer cells with laser beams."

Matt glanced at his watch.

"According to her parents, she's a pacifist who feels caught between two saber-rattling countries," Elliott said. "She jumped at the chance to do something that might improve relations between the U.S. and China."

"Look," Matt said, "this is all very interesting, but I'm in kind of a hurry."

"Bear with us, Mr. Connor," Howard said. "A cleaning woman

found some secret documents from the lab hidden in her apartment and turned her in. The PLA arrested her and put her on trial for spying. She was convicted and sentenced to ten years in a *laogai*, a forced labor camp."

Laogai. Matt had heard the word whispered by refugees from the mainland. There were thousands of *laogai* throughout China. The literal translation was "reform prison," but everyone knew the sentences meant nothing. Most people who entered the camps never came out. And those few who did were never quite the same. He shuddered at the thought of an American woman caught up in that system, then shook the feeling off. It wasn't his problem.

"Tough break," Matt said, "but it seems to me if you go to another country and steal their secrets, they've got every right to throw your ass in prison."

"The documents were planted," Howard said. "That's not why she's in prison."

"Whyever she's there," Matt said, "I can't see what any of this has to do with me." He started to come to his feet.

"We want you to help get her out," Susan Elliott said.

Matt froze. He stared at her for a minute and eased himself back down on the couch. His eyes went back and forth from Howard to Elliott.

"Are you nuts?"

"Now, hold on," Howard said. "Admiral Jacobs said you'd give us a fair hearing. That's all we ask."

"Hell, you're the State Department. She's the daughter of a senator. Surely you can negotiate her release."

Cliff Howard said, "We've tried—repeatedly—but the Chinese are intransigent on the subject."

Matt looked at Susan Elliott. "Well, here's an idea. You're the CIA. You get her out."

"We're an intelligence-gathering organization, Mr. Connor."

"Bullshit. I know what the CIA does."

"Whatever your perceptions of the CIA, there can't be any U.S. government involvement in any of this."

"Okay. What about all those high-powered relatives she's got in China? Her cousin? An uncle who's a top general? Another uncle who's a billionaire? They must have some influence. You just—"

"They say their hands are tied."

"Well, then, there you are." Matt stood up. "She stays where she is." He looked at his watch. "Now if you'll excuse me, I've got a job to get to."

"We know," Howard said.

"What do you mean you know?" Matt said. "You know what?"

Elliott gave him a small, crooked smile. "You said you knew what the CIA does, Mr. Connor."

Matt stared at her.

"We set it up as a cover," she said. "The prison where she's being held is on a small island off the coast of Macau. Escape-proof, like Alcatraz, or so they say. The only way we could get anywhere near it is to stage a shipwreck of a U.S. flag vessel on a neighboring island. That's where you come in."

Matt sank into the soft leather of the couch. He rubbed his face in his hands, feeling more tired than he'd ever felt in his life.

"Are you telling me you ran a damned freighter aground as a cover for this insane venture without even asking me if I'd do it?"

Elliott nodded. "We contacted your salvage agent with instructions to transmit the information only to you. We withheld it from all your competitors."

Matt stared at her, clenching his hands into fists. He could see everything he'd worked for slipping away.

"Why me?" he said finally.

"We started asking around, your name came up," Susan Elliott said. "Repeatedly."

"I can't imagine why. This doesn't make—"

"You're the perfect candidate," Howard said. "You've got the expertise. You've got a way in, and a way out. And there's nothing to link you to the U.S. government. You don't even live in the U.S."

"What do you mean, I've got the expertise?"

"We've gone over your record," the CIA agent said. "All of it. As executive officer of a nuclear sub, you've had experience with covert operations involving SEAL teams."

"That's the expertise you're talking about? All I ever did was haul those guys around on the boat. I'm not a SEAL. I've never gone on a mission like that in my life."

"But you understand the process," Elliott said. "You've managed some operations so sensitive they've been stricken from your record." She moved to the edge of the couch. "The bottom line is, you can do it."

"At my age? Get real."

"You're thirty-eight," she said. "That's the same age Neil Armstrong was when he landed on the moon. Look, we're not suggesting some commando-type raid where you charge in like Rambo, guns blazing. It's an inside job. We've got people under contract who'll deliver her to you. All you have to do is pick her up and sail away, get her out of there. We want this as low-key as possible. We—"

"You people are something else. You believe everything you hear, you scrounge around in records you don't understand, you take a piece from here and a piece from there and add them all up and come up with me. Damn you both—I was counting on that job."

"Look, this *is* a job," Howard said. From his briefcase he retrieved a letter on heavy stationery and slid it across the table. "Senator Grayson is offering five million dollars for the safe return of his daughter."

Five million dollars. With that kind of money, he could get Gray Wolf off his back for good. He picked the letter up.

"Is this for real?"

"Five million," Howard said. "Deposited into any bank account you specify on the day you deliver the girl."

Matt thought hard for a moment, then pushed the letter back across the table.

"This is crazy. Even if I could get her aboard, how far do you think we'd get, once they know she's gone?"

"All you need to do is get out beyond the two-hundred-mile limit. They can't touch you out there."

"The hell they can't. The PLA Navy thinks it owns the South China Sea." Matt shook his head slowly, as if steeling himself against his own impulses. "No. Forget it. I could lose my ship, my crew, my freedom, maybe my head, with a stunt like this."

Susan Elliott leaned forward and looked him directly in the eyes. "We've worked it out very carefully, Mr. Connor. There's not as much risk as you think."

"Like hell. You'd have to send a brigade of marines to break someone out of a Chinese prison."

"It's a forced labor camp, not a full-blown prison," Howard said. He nodded to Susan Elliott, who pulled a satellite photo out of her stack.

"It's an island. Right here." She pointed a red fingernail at the largest speck in a chain of specks.

Matt knew exactly where it was. A dozen tiny islands clustered together fifty miles east of Macau. He'd been plotting his course there behind closed doors since he'd received the fax.

"The locals call it Turtle Island," she said. "Not because it has any, but because it's sort of shaped like one."

"I've seen it from a distance. Fiji has nothing to worry about."

"All it's good for is growing peppers," she said. "The prisoners are usually out working in the fields all day. The Chinese think the prison is escape-proof because it's on an island. Security's light. We've beached the freighter on the island furthest from it so as not to arouse suspicion. We'll have a contact on the island, someone to get her out of her cell and deliver her to the north shore at midnight. All you've got to do is pick her up with a Zodiac, get her aboard your ship, and get out of there."

"You think the Chinese won't be watching us? I've done salvage work in Chinese waters before. They watched us like a hawk, every move."

"They'll watch you, but from a distance. The freighter's an American flag vessel. There's a trade meeting scheduled for next month between the Chinese prime minister and the president. The Chinese don't want anything that looks like an incident right now."

"The more I think about this, the less sense it makes," Matt said. "Even a senator can't dispatch someone from the State Department and the CIA to initiate something like this on his own authority. There's more to this than the senator, and his daughter, and his money." He looked at the pair, eyes narrowed. "Why would the U.S. go to so much trouble to get one person out of a Chinese prison?"

"The senator wants his daughter back and he's willing to pay five million dollars to make it happen," Howard said. "That's all you need to know."

"I don't buy it," Matt said. "Something like this would have to come from a much higher authority."

Susan Elliott smiled, almost imperceptibly, but said nothing. Howard shot her a sharp look.

"How high?" Matt said. "The secretary of defense?"

Elliott grinned and lifted her eyebrows, playing with him now.

"The president?"

Howard glared at Elliott and said, "Unacknowledged and undocumented, of course. The president asked the secretary to work with CIA to find a way to get her out of there. Without any official U.S. involvement."

"Why? I understand Senator Grayson's concern. What I don't understand is why the president of the United States would get involved."

Elliott said, "Senator Grayson is threatening to withhold crucial support from a tax bill the president wants passed unless he sees some movement in getting his daughter out of China."

"Politics? You're asking me to risk my neck so the president can get some bill passed? Come on. I may have been born at night, but it wasn't last night."

Elliott sighed. "That's the story we were supposed to give you if you balked. I didn't think you'd buy it."

Matt felt a touch of relief at her candor. His eyes went back and forth between the two.

"You might as well level with me. I'm not going anywhere unless I know the full story."

Susan Elliott took a deep breath, then said, "I can't be more specific, but we have reason to believe Elizabeth Grayson accidentally learned something during her tenure at the lab in Guangzhou that the Chinese don't want us to know. We have indications that they're up to something. We need to know what it is, and we believe she can tell us."

"If that's true," Matt said, "if she knows something so sensitive, why risk keeping her alive at all? Why don't they just kill her and be done with it?"

"The Chinese can't afford to kill the daughter of a U.S. senator, but they can't let her go, either. Her father has four years to serve before his retirement. Sending her to a forced labor camp is a way to keep her quiet in the short term and kill her in the long term. She'll die quietly in prison, after her father is no longer in office."

"Who else knows about this?"

"A handful at NSA and NGA. Two or three at State. About that many in Langley. Not even the senator's wife knows about it."

Matt had never even heard of the NGA. He looked her straight in the eyes.

"If this thing goes south, you won't even know my name, will you?"

"Afraid not. That's why we've tried to structure it so the reward outweighs the risk."

Matt fell back against the couch and rubbed his eyes. Like it or not he had to make a decision, and the choices were lousy. If he accepted, he could lose everything. If he turned their offer down, there was no telling when the next big job would come along, and he knew he couldn't hold Gray Wolf off for long. As it was, with one payment in arrears, his unsavory Chinese friend could show up at any time and seize his ship.

"I need time to think—"

"Five million," Cliff Howard said. "In cash. We're also authorized to tell you the IRS lien on your ship will be torn up and you won't be hassled any more. You'll be free to go home again."

Home. After almost five years of being out of the country, he missed the U.S. A lot. The deal was sounding sweeter, but. . .

"I'd have to talk to my crew. I can't take them into a situation like this without their okay."

"Not until you're at sea," Elliott said. "There can't be any chance of a leak."

"You won't have a problem with your crew," Howard said. "We've checked them out. They're out for the big score and they'll follow you anywhere."

Howard was right—they'd follow him anywhere, especially if the price was right, especially if the job was challenging and dangerous. Matt knew he was cut from the same cloth, but this time there was something bigger pulling at him.

He looked across the way at the black nuclear sub and suddenly knew why it was there. Jake had sent it, a subtle reminder of the man who'd died on his watch six years ago. His old mentor was offering him a chance to redeem himself.

Some chance. It was all or nothing, a chance to wipe the slate clean or lose everything in one roll of the dice, and he had no choice but to take it. He exhaled a long, weary breath.

"All right," he said. "Let's do it."

Cliff Howard came to his feet and Susan Elliott began stuffing papers into her briefcase. The telephone on the forward bulkhead rang. Matt picked it up.

"Captain."

"Hey, Skipper."

Matt could tell by his first mate's measured tone that there was a problem. Add it to the list. Problems were normal when you were getting a ship as old as *CoMar Explorer* ready to go to sea.

"What's up, Sam?"

"More suits on the quarterdeck," Sam said. "Only this time it *is* Gray Wolf's boys. Six of 'em. Bulges under their coats."

Steady. It was Gray Wolf's usual show of force when Matt was behind on a payment. The old man was probably sitting in the back seat of his gray Mercedes limo on the dock, enjoying the show. All Matt had to do was sit down with him over dominoes and a cup of Oolong tea. He'd always been able to talk his way into an extension. He glanced at the pair of government agents getting ready to leave. As long a shot as it was, this job was his only hope now, and if Gray Wolf seized his ship, even that was gone. He turned away from them and spoke quietly into the phone.

"Don't worry about it. I'll talk to Gray Wolf."

"He ain't here," Sam said. "Not that I can see."

Matt winced. That was a bad sign.

"Who's in charge?"

"That loud-mouth muscle of his, the one with the messed-up face."

Matt felt his stomach slide. Popeye Zhang. The left side of his face had been blown off in an assassination attempt, leaving one eye bulging out. Matt didn't know if it was true or not, but the story was that he'd hunted down everyone responsible and killed their entire families.

"What does he want?"

"I don't speak the lingo," Sam said, "but it looks like he's here to take the ship."

Chapter Two

Elizabeth Grayson heard footsteps. Thudding, arrogant footsteps followed by short, shuffling ones. Four Finger Tang and his stooge, Big Ears Wu. She glanced around the cell. A dusky shaft of light from a slit in the concrete wall illuminated a straw mat in the center of the room. A bucket sat in the opposite corner. Crouching in the corner of her cell, she pulled herself into a protective ball. How many more of these sessions could she take before she broke and signed the damned confession they kept shoving under her nose? It was a miracle she'd held out for three months. She'd seen other prisoners break in as many hours.

It wasn't the questioning that would break her. The struggle sessions went on for hours, but she was still strong enough to handle their simple mind-games. It was the beatings that followed that were wearing her down. The beatings, and the twelve-hour days of stoop labor in the fields, and the miserable diet, and the sleep deprivation from being awakened every hour with someone screaming in her face, demanding that she confess. She didn't know how much longer she could hold out, but she knew she had to—once she signed the confession and read it into a tape recorder, she was as good as dead. She jammed the knuckle of her index finger into her mouth and bit down hard. *Welcome to your ancestral homeland.*

The bolt of the cell door snapped open, causing a sharp pain in her abdomen. She was a scientist. An ordinary sound couldn't cause physical pain. Yet this one always did. She uncoiled, pulled herself erect, and pushed the hair away from her face. She straightened her clothes, a wheat-colored two-piece uniform that hung on her slender body, and wiped her eyes. They would not see her looking defeated.

The steel door swung inward. Elizabeth stood in the center of the cell, head held high. The two "wardens" stood in the darkened hall, shielded from the light coming through the slit high in the wall of her cell. All she could see were their feet, shod in traditional woven slippers, and the business end of the split bamboo rod she'd come to know so well. After standing there the requisite thirty seconds—it was their way of making an entrance—they ceremoniously stepped inside.

At five-feet-nine, Elizabeth towered over Four Finger Tang, which she liked to imagine made him furious. Bowing was forbidden in Communist China, but prisoners soon learned a deferential dip of the head would help stave off beatings. Smiling, she nodded to the portly guard. There was a stump where his right thumb should have been, bitten off, so the rumor went, by a prisoner who had snapped after being tortured for four days. The severed thumb had earned the crazed prisoner what he wanted—a bullet in the back of the head—and the ample Tang a name he despised.

"Good evening, you fat slob." She nodded to Big Ears Wu. "Good evening, you little weasel." She could call her guards anything, so long as she dipped her head and smiled. Neither spoke a word of English.

They both grinned at her. Their grins weren't comforting; they wore them any time they were in her presence, especially when they beat her.

"The west-ocean mongrel looks good tonight, eh, Wu?" Four Finger Tang said in Cantonese.

Big Ears Wu looked down. "Yes, she is pleasurable to look upon."

"She's a banana, yellow on the outside and white on the inside." He glanced at Wu. "I'll bet you'd like to get those big ears of yours between those pale yellow thighs." He howled with laughter.

Wu colored and looked away.

"As for me, I'd sooner fornicate with a goat," Tang said.

Elizabeth held her smile, stomach churning. Since being taken into custody, she'd been careful around her guards not to reveal that she was fluent in Cantonese. She'd learned a lot.

Four Finger Tang pointed to her with the bamboo rod and motioned for her to come. She steeled herself, then walked between the two down the long narrow hall, knowing where she was being taken.

They came to a stop just outside a pair of wooden doors. The Great Room of the People. Big Ears Wu opened both doors and Four Finger Tang shoved her forward. Elizabeth adjusted her eyes to the dimly lit room and stood erect, determined not to show fear. Every prisoner not on duty was there, more than two hundred emaciated Chinese prisoners seated on bleachers formed in a U around a wooden stool in the center of the room, illuminated by a single spotlight. She couldn't count how many times she'd been knocked off that stool for "insolence." The prisoners stared straight ahead, completely silent. Four Finger Tang shoved her toward the stool and motioned for her to be seated.

Elizabeth climbed up on the stool, adjusted her eyes to the spotlight, and gazed at the audience, chin held high. The other prisoners stared back at her, eyes dead. After working in the fields for twelve hours, they showed no hint of compassion, even though most of them had been where she was sitting now and knew what was coming. She could feel their resentment. If the half-Chinese foreigner would just die, they could get some rest.

A door opened behind her. She resisted the urge to turn around. The first time she'd done that, Four Finger Tang had charged like a water buffalo and knocked her off the stool. But after three months in prison, there was no need to look; her senses had become so acute she knew who it was.

The mincing footsteps and whisper of expensive shoes came closer. Lee Hong stepped into Elizabeth's field of vision and came to a stop a few feet in front of her. He stood smiling at her in his tailored sport coat, hands behind his back, cropped black hair set off by white sidewalls. After the camp administrator and his stooges had struck out, they'd brought in their big gun to interrogate her, a fellow scientist who'd known her in California.

He looked and acted very different from the first time she'd met him at UC Berkeley. She'd been teaching an advanced course in laser technology. He'd been one of her students. She remembered him as being affable, eager to ingratiate himself with anyone who could teach him anything. He had a different name then, Henry Lee. She'd been mildly amused at his insistence that everyone call him Hank. Nothing about him amused her now.

"Good evening, Ms. Grayson," he said in English.

Elizabeth nodded. "Mr. Lee."

"Please call me Hank."

"Oh, yes," Elizabeth said. "Hank."

Lee sighed. "Look, we don't want to have another unpleasant evening like the one we had last night, do we?"

"Why don't we go out for dinner instead, maybe take in a movie?"

"It doesn't have to be this way." Lee pulled the same ragged piece of paper from his jacket pocket he'd been waving at her for a week. "All you have to do is sign your name, read this into a tape recorder, and you're out of here."

"I'm not signing or reading anything. I've done nothing wrong, and you know it."

Lee smiled. "If you've done nothing wrong, then why are you here?"

Elizabeth shook her head, then nodded toward the other prisoners. "The same reason everyone else is here, trumped-up charges and slave labor."

"You know better than that. There's no slave labor in China. Under Communism all workers are well paid, even prisoners."

Elizabeth looked around. Who was he playing to? "Sure. The equivalent of six U.S. dollars per month, from which you deduct three for 'food.' The rest goes for 'personal necessities,' like that bucket in my cell."

"Well, of course. Do you think we should give away the people's food and the people's property? Do you think we Chinese are fools?"

Don't, Elizabeth told herself, but the words were out before she could stop them.

"No, I don't. I have the highest respect for the Chinese people. But there are fools in China, just as there are fools in any country. Fools like you, who've enslaved a great nation under the pretense of social equality."

Lee charged at her, fists clenched. His face was so close, she thought she'd fall backward off the stool.

"You think because of your arrogant white blood, you're superior to the Chinese people."

"A thought like that wouldn't even occur to me."

Lee stepped back and said, "Because you look Chinese, you think you can come here and spy on us?"

Elizabeth felt an uncontrollable urge to laugh. She couldn't tell if it was hysteria or the absurdity of the assertion. She stared at him.

"Is it possible to reason with you?" she said finally. "Would the daughter of an American senator be sent here as a spy? Would the niece of the top-ranking general in China be sent here as a spy? Would the cousin of the chairman and managing director of the largest tech company in China be sent here as a spy? Does that even make sense?"

"It makes perfect sense. Who else would have greater access?" Lee took a deep breath. "I've told you before. No questions. You may only speak to answer *my* questions. Now, why were you sent here to spy on the peaceful Chinese people?"

Peaceful. Elizabeth stared back without answering. It was pointless.

Lee nodded, and Four Finger Tang stepped forward with his bamboo rod.

Elizabeth sighed. Repeating her story would at least buy her some time before the torture began.

"I came here at the invitation of my cousin to do medical research."

"And your cousin would be the honorable James Lao, esteemed head of China Aerospace and Technology?"

Elizabeth didn't think her cousin was so esteemed. Where the hell was he? Why hadn't he gotten her out of here by now? She nodded.

"What was the nature of that research?"

"We were trying to determine the feasibility of using microlaser technology to kill cancer cells."

"And you abused your position of trust by stealing secrets from the Chinese people."

"That's a lie, and you know it."

"What did you learn in your spying at the laboratory in Guangzhou?"

She wanted to say, "What you madmen are doing," but it would be her death sentence. She had a tendency to blurt things out when she was angry or frustrated, but she would choose her words carefully.

"I'm a scientist, not a spy."

Lee nodded to Four Finger Tang. "Bind this stinking half-breed," he said in Cantonese.

Elizabeth held her breath. *Please give me the strength to get through this.*

Four Finger Tang produced a length of rope from his little chamber of horrors and tossed it to Big Ears Wu, who tied her hands behind her back. She felt the blood stop flowing to her hands. He drew the rope around her shoulders, under her armpits, and around her neck, then connected it to her hands and pulled it up taut, so that any movement to ease the pressure caused intense pain. She pulled herself erect on the stool, the only way to avoid the pain, but knew from experience she'd only be able to hold that position for a few minutes.

"Now, Ms. Grayson, let's try this again. What secrets have you stolen from the Chinese people?"

"I've done nothing wrong, and you know it." She tried to make her voice sound strong, but heard it break.

On a cue from Lee, Four Finger Tang began waving his arms at the other prisoners. They came to life, chanting slogans and shaking their fists. As Tang pointed to individuals, they sprang to their feet like puppets, pointing fingers at Elizabeth and screeching at her in Cantonese, denouncing her as an American spy and imploring her to confess.

In the midst of the din, Lee advanced on Elizabeth and held his face inches away from hers. The smell of stale sweat and his darting eyes told her he was under intense pressure to extract a confession. She drew back, repulsed by the smell of him.

"Sign the goddamn paper," he said, waving the document in one hand and a small tape recorder in the other. "Then read it into this. That's all you have to do."

Elizabeth tried to pull back from his face and grimaced at the pain that shot through her body. His face moved closer to hers. She felt herself on the verge of falling backward. She'd seen prisoners trussed up like her fall or be knocked off the stool and not get up. Her mouth was dry, but she did the only thing she could think of to get him away from her. She spit in his face.

Lee jerked back. He removed a handkerchief from his pocket and nodded to Four Finger Tang, but the portly guard was already charging like a Samurai with his bamboo rod in the air.

Elizabeth tried to duck the blow but couldn't move more than a few inches. She felt the solid part of the bamboo rod come down across her right shoulder and searing pain as the slivers of bamboo sliced into the side of her neck. She felt herself falling into darkness, away from the pain.

The shock of cold water on her face revived her. She blinked her eyes open and squinted into the overhead spotlight, not sure where she was. She tried to move her hands and remembered. Head pounding, she rolled over on the concrete floor. How long had she been lying there? She saw the black glint of Lee's shoes a few feet away. She must have been out for only a few seconds. Feeling hands under her armpits, she pulled herself into a sitting position. She opened her eyes and saw a camera mounted in the corner. So that was what Lee was playing to. It hadn't been there the night before. During that session she'd also been knocked to the floor and would have seen it. Who was watching her?

Blood seeped into her mouth from somewhere. It tasted like a copper penny under her tongue. She must have bit something. A wave of desolation swept over her. She couldn't last long at this pace, but there were no good choices. If she confessed, they'd use it to keep the Americans who were pressing for her release at bay; if she held out, there was a good chance they'd kill her. Her uncles and cousin must be powerless, or they would have gotten her out by now. She was stuck here unless the U.S. government sent troops to rescue her, and she knew enough about the realities of politics to know that would never happen.

She could tell by Lee's face that the struggle sessions would continue until she confessed or was dead. Some choice. Die quickly or die slowly with lots of pain. Easier to confess and get her death over with quickly, but as long as she stayed alive there was a chance— however slim—that they could be stopped. To hell with it. The stakes were too high for one person's pain to matter much. They'd just have to kill her slowly.

Steeling herself against the pain, Elizabeth made her back erect. She felt hands beneath her, lifting her up on the stool, the ropes cutting into her throat. The worst was yet to come. She mustered all her courage and twisted the grimace on her face into a smile.

"And you call all non-Chinese barbarians?"

Lee took a step back and straightened his coat. He seemed to be trying to regain his composure to try another tack.

"As I said before, it doesn't have to be this way, Ms. Grayson. If you confess your crimes and apologize to the Chinese people, you'll be sent home."

Home. God, how she wanted to go home. She felt tears well up behind her eyes and forced them back.

Lee stepped forward, looking at her eyes.

"You'll be flown first-class by China Air to Cambridge, Massachusetts. You'll be given medical attention and new clothing. You'll be treated to gourmet food along the way, compliments of the generous Chinese people. Your mother and father will be there to greet you in a joyful reunion. All you have to do is sign this." He waved the document under her nose. "Then read it into this tape recorder and you'll be on your way."

A stabbing pain shot through her spine. She twisted on the stool. She couldn't bear the pain much longer without screaming. The only thing she could do to end the session was to provoke him into knocking her unconscious. This time she'd stay down. She pulled her face into a look of contempt.

"Go fuck yourself."

Lee's jaw dropped. He struck her across the face with a backhand.

Elizabeth felt herself falling backward through space, then a great thud, then darkness.

She blinked her eyes open. Assuming she was still lying on the floor of the Great Room of the People, she lay still, feigning unconsciousness, then realized it was dark. She raised her head slightly. A sliver of moonlight fell across her eyes. She looked up. The light was coming through her cell window. She moved her left arm. The rope was gone. She rolled slowly over and gradually moved all her limbs. Nothing seemed to be broken. She pulled herself into a sitting position and felt her head. She winced when her hand grazed a bulge on the left side of her scalp. The wound was sticky with salve. She looked at her fingers, then felt the bulge again. Did she have a concussion?

She crawled to the nearest corner of her cell and leaned into it, grateful to have some back support. She couldn't tell how long she'd been unconscious, but it must have been several hours. She reached inside her bra—the only one they'd allowed her to keep—and retrieved her watch. She held the timepiece up to the sliver of moonlight. Ten after ten. June 10.

Sitting in the dark, she ran her thumb around the diamond-cut, ribbed bezel of the watch, a stainless steel and gold Rolex, her only earthly possession. She didn't care that much about material things, but the watch had been a gift from her parents when she'd graduated from MIT, and she was determined to keep it. She'd dropped it into her underpants just minutes before she was arrested by the PLA and had been able to keep it hidden from her captors for three months by moving it around. She normally carried the watch in her bra, but moved it to a more private area when the situation called for it.

She leaned her head back into the corner but willed herself not to sleep. With a concussion, she might not wake up. In spite of the pain, she drifted off into a thin sleep.

In a distant corner of her mind, she heard footsteps. She heard the key turn in her cell door and jerked awake, praying that she wasn't in for another struggle session.

Four Finger Tang stepped into her cell, while Big Ears Wu stood grinning in the hall. The obese guard pointed his bamboo rod at the bucket in the corner. He motioned with his head for her to pick it up and follow him.

Thank God. Elizabeth pulled herself erect. A dull ache permeated every bone of her body, but she didn't mind. This was the good part. She picked up the galvanized pail and followed her guards out into the night air, down the path to the fields where human excrement was the chief source of fertilizer.

She'd long gotten over her feelings of humiliation and now looked forward to the ritual. It was as close as she could come to being outside at night, alone. She looked up at the sky, happy for the moment to be alive. Stars twinkled over a cloudless night. The sweet scent of pepper plants hung on the air. In the distance, she heard the soft crash of waves break against the rocky shore, smelled the salt spray that drifted over the rim of the island. Although it was two oceans away, she imagined that the water washing ashore was the same water that washed up on the beach of her parent's summer home in Martha's Vineyard. It comforted her to believe they were connected, that home was at the other end of that water.

The guards stood apart from the stench of the barrels, urinating, breaking wind, laughing, jabbering in Cantonese. She tuned them out and looked up at the sky. A shooting star blazed across the eastern horizon. *Star light, star bright. The first star I see tonight.* There would soon be another star in the sky, one far more deadly than any made by nature. Tears came to her eyes. How could she have been so dense?

She blinked back her tears and focused on the moon. Americans had actually walked there. *If we can do that, surely someone can get me out of here.* She didn't deserve to be rescued after what she'd done. Even though her contribution had been completely unintentional, America should disown her. Still, maybe someone would come. *Please, God, let it be in time to stop them.* It was the one thought that sustained her.

A slight movement in the brush caught her eye. Wildlife on the island was said to be nonexistent, wiped out long ago by starving prisoners. More curious than afraid, she inched closer. She looked down, frozen, as a hand emerged from the brush and patted her bare foot twice, as though to comfort her. *What?* She felt a tiny roll of paper being slipped into her left hand, then all was still.

She thrust the note into a pocket, dumped her bucket into one of the filthy wooden barrels, rinsed it out with salt water from a pump, and followed the guards back to her cell. After returning her bucket to its corner, she collapsed across the straw mat and pretended to fall asleep. She lay there for what seemed like hours. Finally, she heard her guard's footsteps shuffle down the hall and fade into silence.

She slid off the mat and crawled to the edge of her cell, where a thin shaft of moonlight splayed against the wall like a distorted movie screen. She took out the note, a thin sheet of rice paper rolled into a tight cylinder. With trembling fingers she unrolled the tiny scroll and held it up to the shaft of light. The words in black ink electrified her.

"Stay strong. We are leaving soon."

Chapter Three

J ames Lao sipped his latte and gazed at the television monitor on the wall. He paused the tape with the remote control, rewound it, and watched his American cousin spit in Lee Hong's face in slow motion. He smiled at the expression on Professor Lee's face. Beth was just like her mother. His mother, too. The Tang sisters took no shit from anyone. He fast-forwarded and again watched Lee backhand her, knocking her to the floor. He shook his head. The inept fool would kill her before he got her to sign a confession.

No matter. Beth's confession would help to hold the family members and American officials clamoring for her release at bay, but even without it they could be dodged for a while longer. He looked at the calendar on the wall. The tenth of June. Only eleven days to go. After that, she could be released. By then, the American government would know what she knew. In fact, the whole world would know.

He switched the monitor off and drew himself a fresh latte, an addiction he'd picked up as an MBA student at Stanford. He whistled across the cup, then took a swallow and let the caffeine work on his headache. Standing at the window, he looked out over Victoria Harbor at the Hong Kong skyline.

The stark contrast between the city created by the British and the squalor created by his own people was a constant source of embarrassment. Tall, elegant office buildings stood side by side, as if linking arms to push back the encroaching Chinese slums. In the harbor below, ancient Chinese junks swirled about luxurious cruise ships like bugs on a pond, their owners selling trinkets, taking leftover food that had been thrown out.

He sighed. Truly he was a man without a country. In the years he'd spent living in the U.S., he'd never felt accepted and had come to despise the arrogant superpower. Yet living in America had made him see China through the eyes of a Westerner, and he now hated what he saw. As a student in the West, he'd learned exactly what the fabled Mao had done. The insane peasant had caused the deaths of 70 million people—in peacetime. Mao was long gone, but the insanity was still there, along with his rotting corpse. Market reform had improved things to some extent, but the country was still decades behind. James detested the Communist fools in Beijing—including his father—who kept the Mao myth alive, clinging desperately to power.

He no longer had any desire to live in China. When his father ordered him back to head up the development of a new weapons system, James had resisted—until he learned what the new weapon was, and how it would be used. It had been an opportunity he couldn't refuse, a chance to set things right, not only for China but for himself. It had taken all the skills he'd learned in America's finest schools, but after an epic six-year struggle, it was finally ready. If his presentation went well tonight, his mother country would soon hold a new place in the world—and so would he.

The door clicked open behind him. There was no need to look. No one but his father would dare to walk unannounced into the office of the chairman and managing director. James's secretary wouldn't challenge him. No one challenged General First Class Lao Jianxing. At the age of eighty-three, standing tall and stiff in his PLA uniform, with a full head of iron-gray hair cut into a severe crew cut, he looked every inch the revered national hero that he was. James glanced over his shoulder.

"Honorable Father."

"How can you drink that American swill?"

That was the general, ever the hard-liner. His father had started his career fighting Japanese invaders as a boy and had become a young Communist leader in the civil war against Chiang Kai-shek, marching side by side with Mao. After the nationalists fled to Taiwan, he'd been sent to the Russian Military Academy and had since risen to the rank of four-star general in the People's Liberation Army. After crushing the pro-democracy movement in Tiananmen Square, he'd been appointed vice-chairman of the Central Military Commission, the top military job in the country. Even after decades of seeing the chaos Communism had caused, he was still convinced that it was the salvation of China. Where were his eyes?

James said, "Not everything in America is bad."

"You have too many Western ideas, Jintao."

He'd been James for so long in the West, his given name sounded strange, foreign.

"Yes, but look where they've gotten us," he said.

"They've gotten our heads on the block. This thing had better work."

"It will, don't worry."

"Someone had better worry." General Lao was pacing. "Prime Minister Wen will be here any minute."

"It's been tested and retested. The demonstration will go fine."

"Even if it does, this could still blow up in our faces. You bring your half-barbarian cousin over here against my wishes and she threatens to expose the entire operation. To make matters worse, you have her thrown in prison! Fornicate all gods, Jintao, couldn't you have found a better solution than that? The whole family's in an uproar."

The family would have been in an even greater uproar if James had followed through on his first impulse, which was to arrange an accident for her. It embarrassed him that he'd been unable to give the order. A weakness like that—when the stakes were this high—could be fatal.

"Calm down, Father. I'm very fond of Beth. She won't be harmed, not in any material way. After the launch we'll arrange for her release."

"Your mother's sister—Amelia, she calls herself in the West—has been telephoning me non-stop. Aiya, that woman won't shut up."

"I know. She's been calling me, too. I tell her we're doing everything possible to obtain Beth's release."

"And that barbarian politician she's married to is high up in the American government—chairman of the senate Armed Services Committee. There's no telling what he might do."

"Relax, there's nothing he *can* do. They don't even know where she's being held. Cousin Beth is very secure and will remain so until after the launch. After that, she'll be the least of their problems."

"What if she gets word out somehow?"

"She's locked up, Father. On an island. And the launch is just eleven days away. What could happen?"

"If you live to be as old as I am, you'll learn that anything can happen."

James tuned his father out. At precisely 10:00 p.m. he'd deliver a presentation that would be the culmination of six years of work, and he needed to stay focused. An entourage of VIP's was flying in from Beijing for the demonstration. His father had flown ahead to make sure everything was ready, and he'd been driving James crazy since he'd arrived. Squinting through the darkened glass of his 32nd-floor office window, James could see the lights of Hong Kong International in the distance. The prime minister would normally travel in an official state aircraft, but the need for secrecy was such that James had dispatched a company jet.

The plane had touched down twenty minutes ago. Bearing the ubiquitous CAT logo, a springing tiger superimposed over a rocket at lift-off, the jet wouldn't attract undue attention. The Boeing 737 had been directed to a private hangar, where company vans with darkened windows were waiting to take the group to the test facility. As head of the state-owned enterprise, James should have been at the airport to greet such important guests, but because of the secrecy surrounding the prime minister's visit, his father had insisted they be taken directly to the test site.

James looked at his watch. 9:40. "We should be leaving now."

He picked up the note cards on his desk and ushered his father into the private elevator adjacent to his office. His father watched the lights change above the door, neither speaking. James could feel the old man's tension. Fear was useful. It was what had enabled his father to survive all these years. The car glided down thirty-three floors, coming to rest below the surface of the earth. James held the door and motioned his father out into a dimly lit passageway, where an electric vehicle resembling a golf cart stood waiting.

They rode in silence. After a ten-minute drive through the dark green hallway, the vehicle began to slow. Ahead, a set of pneumatic doors tripped open with a whoosh. The vehicle entered the basement of the test facility and came to a stop before an elevator. They rode up to the eighth floor, and James steered his father toward the observation room. Through the thick glass walls he could see the group from Beijing approaching from the opposite direction. His timing was perfect: he would be there just ahead of his guests.

Father and son entered the observation room from the rear and came to a stop in the center of the room, facing the double doors of the main entrance. Almost immediately the doors opened and James's guests stepped inside. He was glad to see that they, like himself, wore finely tailored Western-style business suits. The dreadful Mao suits had gone out with Deng, but there were still a few diehards in Beijing who wore them.

James stood facing the man he recognized as Prime Minister Wen, a plump man with a severe haircut and dark-rimmed glasses. He'd never met him, but his photographs were everywhere. The ancient custom of bowing was forbidden under Communist rule. James approved—it was a ridiculous custom—still, some equally ancient instinct made him want to dip his head in the presence of the second highest-ranking man in the country.

"Greetings, comrades," James said in Mandarin. He normally spoke English when doing business in Hong Kong and Kowloon, but when he spoke Chinese in those cities it was Cantonese. He'd been out of Beijing for so long his command of Mandarin, the official dialect of China, was rusty. "You honor us with your presence."

As the one who had organized the trip, General Lao made the introductions. "Prime Minister. May I introduce my son, Lieutenant Colonel Lao Jintao, chairman and managing director of China Aerospace and Technology."

The prime minister extended his hand. "It's an honor to meet you." He glanced at General Lao and smiled. "I've heard so much about you, Colonel."

"The honor is mine, Prime Minister." The military rank was a reference to the commission James held in the People's Liberation Army. With the passing of Deng, the PLA had dramatically increased its influence in China's political decision-making process. James's PLA rank was now an important part of his persona. He smiled. "I hope some of what you've heard has been good."

"The other distinguished comrades you know," General Lao said. He nodded to a group of ten men, heads of various ministries and their aides. James had worked with three of them, Xu Junjiu, minister of the State Commission of Science, Technology, and Industry for National Defense, Yang Deguan, minister of National Defense, and Zhou Yongzheng, minister of Science and Technology. The other ministers he'd met but didn't know well.

"Of course," James said. He waved his hand toward the food arrayed along the side table. Covered dishes of steamed rice, shrimp, and sea bass had been whisked into place just moments before the honored guests had arrived. James had been especially careful to serve fish. The Chinese word for fish, *yu*, also meant "plenty," or "surplus," and it was traditionally served at celebratory banquets. "Your journey has been long. May I offer you some refreshments?"

The senior members of the group approached the table. James and his father hung back at a respectful distance. He watched the others at the trough. You could tell a lot about the discipline of a man by watching him in the presence of food or women. The prime minister picked up a cup of green tea, then stood back while the ministers and their aides filled their plates. James's father, who ate and drank only sparingly, looked at them with poorly concealed disapproval.

James glanced at his watch. If the prime minister wasn't going to eat, there was no need to delay the demonstration. When the others' plates were filled, he said, "Please be seated, comrades." He motioned toward the black leather swivel chairs mounted on posts and arranged in a curve in the front row of the stadium seating. Behind them were rows of ordinary red plastic seats, ascending to the rear of the stadium. The ministers would be seated comfortably, looking down on a stage forty feet wide with a curtain behind it.

The guests mounted two steps and took their seats while James assumed his place behind the podium on the far right side of the stage. He retrieved the set of note cards from his inside coat pocket and set them before him, knowing he wouldn't need them. His headache was gone, and his mind was focused. He looked out over his audience. He knew what the ministers called him behind his back. He was a *gaogan zidi*, a high-cadre child, one born into privilege. Like the sons of all high-ranking cadres—the name the Communists had adopted for bureaucrats—he was also a Red Prince. Most were dilettantes who'd spent years studying in the West and had amounted to nothing. James suspected he'd been tarred with the same brush. Tonight that would all change. He cleared his throat and started speaking in a clear voice.

"The famed German military strategist Carl von Clausewitz, in his classic book *On War*, wrote that, 'War is the realm of uncertainty; three-quarters of the factors on which action is based are wrapped in a fog of greater or lesser uncertainty.' Senior military officers in the United States have long talked of the need for a 'Revolution in Military Affairs' that would dissipate this so-called *fog of war*.

"What the West envisions and is working toward includes a worldwide network of satellites that would allow military commanders to observe the enemy's movements on the battlefield, a system that would enable them to 'see' the battlefield and deploy troops and resources exactly where needed. Obviously, such a system in the hands of the West would not be in China's best interest. In response to this threat, we began work some six years ago on a weapons system that would counteract such a strategy."

James took a sip of water. "More recently, the president's New Year's speech to the Central Military Commission, in which he demanded that the military 'develop a surprise weapon to give China a distinct advantage over the United States,' has caused us to redouble those efforts. You will recall that the president asked us to produce 'a weapon that could be introduced without warning and would provide a decisive victory in a conflict with America.' I'm happy to report that our scientists have achieved a breakthrough in technology, culminating in a weapons system that will meet this goal."

James paused. The "breakthrough" had largely come from an unintentional contribution by an American female scientist.

"After six years of research and development, and a capital investment of approximately 5.6 billion U.S. dollars, we have developed a weapons system that will revolutionize warfare. Mere words are inadequate to describe the power of this weapons system, and so, with your permission, I will let the system speak for itself."

James pressed a button on the podium and stepped back with a sweep of his hand as the curtain began to part.

"Comrades," he said. "I humbly present 'Raptor.'"

The curtain drew back with a hum. The men leaned forward in their seats, peering through the wall of thick dark glass as the light level was raised inside the test building and lowered inside the observation room. Slowly a titanium satellite descended into view, where it hung beneath a gantry crane, supported by a black cable. From the top of the spacecraft, photovoltaic cells stretched out in obeisance to the sun while the lower half bristled with a dozen eyes, each glowing softly, pulsing intermittently.

From the eighth floor they were looking into the abyss of the test building, where hundreds of metal disks the size of dinner plates hung at various levels.

The satellite pulsed and began to rotate slowly. With a blinding flash, a beam of high intensity light emitted from one of its eyes, incinerating its target.

The guests jerked in their seats. Prime Minister Wen came to his feet and walked slowly down to the stage, not taking his eyes off the satellite. Followed by the others, he edged toward the rear of the stage, gazing through the thick dark window as the satellite continued to turn, targeting, firing, incinerating. With each snap the men recoiled, then gaped at a metal disk dangling in ruins. Within minutes all were gone, reduced to smoking scraps of twisted metal. The men stood quietly, staring at the carnage. Of the hundreds of disks deployed for the test, not one had survived.

The men stood silently for several minutes, shaking their heads.

James stepped up to the podium. "The system, which we've code named Raptor, employs multiple, high-intensity laser beams that will destroy enemy communication, photo reconnaissance, surveillance, and electronic spy satellites, including the DSP satellite system used by NORAD, while simultaneously protecting China from a nuclear attack."

He paused and waited for the enormity of that statement to sink in.

"The satellite gives us the ability to destroy the enemy's civilian and military communication satellites, leaving them without the ability to wage war. But in the unlikely event the enemy were able to launch a nuclear strike, the satellite also contains highly sophisticated sensors that collect electronic and infrared emissions, tracking the heat plumes of ballistic missile booster rockets. Any such rockets that have been fired, from anywhere on earth, will be targeted and destroyed before they reach China's air space."

"Raptor," Prime Minister Wen said, almost in a whisper. He turned to James with a new look of respect. "It's an apt name."

A burst of laughter erupted from the group, a release of tension.

James found himself surrounded by ministers offering congratulations in an uncharacteristic display of emotion. His father beamed at him from the rear of the group. He didn't need to say another word—they all understood the implications of this new technology for China.

When the laughter and hoopla died down, the questions began. After the initial exuberance, the ministers were coming to the realization that a shift in power had just occurred. No longer would James be thought of as a *gaogan zidi*. He was now a contender for one of their jobs and as such would have to deal with their petty jealousies. He braced for their questions.

"Very impressive, Colonel Lao," Yang Deguan said. "All well and good in a confined laboratory setting, but how will this system perform in the vast distances of space?"

"An excellent question," James said. "The answer is that there is no loss of force because of distance. The intensity of the beam remains the same, with pinpoint accuracy, whether one mile or ten-thousand."

"What powers this thing?" Zhou Yongzheng said.

"Ultra-efficient photovoltaic cells create hydrogen through an electrolyzer," James said. "Fuel cells then convert the hydrogen into electricity. Simply stated, the satellite is powered by fuel cells that are replenished by the sun."

"Does that mean it will remain viable indefinitely?"

"Unfortunately, no. The fuel cells will deteriorate over time and will eventually cease to function. That is the one weakness of the system."

"But how long will it last?"

"At least twelve months, long enough to accomplish all our objectives. By then a newer, more powerful satellite will be launched into orbit to replace it."

"How will you deploy?" Xu Junjiu asked.

"The details of the launch have been classified Most Secret," James said. "Suffice it to say that the satellite will be launched in an entirely untraditional way in order to evade detection, both pre- and post-launch."

The questioning went on for the better part of an hour. James stood at the podium and fielded each query with confidence and poise. His father looked pleased.

"Thank you, Colonel," Prime Minister Wen said. "I congratulate you on a most impressive achievement." He nodded to James's father. "Perhaps General Lao can give us an update on the post-deployment plan."

The general stepped up to the podium. "After the satellite has been successfully launched into orbit, ours is a three-step plan. First, we will destroy all American civilian and military communication satellites, leaving the American forces as well as the U.S. civilian population in the dark. Second, we'll make it known to the White House through the U.S. ambassador that we have targeted specific American cities—Los Angeles, Chicago, and New York—with CSS-4 intercontinental ballistic missiles armed with five-megaton nuclear warheads as added insurance against the unlikely event of an American nuclear attack. Third, with the U.S. military unable to respond, we will launch a 'no-warning' lightning missile attack against Taiwan."

"What about Taiwan's missile defense system?" Wen said.

"Approximately seven hundred missiles will be launched from various angles to overwhelm missile defenses," General Lao said. "These will be targeted at ports, ships, airfields, command posts, fuel depots, and weapons storage facilities, immobilizing Taiwan's air and naval forces. We will also target Taiwan's political and military leaders by destroying the presidential palace and the defense ministry. Within forty-five minutes, Taiwan will be paralyzed. Infantry divisions of the People's Liberation Army, which are even now quietly massing along the coast, will sail across the Taiwan Strait and occupy the island. Because of the information blackout we expect minimal resistance."

"And once the occupation is complete?"

"We have plans to immediately convert the Taiwanese defense forces to PLA forces once the flag has been lowered and the PRC flag is in place. Those who resist will be shot. Senior political leaders will be immediately replaced with a team standing by in China. Lower level government functionaries will be given the same option as the Taiwanese defense forces and will suffer the same consequences if they refuse. It will all be over before the Americans know what has happened. By then, there will be nothing for them to defend. China will be one again."

A burst of applause went up, but the ministers' approval had little to do with being one again. The old cadres, including James's father, were struggling to remain relevant. Market reform and encroaching capitalism were eroding the power of the Communist party. Taiwan, like Hong Kong before it, was exporting capitalism onto the mainland. Retaking the island would solidify their support, but it was a risky business. After the initial exuberance, the room drifted to silence. The ministers seemed to be contemplating the long-term implications of what they were hearing.

"You mentioned that American civilian satellite systems will also be destroyed," Minister Zhou said. "Why is this needed? We don't want to provoke the Americans any more than is necessary."

James stepped to the podium. "The destruction of civilian communication satellites is essential for two reasons. First, in order to have a complete news blackout over the United States, including American Forces Radio and Television Services, and second, to prevent non-military communication systems such as cell phones from being used to conduct military operations in an emergency."

"What impact will the destruction of these satellites have on the

American economy?" Zhou asked.

James hesitated. The American economy was interdependent. It didn't take much to disrupt it. Nine-eleven had proven that. Even before 9/11, the malfunction of the U.S. satellite known as Galaxy IV had shut down nearly every pager in the country. It had also disrupted cable and broadcast video feeds, credit card authorization networks, and corporate communications systems for weeks. The impact of the simultaneous loss of every U.S. satellite could only be imagined. He was convinced that the securities markets would collapse, triggering wholesale unemployment, which would cause an economic depression worse than the 1930s. But there was no way he was going to tell the ministers that. He had to get his plan approved. Tonight.

"There will be some short-term disruptions," James said, "but the U.S. economy is resilient. "It should make a reasonably quick recovery."

"It's the price the Americans will have to pay for meddling in China's internal affairs," Yang said.

"What about China's economics?" Zhou said. "America is China's biggest trading partner."

Prime Minister Wen said, "There are some instances in which a nation must place national sovereignty ahead of economics. I believe this temporary economic loss will be a small price to pay for China's unification."

"What will the Americans do?" Minister Xu asked.

General Lao shrugged. "What can they do? Invade China? Land of more than one-point-three billion people? The U.S. understands that in war, China is prepared to take unlimited casualties. The Americans, as demonstrated in Viet Nam, are not. For all their adventures in Afghanistan and Iraq, they won't invade another Asian country— they've learned their lesson well. Launch nuclear strikes? Let them. We're now protected, and they aren't. If they launch strikes over China, we'll be protected by Raptor and will be wholly justified in launching strikes over Los Angeles, Chicago, and New York. It's a mistake they'll never repeat."

"In short, comrades," James said, "there's not only nothing they can do, there's nothing they *will* do. I've lived and studied in America for years. The Taiwan issue is driven by their politicians. The American public cares nothing about Taiwan. The risks are low and the rewards are high. The net effect of this operation will be a tremendous loss of face for the Americans, a weakening of their military and economic strength, and a shift in the balance of power in the Pacific from the U.S. to China."

Prime Minister Wen nodded. "What we've seen and heard in this room tonight will mark the beginning of a new world order, one in which China is finally accorded her rightful place after a century of domination by the West." He extended a hand to General Lao in an unusual display of warmth. "The acorn does not fall far from the tree," he said with a smile. He turned to James. "Lieutenant colonel, is it?" he said, gripping James' hand. "I think senior colonel is much more appropriate for one with such responsibilities." He glanced at James's father. "See to it, General."

"At once, Prime Minister."

"Much is at stake here, Senior Colonel," the prime minister said in a low voice, still gripping James's hand, gazing intently into his eyes. "I need your full assurance that you will not fail the People's Republic."

James couldn't believe what he was hearing. An on-the-spot promotion from the prime minister himself. A two-grade jump, from lieutenant colonel to senior colonel, bypassing the rank of colonel altogether. Wonderful. He could use the added status it would give him to implement his plan—though if the prime minister knew what James had in mind, he'd also know he didn't need to offer an incentive to make it work. This was Phase I. Phase II would be secretly implemented in the morning. Once set in motion, the launch had to go off as planned. If it didn't, James would be a dead man. He gripped Wen's hand.

"You have my word, Prime Minister."

The group of ministers gathered their portfolios and stood in line to congratulate James on his presentation and his promotion. After repeated thank-yous and goodbyes, they headed for the door.

James threw a satisfied glance at his father, who was queuing up to leave for Beijing with the ministers.

He waited until the last minister was at the door. "I wouldn't celebrate that promotion just yet, Senior Colonel," he said, looking James in the eyes. "You still have to get that thing in the air."

James smiled. "I assure you, Father, the launch will go off exactly as planned."

"It had better. If you go down, I go down with you."

Chapter Four

Matt Connor wound his way up to the main deck of *CoMar Explorer*. What in hell was he going to tell Gray Wolf? He'd built a relationship with the famous leader of the Great Wall Triad by always telling him the truth. But if he revealed the rescue plan, not only would he be compromising a top-secret mission, Gray Wolf might also refuse to allow the ship to be used for such a dangerous purpose. On the other hand, if he said he had no job and no prospects, the underworld leader might seize the ship and sell it out from under him to recover his investment. In either case, he'd be finished.

Matt paused on the ladder and rubbed his eyes. He'd tell Gray Wolf the truth, just not all of it. He'd tell him he had a lucrative job, a freighter run aground on an island east of Macau. No need to mention that the job was a cover for a CIA-sponsored rescue mission. He hated to compromise himself, and he knew the risk in being less than straight with Gray Wolf, but it was his only shot at keeping Connor Marine together.

By the time he got to the main deck, Sam had been joined by five other crew members. The six men stood on one side of the quarterdeck, arms folded, facing down Gray Wolf's foot soldiers on the other. Popeye Zhang and his clones, dressed in their trademark black suits, white shirts, black ties, and sunglasses, stood glaring at Matt's motley crew dressed in the mismatched rags of men who did real work. As Matt approached the quarterdeck, Popeye Zhang leveled a crooked finger at him.

"You come."

Sam stepped across the imaginary line that separated the two groups, arms folded across his chest.

"Who are you, little man, to be telling my captain to come?"

Zhang's hand moved inside his coat.

"I wouldn't reach for that," Sam said. "You won't be any good to your leader with one arm."

"*Hei ren.*"

Sam had heard all the Taiwanese epithets for black people in the five years he'd been with him on Taiwan and had learned how to handle those, but Matt wasn't sure how he'd handle being called "black man" as though it were an insult.

Sam's eyes narrowed. "Right on both counts. I'm black. And I'm a man. A better man than you, you little pissant. Want to put that to the test?"

Popeye Zhang glared up into Sam's fearsome features. The ex-Navy SEAL was a man, all right—six-feet-four and 220 pounds of man. Matt was tempted to let Sam have at him, but it was enough to see the fabled Zhang quavering in his shoes.

"It's okay, Sam," Matt said, stepping in between them. Popeye Zhang looked relieved. Backing down in the face of an enemy would be a loss of face he'd never recover from.

"What do you want, Zhang?"

"Gray Wolf say you come."

So they weren't here to take the ship. That was the good news. The bad news was they were here to take him. He flirted with the idea of giving Sam the signal to disarm them and send them packing, which his crew could easily do, but he didn't want Gray Wolf on his tail or his unarmed crew in danger. He shrugged.

"No problem."

"We better go with you, Captain." Sam nodded toward the six gangsters as though at a pile of dung. "These pissants might sting you."

"I'll be okay, Sam." Matt forced a smile. "Gray Wolf can't hurt me, I owe him too much money."

He ordered Sam to continue with the preparations to get under way and walked down the gangway, surrounded by Zhang and his men. They moved toward a gray GMC Suburban parked on the dock. Matt strained to see inside but the windows were so dark they were almost black. Not keen on going for a ride with Popeye Zhang and his hooligans, he hoped Gray Wolf was waiting inside, but the van turned out to be empty.

"*Shang che.*" Get in. Two of Zhang's soldiers shoved him into the middle seat where he sat with one on either side of him, two in the seat

46

behind him, and two in front, Zhang riding shotgun. Literally. The doors locked with a clunk and Matt immediately felt closed in. He told himself to calm down and breathe.

The van pulled away, heading east on Penglai Road. Matt glanced up at the roof a few inches over his head. He shoved against the two thugs to give himself some shoulder room and pulled more air into his lungs. Wherever they were taking him, he hoped this would be a short ride. He hated being inside anything he couldn't quickly get out of.

At a shade over six feet, he was a bit taller than the men who were flanking him. They appeared to be in their early twenties and were trying hard to look tough. The one on his left looked him over, posturing.

"Look at the hair on this monkey," he said in Mandarin, staring at Matt's forearms.

"What a stinking mess," the one on his right said, turning up his nose. "Smells like a piss-spraying eunuch."

They all laughed.

Popeye Zhang turned his head to the side, exposing his mutilated face.

"Didn't you whores know? All west-ocean foreigners are half monkey. They piss down their legs when they're captured."

They all knocked themselves out laughing, sucking up to their leader.

The van pulled out onto Kushan 1 Road, merged into traffic, and headed north. The feeling of being closed in started to surface again, and Matt forced it back down. *Breathe. Look out the window.* To the east, couples strolled in Shoushan Park while small children raced around them, laughing and playing. He focused on the families, wondered what it would be like to live a normal life, then told himself to knock it off.

The van slowed and turned onto Kushan 2 Road, drove northeast for a few miles and turned left into a narrow road just south of Chenghuang Temple. He'd heard Gray Wolf mention the temple before and knew it was somewhere near his residence. Was he being taken to

Gray Wolf's place?

The van approached a gated opening in a high stone wall. The wrought iron gate had a wolf's head logo in the center. It had to be Gray Wolf's house. Strange. All his prior meetings with the underworld leader had been in the private back rooms of various bars on the waterfront, or in the back seat of his limo, parked on the dock near *CoMar Explorer.* Strange, but good. The triad leader wasn't averse to using violence when it suited him, but he'd be unlikely to condone it in his home. Matt began to relax a little.

The iron gate swung inward and the van pulled into a courtyard. Popeye Zhang stepped out and opened the side door.

"*Lau wai.*" Zhang jerked his thumb, motioning Matt out of the van.

Old foreigner. It was a favorite insult for Westerners, probably the least offensive one he'd heard. The Taiwanese were convinced they looked younger than their Western counterparts. In Matt's case, they were probably right.

He stepped out into the gravel courtyard and breathed deeply, relieved to be out of the van. He looked around, impressed by the sheer size of the place. Gray Wolf's home looked more like a Buddhist temple than a private residence. It was hidden by the cypress trees and high wall that surrounded it—he could have driven by that iron gate a hundred times without seeing the house. The gate clanged shut behind him with a finality that made him look over his shoulder. The top of the stone wall was lined with pieces of broken glass embedded in concrete. One thing was certain. He wasn't leaving until it was Gray Wolf's idea.

"*Ang mo.*" Zhang drew the expression out, prompting his goons to snicker. He pointed to the double doors of the main entrance.

Red beard. Another favorite insult for Westerners, alluding to their relatively hairy bodies. When he first heard the term, Matt had protested that his hair was black and he didn't have a beard, but it didn't matter. All Americans were *ang mo* to the Taiwanese. Popeye Zhang's arrogance was beginning to annoy him. He toyed with the idea of dropping him to his knees, just to teach him a few manners, but decided this wasn't the place.

The double doors of the entrance opened wide. Two male servants dressed in black mandarin gowns stood in the foyer, one on either side of him, pulling the heavy doors inward. Matt wasn't confused by the gowns. Obviously Gray Wolf's personal bodyguards, the two men looked like they could eat Popeye Zhang and his thugs for breakfast. With one in front and the other behind, Matt walked down a long tiled hallway with a smaller set of double doors at the end. The man in front knocked on the door softly, opened it, and exchanged a few words of Mandarin with a voice inside. He pushed the door inward and held it for Matt, eyeing him.

Matt stepped inside. His years aboard a sub allowed his eyes to adjust to the dim light quickly. He glanced around at what appeared to be a strikingly tastefully furnished study. Rich tapestries adorned dark paneled walls. Flower arrangements sat atop lacquered tables on the perimeter. Joss sticks smoldered in the corners, masking a strange animal smell of some kind. Gray Wolf sat behind an ornately carved teak desk, writing with a fountain pen. Matt stood quietly. Gray Wolf finished the last few strokes of whatever he was writing, rolled a blotter over it, and looked up.

"Mr. Connor," he said, coming to his feet. "I apologize for not greeting you properly. Kindly forgive me for being a poor host."

Relieved, Matt flashed a smile.

"No need to apologize."

Something moved on either side of Gray Wolf's desk. At first he thought it was two dogs, the strange animal smell. They came to their feet, shoulders level with the desk, heads erect above it. Matt flinched. Were they wolves? He'd seen wolves in a zoo before, but never this close. Obviously males, they looked as big as lions. The pair lowered their heads and crept toward him, exposing fangs that gleamed like knives, growling gutturally. The hair on the back of his neck stood up.

"Saddam. Osama. *Zhanzhu.*"

The pair stopped in their tracks.

"You must forgive them," Gray Wolf said. "They're no more trustworthy than their namesakes."

Matt froze, not taking his eyes off the pair. The Taiwanese

routinely named vicious dogs after infamous people, but wolves? He stared at them. They'd stopped growling, but their fangs were still exposed. Their canine teeth above and below had been replaced with what appeared to be steel spikes. It took all his discipline to stand still.

Gray Wolf snapped another command in Mandarin and the pair abruptly lowered their muzzles and dropped to their hindquarters.

Matt stared, amazed that wild animals could be controlled to such an extent. Gray Wolf watched him with an amused expression.

"They both had canine teeth broken off during training exercises," Gray Wolf said. "I had them replaced with titanium spikes." He smiled. "Impressive, aren't they?"

Matt nodded, still staring at them. "I didn't think wolves were trainable."

"They're half German shepherd and half timber wolf. The dog part is trainable, the wolf part is not," he said with a shrug. "I never turn my back on them." He walked around from behind the massive desk and extended his hand, smiling. "It's good to see you again, younger brother."

"And you," Matt said, his eyes still on the matched pair sitting on their haunches before him.

Gray Wolf snapped another command in Mandarin, and the wolf-dogs slunk back to their resting places by the desk.

"*Ni chr bau le ma*?" Have you eaten your fill? It was the traditional way of asking, "How are you?" in Taiwan, a land that had seen its share of famine and hard times.

Matt said "Yes" in Mandarin and asked the same of Gray Wolf, although the answer was obvious. The leader of the Great Wall Triad wore a gray Italian-cut silk suit over a crisp white shirt and silk maroon tie. He had to be in his mid-seventies, but a thin layer of fat made his skin as smooth as polished amber. Even in the dimly lit room, he exuded prosperity.

"Your Mandarin lessons have served you well," he said.

"Progress has been slow for this thick head," Matt said in Cantonese, showing off his ability to speak both.

"I'm glad to see you keeping up with Professor Liu's lessons."

It would have been impossible not to. Gray Wolf had hired a retired university professor to teach him Mandarin and Cantonese, and she'd taken to the job like a drill sergeant. The old man's insistence that Matt learn both dialects as a condition of the loan had initially puzzled him, but his mentor was right. It had served him well. He grinned.

"It's hard when we're at sea, but I manage. Professor Liu is a strict taskmaster."

Gray Wolf laughed. "Let's sit over here, Matthew, where we can relax over *lau ren cha*.

Pensioner's tea. It was an involved ritual and the first indication that Matt was going to be there awhile. It was so called because old people who had nothing better to do liked to sit around with their friends, sipping tea, snacking on whatever was available, and talking. For hours. He stole a glance at his watch. He was eager to get whatever Gray Wolf had on his mind resolved and get back to the ship, but it was considered rude to come to the point quickly.

Gray Wolf steered Matt to a corner of the room with a pair of comfortable-looking sofas. A lacquered table between them held a tray of fresh dim sum and a small gray box.

Gray Wolf took a seat on the opposite sofa, not taking his eyes off Matt. An elderly female servant appeared, carrying a tray loaded with paraphernalia. Matt dutifully watched her take a small teapot, fill it with leaves from a brick of tea, and place it inside a terra-cotta bowl along with two demitasse cups. Holding a towel, she picked up a steaming cauldron from the tray and poured hot water over the tea leaves to activate them, then over the cups to heat them. Using a pair of bamboo tweezers, she rolled the cups in the scalding water, then removed them to let them stand and dry while the tea steeped. After a few minutes, she poured tea into one of the cups and presented it to Matt with both hands, head lowered.

"You prefer Oolong, as I recall," Gray Wolf said.

"Yes, thank you." Matt took the cup with both hands in the old way, showing respect. He waited until Gray Wolf had been served, then went through the ritual he was expected to perform as a guest. He savored the aroma under his nose, noted approvingly that there were no leaves in the tea, then took a sip. The bitterness behind the aroma turned to sweetness in his mouth when he swallowed. He nodded.

"This tea is excellent."

Gray Wolf shrugged. "The water was too hot."

"Sorry to disagree, but it's the best I've had."

A slight smile lifted Gray Wolf's eyes.

"You're not Taiwanese, yet you instinctively understand *ren ching wei.*"

The flavor of human emotions. It roughly meant a sincere demeanor, combined with a certain outward charm or appeal that stayed within the bounds of Confucian humility. Next to face, it was the most important concept to understand for getting along in Taiwan. It was a rare compliment for a Westerner. Matt nodded but said nothing.

Gray Wolf sipped his tea, watching him.

"The winds say you're getting under way."

Matt felt something move in his stomach. He nodded.

"That's right."

"You were leaving without saying goodbye?"

"I didn't know that was a requirement," Matt said. As soon as the words were out, he knew it was the wrong thing to say.

Gray Wolf's mood darkened.

"You've embarrassed me, younger brother. I've lost much face. My friends think I'm a fool for doing business with a foreigner, and then you prove them right by slinking out of port at midnight."

"I wasn't slinking out," Matt said. "There's a shallow draft in Kaohsiung Harbor. That's when the tide comes in."

"I see." Gray Wolf sipped his tea, studying Matt's face. "May I ask where you're bound?"

"I have a job," Matt said.

Gray Wolf raised his eyebrows. "Oh?"

"A freighter aground on an island east of Macau," Matt said. "It came up without any warning, the way they always do, but it should be a lucrative job, worth maybe five million U.S. I know I'm behind on a payment, but if you can bear with me a little longer—"

Gray Wolf raised the fingers of his hand, cutting him off.

Matt flushed. What an idiot. He hadn't been there five minutes and already he was babbling about money.

Gray Wolf's face eased into a smile.

"Such good fortune. A job and visitors, all in the same day."

Matt felt the movement in his stomach return. Don't react. The two government agents had only been aboard an hour, and he'd taken them off through the cargo loading bay to keep them from being seen by Popeye Zhang and his men. Many people came aboard *CoMar Explorer* in the course of a day. Gray Wolf could be referring to anyone. He raised his eyebrows.

"Visitors?"

"The black man and white woman."

"Oh, them. They're from America," Matt said, stating the obvious, implying they were friends, hoping Gray Wolf would drop it.

Gray Wolf sipped his tea.

"Did you know your friends from America were *jianshi juzhu*?"

Under surveillance. It didn't bother him to learn that the two were being watched—foreigners on Taiwan were routinely followed by the government—but it bothered him that Gray Wolf was watching him and his ship so closely. He shrugged.

"How would I know that?"

"You wouldn't, of course," Gray Wolf said. "There must be some other explanation."

"For what?"

Gray Wolf leveled his gaze at Matt. "Why you felt it necessary to remove the two agents through the cargo loading bay."

Agents? Christ. How did he know? Matt felt transparent, as though Gray Wolf could see right through him. He should have known better than to try to deceive the man. The underworld leader had eyes everywhere. Matt squirmed in his seat. It was obvious Gray Wolf knew what was going on. If he leveled with him now and asked for his help, he might even get it. The worst he could do was refuse and cut him off. But if he lied to him, he could get himself killed. He couldn't risk dancing around with Gray Wolf any longer. He sighed.

"I need your wise counsel."

A gratified look came over Gray Wolf's face.

"Oh? Is that so?"

While his host listened intently, Matt told Gray Wolf about the meeting with the two government agents and explained the details of the rescue plan. There was no need to hold anything back. It was obvious that Gray Wolf knew who the agents were. That's why he'd been brought here. Gray Wolf had been playing with him, giving Matt every opportunity to save face for both of them by telling him on his own. Now that he had, his mentor seemed pleased.

"*Hen you yisi.*" Very interesting. "From Macau I hear rumors of a foreign woman, a half-Chinese American scientist, being held in a *laogai* somewhere in the south of China. That has now been confirmed by you. From Hong Kong I hear rumors of a scientific breakthrough in laser research by China Aerospace and Technology, and from Beijing I hear rumors that the PLA is boasting of a new weapons system, a *sha sho jian.*"

Matt wasn't sure he'd translated the words correctly. "Assassin's mace?"

Gray Wolf nodded. "It's a term used by the president of China during his New Year's speech to the Central Military Commission. He ordered the military to develop a surprise weapon that would give China a decisive advantage over the United States during any regional conflict."

"The agents didn't say anything about a weapons system."

"No, of course they wouldn't," Gray Wolf said, "but I'm convinced those events are related."

"What kind of weapons system?"

Gray Wolf shrugged. "I'm told it's something that will knock out the U.S. military, temporarily, making it possible to take Taiwan, something that wouldn't be in my best interest. My brother triads in Hong Kong and Macau haven't fared well under Communist rule."

Matt shook his head. "Forgive me, but I doubt very much that China could develop a weapons system that could do that."

Gray Wolf steepled his fingers. "Americans think only they can innovate. But while America rests on its cold war laurels, working to improve its conventional military power, other nations are working at ways to overcome it."

Matt studied his eyes. It was common knowledge on the docks that Gray Wolf was one of the biggest arms dealers in Asia. What did he know?

"Like how?"

"You're a student of military history, Matthew. There've been many revolutions in warfare. Some quite basic, like the stirrup, which made mounted troops effective, then the long bow, then gunpowder. In our time the revolutions have become increasingly sophisticated— radio, aircraft, sonar, radar, nuclear weapons. Each was a major revolution in the art and science of war. Another revolution is at hand, with the rise of the information age. While the Western powers have been asleep, I believe China has leapfrogged ahead."

"With all respect," Matt said, "that's nonsense. How can you compare China's military with the high-tech weaponry of the U.S.? Look at Iraq. We toppled Saddam in ten days. He didn't know what hit him."

Gray Wolf waved his hand. "A late industrial-age skirmish. Nothing more. Tomorrow's wars will be fought in the information age. The battlefield of tomorrow will look very different, and the West isn't prepared."

"There's just one flaw with that argument," Matt said. "It would take billions to develop a weapons system that could do all that. China's an emerging power, but they don't have that kind of money."

"So they would have you believe," Gray Wolf said. "Under General Lao Jianxing the PLA has been selling conventional weapons—planes, tanks, and artillery—to countries like Iran, Iraq, and North Korea, for hard cash, which they then used to develop RMA weaponry. That's why Lao installed his American-educated son as chairman of China Aerospace and Technology. The West gets upset at such sales, but those weapons are largely obsolete. While you've been fixated on their sale of yesterday's weapons, they've leapfrogged you into the twenty-first century."

"You're saying that China is preparing for war against America?"

"Of course," Gray Wolf said. "China is five thousand years old. Do you think it'll allow itself to be dominated indefinitely by an upstart nation barely two hundred years old?"

"Do you think the leadership of China is crazy? They aren't about to engage the United States in a war."

"War is like death," Gray Wolf said. "No one thinks it'll come, and when it does, no one can believe it's happened. But war, like death, always comes."

"Okay," Matt said. "Let's assume they have this innovative new weapon. What do you think it is, and how do you think they'll use it?"

"No one knows," Gray Wolf said. "I've offered huge sums to find out, with no results. The security surrounding this weapon is the tightest I've seen. But the indications are that it'll be used initially to take Taiwan."

Matt shrugged. "If that's all they do with it, that may evoke a big yawn from the rest of the world. The only country that even says they care is the U.S., and they've worked themselves into a corner. On the one hand they've adopted a 'One China' policy, on the other they've declared they'll defend Taiwan if she's attacked. I suspect if China took the island quickly and with minimal bloodshed, a lot of folks on Capitol Hill would be relieved to see it go. They'd say the right words publicly, but privately they'd be glad to be rid of the problem."

"They're seriously misguided to think it's just the fate of Taiwan at stake," Gray Wolf said. "What China wants is not Taiwan, but hegemony in the Pacific. Once China takes the island, the U.S. will be forced out of the Pacific and China will be the dominant power in Asia."

Gray Wolf let that sink in while he sipped his tea. "Apparently, the only person outside the PLA who knows what the weapons system is and how it'll be used is the American woman scientist who somehow discovered what they were doing. That's why she must be freed—why you must go."

Matt leaned back and rubbed his eyes. Gray Wolf was getting old. He was adding three separate bits of information and getting a giant, fantastic conspiracy. But at least he wasn't standing in Matt's way. He was actually encouraging the mission, though for a different motive. Well, the agents had theirs, Gray Wolf had his, and Matt had his—to save his neck.

"I'll go and get the woman, but not because of any weapons system," Matt said. "If they have such a thing, the U.S. obviously knows about it. With all their intelligence, they have to. Whatever China's got, whatever they're planning, the U.S. will preempt it."

"Governments seldom preempt anything," Gray Wolf said. "Nations always wait until they've been attacked and then react. Preemptions, throughout history, have almost always been done by solitary individuals. Like you, Matthew."

Matt looked into Gray Wolf's eyes, and it hit him. The underworld leader had been grooming him from the start for something like this, some unknown mission that an ex-naval officer and a team of ex-warriors could pull off, something that would serve his vast interests.

"I'll be damned. So that's it. That's why you wanted me to speak Chinese. Why you financed me."

"I invest in many people who I think may one day be useful," Gray Wolf said. "Most never are. Fate has chosen you, Matthew. It's your *joss*."

He gazed at Gray Wolf, amazed that he hadn't seen his true motivations before and amused by his conspiracy theory. *Joss* included a whole panoply of forces, both good and evil, that came to bear on one's life, a superstitious mixture of fate and luck. Matt didn't believe in either. Fate and luck were what you made them. *Call it* joss *if you like, my friend, but I'm going for the gold.* He placed his teacup on the table.

"In that case, I'd better get started."

Gray Wolf smiled gently. "I knew you'd come to the right decision. Is your ship armed?"

Matt shrugged. "Couple of rifles to keep the sharks at bay when our divers are down. That's about it."

"I thought as much. I've arranged to have a few items that may be useful delivered, they should be there by the time you return." He picked up the small gray box that had been lying on the table and handed it to Matt. "This is for you."

Matt opened the lid. An automatic pistol, very small, dark and menacing, lay in its green velvet liner.

"It's a custom nine-millimeter, made by an acquaintance in Shanghai. It's loaded with hollow-point ammunition. Small but quite powerful. The pistol and the ammunition are made of materials that won't be revealed by a metal detector. It's unique, one of a kind. The group that ordered it managed to blow themselves up before it was picked up. I thought you might find it useful."

Matt didn't believe such a thing could exist. Out of curiosity, he picked it up and ejected the magazine. The cartridges appeared to be made of some space-age material he'd never seen before. He'd seen pistols made of polymers, like the Glock, but he'd never even heard of ammunition made of anything other than metal. He hadn't thought it was possible. It was an airline pilot's worst nightmare. Maybe Gray Wolf was right; maybe there were things going on in the world he wasn't aware of. He snapped the clip back in place with the heel of his hand.

"I can't accept such a generous gift."

"It would please me if you'd accept."

Matt didn't want it, but he'd rather have the pistol than see it in the hands of some terrorist group. Once they were at sea, he'd throw it over the side.

"Thank you."

They both came to their feet. Gray Wolf extended his hand.

"Go and find the young woman, Matthew. But remember, she's not important. Only what she knows is important. The first thing you must do when you make contact is find out what she knows. No matter what happens to her, you must bring back the information."

Bullshit. With a five-million-dollar reward on her head, there was no way he wasn't going to bring the senator's daughter back. He tucked the pistol inside his shirt, under his belt.

"I'll bring her back."

Gray Wolf walked him out to the van, giving him tremendous

face. Popeye Zhang and his soldiers, who'd been sitting on their haunches around the van, came to their feet.

"I sent these men to protect you," Gray Wolf said in Mandarin. "I ordered them to be courteous and treat you with respect."

Popeye Zhang and his soldiers looked shaken. Why was their great leader speaking to this barbarian? Everyone knew the *kwai lo* couldn't talk.

Matt didn't react. He didn't especially want these goons to know he spoke Mandarin.

"Did they comply with my wishes?" Gray Wolf said, again in Mandarin.

The color seemed to drain from Popeye Zhang and his men. They stared at Matt, mouths open, waiting for the answer that could cost them their heads.

Matt paused for a long moment. Gray Wolf must be outing him as a way to make Zhang and his men keep their mouths shut. "These honorable soldiers?"

"These miserable sons of whores."

"Now that you ask, they made me feel . . ."

Matt could see Zhang tense up.

". . . really welcome."

After Gray Wolf's warm send-off, Popeye Zhang and his men drove Matt back to the ship in silence. They sat slumped in their seats like beaten dogs, avoiding any eye contact. The driver raced down streets that were now dark, eager to be rid of the foreign devil who'd nearly gotten them killed.

The van slid to a stop near the gangway of *CoMar Explorer*. Popeye Zhang hopped out and opened the side door. He looked at Matt as he stepped out onto the dock. There was a new look in his one good eye: respect, and a grudging speck of gratitude. He'd lost much face, but he still had his head.

Matt looked at him and saw that they both understood: *You owe me.*

The doors slammed shut and the van roared off. The sound of Popeye Zhang shrieking at his men, shifting the blame to them for not knowing the *waiguoren* could talk, faded down the docks.

He looked up at *CoMar Explorer*. The tide was coming in and she rode high against the dock, cranes towering above her. It was dark now and floodlights lit the ship with a carnival atmosphere. He felt a surge of pride. With her sleek lines and water cannon forward and aft, she looked more like a ship-of-the-line than an ocean-salvage vessel. He took a long last look at her, sobered to know that he was risking everything on one roll of the dice. Depending on the success or failure of this venture, it would either be the beginning of a fleet of such ships, or the end of the line.

Chapter Five

Elizabeth Grayson awoke face down across the straw mat in her cell, her forearm throbbing with pain. Her eyelids felt stuck together. She blinked them open. A smoky orange light, the first hint of dawn, came through the slit in the wall. She rolled over and freed her pinned arm. Her hand was clenched into a fist. *The note.* Was it real or had she just been dreaming? She opened her hand. The tiny scroll, damp with perspiration, was still there. She glanced at the cell door, then unrolled the note and brought it into focus.

Stay strong. We are leaving soon.

The note was real. Real and dangerous. She leaned her head against the wall and closed her eyes, the lids trembling. She should have gotten rid of the note last night, but couldn't bring herself to destroy it.

She looked at it again. What did "we" mean? One thing was certain. It wasn't a negotiated release. It had to be a rescue attempt of some kind. Who was behind it? Her father? Her uncle Lao? Her uncle Wang? Her cousin James?

It had to be James. He was responsible for bringing her over, and he was close by, in Hong Kong. James was a few years older, and had always been an odd sort, but they'd been close as children, playing at her parent's summer home on Martha's Vineyard. He'd even had a crush on her. Poor guy. He'd made a few clumsy attempts to be kissing cousins, but she wouldn't go there. He'd evolved into a real loner as an adult, but it now seemed clear that he loved his American cousin and wouldn't rest until he got her out. She could understand what had taken so long. James was the type to follow all the procedures. He'd exhausted all the proper channels and had struck out. Somehow he'd found out where she was being held and was now doing the only thing he could—sending someone to rescue her.

She tried to picture who it would be. Someone like the handsome marine captain she'd seen at a White House dinner with her parents? God. What would he think when he saw her? She felt her hair, stiff with grime, scrape against the wall like a brush. The weekly two-minute shower in cold water barely got the dirt off. She'd kill for a hot bath. She'd never been big on makeup but wished now she at least had the basics, some mascara and a little lip gloss. She hadn't looked in a mirror in three months, but she could tell by her ribs she was skin and bones. Whoever came through that door would probably take one look and run for his life.

The light breaking through the window grew brighter. She braced herself for the dawn, when the gates of hell would open. Trumpets would blare and gongs would sound, calling the penitents to the fields to atone for their crimes. Four Finger Tang would hammer on the door, strut into her cell, and cover every inch of it, poking her with his bamboo stick, shouting slogans, looking around. She wanted to keep the note, but if Tang found it she'd be finished. They'd take her off the island, into the Chinese interior, and she'd never be heard from again.

But without the note, it would all be a dream. Still . . . She tore the rice paper note into four tiny pieces, placed them under her tongue, and let them dissolve in her mouth. She could feel her body absorb the strength of the words. She leaned her head against the wall, closed her eyes, and drifted off into a nether world, neither asleep nor awake, dreaming of home, fantasizing about her rescue.

A trumpet blaring through a tinny loudspeaker knocked her out of her reverie. It was the opening blast in a cacophony of drums, cymbals and gongs, guards shouting, inmates groaning, cell doors clanging. She heard the bolt on her cell door snap open, felt the same sharp pain in her abdomen.

"Reform through labor, reform through labor," Four Finger Tang said, bursting into her cell.

"Must work, must work, must reconstruct socialism with two hands," his shadow, Big Ears Wu, said. Elizabeth wondered how long it had taken this dimwit to memorize such a long slogan. It must have taxed his brain, because it was the only thing he ever said.

They walked around her cell, looking over every nook and cranny, even picking up her bucket and looking beneath it. Satisfied, Four Finger Tang shoved her out the door. She fell into the long gray line of skeletal prisoners shuffling by in silence, stretching stiff limbs, hawking and spitting, steeling themselves for another twelve-hour day in the withering sun.

"Look, the west-ocean mongrel from the Golden Country is still alive," the prisoner in front of her said. "Another day and you lose your bet, old Wang."

"Eh, she won't live another day," the man behind her said. He appeared to be in his late sixties, with a face the color of an old saddle. "Look at her. She's as bony as a carp."

"And just as pale and smelly," the young man in front said. "But she will live another day. Each night I enter her jade gate with my jade spear and fill her with life. I only do her to win the bet, of course."

"*Diu neh loh moh.*" Do your mothers.

A stunned silence came over the prisoners surrounding her. It was the first time she'd spoken Chinese in front of them. Probably a mistake, but she couldn't help herself. She'd listened to an unending stream of vulgarities and insults for three months. Besides, the note had given her hope that she'd be leaving soon. There was no longer any need to practice the fine art of what the Chinese called *jia chi bu dian*, playing stupid while being smart.

The line shuffled out into the daylight and snaked around to a steam table and huge cauldron. She didn't have to wonder what was being served for breakfast. It was the same meal, twice a day, seven days a week. *Mantou* and *tangmian*. Plain steamed buns and heavily salted noodle soup. Every Friday, during the evening meal, a chunk of stewed pork fat was plopped into the soup with great ceremony. The prisoners ate it with relish, but Elizabeth was repulsed by it. She was most popular then. The others clustered around, waiting for her to leave the greasy, flabby lump, then fought over it.

She took her morning ration and sat on a pile of leaves, away from the others, and forced herself to eat. She looked around at the human discards squatting in the dirt. Mostly political prisoners, along with a handful of drug dealers, vagrants, murderers, rapists, thieves, and embezzlers. The two men she'd just shut down were sitting as far away from her as they could get.

She noticed a prisoner she hadn't seen before moving in her

direction with his tin cup and steamed bun. He disappeared behind some shrubs briefly and then reappeared beside her, squatting behind the bush on her right, out of sight of most of the others.

"*Dong Zhongwen-ma?*" he said. Do you understand Chinese?

Elizabeth glanced at him sideways. He was young—late twenties, maybe—and soft-spoken. He looked well fed and in good condition, like someone who had only just arrived. Her instincts told her he meant no harm.

"*Dong,*" she said. I do.

"They didn't tell me," he said in English.

"Who didn't tell you?" Elizabeth said. "Who are you?"

"A friend. I liked the way you nailed those jerks, but don't speak any more Cantonese. If you feel compelled to say something, tell them to get stuffed in English, like you did Professor Lee last night."

"You were there?"

He nodded. "I was afraid you were near your breaking point. I had to get word to you to hold on."

Elizabeth gasped. "My God. It was you, last night, you touched my foot."

He looked embarrassed. "Sorry. I wasn't trying to be familiar."

"Please don't be sorry." Women's feet were considered erotic to Chinese men, for reasons Elizabeth had never figured out. This guy could touch her foot any time he wanted. "Who sent you?" she said. "My cousin James, right?"

"Who sent me's not important. That note could get us killed. I hope you disposed of it."

She touched her chest. "I swallowed it."

"Good girl. The next time you see me, do exactly as I say. We'll go together. I've been here three days, and I can't stomach any more of this slop." He poured his soup into the bushes, then offered his steamed bun.

She shook her head, too excited to eat. "No, thanks. When will that be? When will I see you?"

He broke the bun in half, sniffed it, made a face, and took a bite. "It's best if you don't know."

"How will we get off the island?"

"Best not to know. When I show up, just do as I say. You'll be in safe hands."

"What's your name? I have to know your name."

"My friends call me Charlie," he said. "Charlie Chan." He grinned and then he was gone.

James Lao sipped his morning latte and dabbed at his forehead with a napkin. He looked at the damp paper. Was it the coffee or was it nerves? No one could blame him for being nervous. He'd just activated Phase II of his plan. Everything had been prearranged. All it had taken was a simple phone call, but he'd reached for the phone three times and pulled back three times before he'd finally had the balls to go through with it. There could be no pulling back now. He glanced at his calendar. June 11. L minus ten. If his plan was discovered before the launch, it would mean his death. But with only ten days to go, he felt the risk was virtually nonexistent.

The intercom on his desk buzzed. He looked at his watch. It was early for a call. He pressed the button.

"Yes?"

"Good morning, Senior Colonel," his secretary said in English. "Your Aunt Amelia on line one."

Oh, Christ. Not again. Beth's mother was the last person on earth he wanted to talk to right now. He thought about making an excuse, then picked up the handset and pressed the flashing yellow button.

"Good morning, Auntie. What a pleasant surprise."

"Don't 'Auntie' me. What have you done to get my daughter out of that dunghole of a prison she's in?"

"Now, Auntie, I told you yesterday, we're doing everything we can. These things take time. We—"

"Time? You've had three months. How long do you think a young woman as refined as your cousin can live in a place like that?"

"I know it's dreadful. But we're making progress. I just spoke with my father about it yesterday."

"Your father. Humph. He won't take my calls any more. My

sister tells me he won't even take hers!"

"That's because he's very busy working for her release. As I said, these things take time. We're still trying to find out where she's being held."

"Even I know that."

"You…do?"

"Of course. I overheard my husband say she's being held in a *laogai* on a small island off the coast of Macau. Turtle Island, he called it."

James managed to hold back a groan. How the hell did the senator know where she was? "That's only a rumor, Auntie. We've heard that she's being held in a dozen places."

"This is no rumor. This has been confirmed."

"By whom?"

"By the CIA."

James swallowed. "Are you certain?"

"Absolutely."

"That's wonderful news," James said. "That will help us immensely. I'll transmit the information to my father. I have to go, Auntie, an important call."

He hung up the phone, his mouth dry. So they know she's on Turtle Island. Goddamn it. He'd kept her location top secret. There had to be a leak somewhere. No matter. The launch was still only ten days away. It would all be over before anyone could react. Still, the leak bothered him. He pressed a button on his intercom.

"Yes, Senior Colonel?"

"Ask Major Zhu to come in."

"At once, Senior Colonel."

James finished off his coffee and flipped through his morning briefing report, waiting for his chief of security to arrive. He skipped past the launch details and turned to the security section of the report. Everything appeared to be in order. A footnote caught his eye. A freighter had run aground on an island near the *laogai* on Turtle Island. Not unusual. There were treacherous currents around the islands that made the *laogai* escape-proof. The currents had pulled more than one ship into the islands when their engines failed or someone was asleep on watch. A U.S. flag vessel. That was unusual. There weren't many of those left, thanks to America's greedy labor unions. Nevertheless, because it was a U.S. flag vessel it would take special handling. Something to be aware of.

He glanced at his watch—where was his security chief? As though on command, the intercom on his desk buzzed. He pressed the button.

"Yes."

"Major Zhu is here, Senior Colonel."

"Send him in."

The door clicked open and Zhu Lanqing entered the room carrying several manila folders.

"Good morning, Senior Colonel. May I congratulate you on your promotion?"

James waved him toward a chair in front of his desk.

"Give me a full status report on the American prisoner," he said.

"She's secure in the *laogai* on Turtle Island," Major Zhu said, searching for the right folder. "No confession as yet, but we'll have one before long."

"I know all that. Tell me about the counter-intelligence measures. Bring me up to date," he said, probing for something, not certain what.

"Yes, Senior Colonel." Major Zhu opened a folder. "As you know, we have several agents in the U.S. State Department."

James nodded. The CCP sent promising young men and women to America as college students with the express purpose of becoming government agents. Known as *chen diyu*, deep-sinking fish, they were encouraged to become naturalized U.S. citizens and seek high-visibility jobs in government. As a member of the selection committee, he'd recognized a few of his *chen diyu* on the campus at Stanford.

"One of our people recently overheard a conversation in which the name Elizabeth Grayson was mentioned," Major Zhu said. "We assigned an agent to the official she suggested we watch. We followed him, a black man named Clifford Howard, until he made contact with an agent from the Central Intelligence Agency, a woman named Susan

Elliott. A team of agents has since followed them everywhere, before they left Washington and after."

The State Department and the CIA. No surprise there after his revealing conversation with his aunt.

"And?"

"We failed to see any connection with the American prisoner," Major Zhu said. "We concluded that it was a false alarm."

"Did you?" James said. "Where did they go?"

Major Zhu looked at his notes. "While in Washington, they had lunch or drinks with several naval officers. Their only other contact was a meeting at the Pentagon with the Chief of Naval Operations."

Odd. Why would they go to see the Chief of Naval Operations? Surely they weren't planning on sending the Navy in to rescue his cousin. The Americans were arrogant, but they weren't stupid.

"Where did they go from there?"

Major Zhu retrieved a sheet of paper from his folder and handed it to James.

"Here's a list of their stops."

James ran his eye down the list. United Airlines flight 881 from Dulles to O'Hare, then flight 895 to Hong Kong International, then China Air flight 628 to Kaohsiung. James shook his head. Kaohsiung was a shithole of a town. Other than boasting the largest seaport in Taiwan, there was nothing there. He looked at Major Zhu.

"Why did they go to Kaohsiung?"

Major Zhu looked at his notes. "They stayed at the Linden Hotel on Sszuwei Third Road, separate rooms—"

"I don't care where they stayed. Who did they see?"

"They went aboard a ship, the . . . let me see . . . the *CoMar Explorer*."

"Did the ship sail?"

"No, Senior Colonel, they left after one hour and twelve minutes."

"What nationality is the ship?"

"Panama. It had a Panamanian flag."

"That's a flag of convenience, that means nothing," James said.

"Who's the owner?"

"The ship has a questionable title," Major Zhu said. "A major financial backer is a lying thief known as Gray Wolf, a Taiwanese gangster involved in gun-running, smuggling, and loan-sharking. Head of the Great Wall Triad."

Ah yes, the triads. Chinese organized crime that went back centuries. They could be useful, but in an outlaw province like Taiwan they'd spread like flies. The first thing the Communist party would do when they retook the island would be to round them up. Keep the ones who could do them some good and exterminate the rest.

"I don't see the connection," James said. "Who did they see aboard the ship?"

Major Zhu turned a page. "According to our agent, they met with a man believed to be the ship's captain. An American. One Matthew Baines Connor."

An American. Why would agents from the State Department and the CIA take the long trip from Washington for a one-hour meeting with an American ship captain in Taiwan?

"You don't know what was discussed?"

"No, Senior Colonel. Our listening devices wouldn't penetrate the steel of the ship."

"What do we know about the captain?"

Major Zhu turned the page. "Former U.S. naval officer. Resigned in disgrace. Expatriate to Taiwan. Unable to return to the U.S. because of a tax lien against his ship."

Not surprising. He was exactly the kind of outlaw scum that belonged on Taiwan. Water seeks its own level.

"What else do you know about him?"

"He was related by a former marriage to the American Chief of Naval Operations," Major Zhu said.

Related to the Chief of Naval Operations. Curious. Perhaps a coincidence, but his experience told him that any time something came up twice in the same conversation it was no coincidence.

"Interesting," James said. His instincts told him there was something there, but he couldn't quite see it. They stared at each other, neither speaking. Grasping at straws, he said, "What kind of ship is it, a freighter or a passenger ship?"

"Neither, Senior Colonel," Major Zhu said. "It's an ocean-salvage ship."

James felt the blood drain from his face. He picked up his daily briefing report and started flipping pages, his mind racing. His aunt's call. Their knowing where Beth was. An American captain. Former naval officer. Related to the CNO. Expatriate to Taiwan. Ocean-salvage ship. The footnote he'd just read. A U.S. flag vessel run aground on an island near the prison.

He threw the report across the desk, striking Major Zhu in the face.

"You idiot! Don't you see what they're doing?"

Major Zhu jumped to his feet. "Please, Senior Colonel. I don't understand what—"

"Of course you don't." James pushed himself up from his chair and began to pace behind his desk. It was crystal clear to him what the Americans were doing, and his half-witted security chief still didn't see it. He could be wrong—he could be adding two and two and getting five—but he couldn't take a chance. There was too much at stake.

He was in enough trouble with his father for bringing his American cousin over in the first place, then having her thrown in prison. To now admit that her security had been breached would send him over the edge. On the other hand, if the Americans were successful in reaching her . . . He dared not think about the consequences, especially after what he'd just done.

"Where's the ship?"

"Right now?"

"Yes, you fool, right now."

"I don't know, sir, but I'll find out."

Major Zhu began stabbing out phone numbers. After several minutes of working the phone, he hung up, his face ashen.

"The ship sailed from Kaohsiung Harbor last night at high tide, approximately eleven forty-five p.m."

"Which direction?"

"On a course toward Macau."

That confirmed it. He was right. *Calm down and think.* He looked out the window, hands behind his back. He had to find a way to circumvent this, all without his father finding out. He couldn't rely on his incompetent security chief, who still didn't realize what was going on. He was on his own.

His first impulse was to simply move his cousin from the island, but if spies had reported her location once they'd do so again. Besides, if he moved her, his father would know that her security had been compromised and he'd be even angrier. That was not an option. The only other course was to stop the Americans in their tracks. With the launch only ten days away, the U.S. wouldn't have time to react, to put another mission together.

That was the answer, but how to do it? Sink the ship? Even with the rank of senior colonel he couldn't order it on his own, but he might be able to order it by invoking his father's name. The only problem was, his father would be sure to find out. Besides, sinking a ship commanded by an American, even if he was an expatriate, could cause an international incident that would focus too much attention on China. The ship had to be stopped, but it had to be stopped quietly.

He watched an ancient Chinese junk crawl across the harbor below like a slow-moving water bug, inching its way toward a luxury liner.

In an instant he knew what to do. A strategy his father was fond of quoting came back to him: *When weak, appear strong; when strong, appear weak.*

Yes. He knew exactly what to do.

Chapter Six

Matt jerked awake, drenched in sweat. He'd heard that dreams only last a few seconds, a minute at most, but he didn't believe it. His personal nightmare had returned with a vengeance, playing over in an endless loop for what seemed like hours. The same terrified faces melted into the same roaring flames. The same anguished eyes stared at him, pleading for him to save them. And as always, he stood rooted to the spot, unable to move, no matter how hard he tried.

He covered his eyes with his forearm, still numb from the green and white capsules Doc had given him. He felt like he hadn't slept at all, but it served him right. He didn't deserve sleep. In spite of everything, he hadn't learned. Without asking anyone, he'd just committed his entire crew to break someone out of a Chinese prison, for God's sake. How many men would die on his watch this time?

He raised his arm and squinted at the beam of sunshine streaming into his sea cabin. The angle of the rays told him it was way past the time he'd told Francisco to call him. He brought his watch into focus. Almost ten. Damn. He came upright in his bunk and scrubbed his face with his hands. His first impulse was to skin Francisco alive for not calling him, but he couldn't blame the cook. He should have had the discipline to wake on his own.

He sat on the edge of his bunk for a minute and cleared his head, breathing in the stale air of his sea cabin. He glanced up at the porthole. He knew he'd opened it last night—he had to have a steady supply of fresh air—but Francisco must have closed it after he'd gone to sleep. He shook his head. His new cook had a mind of his own.

He stretched and yawned and told himself to concentrate on being at sea again, away from the chaos of Kaohsiung. Out here he was lord and master, captain of his own ship, the purest form of dictatorship on earth. He glanced at his watch again. More than guilt for sleeping in, he felt a little jealous that the ship seemed to be functioning well without him. He could tell by the vibration in his feet that the pitch on the props was optimized and that all four engines were running smoothly. Based on the rate of swell passing by the porthole, he estimated *CoMar Explorer*'s speed at around fourteen knots, her cruising speed.

With the light of day pushing the shadows of doubt back, the plan suddenly seemed to make sense. His crew would understand that he'd had no choice, that this was the only option left open to him to keep Connor Marine together. And this time he'd make damn sure that everyone came back alive. He should relax and enjoy the ride. The sea was calm, the winds were fair, the sun was up, and he was on his way to a job that could solve all his problems.

Traveller lay curled up in his usual spot. He opened one eye and looked at Matt.

Matt slapped his thigh and the dog sauntered over, stretched, yawned, and laid its muzzle in Matt's lap. The poor old mutt still looked terrible, but he'd come a long way since Matt had found him, emaciated and near death, on the dock in Kaohsiung. Matt scratched the dog's ears and looked into the depths of its black eyes.

"So, what do you think, Trav? Think we're going to like being rich?"

Today was the eleventh of June. If everything went according to schedule, he'd pick Elizabeth Grayson up on the north shore of the island on midnight of the thirteenth and have her safely back in Kaohsiung within two days or so, Gray Wolf and his conspiracy theories notwithstanding. He'd personally put her on a plane, escort her to Cambridge, Massachusetts, and accept five million dollars from the grateful parents.

End of story. No negotiating with Lloyds, no arbitration period, no waiting for months for a check, as he would have had to do with a normal salvage job. After that he'd pay Gray Wolf off, get clear title to *CoMar Explorer*, and begin a search for a second salvage ship. Sam was ready for command, and a second ship would be an extension of himself, covering parts of the Pacific he couldn't reach in time to beat out his larger competitors.

But first there was the little matter of briefing his crew on the mission and getting everyone to agree. He knew he'd meet with some opposition, and he knew exactly who'd lead it. Matt had wanted to brief his obnoxious chief engineer first to keep him from spooking the rest of the crew, but after sleeping in, there was no time. It wasn't fair to withhold the mission from the crew any longer. And now he'd missed breakfast. He hated thinking about Scootchy Carter on an empty stomach.

He came to his feet, dropped, and did fifty push-ups. An old habit from his Navy days, but he'd noticed lately that they were getting harder to do. Breathing hard, he ran a hand through his hair and pulled on the pair of khakis he'd draped over a chair. He'd taken a quick shower before he crashed at 0200, and he never bothered to shave when they were at sea, so he was good to go.

The pistol Gray Wolf had given him was still sitting on the chair where he'd placed it. He hefted it once, then slipped it into his hip pocket. He'd pitch it over the side tonight when he had the watch. He picked up a clean tee shirt from a stack in his closet, pulled it on, then heard a rap on the door.

"Come."

The door to his sea cabin opened a crack and Francisco's round face peered in.

"Hey, Boss-man, time to—"

"You're a little late, Francisco. I told you to call me at 0600."

"Too early. Four hour sleep not enough. Boss-man need sleep, now Boss-man need food."

"No time for that," Matt said, rummaging in his closet for a sweatshirt.

"Boss-man need food." Francisco pushed the door open and walked in with a tray.

Matt stared at him. "Don't you ever follow orders?"

"Why should I?"

"Well, it's like this," Matt said. "I'm the captain of a ship, and you're a member of my crew."

"Baloney."

"And another thing. How many times have I told you? Stop calling me Boss-man. Makes me sound like an overseer on a southern plantation."

"Okay, Boss-man."

Matt shook his head. He'd been having the same argument with the Filipino since he'd taken him on as ship's cook during a stop in Manila. Francisco had been executive chef of an upscale restaurant in Cavite City that had burned down under mysterious circumstances. He'd seemed to be in a hurry to get out of town and had never been at sea before, but Matt needed a cook and hired him in spite of his misgivings.

His instincts had turned out to be correct. Francisco was the most insubordinate crewman he'd ever known, but even if he'd wanted to, there wasn't much he could do about it now. The crew of *CoMar Explorer* had fallen in love with the wily Filipino. He always made extras of his Filipino pastries as cumshaw for the crew when they passed by the galley. The men pretended to filch the goodies and Francisco pretended not to see, always with a sly smile on his face.

Now he shoved paperwork to one side and set the tray on Matt's desk.

"You eat now."

The ship took a slight roll, and Francisco froze with a stricken look on his face.

Matt grinned. "How do you feel?"

"Death would be merciful."

Matt glanced out the porthole. It was one of those halcyon days when the South China Sea looked like a sheet of green glass, but he didn't want to tell Francisco that.

"You'll get used to it."

"Like earthquake that never stop." Francisco pressed a napkin to his forehead and poured coffee. "Men want to know where we go, what job is," he said. "Everybody ask."

"There'll be a meeting in the crew's lounge in fifteen minutes," Matt said, pulling on a faded 49ers sweatshirt. He punched a button on his speakerphone.

"Bridge," Sam's resonant voice came over the speaker.

"Morning, Sam. How's everything going?"

"No problems, Skipper. We're right where we're supposed to be."

"How's the number four?"

"Scootchy's got the watch. Says it sounds like a sewing machine."

"Good," Matt said. With Scootchy Carter in the engine room, he might be able to brief the crew without being interrupted every five seconds. "Tell him to stay there and keep an eye on it, I'll brief him later. Pass the word over the PA system. There'll be a meeting at ten-thirty in the crew's lounge for all hands not on watch. Have Jason relieve you. I want you there."

"Aye aye, Skipper."

Matt switched off the speakerphone. A lot was riding on this meeting, and his brain still felt numb. He felt mildly hungry but didn't want to be slowed down with a heavy breakfast. Thinking he should at least have some coffee to clear his head, he picked up the cup Francisco had poured and took a sip. Jesus. No one made coffee like Francisco. The pungent flavor of the coffee on his tongue sharpened his appetite. His nostrils caught a scent of the aroma drifting up from the tray. He lifted the cover. Steam rose from a cheese omelet drizzled with Madeira sauce and thin slices of polenta, fried golden brown and still sizzling. He picked up the plate and took a bite of the omelet.

"Hey, what's a matter? You no like my scones?" Francisco picked up a wicker basket and drew back the white linen cover.

Matt picked up a freshly baked scone embedded with walnuts. *Insubordination be damned. This guy can cook.*

"I love your scones." He downed it in two bites and washed it down with a slug of black coffee.

"Hey, take it easy, Boss-man. Eat slow. Food meant to be tasted."

Matt finished off the omelet and half the polenta, nodding his approval. He picked up a pair of scones and headed for the door. He paused with his hand on the latch, feeling better than he'd felt in a while. Even without much real sleep, a belly full of eggs, corn meal, and coffee had worked wonders. He turned and smiled.

"Thanks, Francisco. You're amazing."

Francisco grinned, his moon face flowering.

"I know."

Traveller darted out the door beside Matt. As Matt walked away, he tossed one of the scones to the dog.

"Scones for you. Not for dog," Francisco shouted over the clatter of dishes from the sea cabin. "Scones too good for dog."

Matt watched Traveller bolt the scone down in two gulps while he finished his own, savoring each bite.

"No offense, Trav, but he's right."

He walked aft to the crew's lounge, rehearsing what he was going to say. He stepped over the coaming and saw that most of the crew was already there. They milled around, bantering, drawing coffee from the urn, waiting for the show to begin. Francisco came bustling in with a tray of Filipino pastries and set them on the table by the coffee. The crew converged on the tray, murmuring their approval at rows of fresh hot pandesal, pan de ube, ensemada, and cheese rolls, while Francisco beamed.

"Well, if it ain't sleeping beauty," Scootchy Carter said. "What brings you up, Cap'n? It ain't even noon yet."

Matt felt the muscles in his abdomen constrict, looking into his chief engineer's weasel face. His real name was Raymond, but everyone called him Scootchy. The scuttlebutt was that someone had once caught him in the engine room scooting against a steel deck plate to relieve the pain of his hemorrhoids, like a dog on grass. He'd been dubbed Scooter, which had evolved into Scootchy, and the name had stuck. It was the way of the sea. The first rule every seaman learned was never get caught saying or doing anything embarrassing aboard ship, because it would never be forgotten.

"What are you doing out of the engine room?"

"Them Cat 399s don't need me. They'll run forever."

"Who relieved you?"

"That new kid, Kuntz. Been breaking him in to stand engine room watches."

Matt flushed. "Kuntz is a diver, not an engineer. We just overhauled the number four engine. I want it monitored closely for the first hundred hours. You need to be down there."

"Bullshit, I already told Sam, it's running like a two-dollar watch," Scootchy said. "Anyway, I'm a ship's officer, I got a right to know. I ain't gonna get it second hand. I want to hear it from the horse's ass—I mean mouth." He grinned, exposing his rat teeth.

Matt's eyes flashed. "One of these days, your mouth is going to get you into more trouble than you can handle."

"Hey, it was a joke, for chrissake."

Sam walked up. "Morning, Skipper." He turned to the chief engineer. "I thought I told you to stay below, Scootch."

"And miss the scoop? No chance."

"All right," Matt said. "You can stay. But keep your opinions to yourself during the briefing. If you've got a problem with anything I say, I'll talk to you about it privately."

Scootchy shrugged. "Why should I have a problem with a salvage job?" He walked toward the coffee urn.

Sam counted noses. "Looks like everyone's here that can be, Captain."

Matt nodded. "Let's get started."

"All right, you slugs, knock it off and sit down," Sam said. "Captain is on deck."

Matt walked up to the aft bulkhead and pulled down a map of the South China Sea. He turned and looked out over his crew. Fourteen members were present, including Sam and himself, and four were on watch. A crew of eighteen was lean for a ship of this size and capability, but they were all good men, even Scootchy. They'd all signed on as specialists, and Matt had insisted that every member of his crew be trained to do any job aboard ship. The years of cross-training had paid off, and Connor Marine had a reputation for having one of the most efficient salvage crews in the industry. He smiled at them, as proud of his crew as he was of his ship.

"Good morning," he said with a sheepish grin. "I hope you guys slept as well as I did."

They all laughed. There were no secrets aboard ship, and they seemed to enjoy the fact that the captain had dogged it.

"About this job. . ." Matt said.

"This better be a good one," Scootchy said, munching a cheese roll. "I need the money. There's a ranch I want to buy."

"It's actually more of a mission than a job," Matt said, "but there'll be bonuses for everyone if we can pull it off."

"A mission?" Scootchy said. "What the hell does that mean?"

"If you'll shut the hell up, Scootch, maybe the captain can tell us," Sam said.

"There's a freighter aground on an island off the coast of Macau," Matt said, pointing to a black speck on the map. "We're going to go through the motions of debeaching the ship, but it's just a decoy. The real assignment is to pick up a woman from a neighboring island."

"A woman?" Scootchy said. "For what?"

"She's an American citizen being held by the Chinese. Other people will deliver her to us. Our job is to bring her back."

"Being *held*?" Scootchy said. "Jesus Christ, you mean we're going to break her out of some Chink prison?"

"Nothing like that." Matt glared at him. "Our role in this is a relatively small one." He spent the next twenty minutes going over the details of the rescue plan, and the bigger than usual bonuses they'd all get, while the crew sat mesmerized. To his surprise, even Scootchy kept quiet, apparently too flabbergasted to speak. When he'd finished, he leaned back against the table and folded his arms.

"That's about it. Any questions?"

There was a long silence.

"Holy shit," Scootchy said, rubbing the back of his neck. "I don't know about the rest of you boys, but this ain't what I signed on to do."

"I never thought I'd agree with Scootchy on anything, Captain, but he's right," Doc Miller said. "This is over the top."

"I know it's out of the ordinary," Matt said, "but business is a little slow right now. If we want to keep the crew together we're going to have to take some risk."

"Risk?" Scootchy said. "Jesus Christ Almighty, we're liable to have half the goddamn Chinese Navy down on our backs. If they catch us, we're screwed. I don't fancy spending the rest of my days in a Chinese prison."

"Scootchy's got a point," Gene Harvey said.

The rest of the crew sat quietly, watching Matt and Sam.

"I've tried to give it to you as straight as I can," Matt said. "Yes, there is some risk involved, but I think it's manageable. You guys will have to decide. If you want, we'll abort and return to Kaohsiung and wait for another job. It may come in time to keep us together, it may not."

They all looked at Sam, waiting for his opinion. Matt hadn't discussed it with him, but he thought he knew how he'd vote. If Sam agreed, the rest of the crew would go along.

Sam stepped forward. "Let me remind you jokers that none of us were doing so hot until the skipper here brought us together. Under his leadership over the last five years we've all had more fun and made more money than we ever did in our lives. Some of us even got our self-respect back. Now, the captain's thought it through. If he says it's the right thing to do, then I'm in."

"Well, what the hell," Doc Miller said. "I guess we could use a little excitement around here."

"You can have the excitement," Gene Harvey said. "I'll take the money."

Matt saw heads nodding in agreement. A chorus of "Suits me," and "I'm in," went up from the crew.

"Well, I guess that makes me odd man out," Scootchy said. "I'll go along, but I still don't like it. Even if we pick her up without getting our heads shot off, we still gotta have a woman around. Women are bad news on a ship."

"How would you know, Scootchy?" Doc Miller said. "You never had a woman in your life."

"Hell I didn't," Scootchy said over the laughter. "I had a woman once. Women are only good for two things. Screwing and complaining. And when they ain't screwing, they're complaining. Never again. I want gash, I buy it."

"All right, knock it off," Matt said. "We're going to have a woman aboard, and I expect you all to be on your best behavior."

"Ass for gas," Scootchy said. "If she wants to ride, she's got to—"

"You heard the captain," Sam said. "There'll be no more of that kind of talk."

Matt spent the rest of the day moving around the ship, briefing the watch standers who'd missed the meeting of the ship's company and talking with crewmen individually, reassuring them. By the next morning they all seemed to be solidly behind him, though Scootchy Carter, he'd heard, was still taking shots behind his back. He had to get it resolved. He found Scootchy in the crew's mess just before noon, sitting alone at his usual table. Matt drew a cup of coffee and joined him.

"Scootch, I'm hearing scuttlebutt that you're not with me."

"On what?"

"This mission."

"I wouldn't exactly say that," Scootchy said, tearing into a roll. "I just think it's nuts, is all."

"I can't have you getting the crew upset. I told you before the briefing yesterday that if you had any problems with it, I'd talk to you about them privately."

"You ain't been around to talk privately."

Before Matt could respond, he heard Jason Tyler's voice rattle through the ship's loudspeaker system.

"Cap'n to the bridge. Radar reports low-flying aircraft approaching from the stern."

"See, I told you," Scootchy said, his voice rising. "It's probably a Chink fighter. They're probably wise to us already. They could drop a bomb on us out here and no one would ever know."

"Shut up," Matt said, listening. In the distance, the faint thump of helicopter rotors beat the air. "Go to emergency stations."

The crew broke and scrambled for their assigned stations, and Matt ran for the bridge. He grabbed a pair of binoculars from a hook in the pilothouse and stepped out onto the bridge wing. He adjusted the focus and followed a small speck in the airspace over the stern of the ship as it approached. It was a military helicopter and it appeared to be coming straight toward them.

"Can you make it out, Captain?" Sam asked.

"Starting to. They're gaining altitude."

"What does that mean?"

"They're either going to sink us or fly over us."

"What is it?"

"Looks like a Z-8."

"What the hell's that?"

"PLA Navy chopper. Chinese copy of an old French design called the Super Frelon. They bought a few and developed their own version of it."

"Whatever it is, that son of a bitch can move."

Matt nodded. "Medium-size bird with three turboshafts. Cruises around two-fifty kilometers per hour. They fly off DDGs on anti-sub missions."

"Think they're going to drop a bomb on us?"

"They don't carry bombs, but they could sure as hell sink us if they wanted to. They carry one torpedo, usually an American Mark 46."

"Be a bitch if they sunk us with one of our own torpedoes."

Matt strained his neck to look up. The helicopter roared straight overhead, the red star on its fuselage clearly visible. It decreased its altitude and kept going in a straight line, appearing to take no notice of them.

"What the hell was that all about?" Sam said.

"Beats me," Matt said, watching the steel-blue helicopter disappear over the horizon. "They look like they're searching for something, but whatever it is, it's apparently not us."

"Suits me fine," Sam said.

"You got that right," Matt said, and whistled a sigh of relief. "Pass the word to secure from emergency stations."

"Aye aye, Captain."

Matt stayed on the bridge for another hour or so, scanning the horizon, making sure the helicopter didn't come back. Suddenly feeling hungry, he looked at his watch. One-thirty. He decided to join the late lunch crowd in the crew's mess before it was closed. There had been a small officer's mess on the ship, but Matt had converted it into a storage area. He insisted that every member of the crew eat together.

"Any more of them Chink birds flying around out there, Skipper?" someone asked as he walked into the crew's mess.

"Nary a one," Matt said, picking up a steel tray. Francisco was busy in the galley, so he went down the line and served himself a slab of meatloaf, a scoop of au gratin potatoes, and a side of green beans. He finished his lunch, then went to his sea cabin to catch up on some paperwork. By the time he finished, it was three o'clock. Before he could clear off his desk, the speaker on the bulkhead crackled.

"Captain to the bridge, captain to the bridge!"

Matt dropped the papers and sprinted for the bridge, hoping it wasn't another encounter with the PLA Navy. He burst through the door of the pilothouse and saw Sam and Jason Tyler staring through binoculars at an object two points off the starboard bow.

"Better have a look at this, Skipper." Sam handed Matt his binoculars. "Looks like some poor joker out there on a raft."

Matt focused the binoculars on what appeared to be a nearly naked man lying face down, clinging to a crude raft that was half submerged.

"Must be what the Chinese were searching for this morning," Matt said.

"I wonder how they missed him?" Sam said.

"It's easy to miss a speck from the air, especially when you're flying at that speed."

"If that's the guy the Chinese are searching for, I don't think we want him aboard," Jason Tyler said.

Matt silently agreed, but he'd pick him up if he was still alive. It was the oldest law of the sea.

"Doesn't matter who it is. We can't just leave him."

"He's not moving," Jason Tyler said. "Maybe he's dead."

"Let's get a closer look," Matt said. "I've got the conn, Jason. Right standard rudder. All ahead slow."

"Captain has the conn. Right standard rudder, all ahead slow, aye, sir."

As *CoMar Explorer* inched closer, the man shifted his weight, struggling up higher on the raft, trying to get his feet out of the water.

"He's alive," Matt said. "All engines stop."

"All stop, aye, Captain."

"Pass the word," Matt said. "Stand by to recover a man on a raft. Starboard side."

"You want the raft too?" Sam asked.

"Leave it. If the Chinese find it they'll think he's drowned and stop looking."

Within minutes of the All Stop order, two divers wearing masks and fins were in the water, swimming the raft toward the ship. They lifted the man into a sling suspended from the aft cargo boom, positioned themselves on either side, and gave the thumbs-up sign. The boom operator hoisted the sling aboard, dripping seawater, and gently lowered it to the deck.

"Secure from recovery operations," Matt said, watching from the bridge wing. "Jason, you have the conn. All ahead full. Return to your original course."

"I have the conn, aye, Captain," Jason said, twisting the wheel. "All ahead full. Course two-six-three."

Matt felt all four Caterpillar engines come to life at the same time. The ship shuddered and surged ahead through green water.

"Call Doc to the infirmary," he said. "Come on, Sam. Let's go see what we've got."

By the time Matt got to the ship's infirmary, Doc Miller was bending over the castaway, trying to stick a thermometer in his mouth. Doc had been a Navy hospital corpsman until he got bored with it and became a diver. He was the only member of the crew with any medical experience at all, so he got stuck with looking at every sprained wrist and ingrown toenail. "Can't get a thermometer in his mouth," he said. "Bastard won't hardly let me look at him."

"How is he?"

Doc shrugged. "Looks okay to me. A few contusions and abrasions that look fresh. I'd expect him to be dehydrated, but he doesn't seem to be. He must have had some fresh water on his raft."

Francisco came rushing in with a tray holding a steaming teapot and single mug. "Man need tea now, not food." He said it firmly, as though expecting an argument.

Matt looked down on the man. He appeared to be Chinese, about forty. He sat up in bed to take the mug of tea Francisco offered him, and the thin blanket that had been covering him fell away. The guy had a body like an athlete. Aside from a few bruises here and there, he looked to be in perfect physical condition.

"*Nin gui xing?*" May I ask your name?

The man looked up, startled, and sloshed tea on the blanket. He stared at Matt.

"You can talk?" he said in Mandarin.

"My Chinese is poor," Matt said, "but I can talk a little. How are you called?"

"You speak very well," the man said. "I've never known a west-ocean person who could talk." He looked down at the blanket, then at Francisco. "Please tell this foreign brother I apologize for spilling his tea."

"It's nothing," Matt said. He stared, waiting for an answer.

"Forgive me. I am called Yang Zhi."

"Where are you from, Mr. Yang, and how did you come to be on a raft in the South China Sea?"

"I am from Dalu, a small village in Quangxi Province. I was sentenced to fifteen years in prison for speaking against the government. I was sent to a *laogai* on an island off the coast of Macau. Everyone said it was escape-proof, but I got away."

Matt blinked. "Turtle Island?"

Yang stared at him. "Do you know the place?"

"Only from a distance. You say you escaped from Turtle Island?"

"I could not have done it alone. I was working on the periphery of the fields in an out-of-the-way place, and with the help of a friend was able to construct a raft."

"How did you get away on a raft?" Matt asked. "There are strong currents around that island."

"As a man of the sea you would know this," Yang said. "But my friend and I found a part of the beach shielded from the strong currents by a natural sea wall. There we were able to push off at night and get away."

"What happened to your friend?"

"We were hit by a storm three days ago, he was washed away. Very sad."

"A PLA Navy helicopter flew over this morning," Matt said. "They appeared to be searching for something."

"Yes, I saw the helicopter. They're searching for us."

"Why didn't they see you?"

"We had a gray blanket we pulled over the raft to disguise it from the air."

Made sense. Still, something bothered him. Traveller sauntered in, sniffed the air, and growled at the stranger. Matt shushed him by stroking the dog's ears.

"Life in a forced labor camp must agree with you," Matt said, nodding at his muscular chest. "The food must be good."

Yang Zhi made a face. "The food was execrable. Steamed buns and salty noodle soup twice a day. Everyone is emaciated. I was only there a short time, but I had to get away. I knew that if I stayed, I would die like so many others."

Matt nodded. If he was only there a few days, that would explain his condition.

"Rest now, my friend. You're in safe hands."

The man took a deep breath, let out a long sigh, and closed his eyes.

"He'll probably sleep now," Matt said. "Let's leave him alone. Check on him later, will you, Doc?"

Sam returned to the bridge and Matt to his sea cabin, thinking about his unwanted guest. He might be able to get some lemonade out of this lemon. If the man knew a section of the beach that was shielded from the strong currents, he might have other useful intelligence about the island and the prison. After he'd slept for a while, Matt would find out what else he knew.

He pulled off his shoes and lay down. He felt tired again. Those damn capsules. . .

Something brought him awake, a change in the rhythm of the ship. He glanced at his watch. He thought he'd just closed his eyes, but he'd been asleep for over two hours. The phone on his desk rang, the light from the bridge line blinking. When he sat up he could tell by the vibration in his feet that one of the engines was down, probably the number four. Goddamn Scootchy. He slipped into his shoes and pressed the button on his speaker phone.

"Captain."

"Number three's down, Skipper," Sam said.

"Not the number four?"

"No sir, the number three. Engine room's not responding."

"Damn it."

"You want me to go down with you?"

"No, stay on the bridge. Adjust the props to compensate. I'll take care of it."

Matt hurried down the ladder to the engine room. He paused at the entrance: something didn't feel right. As noisy as the engine room was, there was always the sound of voices over it, quarreling, good-natured bantering, *something*. This time there was only the out-of-balance clatter of three diesel engines.

He stepped inside. The lights were out. An emergency battery-powered lantern cast ominous shadows against the port bulkhead. He pulled a flashlight from a clip by the door and walked toward the engine room console, playing his light around.

The beam flashed on a pair of feet by the engine room console. Closer now, he saw Scootchy Carter lying face down, his head in a pool of blood. With a head wound that severe he had to be dead. He glanced at the console. The number three engine had been shut down. He shined the beam of his light toward the console and reached for the black telephone handset.

The shadow of an arm rose above his head. He ducked instinctively and felt a glancing blow behind his right ear. He went down to his knees and rolled over on his back. He looked up, head splitting with pain, and saw the fuzzy image of Yang Zhi standing over him with a wrench in his hand.

Wearing only a loincloth, the escaped prisoner straddled Matt. He raised the wrench over his head and brought it down in a sweeping arc intended to be the final blow. At the last instant Matt rolled to the side. He felt the wind of the swing and heard the clang of the wrench on the steel deck plate. Darting out from between his attacker's legs, he scurried backward. He had to get to his feet. Another blow from that wrench and he'd be finished.

Matt crabbed backward another few feet and managed to pull himself upright by clinging to the engine room console. Yang Zhi walked slowly toward him. He seemed to be supremely confident that he could kill him at his pleasure. Matt looked frantically around for something to fight with, then remembered the pistol. He still had it in his pocket. Backing up, he shook the darkness out of his eyes, ears still ringing from the blow, and probed for the weapon with his fingers. Somehow he managed to get the pistol out, upside down. He righted it and leveled it at Yang.

"That's far enough," Matt said. His voice sounded distant.

Yang shook his head. "You're not the type to keep a gun cocked and ready to fire."

Oh, shit. Matt fumbled for the slide with his left hand. Before he could cock the pistol, Yang grabbed his wrist in a lightning move and wrested the pistol from his hand. It slid down between two deck plates and disappeared into the bilge.

"Why are you doing this?" Matt said in Mandarin.

Yang smiled.

"Tell me," Matt said, buying time for his head to clear. He felt the back of his head. Blood was gushing from a wound at the base of his scalp.

"You have your destination and I have mine," Yang Zhi said, advancing.

That was why he'd shut down only one engine. If he'd shut them all down, the whole crew would have been down there. He didn't want the whole crew. The son of a bitch was going to pick off one or two men at a time, then commandeer the ship with what was left.

Yang lunged and swung the wrench.

Matt raised his arm to fend off the blow and felt a sharp pain in his forearm. Grimacing, he allowed his attacker to back him toward the ladder leading to the catwalk around the engine room. He had to clear his head before he engaged this guy. Gripping his arm, Matt backed his way up the ladder with Yang Zhi advancing as though he had all the time in the world. As they emerged onto the catwalk, Matt lunged for the wrench. He grabbed Yang's arm and slammed his wrist against the handrail. The wrench went clattering to the deck below.

Unfazed, Yang spun around with a kick that caught Matt under the chin.

Dazed, Matt went into a fighter's crouch and swung with his right. He scored a direct hit on Yang's jaw, but the man moved with it, avoiding the full impact.

Yang smiled again. He crouched and swung upward from his center of gravity, catching Matt in the stomach.

Matt felt the wind go out of him. Yang came up under Matt's chin with his bare knee, knocking him backward. Matt shook the clouds out of his head. He feinted with his left and swung with his right, catching the man with a direct hit that made him stagger. Yang shook his head and smiled. They fought back and forth, exchanging blows for several minutes. *Who the hell is this guy?* He took straight shots to the head that would knock a mule down and kept on coming. He'd said he was in prison for speaking out against the government, but Matt didn't think so. He looked and acted like a professional killer, someone who loves his work.

Over the noise of the engines below, Matt heard the horn on the engine room console blare, indicating that the phone was ringing. Yang Zhi looked down at the blinking overhead light, pulsing in unison with the horn. He had to know that an unanswered phone would bring people to the engine room, so he moved in to make the kill. He charged and spun Matt around. Matt felt his neck being twisted to one side. He recognized it as the move Sam had taught him when they were fooling around one day. It was an old SEAL tactic, a way to kill a man with your bare hands.

Sam had also taught him how to break it and throw your attacker off balance.

He slammed his left elbow in Yang's ribcage and reached over his head, grabbing him by the back of his neck. He tucked his body in and pulled, flipping Yang over his head. Yang's back landed squarely in the center of the hand rail. Matt could hear his spine snap over the noise of the engine room. He lay dangling over the steel rail, screaming in agony. Matt placed his fingertips under Yang's head and flipped him forward, over the hand rail. He watched him fly twenty feet down into the engine room in slow motion and land face up on top of the number three engine.

Matt leaned against the handrail, gasping for breath. He stared down on his attacker, sprawled across the yellow Caterpillar engine. Looking closer, he saw a steel rod protruding from his stomach, blood seeping up around it. The sight of a man impaled alive sickened him. Yang shuddered. His arms twitched, and then he stopped moving. Matt felt like vomiting, but he was grateful to be alive. Another five seconds and it would have all been over.

He touched the wound on the base of his skull and looked at the blood on his fingertips, his mind racing. Nothing about this guy added up. Was he really an escaped prisoner, or was he something else? Was the Chinese helicopter really searching for him, or had they flown over the horizon and dropped him in their path, knowing that an American ship captain would automatically stop and render assistance? The man didn't look like someone who'd been drifting at sea for very long. Maybe he came from that helicopter. If he did, if he was a plant, then that meant the Chinese were on to him. And if the Chinese were on to him, he should abort and get the hell out of there.

He told himself to calm down and think. There were only a few people who knew about the mission: Senator Grayson, himself, Gray Wolf, and a handful of government agents. There was simply no way for the Chinese to know, and if they did they wouldn't do something as idiotic as this. The guy was probably a hit man for one of the triads who'd had a taste of prison and wasn't about to go back.

No, if the Chinese were on to him they'd send the PLA Navy out to sink him and be done with it, not pull some stupid trick like this. He would proceed as planned. Clutching his arm, he inched his way down the ladder, toward the ringing telephone.

Chapter Seven

E lizabeth hoisted her wicker basket to her shoulder, let out a sigh, and trudged up the row of plants toward the collection bin. She blinked into the breeze coming from the ocean. Her eyes stung from the acid in the peppers, but she'd learned not to rub them. She glanced around the fields, looking for the man who called himself Charlie Chan. She'd been trying to spot him among the prisoners since their meeting at breakfast, but he was nowhere to be seen. The sun hung low on the horizon, not much daylight left. How did he manage to evade the guards all day?

She placed her basket on the scale. Old Wu, the tally man, an ancient prisoner with a gaping hole where his right eye should have been, flicked the counterweights back and forth, squinting at the indicator marks on the brass bar. He grunted, then entered her contribution on a sheet of rice paper.

Elizabeth turned her head sideways to read the total scrawled in Chinese characters on the tally sheet. Nine kilos. About twenty pounds. She'd met her quota. She could coast for the rest of the day. The tiny red peppers didn't weigh anything—it took a million of them to make a kilo—but she was now determined to meet her quota and stay out of trouble. When the time came to leave, she didn't want to be beaten so badly she couldn't move, or hung from the rail, or locked up in one of the steel boxes that ringed the fields.

Old Wu peered at her with his one good eye.

"Your quota has been increased to twelve kilos per day. It is only two hours until dusk. You must work harder or you will be beaten."

Elizabeth felt her face flush. Every time her quota was increased and she met it, it was increased again. It was torture to meet it and it was torture to refuse. She glanced at the periphery of the fields. Two prisoners who hadn't met their quotas, or had simply collapsed, were hanging by their hands from a wooden rail that resembled a goal post. They'd been hanging there all day, twitching and moaning, excrement running down their legs, a living example for all to see. Which would be worse, being hung from the rail or being bent over nearly double in one of the claustrophobic steel boxes with only a tiny hole for air? After a day of either, the prisoners were often dead. She forced a smile and dipped her head.

"There is nothing this lesser person would rather do."

"I do not think you are sincere."

"No shit," Elizabeth said in English.

She made her way back to the spot in the row where she'd left off and squatted down behind the plants to rest for a moment. Americans had never been good at stoop labor, and she was no exception. The pain in her back became unbearable after ten minutes or so. She couldn't work on her knees. They'd be scraped bloody, and the moist black earth was permeated with night soil. God only knew what strains of bacteria were lurking in there. She steeled herself and went back to work, duck-walking down the row of plants, pulling her basket behind her. No doubt she'd have the best-developed set of glutes in Cambridge, Massachusetts, when she got back home.

Home. She blotted out her surroundings and tried to imagine what her homecoming would be like. Her father would try to maintain his senatorial dignity, but she would fall into his arms and he would melt as he always had. Her mother would be standing to the side, weeping silently before launching into another of her sermons about getting married and settling down. Looking at the mess she was in now, it'd be hard to argue with that. She had no problem with getting married and having children. She'd thought about it a lot, but the only men she'd met were soft academic types, all brains with no sense of adventure. None had held her interest for more than ten minutes.

Lost in her reverie, she watched the daylight slip away. Then, parting the leaves to search for peppers in the waning light, Elizabeth caught glimpses of the prisoner working the row next to her. She appeared to be a woman in her mid-fifties, perhaps older. Unusual. Women made up only a small percentage of the prisoners on the island.

They worked side by side for ten minutes or so, the only sound the dry rustle of the leaves and the mournful squawk of an occasional seagull floating overhead. Elizabeth reached behind her to pull the basket forward and heard a groan from the next row. She spread the leaves with her fingertips. The woman was on all fours, shaking her head.

"What is it?" Elizabeth said in English.

The woman's head snapped to the side. She looked sick and frightened.

Elizabeth switched to Cantonese. "Are you ill?"

"Who are you?" the woman said.

"Just another poor prisoner."

The woman peered at her through the leaves. "Are you a foreign person?"

"I'm American."

"From the Golden Country? You look . . . different."

"My mother is Chinese," Elizabeth said. "What is it, old mother? What's troubling you?"

The woman looked down at the dirt and shook her head. "I'll never meet my quota."

"You're too sick to work."

"I have to. If they hang me from that rail I'll die."

The woman began grabbing clusters of peppers, taking whole handfuls of leaves with her, throwing them toward her basket, missing. Elizabeth watched her, furious at the cruelty of a system that made people work even when they were deathly ill. The woman turned her head and coughed again, pink foam emerging from the corners of her mouth. She reached for another handful of peppers, lurched, and collapsed face down in the dirt.

Elizabeth struggled through the dense row of plants, across to the row where the woman lay. Keeping her head down so the guards wouldn't see her, she cradled the woman's head in her lap and gently patted her face. After a few minutes, the woman moaned and opened her eyes.

Elizabeth felt hot tears of anger stinging her eyes. "I'm so sorry, I don't even have water to give you."

"Please don't trouble yourself, my daughter. I'll die soon."

"You're not going to die," Elizabeth said. "Not if I can help it." She rubbed the woman's hands and patted her face. "How are you called?"

"I'm Wei Ling, from Guangzhou."

"I haven't seen you before, Mother Wei."

"I arrived yesterday."

"Why are you here?"

"I was arrested for being a member of the Falun Gong. They held me for two months at the Guangdong Province Number One Prison in Guangzhou. They beat me every day to make me renounce my faith, but I refused. They didn't want me to die there so they sent me here." She put her hand over her ribs. "I think something is broken inside. If they hang me up like the others, pray that I die quickly. I don't think I could bear the pain."

"Don't worry, I won't let them hurt you," Elizabeth said, not knowing how she'd stop them. She scooped a pile of dirt under the woman's head to make a pillow. "You lie here and rest. I'll fill your basket."

"Please don't make trouble for yourself."

"It's no trouble, I've already met my quota for the day," Elizabeth said. She began duck-walking down the row, picking peppers furiously, filling the woman's basket. After a few minutes, she heard a commotion, shouting from one of the guard towers. The guard in the east tower was pointing in her direction. On the periphery of the field, Four Finger Tang came to his feet from his resting place and came crashing through the rows of pepper plants, running toward her, shouting.

Oh, no. He was headed for the woman, lying nearly unconscious in the row behind her. Elizabeth left her basket and scrambled back to the woman in time to nearly collide with Four Finger Tang.

Tang raised his foot to kick the woman. "Get up, you lazy whore."

Elizabeth darted between them.

"No! She's ill," Elizabeth said in Cantonese.

Tang grabbed Elizabeth by the hair. "So it's true. The west-ocean mongrel does talk." He pulled her away. "Get back to your station." He kicked the old woman in the side. She groaned but didn't move.

"Stop it. You'll kill her."

Tang raised his boot to kick the woman again and Elizabeth locked her arms around his stubby leg.

"Please. She's an old mother. Think of your own mother."

Four Finger Tang paused, just for an instant. The whistle screamed, signaling the end of the work day.

"Eh, she'll be dead before nightfall," he said. "Not worth bothering about. If you're so interested in her welfare, she's yours." He turned and walked away.

Elizabeth patted the woman's face. "Mother Wei. Are you all right?" The woman didn't respond. Frantically, she glanced around at the prisoners leaving the field and waved to one of the men. "Brother, can you help me?"

The man shrugged and came over. The two got Wei Ling to her feet and merged into the procession of prisoners returning to their cells. When Elizabeth's cell came into view the man melted away into the crowd, leaving her to carry the full weight of the woman. She struggled through her cell door and eased the woman down to the concrete floor before collapsing beside her. Four Finger Tang closed the door behind them and glanced through the barred window.

"Please," Elizabeth said. "Some water for the old mother."

Tang shrugged and walked away. A few minutes later the cell door opened and Big Ears Wu shuffled in, carrying a plastic pail of water and a cup.

"Thank you, brother," Elizabeth said in Cantonese.

Wu stared at the two women, then shuffled out, clanging the cell door closed behind him.

Elizabeth made a pillow of straw and placed it under Wei Ling's head. She drew a cup of water, supported the woman's head, and placed the cup to her lips.

"Drink, mother."

The woman took a sip, coughed, and sighed. "I cause you too much trouble."

"Don't talk polite." Elizabeth tore a piece of cloth from the hem of her prison uniform, soaked it in water, and placed it on Wei Ling's forehead. "Lie quietly, now. I think you may have a broken rib. You must let it heal."

Wei Ling closed her eyes and after a few minutes seemed to fall asleep.

Elizabeth crawled to the nearest corner and leaned into it, arms locked around her knees, then watched the old woman sleep. It felt good to have another human being in the cell with her. After three months of forced isolation, she was puzzled by the sudden change of heart, but she wasn't going to look a gift horse in the mouth. Just the sound of Wei Ling's breathing was comforting. She felt exhausted from working in the fields all day, but she resisted sleep. What if Mother Wei woke up and needed her? After watching her sleep for the better part of an hour, she tilted her head into the corner and closed her eyes, just to rest them for a minute. . . .

The clink of something skipping across the floor brought her awake. The angle of the moonlight coming through the slit in the wall was higher now. She must have been asleep for several hours. She glanced around and saw what looked like a small pebble with a piece of brown paper wrapped around it, bound with white thread. Wei Ling moaned and shifted her position. The pebble must have struck the old woman when it was tossed through the window. Elizabeth crawled noiselessly to where the object lay, snatched it up, and crabbed back into her corner. She cut the thread with her teeth, unrolled it, and held the paper up to the moonlight. She instantly recognized the familiar letters. Her breath caught in her throat.

"Midnight tomorrow. Be ready."

She clutched the note to her breast. Tomorrow at midnight. *So soon.* She couldn't believe it. She looked at the date on her watch. June 12. She would actually be leaving this hellhole in a little over twenty-four hours. She couldn't imagine how it would happen. Would marines storm the island? Would paratroopers fall from the sky? She felt instantly energized, but her joy was overshadowed by the responsibility she'd just taken on.

Elizabeth looked at Wei Ling sleeping peacefully. How could she leave the old woman? Without someone to look out for her, she'd surely die. On the other hand, she'd probably die anyway. And if Elizabeth insisted on bringing her with them it could put the rescue in jeopardy. She could only imagine Charlie's reaction to that proposal.

She watched Wei Ling breathe softly for a few minutes and came to her decision. It would break her heart, but she'd have to leave her new friend behind. The stakes were simply too high. She wiped a tear from her eye, tore the note into pieces, placed them under her tongue, and fell into an uneasy sleep.

James Lao peered through the windshield of the Z-11 helicopter as it broke through the yellow haze over Guangzhou. In the dusky light he recognized the layout of the CAT laboratory compound on the bank of the Pearl River. To the south he could make out the payload processing facility, the H-shaped building closest to the water's edge. The command and control ship *Zenith* stood moored to a dock near the facility, waiting to receive the payload. Inside that odd-looking building, and soon to be aboard that ship, was a device that would change the world and his place in it forever.

The light helicopter hovered over the asphalt landing pad in a whirl of dust and leaves and settled down with a whoosh of hydraulics. The single turboshaft engine throttled down and the copilot scrambled to open the door. James gathered up his briefcase, released his seatbelt, and stepped off, glad to be free of the infernal thing. He had little confidence in Chinese-built aircraft. He instinctively ducked his head and quickly walked to the edge of the heliport, where a contingent of dark-suited executives stood waiting to greet him.

"Chairman Lao," Chin Fei said over the idling helicopter. "Your visit brings us great honor and joy."

James stared at the line of dark suits. He'd made it clear that he wanted to dispense with protocol on this visit. He didn't want to be tied up with a series of formal briefings by these bureaucrats, each bent on protecting his own turf.

"You're very kind, Director Chin," James said, "but I fear my visit is a great trouble for you."

"On the contrary, it's a great pleasure. May I be among the first to congratulate you on your promotion to senior colonel?" Chin looked at him curiously. "It would be a great honor for anyone, but especially for one so young."

Bad news travels fast. Envy and mystification chased each other across Old Chin's face. The rank of senior colonel in the PLA was equivalent to a brigadier general in the West. How did one get promoted from lieutenant colonel to senior colonel in one jump? And especially at age thirty-two? If Chin knew it had been a direct promotion ordered by the prime minister himself, he'd die of jealousy. James watched him squirm.

"Thank you for your kind thoughts."

"I hope your trip was a pleasant one," Chin said.

Business trips were never pleasant, they were either efficient or inefficient. By that measure, James considered himself off to a good start. His personal Cessna Citation had departed from Hong Kong International on schedule and had landed at Baiyun Airport in Guangzhou slightly ahead of schedule. A PLA helicopter was sitting at the end of the runway where it was supposed to be, engine running, waiting to fly him to the lab. That was the level of efficiency he had to achieve at every stage of the operation, from now until the successful completion of the launch.

"Yes, thank you."

"Come. We've prepared food and drink for you."

No doubt. To a small division of China Aerospace and Technology, a visit from the chairman and managing director was nerve-racking. They'd try to keep him out of the way and under control with the usual gambits: briefings, food, and the endless toasts of *bai jiu*, the explosive 120-proof rice drink old Chin loved. James had permitted himself that frivolity on a previous visit, but not this time. There was too much at stake.

The only way to ensure a successful launch was to be highly visible at every step of the way, from the lab that built Raptor, to the payload processing facility, to the command and control ship, to the launch platform on the equator. There was no substitute for being there, probing, questioning, showing interest. The Americans called it

MBWA, management by walking around. It was a technique he'd learned at Stanford.

"Thank you, no. I'd like to see the payload now."

"But the department heads have prepared briefings for you, Chairman Lao."

Briefings that would drone on and on and tell him nothing except what they wanted him to hear. James needed to see and touch the payload, and meet the technicians who worked on it, and look them in the eye as he discussed the progress of their work in their normal work environment. It was the only way to see what was really going on, find out what if any the problems were. In America this kind of interaction between executive and worker would be called leadership, but in hidebound China it was considered unseemly. If China was going to find her proper place in the world, China would have to change.

"Perhaps another time. I don't wish to keep these honorable comrades from their families any longer."

"As you wish," Chin said. The director nodded the line of mandarins away, the loss of face evident in their expressions. Chin waved his hand, and a white Ford van with the CAT logo on the door pulled up to the entrance of the heliport. James would have preferred to walk the short distance to the payload processing facility, but he held his tongue. There was no point in upsetting protocol any more than was necessary.

The van pulled up to an H-shaped building that resembled a blimp hanger. A safety horn sounded, and a steel tambour-type door on the left side of the building groaned and began to move up on motor-driven tracks. James left the van and walked toward the shadows of the cavernous entrance, Chin scampering behind. He adjusted his eyes to the light. Technicians in blue jumpsuits swarmed around a large cylindrical body positioned on a stainless steel dolly.

"Here the satellite's being prepared to be mated to the launch vehicle," Chin said behind him, catching his breath.

Raptor looked very different from the last time he'd seen it. The satellite had been transported to Hong Kong for final testing and James's demonstration to the prime minister, then shipped back to the payload processing facility in Guangzhou for final preparations. He retrieved a schedule from his coat pocket and ran his eye down the list.

"Has fueling been completed?"

"Yes, Senior Colonel. An hour ago. The technicians you see here are in the process of encapsulating the satellite within the payload fairing."

The payload fairing, a device similar to the nose cone of a rocket, served double duty. It would protect the satellite from the elements, and attach it to the launch vehicle.

"When will that be completed?"

"By eleven p.m. tonight," Chin said. "The encapsulated payload will then be transferred to the *Zenith*." He dabbed at his forehead with a handkerchief and nodded toward the giant ship's superstructure, visible from where they stood. "That will end our responsibility."

James felt sure old Chin would be glad to see it go. Raptor was a hot potato that had brought too much high-level attention to his lab.

"From there on, it's a great puzzle to me," Chin said. "My expertise is in laser technology, not rocket science. Is it true what we hear, that the rocket is two hundred feet tall and will be launched at sea? How is this possible?"

James smiled noncommittally, gratified by the director's puzzled expression. His strategy was working. He'd insisted on a launch at sea. Launching on the equator was a straight shot into orbit, and the fuel savings would permit a heavier payload to be launched into the higher altitude required by Raptor. But a sea launch also lent itself to breaking the project up into several small pieces. He wanted as few people as possible to have the full picture.

Chin rubbed the back of his neck. "It sounds fantastic."

James had to admit that it did, like a scene out of an American movie. The launch pad, a converted deep-sea oil-drilling rig, had been modified at a shipyard in Indonesia and was on its way to the launch site as they spoke. At 500 feet long and 300 feet wide, with a submerged draft displacement of 60,000 tons, it was the largest self-propelled, semi-submersible vessel in the world.

"Don't believe everything you hear," James said.

The lab director stroked his chin.

"For such personal attention from the chairman himself, this satellite must be of singular importance."

James eyed him, cautious now. Chin knew more than he should about the launch, but he and the other scientists who knew the satellite's capabilities assumed that it would be launched as a purely defensive measure. They had no idea that it would be put into use almost immediately, and that its launch would be a world-changing event.

"All our projects are important," James said.

"Yes, of course," Chin said.

Above the noise of the factory, James heard his cell phone chime. Glad to be free from the inquisitive Chin, he flipped it open and looked at the screen. A call from Beijing, not one to be ignored. He pressed the phone to his head and walked outside into the cool air.

"Senior Colonel Lao speaking."

"So it's Senior Colonel Lao, is it?" General Lao's voice came clearly through the headset. "Enjoy it while you can, Senior Colonel. If that launch doesn't go off as scheduled, it'll be Private Lao, cleaning fish at a post in Tibet, and I'll be alongside you."

James smiled at the apprehension in his father's tone. Parents always thought their children were incompetent idiots.

"It's good to hear your voice, Father."

"You won't think so when I tell you what's happened. Your American cousin is causing big trouble."

"What are you talking about?"

"Fox News Channel reported that an American senator's daughter is being held in a Chinese prison. CNN and the networks have picked it up. They're doing hourly bulletins about her, whipping up public sentiment. The whole country's clamoring for her release."

"Let them clamor," James said. "Cousin Beth is quite secure and will remain so until well after the launch."

"She'd better be. Obviously we can't release her, no matter how much pressure they bring to bear, but the leadership is concerned. Questions are being raised about moving up the launch date, perhaps shifting to a land-based launch to speed things up."

"No," James said, a little too loudly. "A conventional land-based launch isn't possible, given the technical constraints of the satellite. It must be done from the equator."

"Can you assure me that Elizabeth Grayson is secure?"

James hesitated. To mention the American ship that had set out in an amateurish attempt to rescue his cousin would only panic the leadership into doing something that might upset the entire plan. And the rescue would never happen. He'd planted Zhao Lan, the most experienced assassin in the PLA, aboard the American ship. The "escaped prisoner's" empty raft had already been sighted by the helicopter that had dropped it in the ship's path. He looked at his watch. The captain and half the crew were no doubt dead by now and Zhao in command.

"Yes, Father. You have my personal assurance that she'll remain secure."

"You'd better be right," General Lao said. "Americans are unpredictable. They'll stand by while half a million people die on another continent, yet a small thing like one of their citizens being held can compel them to do something foolhardy."

James agreed. He understood Americans, knew what they were capable of. He'd be glad when the launch was over and his cousin had ceased to be an issue. Then the Americans would have much bigger things to worry about.

"Please assure the leadership that she's secure and the launch will go off exactly as planned."

"Assure them yourself," his father said. "I want you here for the next meeting of the CMC. It'll be held before the full commission in the Huairentang at Zhongnanhai on the fourteenth, beginning at 0800. You'll make a presentation to the commission, assuring them that security has not been compromised and that the launch is on schedule."

James felt a web of fear in his stomach he knew would spread throughout his body. His father was vice chairman of the Central Military Commission, but the chairman was none other than the president of China. To be called to Zhongnanhai, the power enclave where the party leadership lived and worked, was considered a great honor among the uninitiated, but James knew better. He'd grown up in the famous compound and knew that many people called to Zhongnanhai never made it out alive. Mao's own secretary had committed suicide there during the Cultural Revolution. He hesitated, but it was impossible to object.

"It would be my honor to address the commission."

James pressed the end button on his phone. He wasn't worried about the launch, but his cousin's security was now more important than ever. He brought up his security chief's number on the screen.

"Major Zhu speaking."

"Major, this is Senior Colonel Lao. I want the current status of the American ship."

"Yes, Senior Colonel." There was a pause. "The ship is traveling at a speed of approximately fourteen knots. It's currently one hundred and ninety miles from the easternmost island in the chain. We calculate that at the present rate of speed, it will reach Turtle Island tomorrow morning at—"

"What the hell are you talking about? Why hasn't the ship turned back?"

"I don't know, Senior Colonel."

"You don't know? What do you mean, you don't—when did the ship take our man aboard?"

"We have no way of knowing the exact time of the pickup, Senior Colonel, or even if in fact there was a pickup. All we know is, the empty raft was sighted approximately eight hours ago."

Eight hours. Something had gone wrong. It wouldn't take the fabled Zhao Lan that long to dispose of enough unarmed civilians to take control of a small ship. Think. An empty raft didn't necessarily mean what he'd thought it meant. Maybe Zhao hadn't been taken aboard at all. Maybe the fool had slipped off the raft and drowned. He didn't want to think about the only other possibility—that he'd underestimated the American ship captain.

He terminated the call, his breathing shallow. For reasons he couldn't fathom, Zhao Lan hadn't performed. The ship was still on its way. He had to do something. The South Sea Fleet was engaged in maneuvers off the coast this time of year. When last he checked there were two frigates and two destroyers, the *Zhuhai* and the *Harbin*, operating in the vicinity of Macau, not that far from the *laogai* on Turtle Island. One of the high-speed destroyers could be there in hours. With the rank of senior colonel and his status as a Red Prince, he could request that a PLA Navy destroyer be diverted to patrol the islands as a temporary security measure. No one would question that move, but he would also have some private, off-the-table orders for the destroyer captain.

He punched out the numbers to the PLA Navy South Sea fleet command in Zhanjiang. He had just one more shot. This one would have to work.

Chapter Eight

"You got any more bright ideas?" Scootchy Carter said in a muffled voice, his face buried in a pillow.

Matt sat on the edge of a bunk in the ship's infirmary, waiting his turn for Doc Miller to look at his wound and change the bandage. The base of his skull throbbed, sending a ribbon of pain up the back of his head, into his temples. He'd had almost no sleep and was in no mood to listen to Scootchy complain. He took in a deep breath and slowly exhaled, the pain in his arm still throbbing.

"Shut up, Scootchy."

Scootchy twisted his head around, his whole body turning.

"Shut up? That's it? That's all you can say?"

"Hold still," Doc Miller said, lifting Scootchy's bandage off.

Matt winced. The words clattered inside his head like ball bearings in a coffee can. He rubbed his temples. He'd been up all night thinking and he had doubts of his own. Maybe the Chinese *were* on to them, and for reasons he couldn't understand were playing games. Maybe, but he wasn't about to share his doubts with his crew. He'd come this far and he wasn't turning back, at least not yet.

"I want to know who that son of a bitch was," Scootchy said, turning back.

"Just a disturbed passenger."

"Disturbed? That son of a bitch damn near killed me. And you. I didn't know what hit me. Didn't even see him come into the goddamn engine room."

"What was that guy's problem?" Doc Miller said, tearing off a strip of white tape.

"He was just an escaped prisoner with his own agenda," Matt said.

Scootchy shot an incredulous look at Matt.

"You really believe that?"

"Sure," Matt said. "What else?"

"Hell, it's obvious, man. Wake up. The Chinese know exactly what we're doing. They planted that son of a bitch right in our path, knowing we'd pick him up." He dropped his face back into his pillow. "I'd of picked him up, all right. I'd of run right over the son of a bitch."

Doc Miller looked at Matt. "Think he was dropped, Skipper?"

"Of course not."

"Well, you're the only one who doesn't," Scootchy said. "I say we turn this thing around and get the hell out of here while we can."

"Look, I don't have any reason to believe that guy wasn't exactly who he said he was." Matt looked at his watch. "We should be on site in a couple of hours. If the Chinese knew what we were doing, we'd never have gotten this far."

Scootchy screwed up his face. "Man, whatever you're smoking, I'd like to have some of it. The Chinese ain't here because they thought that goon would take care of us. When they find out he didn't, what do you think they're going to do? They're going to blow us right out of the goddamn water."

Matt bristled. Scootchy was making just enough sense to be dangerous. If he spread that theory all over the ship, Matt could have a mutiny on his hands. He turned his head with difficulty.

"Listen to me, Scootch. I'm only going to say this once. If you say anything like that to any member of the crew, I'll consign you to the brig until we finish this job and get out of here."

"You ain't locking me in any brig. When that Chink torpedo comes, I want to be the first one off this thing."

"Then you'd better keep your mouth shut."

Scootchy gave him a long, measuring look. "By God, I think you're serious," he said finally.

"Count on it."

Matt gripped the chain on the bunk and pulled himself to his feet. He still felt unsteady, but he had to get away from Scootchy's carping.

"I'm going to the bridge, Doc."

"Better let me look at that before you go, Skipper. Change the bandage."

Matt touched it. "It's all right for now. Maybe later."

"Aye, Captain." Doc looked at Matt leaning against the rail of the bunk. "I'd take it kind of easy for a while, though."

No problem there. He felt terrible. All he wanted to do at this point was make his pickup and get the hell out of there. He stepped onto the bridge, nursing a headache.

"Captain is on the bridge," Sam said in his booming voice.

Matt winced, the words vibrating in his head.

"Not so loud, Sam."

"Sorry, Skipper. How's your head?"

"Loud. But I'll live."

Matt drew a cup of coffee the color of asphalt and swept the horizon with his eyes. The sun blazed on the port side of the ship, a great orange ball rising out of the sea. Feathery cirrus clouds drifted high in the sky. He checked the direction of the wind. Northeast. A wind from the south, east, or northeast—in combination with high cirrus clouds—was a near perfect predictor of rain in the next twenty-four hours. Hopefully, it wouldn't be heavy enough to slow them down. He squinted at the islands just off the starboard bow, a ragged line above the horizon.

"What's our ETA?"

"We're about twenty nautical miles from the easternmost tip of the island where the freighter is," Jason Tyler said. "We should be on site in about an hour and twenty minutes."

"If you look real close you can see the freighter," Sam said, fine-tuning his binoculars. "A little gray speck on the beach."

Matt felt faint. The ship rolled and he leaned into a stanchion to keep his balance. He tried to make it look natural, but Jason asked him how he was feeling.

Matt touched the back of his neck. The crusty bandage felt as thick as a horse blanket. He pressed down and grimaced.

"Like I've been hit by a truck."

"That's what you get for picking up hitchhikers," Sam said.

"No good deed goes unpunished," Jason said. "How's Scootchy?"

"Doc thinks he may have a concussion, but it hasn't stopped his bitching."

"Who the hell was that guy?" Sam said.

It was the fifth time he'd asked the question. "Just somebody who didn't want any part of that island," Matt said.

"Scootchy swears he was a plant by the Chinese to keep us from getting there," Sam said.

"Scootchy's a moron. If the Chinese knew what we were up to, why would they pull a lame-brained stunt like that? They'd just send a destroyer out to sink us."

The bridge got quiet. Sam continued to sweep the horizon with binoculars. After a few minutes he lowered them.

"Looks like that may be what they have in mind, Captain."

Matt picked up a pair of binoculars and peered in the direction Sam pointed. He adjusted the focus and saw a plume of black smoke, then the side profile of a ship on the horizon. Sleek lines, low to the water, twin stacks, red flags fluttering above the superstructure. She was clearly a destroyer, and coming from the vicinity of the islands, she could only be Chinese. The ship made a sharp turn to port. With only the bow in view now, there was no doubt where she was headed. The destroyer was on a collision course with *CoMar Explorer* and was closing the distance fast. His gut tightened.

"Let's go to emergency stations, Sam."

"Aye, Captain." Sam pressed the key on the bridge microphone. "All hands man your emergency stations."

"Right standard rudder," Matt said.

"Right standard rudder, aye, Captain," Jason Tyler said, turning the wheel to the right.

"I see red flags," Sam said, peering through his binoculars. "Must be Chinese."

Matt watched the gap between the ships grow smaller. As *CoMar Explorer* eased to the right, following the international maritime rules of the road, the black numbers on the light gray hull of the destroyer came into view. 1-6-6.

"She's the *Zhuhai*," he said, watching her come. "Luda class destroyer. Upgraded to a Luda III class. Modernized for ASW missions. All new electronics."

"What do you think they want?"

"Beats me," Matt said. "If they wanted to sink us, they wouldn't have to get this close. The *Zhuhai*'s got four twin missile launchers, C-801 Sardines."

"Maybe they don't want to waste a missile on us."

"She's got torpedoes. And if they don't want to do that, she's got twin 37-millimeter guns that could make short work of us from a long way off."

A signal light began blinking from the bridge of the destroyer.

Jason Tyler adjusted his binoculars, translating the pulses of light.

"Heave-to-or-I-will-fire."

"Not very friendly, are they?" Sam said.

"No reason they should be," Matt said. "We're in their territory now. They want to know who we are and why we're here." He nodded to Jason Tyler. "All engines stop."

"All engines stop, aye, Captain."

CoMar Explorer drifted to a stop and hove to, green waves slapping against her hull. A lone seagull swooped toward the ship, squawking. The PLA Navy destroyer approached and stood off about three hundred yards, crews maneuvering to keep her guns aimed directly at the bridge. Matt watched a small boat fill with a boarding party. Seven marines in combat gear, headed by a naval officer wearing a side arm. He wasn't surprised to see marines. Most of the PLA Navy's fifty thousand marines were attached to the South Sea fleet command because of the never-ending territorial squabbles over Taiwan, the Spratleys, the Paracels, and the Senkaku Islands. The signal light from the bridge resumed blinking as the boat was lowered away.

"Stand-by-to-be-boarded," Jason said. "Do-not-resist-or-I-will-fire."

"Tell them welcome aboard," Matt said. "Lower the Jacob's ladder. They're probably looking for the escaped prisoner."

"Let 'em look," Sam said. "He's three miles down, a long way back."

Matt's stomach flipped. The weighted body of the man who called himself Yang Zhi being rolled off the fantail into the inky depths of the South China Sea was a sight he'd never forget.

"If that's what they're after, they may want to search the ship." He looked at Sam. "Where did you stash the crate from Gray Wolf?"

"It's in the engine room, under some heavy pipe," Sam said. "Even if they saw it, they'd have to work their asses off to get to it."

"They've got all the guns," Jason said. "They might make *us* work our asses off to get to it."

"Not much we can do about it now," Matt said. "Take the conn, Jason. Come on, Sam. Let's go and greet our visitors."

By the time Matt and Sam got to the quarterdeck, two of his crew had lowered the Jacob's ladder and a boat fender. Matt watched the small boat from the Chinese destroyer chop its way across the divide. One of the marines stood in the stern with an assault rifle aimed at the crew on deck. The naval officer sat in the bow. The PLA Navy, with all its supposed equality, was no different. Officers were last in, first out. One of the marines tied the boat up to the ladder and held it. The naval officer came up first, followed by the marines.

"Request permission to come aboard," the officer said in perfect English, stepping onto the quarterdeck.

"Permission granted," Matt said, as though he had a choice. The officer appeared to be several years younger than Matt and looked strangely familiar.

"I'm Commander Chen, PLA Navy, commanding officer of *Zhuhai*."

The CO. Matt had never heard of a commanding officer, in any navy, leading a boarding party. *Whatever they want, they're serious about it*. He extended his hand.

"Happy to meet you, Captain. I'm Matt Connor, captain of *CoMar Explorer*."

Captain Chen glanced at the Panamanian flag snapping in the breeze, then at Matt. "What's your nationality?"

"American."

The Chinese officer shook hands and smiled. "I studied in your country. Annapolis, Maryland. U.S. Naval Academy."

Matt stared. That's where he'd seen him before. A couple of midshipmen from Taiwan had been admitted to the class three years behind him. It had been an experimental program to strengthen the Taiwanese Navy that had blown up and embarrassed a lot of people in Washington. Everyone had heard the story. It was discovered after graduation that one of the midshipmen was actually a spy from the mainland. After getting a fine education in the way the U.S. conducts war, he'd returned to China and was now an officer in the PLA Navy. Matt had assumed that part of the story was apocryphal, a tale concocted by xenophobic classmates, but apparently it was true. *I'll be damned.*

"I hope your stay in America was pleasant."

"For the most part." Chen's left eyebrow went up almost imperceptibly. "Why do I get the feeling I know you?"

Matt shrugged. He didn't think Chen would recognize him. As an upperclassman he'd had no contact with the two Taiwanese plebes other than seeing them here and there. Besides, both men had changed a lot over the years. Chen and his running mate had looked like they were about twelve years old back then, and Matt had a lot more miles on him now.

"I have one of those typical American faces."

"On the contrary," Chen said, "I'm sure I've seen yours before."

"I'm sure I'd remember you," Matt said.

"Connor, Connor. . ." Captain Chen folded his arms and rubbed his chin. "Even the name sounds familiar."

"It's a common name in America. My ancestors weren't very good at growing potatoes."

Captain Chen looked at him for another few seconds, apparently unconvinced but unable to place him. Time to get him off the subject.

"How can we be of assistance, Captain?"

All business again, Captain Chen said, "Please assemble your crew on deck."

"No problem." Matt nodded to Sam.

As Sam walked toward the bridge to make the announcement, a marine fell in behind him with an assault rifle at the ready. What Matt had originally thought were AK-47's were in fact AK-74's, a newer version of the Kalashnikov designed to use the new 5.45 mm cartridges. The Soviets had come up with it, trying to find one even more deadly than the 5.56 mm NATO cartridge. The bullet had a soft jacket with an air gap in the nose that made it shatter on impact. During the Soviet invasion of Afghanistan the Mujahideen had called it the "poison bullet," because almost nobody who was hit by one survived. He glanced at the thirty-round magazines. In the hands of seven tense marines, it was a formula for disaster. He hoped none of his men made any sudden moves when they came up on deck.

Captain Chen turned to the sharp-eyed marine who hovered near him. One broad stripe with three smaller ones. The CCP had abolished all ranks a few years ago, then reinstated them when the plan proved to be unworkable. It had been a while since Matt had studied Chinese military ranks, but he thought the markings indicated a sergeant first class, a heavy hitter in the PLA marine corps. Whatever his rank, he was obviously the senior enlisted man.

"Disable the radio and search this hulk," Chen said in Mandarin. "Bring me the ship's log. Confiscate any communications devices or weapons you find."

Disable the radio? Matt held himself in check. He couldn't object without revealing that he spoke Mandarin, and that would cost him the only advantage he had. Damn. He shoved his hands in his hip pockets and felt the pistol he'd fished out of the bilge. He'd rethought his intent to throw it over the side after his little encounter with the escaped prisoner in the engine room. With all the guns trained on them now, he was convinced he'd made the right decision.

The crew came up on deck a few at a time, prodded by marines, blinking into the sun. Doc Miller came up with Scootchy Carter draped over his shoulder. Scootchy looked panic-stricken. At least he was keeping his mouth shut, probably too frightened to speak. Jason Tyler and Sam came from the direction of the bridge. The marine nudging them from behind had the ship's log under one arm. He handed it to the sharp-eyed sergeant, who opened it to the latest entry and handed it to Captain Chen.

Chen read the last two pages in the log, then closed the book, his index finger marking his place. He glanced at the assembled crew and frowned.

"Did you ever see such a stinking mess?" he said in Mandarin. The Chinese marines laughed.

Matt said, "Does my crew amuse you, Captain?"

"Forgive them, Captain, they laugh at anything," Chen said. "We're searching for a man adrift on a raft. Have you seen such a person?"

Matt tried to relax his face. He wasn't very good at lying. He made eye contact with Chen and shook his head.

"No."

Captain Chen opened the log. "It says here you sighted a raft adrift yesterday at 1130 hours."

"That's right," Matt said, "but there was no one on it."

"The raft was empty?"

"Yes."

Captain Chen peered around at the bandage on the back of Matt's head. "You are injured, Captain."

"I fell down a ladder."

He nodded toward Scootchy. "Another member of your crew has similar injuries. Did he fall down the same ladder?"

"Yeah, we'll have to get that fixed," Matt said. "I'll trouble you to explain why you've boarded my ship, Captain."

Captain Chen said, "It's not up to me to explain anything to you, Captain Connor. It's up to you to explain why you bring an armed ship into Chinese waters."

Armed. No one had reported to Chen, so he couldn't know about the cache of weapons. Matt had finally gotten around to looking at it. The coffin-shaped case of weapons Gray Wolf's men had delivered contained Stinger missiles and rocket-propelled grenade launchers. Goddamn Gray Wolf and his conspiracy theories. Matt was there to pick someone up, not start a war. He should have thrown the damn things over the side. If the Chinese found them, there'd be hell to pay. *Bluff it out.* He shrugged and swept his arm around the deck.

"Armed? We're not armed." He heard one of the marines come up behind him. He stepped past Matt carrying a pair of rifles.

Matt let himself breathe. The shark rifles.

The marine handed one of them to Captain Chen. He snapped the bolt back and inspected the chamber. He squinted at the inscription on the side of the barrel. "Winchester Model 70 in .243 Winchester caliber." He looked at the telescope. "These appear to be sniper rifles."

"Hardly," Matt said. "We're an ocean-salvage company. We need the rifles to protect our divers from sharks."

"You won't need them here," Captain Chen said. "There are no sharks in these waters." He tossed the rifle back to the marine and nodded them away.

One of the marines appeared on deck, carrying Matt's naval officer's sword. Damn. How would he explain that? The marine handed the sword to Captain Chen.

"Where was this?" Captain Chen said in Mandarin.

"The captain's sea cabin, sir."

Captain Chen pulled the engraved sword from its sheath and examined it. "A U.S. naval officer's sword. Exactly like mine." He looked at Matt. "How do you come to have this?"

Matt shrugged. "I saw it in a flea market in Shanghai and bought it."

Captain Chen squinted at the inscription engraved on the blade. "Onward and upward." He gave Matt a questioning look.

Matt didn't like to hear this arrogant jerk saying the words his father had said to him so many times. His father had been a career naval officer, a pilot who'd ended up commanding an aircraft carrier before he made flag. Every time they'd parted company those were the last words he said to Matt. His father hadn't talked to him since Matt resigned his commission, but the sword was a reminder of better days. Thank God his father hadn't engraved the sword with Matt's name or initials, as was the usual custom. He gave Chen a palms-up shrug.

Captain Chen passed the sword back to the private, never taking his eyes off Matt.

"Why are you here?"

"A U.S. flag freighter's run aground on an island off Macau," Matt said. "We have permission from Lloyd's and the American owners to salvage the ship."

"Ah, yes. The American freighter. If that's an example of American seamanship, it's no wonder the U.S. merchant fleet has dwindled to nothing. They appear to have driven the thing right up on the beach."

"I'm told the currents are tricky around these islands," Matt said.

"These islands don't concern you. You're confined to the exact proximity of the freighter and are expressly forbidden to approach any of the other islands. Do you understand me?"

Matt shrugged. "Sure."

"That freighter's been nothing but trouble," Captain Chen said. "The crew had to be taken off by helicopter and flown to Guangzhou. I want that filthy thing out of here."

"In that case, we should get started," Matt said.

Captain Chen glanced around the ship, eyebrows raised.

"You intend to move it with this?"

Matt held his pride in check. *CoMar Explorer* displaced only 3300 tons, but with her four Caterpillar engines she could tow a *Nimitz*-class carrier a thousand miles at a speed of five knots. The *Zhuhai* was probably over 3700 tons, and she'd be hard-pressed to do that.

"We can handle it."

"Really. And just how will you go about such a Herculean task?"

Chen was testing him. "It depends. The size of the ship, how it's grounded, whether the hull's been damaged, the cargo, the weather. The first thing we'll need is a damage report and the cargo manifest."

"You must already have that from the ship's owners and the insurance company."

"Unfortunately, we don't. When we get on site we'll check out the cargo manifest. Hopefully, we won't have to unload her." He nodded toward the two 35-foot aluminum workboats secured to their davits. "We'll survey the vessel using small craft and divers. If any repairs are needed, we'll make them. Then we'll conduct a beach survey to inspect the bottom around the vessel and the path we'll have to use to extract her. We don't want to drag her back across the rocks."

"Of course."

"During the survey, our divers will use buoys to mark a survey line that we won't let *CoMar Explorer* cross. We don't want two ships aground."

"Very sensible. What then?"

"Once we've got the survey completed and the lines marked, we'll rig beach gear. We'll do the calculations later, but for a ship of this size, two legs on each ship will probably do it. Then we'll get into harness and take a light pull to stabilize her. When conditions are right, we'll make the actual pull."

"Your engines are large enough for this?"

"We may not even need the engines," Matt said. "We'll use hydraulic pullers first, save the engines for later."

"And if you're successful in extracting the vessel from the beach?"

"That's when the fun begins. We'll have a very large vessel free in a very bad place—the place where she ran aground. Ideally we'd have a tug or two to help, but we don't have that luxury. We'll pull her away from the beach and stabilize her as best we can while we get out of harness. We'll have people aboard to verify the condition of the vessel, see if the retraction caused any additional damage. If so, we'll do the repairs, shore it up, or whatever it takes. Then we'll begin the tow."

"And the ship will be towed where?"

Matt didn't have a clue. That wasn't part of the plan. He shrugged.

"A shipyard in Keelung."

Captain Chen seemed satisfied that Matt knew what he was talking about. "You have permission to remain in these waters only as long as it takes to remove that ship from Chinese territory." He looked at his watch. "You have a full day to accomplish your task. I want you and that ship out of here by nightfall."

Matt stiffened. He had to be here at least until midnight.

"There's nothing I'd like better, Captain. But as you said, that's a very big ship and ours is small. We won't know how long the operation will take until we do a survey of the vessel and the beach. We may not be able to accomplish the job in one day."

Captain Chen glared at him for what seemed a full minute.

"Very well. If the job is that big, we'll provide you with assistance. We Chinese are always willing to help our Western friends and to learn new methods." Chen nodded to the sharp-eyed sergeant and pointed to four of the marines.

"You and your men will remain aboard," he said in Mandarin. "Your orders are to prod these lazy barbarians into action. See that they get that ship off the beach as quickly as possible. I want them out of here by nightfall. We'll pick you up tomorrow."

The marines snapped to attention and stepped off to the side. Captain Chen turned back to Matt.

"Sergeant Li is trained in engineering at Guangzhou University. He also knows these waters quite well. He and his men will remain aboard to provide assistance."

Damn. Matt was scheduled to rendezvous at midnight on the north shore of Turtle Island to pick up his passenger. How the hell was he going to do that with a contingent of marines watching his every move? He needed to know if any of them spoke English, especially the sergeant.

"Your assistance would be most welcome," Matt said, "but unfortunately it wouldn't be productive. I'm embarrassed to admit that I don't speak Chinese."

"No problem," Captain Chen said. "Sergeant Li speaks English, don't you, Sergeant?"

Sergeant Li nodded, managed a half-smile, and said "Yes, Captain."

Matt returned the nod.

First a crazed prisoner and now this, a contingent of armed marines aboard, the leader of whom was a hard-looking character who spoke English. It was either very bad luck or Scootchy was right: they knew exactly why he was there and were throwing up roadblocks to stop him. If that were the case, he needed to make an excuse to get the hell out of there.

Get a grip. If the Chinese knew why he was there, they wouldn't be playing games. They'd sink his ship or at least impound it and take them all prisoner. No. He'd spent the last bit of capital he had just to get here. He wasn't leaving five million dollars on the table because of Scootchy's paranoia—or his own. He'd wait until nightfall and proceed as planned. Sam was already looking the marines over, sizing them up. He glanced at him and Matt saw the look. Sam and a few others could handle these five.

"Glad to have them," Matt said, extending his hand to Captain Chen. "We'll try to teach them a few things."

Chapter Nine

Matt watched Captain Chen and the two remaining marines scramble down the Jacob's ladder and cast off. Chen had Matt's sword tucked under one arm and each marine had one of the Winchester rifles slung over his shoulder. The spoils of war. The shark rifles could be replaced, but it pained him to lose the sword, the only memento he had of his father and his naval career. Still, all things considered, they had gotten off light: the loss of a few small arms and a contingent of marine "observers" placed aboard. Both were obstacles he could overcome.

He looked at the scene around him. Standing on the quarterdeck of *CoMar Explorer*, the Chinese marines and Matt's crew seemed frozen in time, watching the small boat chop its way back to the destroyer. Each group eyed the other warily. Both sides seemed to sense that the departure of the boat signaled a change in their status; they had each crossed the threshold into uncharted territory.

Matt glanced at the faces of his crew, trying to assess how they were reacting to their uninvited guests. Scootchy Carter glared back at him, still supported by Doc. It was obvious by the look in his eyes that he was now more convinced than ever that his theory was right: the Chinese knew why they were there and had placed the marines aboard to prevent them from doing it. Matt saw uncertainty in a few faces, anxiety in a few others, but the only member of the crew that concerned him was Scootchy. The poison his chief engineer could spread could undermine everyone's confidence to the point that the mission could fall apart. He needed to get everyone together again and reassure them, but that would be impossible now with the observers aboard. He'd warned Scootchy to keep his mouth shut. Hopefully he would. If he didn't, it was something Matt would have to deal with.

Know your enemies. Matt took stock of the Chinese marines. All young except Sergeant Li. Based on the comments he'd heard, he was able to figure out their ranks. Two garden-variety privates, one private first class, one corporal, and the sharp-eyed sergeant first class. With the exception of the sergeant, not a very impressive lot.

And only five. That puzzled him. Did the Chinese really think that a contingent of five marines, armed or not, could keep a crew of eighteen men under control? There was a limit as to where five men could be at any one time on a ship the size of *CoMar Explorer*. The more Matt thought about it, the more convinced he became that he was right: if the Chinese knew or even suspected what *CoMar* was up to, they'd have sunk her or had marines crawling all over the ship.

And of the five, the only one that caused him any real concern was the sergeant, who looked like he could whip his weight in mountain lions. Obviously educated. Too smart to let himself be stranded on an alien ship without a way to communicate with his own. Matt didn't see one, but he had to have a radio somewhere, probably in his backpack. If there was any pattern to his communications with *Zhuhai*, Matt would have to find out what it was.

The other four looked young and inexperienced. Like their esteemed sergeant, three of the four were poker-faced. The only one he could read was the younger of the two privates, the one called Fong. Nervous in the midst of the barbarians, his head spun around at every sound. Matt thought he looked like an owl. He made a mental note to watch him. Private Fong was a weakness he might be able to exploit.

He began to form a three-part strategy. The first order of the day would be to lull the Chinese marines into a sense of complacency by going about his business and convincing them he was there simply to salvage the freighter. He would spend the day putting on a show for their benefit, going through the motions of debeaching the ship. If he made it convincing enough they'd let down their guard. Second, he'd make the "observers" work their tails off just to keep up with him and his crew. Debeaching a ship was exhausting work. By nightfall they'd not only be convinced that he was who he said he was, they'd be too tired to care. And third, he'd divide and conquer. He'd split them up and take them tonight when they were bone tired and their defenses were down. He cupped his hands.

"All right. Show's over. Everyone back to your stations. Let's get moving."

Matt's crew scrambled back to their duty stations, obviously relieved to get away from the tense-looking marines whose fingers never strayed from the triggers of their assault rifles.

Sergeant Li jumped to life, shouting commands in Mandarin.

"Wake up, you whores. Corporal Wu, cover the bridge. Private First Class Ling, cover the engine room. Private Fong, patrol belowdecks. Private Yu, patrol the upper decks. Move your asses. Let nothing escape your view. Keep a sharp eye out for these filthy barbarians. They're crafty and can't be trusted. Report anything suspicious to me. Move! *Diu neh loh moh.*"

Do your mothers. Matt had heard the Cantonese obscenity many times around the docks of Kaohsiung. It was a favorite of street gangs in Guangzhou and Hong Kong that had spread throughout China, even into areas that spoke Mandarin. Sergeant Li's men didn't react to it. They'd obviously heard the insult many times from the good sergeant.

They also didn't react to the more subtle insult of being called by their ranks. Even though the once-abolished military ranks had been restored in the People's Liberation Army, it was considered impolitic to call a superior by his rank and demeaning to call an inferior by his. Regardless of their actual rank, in all branches of the theoretically classless PLA, officers were addressed as "Leader" and enlisted men as "Fighter." Only at the most senior levels were officers addressed by their ranks.

That little display revealed much about Sergeant Li. He exerted his leadership through intimidation rather than respect. He was a bully, and bullies usually turned out to be cowards when the chips were down. And he was arrogant. The sergeant spoke English, but it never occurred to him that a "barbarian" like Matt might speak Chinese.

Sergeant Li's men scrambled to obey. Corporal Wu raced to catch up with Sam and Jason, who were heading for the bridge. The sergeant stepped toward Matt, flashing an obsequious smile. The phony bastard. It was clear what his assigned duty station was. He was going to stick to Matt like glue. Good. That would give him a built-in audience. He decided to begin the show right now.

"Jason. Get some rest, I'll take the conn. Sam and I'll take her in."

Jason threw a mock salute, and Matt started for the bridge.

Sergeant Li fell in beside him. By the time they got to the bridge, Sam was already there. Corporal Wu had taken up station in a corner of the pilothouse with his assault rifle at the ready. He stood staring at Sam as though not quite sure what to make of the black giant, his head jerking at every movement. With his finger on the trigger, he made Matt nervous. It would be a good opportunity to test Sergeant Li's knowledge of conversational English.

He nodded toward Corporal Wu and said quietly, "If that thing goes off, this will be the shortest salvage operation in history."

Sergeant Li spun on Wu. "How did you get promoted to corporal, you dog bones?" he said in Mandarin. "Point that piece away."

Interesting. The sergeant understood conversational English perfectly. He needed to alert Sam to that fact before his first mate said something he shouldn't. He nodded to Sergeant Li.

"Sam, this is Sergeant First Class Li."

Sam nodded to the marine but said nothing.

Sergeant Li looked at Matt curiously.

"Unusual for a foreigner to know Chinese military ranks," he said in English.

Stupid. Captain Chen had called the man "sergeant," but only someone who'd studied PLA military ranks would know he was a sergeant first class. He had to be more careful. It wouldn't do for the sergeant to know his background as a U.S. naval officer. If he relayed that bit of information to Captain Chen, the commanding officer of *Zhuhai* might remember where he'd seen him, and that would arouse suspicions.

"Just a lucky guess," Matt said.

Sergeant Li looked skeptical but said nothing.

"All ahead one third," Matt said.

"All ahead one third, aye, Captain." Sam rang it up on the engine-order telegraph.

CoMar Explorer shuddered and began to slice through the green water. Matt took the helm and steered in the direction of the easternmost island. The Chinese destroyer was already under way, gaining speed. He knew from past experience that *Zhuhai* was fast.

She'd chased his Los Angeles-class attack boat around the South China Sea enough in the old days for him to know she could make 32 knots, fully loaded. He'd be lucky to pull 16 knots out of *CoMar Explorer*, and couldn't sustain even that for long. There would be no contest in a race. He had to hope it never came to that.

He noticed that the destroyer was traveling on a southeasterly course, away from the islands. Where was she headed? Probably doing what all peacetime navies do, a never-ending round of war games. She'd probably been diverted to supervise the salvage operation and now, having secured the barbarians with a contingent of marines, was returning to duty. He felt relieved to see her go. His worst nightmare would be to have the destroyer anchored nearby. Captain Chen had said they'd return tomorrow to pick up the marines. If things went well tonight, the arrogant Chen would find the disarmed marines standing on the beach next to the freighter and Matt would be long gone with his prize.

They cruised in silence. Sergeant Li stood at parade rest behind Matt, watching every movement on the bridge, scanning the horizon. Corporal Wu began to settle down, though he couldn't seem to take his eyes off Sam. Closer now, Matt did a preliminary survey through binoculars. The eastern tip of the island, where the freighter was beached, jutted out into the sea like a small knob. He saw no signs of civilization. Nothing but scrub brush and tangled trees, ringed by a narrow beach, coarse brown sand rising up out of pink coral. The freighter sat heavily on the beach, about one-eighth aground at the bow.

Matt fixed his binoculars on a high wave and watched it roll in to see how solidly aground she was. The wave broke white against her stern, and the ship didn't budge. She appeared to be a derelict, an ancient flat-bottomed freighter probably built in the 1930s. The ship's company had lowered a Jacob's ladder off her stern to accommodate the salvors. Very thoughtful. He brought the ship into focus. Not much there. The CIA certainly hadn't overbought. He could make out the name welded on the fantail, just below the taffrail. *Leyte Gulf.*

He was sorry he couldn't stay and salvage her for real. The death of a ship was like the death of a town. When he pulled out tonight, the ship would probably stay right where she was until passing scavengers picked her clean and the wind and waves pulled her back into the sea. It would be an inglorious end to a fine old ship.

A gust of wind unfurled the flag on the freighter. The Stars and Stripes billowed out, snapping in the wind. A small shiver passed through him. Seeing the American flag in a foreign country always did that to him. Cliff Howard's words came back. If he pulled this off, the tax lien on his ship would be torn up and he'd be free to go home. After nearly five years of exile, he'd never been more ready. He'd find a way to lower the flag on the freighter and take it with him. Might raise some suspicions, but he couldn't just leave it behind to be shredded by the wind and defiled by scavengers.

Matt shifted his view as far to the right as he could without attracting Sergeant Li's attention. He could just make out the clump of land furthest to the west. Relatively level above the beach, and cleared for farming. It had to be Turtle Island.

He spent the next two hours maneuvering *CoMar Explorer* into a stern-to-stern position with the stranded freighter. The inshore maneuvers were tricky because of the strong currents around the island, but he was able to get her in position using the bow thrusters. By the time he dropped anchor it was almost 10:30. He secured the bridge and looked around, satisfied. Stern-to-stern was the usual position for pulling a stranded ship off the beach, but it was also a good position for a quick getaway.

From where they were anchored, he estimated that he could reach the north shore of Turtle Island in one of the inflatable boats in about twenty minutes. He'd normally use the 35-foot aluminum work boats to survey and rig a ship the size of the freighter, but the inflatable work boats were dark and fast and he wanted at least one in the water for use tonight.

"Lower away the eighteen-foot inflatables, Sam."

"Aye, aye, Skipper," Sam said. He keyed the microphone and gave the order over the ship's loudspeaker system, followed by the order to lower the Jacob's ladder.

As usual, Sam was one step ahead of him. The accommodation

ladder would take too much time to get back on board. The Jacob's ladder would allow them to be ready for a quick departure.

"Pass the word, Sam. Jason Tyler and Scootchy will do the survey of the ship." Matt would normally have had a survey team that included specialists in all disciplines, but this one was all for show, and he needed to isolate Scootchy from the rest of the crew with someone who couldn't be corrupted. "You and I will do the beach survey. All remaining hands will begin rigging beach gear on the main deck."

"Aye, aye, Skipper."

Sergeant Li turned to the corporal. "Fighter Wu. Two other barbarians will inspect the freighter. Accompany them when they board. Watch them closely."

Corporal Wu seemed to grow taller at being called "Fighter." Jason and Scootchy would be in good hands. He nodded to Sam.

"Let's do it."

The four scrambled down the ladder from the bridge and arrived at the quarterdeck just as Jason and Scootchy were emerging from the after hatch. Scootchy was walking on his own but still looked shaky. Matt caught Jason's eye.

"It will take you all day to complete the survey, Jase. I think this job is exactly like the freighter we salvaged a year ago in Luzon." He hoped Jason would get both messages. First, he wanted him to keep Scootchy aboard all day. The less contact he had with the rest of the crew, the better. Second, he wanted Jason to return with a report that the freighter had a tear in the bow, just like the freighter in Luzon. He needed an excuse not to do the pull tonight.

"Yes, sir," Jason said. "I reckon it's exactly like that."

Good. Jason understood. It helped to surround yourself with bright people.

"You know the drill. Inspect the hull for damage internally, check the holds for cargo and any hazmat." The fax from his salvage agent had indicated the freighter was loaded with manganese, but Matt knew from the CIA briefing that it was actually empty.

"When you complete the survey belowdecks, inspect all the bits and padeyes on the stern, make sure we've got something to attach the blocks and holding stoppers and fairleads to. We'll rig first, two hydraulic pullers on the main deck, port and starboard, then we'll shoot a line over to the freighter, followed by the bitter end of the beach gear wire. Secure it with a carpenter stopper."

"Aye, aye, Skipper," Jason said.

Sergeant Li looked uneasy, listening to salvors whose argot he couldn't understand. Matt decided to seize the opportunity to grab the flag.

"By the way, Jason, I don't think we've ever salvaged an American ship before. That flag will be a nice addition to our collection."

"What flag?" Sergeant Li said.

"It's a little tradition of ours," Matt said. "We collect the flags of all the ships we salvage and display them in our corporate headquarters." He turned back to Jason. "Pick it up when you leave, will you?"

"Sure thing, Skipper."

Matt smiled, pleased with himself and his little aggrandizement. They were standing on the only corporate headquarters Connor Marine was likely to have.

Scootchy glared at him, snorted, then started shakily down the ladder with Jason Tyler and Corporal Wu close behind. Scootchy cast off while Jason took the rudder and steered toward the freighter.

Matt watched them leave, then followed Sam down the ladder with Sergeant Li on his heels and shoved off in the second work boat. Sam took the rudder and steered the small craft around coral reefs, maneuvering into shore as close as he could get.

Sergeant Li was the first one out. "The weather around these islands has been calm for a month," he said as he waded ashore. He looked up at the black bow of the freighter. "I don't understand how the ship was beached."

"The ship was stranded, not beached," Matt said, tugging the inflatable up on the shore.

"What's the difference?" Sergeant Li said.

"A ship that's been intentionally run aground has been beached,"

Matt said. "If she's unintentionally run aground, she's been stranded."

"Whatever you call it, I want that ship removed as quickly as possible," Sergeant Li said. "How long will this take?"

"We won't know until we do the surveys," Matt said.

"My orders are for you to be gone by nightfall."

"Look, Sergeant," Matt said, "time is money. We don't want to be here any longer than we have to, but we won't know what we're up against until we do a survey of the ship and the beach."

Sergeant Li looked up at the bow of the freighter, then walked around, inspecting the portion of the hull that was aground. "The ship doesn't appear to be damaged. Just pull it off the beach and get it out of here."

"It's not that simple," Matt said. "In the first place, there may be damage in an area we can't see. That's what the survey team aboard will find out."

"What are *we* doing?"

"We need to determine the ground reaction and calculate the freeing force so we'll know what it will take to move her."

Sergeant Li blew out a long exasperated breath. "And what does that entail?"

Matt looked up at the bow. "This one isn't too bad. The worst possible scenario is broached to, when you've got the whole freighter sitting sideways on the beach."

He waded into the surf and took some measurements with Sam holding the tape on the beach. "In this case we've got a 450-foot freighter one-eighth aground at the bow. That means she's a little over fifty-six feet aground with a center of ground reaction of approximately twenty-eight feet aft. For an eight-thousand-ton freighter, that means we've got approximately a thousand long tons of weight sitting on the beach. We need to know that in order to calculate freeing force."

"What does that mean?"

"That's the total tons of pressure required to free the ship," Matt said. "It's measured in short tons because it's a lifting force. That's why ground reaction has to be converted from long tons to short tons. It's fairly straightforward. You just multiply the ground reaction by 1.12 to convert it to short tons. Then you have to factor in the coefficient of friction."

Sergeant Li rolled his eyes.

"It's the amount of drag the bottom type puts on the hull. There aren't any exact figures available, but in general the coefficient of friction for sand is between 0.3 and 0.4. For coral it's between 0.4 and 0.8." Matt walked to the water's edge and scuffed the heel of his boot in the coarse sand, digging down to the coral. "Based on my experience with this combination of sand and coral, I think we should use 0.6."

"Just get on with it," Sergeant Li said.

"No problem." Matt took a small calculator out of his pocket. "Let's see, now. Freeing force equals 1.12 times U times R, where U equals the coefficient of friction for the bottom type, in this case sand and coral, and R equals ground reaction, or total tonnage aground." He smiled at Li. "Once you know the variables, the calculation is pretty simple. It's a matter of multiplying 1.12 times 0.6 times a thousand," he said, punching in the numbers. He shielded the display with his hand and showed Sergeant Li the answer. "In this case it equals 672 short tons of force required to free the ship."

"Then make your connections and pull it off."

"It's not that easy," Matt said. "Each leg of beach gear can only pull fifty tons. We can rig two legs aboard *CoMar Explorer* and two legs aboard the freighter. That makes a total of two hundred tons of freeing force. That leaves us 472 tons shy of being able to move the ship."

"Then Captain Chen was correct. Your ship is too small. It's impossible for you to do the job. You should pack up and leave now."

Matt flashed an indulgent smile. "Few salvage ships in the world can bring more pulling power to bear than *CoMar Explorer*. All salvors have to rely on other factors, such as the tide. In this case we're lucky. High tide will more than compensate for the 472 tons we're shy. All we have to do is rig the beach gear and wait."

"For how long?"

Matt shrugged. "By midnight the conditions should be about right, assuming there's no damage to the freighter."

"That's not possible. My orders are for you to be gone by nightfall."

Matt gave him an open-handed shrug. "Sorry, that's the best we can do."

"Sitting around until midnight is unacceptable."

"Oh, we won't be sitting around. It'll take all day to do our surveys, set up beach gear on both ships, and get into harness. Setting up beach gear on two ships is a big job. I'm glad you and your men are here to help."

"My men are not here to work."

"Did I misunderstand Captain Chen?" Matt said. "Let's see. I believe his exact words were, 'If the job is that big, we'll provide you with assistance.' But I could be mistaken." He took a step toward Sergeant Li and pointed to his backpack. "Let's get him on your radio."

Sergeant Li stepped back defensively, then glared at Matt.

"Very well," he said. "My men can help if that's what it will take to get this stinking hulk out of here."

"Good," Matt said. "Even with your men helping it'll be a full day's work, but we'll be ready by tonight. Assuming, of course, there's no damage to the freighter."

After completing the beach survey, Matt spent the rest of the morning directing the setup of beach gear on the main deck. Now that he'd established the fact that Sergeant Li had a radio in his backpack, he watched him closely to see what his check-in pattern would be, who he called, what he said, the time, the frequency. So far he hadn't been able to catch him at it.

Li's men stacked their weapons on the quarterdeck and turned to. Gene Harvey, a rigger from Los Angeles, connected his portable to the ship's loudspeaker system and blasted a Rolling Stones CD throughout the ship. Just before noon, Francisco appeared on deck with a tray of sandwiches and a coffee urn. Traveller came up with him. The dog walked around sniffing the legs of the Chinese marines, then settled himself in the sun to watch the show.

Matt looked around at the scene. The food, music, and bantering laughter of the crew was typical of the party atmosphere he tried to create when they were salvaging a ship. He was glad to see the Chinese marines working. Reticent at first, they'd gotten into it and almost seemed to be enjoying themselves. Good. By tonight they'd be so worn out, they'd be vulnerable. He felt like a predator, but he knew it would be best for them, too. He didn't want any shooting. If he handled things right, no one would get hurt.

The sergeant was another matter. He hadn't even removed his backpack. Didn't want to get too far away from his radio. He stood with his AK-74 at the ready, watching everything. If any member of the crew strayed close to the stacked weapons, he tensed up. In spite of Matt's best efforts to engage him in the process, it was becoming clear that Sergeant Li would never relax his guard. No matter. Matt hoisted his khakis and felt the small pistol. It would make things more difficult if the sergeant had his guard up, but he would still take him. Matt had the element of surprise, which gave him a huge advantage. If his pickup was where she was supposed to be tonight, the deed was as good as done.

The only open question at this point was Sergeant Li's call-ins. It was critical to know the frequency. Hopefully, there'd be an interval of at least a few hours between calls. The check-in time would logically be on the hour. Matt looked at his watch. A few minutes before noon. He had to find a reason to get closer to Sergeant Li, who was never far away from his men. He saw one of the Chinese marines, the young private named Yu, struggling with a standing block on the port beach gear leg after the rigger he was helping stepped away.

"No, not like that," Matt said, walking over. "The tensiometer goes between the attachment point and the standing block, then rig the purchase between the standing block and the traveling block." He pointed to where everything went, making gestures. "That's right. Then the holding stopper and the ground leg."

Sergeant Li turned his back, and Matt heard him say in Mandarin, "Aerie, this is Eagle." He paused for a minute, then said, "The barbarian ship and crew are secure at twelve hundred hours." So check-in time was on the hour. No surprise there. The big question was, what were the intervals?

Over the next hour, Matt watched Sergeant Li out of the corner of his eye, sweating it out. At exactly 1300 the sergeant reached over his shoulder, threw a switch, and said the same words into a tiny microphone attached to his lapel. It *was* every hour. And if Li didn't check in every hour on the hour, the *Zhuhai* would come back and blow them out of the water. Matt looked toward Turtle Island. Even if they took the marines right after Sergeant Li reported in, there was no guarantee they could get there and back in an hour, before the next call-in was due. Matt could take control of the radio and he spoke Mandarin, but he didn't sound Chinese. He'd never be able to pull it off. He slumped against the lifeline and rubbed his face in his hands. Damn it. He'd made the classic mistake he'd been taught never to make: he'd underestimated his enemies. *Get over it and think.* There had to be a way around this, and he had to find it before midnight.

Elizabeth took her evening meal and steered Mother Wei toward a log near the tool shed, away from the others. She eased the old woman down on the decaying log and sat down beside her, grateful for a place to sit. It was difficult for her to squat on the ground the way the others did. She looked at the thin soup and the steamed bun. In spite of her starvation diet she felt surprisingly strong, probably the adrenaline coursing through her. Since last night she'd been unable to think of anything but the note. *Tomorrow at midnight. Be ready.* She was definitely ready, but she hated the thought of leaving Mother Wei behind in the shape she was in. The old woman needed more food if she was going to have any chance of surviving. She broke her steamed bun in two pieces and held out half.

"Here, Mother Wei."

"No, girl-child, I can't take your food. You must eat."

"I'm not hungry. Really."

Elizabeth took a sip of her soup and poured the rest into Mother Wei's cup. With her arm outstretched, she looked at her biceps. She could tell by her shadowy skin and shrunken muscles that her body had entered the preliminary stages of starvation. Like the others, she was slowly dying of malnutrition. For her it didn't matter—she'd be leaving this place tonight, God willing. But she had to find a way to get Mother Wei some real food. Just one decent meal, one infusion of some good quality carbohydrates and protein might make the difference between life and death. If she could find a way to get them, she wouldn't feel so guilty about leaving her behind. There was only one way. She looked around for Tang.

The overweight guard sat squatting on the other side of the tool shed, watching the prisoners, poking the dirt with his bamboo rod. She'd learned the rule for addressing guards by listening to the other prisoners. Even the lowest ranking guard was referred to as "Warden." She approached Tang with her head lowered in deference.

"Honorable Warden Tang," she said in Cantonese. "This lesser person would speak."

Four Finger Tang came to his feet with a wary, disgusted look on his face.

"Insufferable foreigner! I've heard the words you speak. Get back with the others."

Nothing melted the Chinese like an apology. Elizabeth thought the words would choke her, but she managed to say, "I apologize for my past indiscretions, Warden, and humbly ask to be forgiven."

Tang looked at her. "Speak, then, but watch your tongue."

"In private, please. It's a personal matter that one of your great sensitivity would appreciate."

Tang hesitated. What trickery was this, his eyes seemed to be saying. Finally, his curiosity got the better of him. He looked toward the small corrugated tin shed used for storing tools.

"Around the corner, then, but no tricks."

When they were out of sight of the others, Elizabeth lowered her head in obeisance. "Honorable Warden Tang, this unworthy person would ask a favor. The old woman, the prisoner known as Wei Ling, is not well. She must have more food or she will die."

"What nonsense is this?"

"Please, just a bowl of rice and some meat or fish."

"All prisoners have adequate rations. It's not possible."

Elizabeth locked eyes with the fat guard and reached into her bosom.

Four Finger Tang recoiled, gaping at Elizabeth's grimy fingers probing inside her bra. A confused, repulsed look came over his face. He raised his bamboo rod.

"Foreign devil!"

Elizabeth retrieved her Rolex and held it out. The late afternoon sun glinted off the diamond-cut bezel. *Gold*. The universal language. She could see Tang's eyes going over it.

"This watch is worth a great deal of money," Elizabeth said. "At least two thousand U.S. dollars." She knew that was more than Tang would make in a decade. "It's yours for a supply of rice, some vegetables, and some meat."

Tang lowered his rod. Even the lowliest peasant in China knew the value of a U.S. dollar. He licked his lips and reached for the watch. His missing thumb made his right hand look like a claw.

Elizabeth snatched it away and stuffed it back inside her bra. Tang would never touch her there, but he'd seen enough.

"When you deliver the food. Bring it early tonight and the watch is yours." She turned and walked back to Mother Wei.

Elizabeth watched the old woman drink the last of her soup, then helped her get into the queue for returning to their cells. Along with the other prisoners they deposited their tin cups in a large steel cauldron filled with boiling water and acrid-smelling soap, then trudged back to their cells, Elizabeth and Mother Wei spinning off at cell number sixteen.

Elizabeth paced the cell for the next hour, anxiety rising. Retrieving her watch, she checked the time. A few minutes before 8:00 p.m., June 13. According to the man who called himself Charlie, the rescue was hours away. Elizabeth heard a key in the door and flinched. Four Finger Tang stepped in, glancing back over his shoulder. Under a faded copy of the *South China Morning Post* was a bowl of steamed rice with a few carrots and a gray slice of pork.

Without a word Elizabeth took the bowl and handed it to Mother Wei, who was seated on the floor. Then she took Tang by the arm, turned him around so the old woman wouldn't see, and handed him her watch. He put it in his pocket and was gone as quickly as he'd come.

Mother Wei gazed up at her with an amazed look. "Why did he bring this?"

Elizabeth smiled and shrugged. "I think he likes you."

The old woman shook her head. "I think I cause you too much trouble."

"Nonsense," Elizabeth said. "We know each other too well to talk polite, is it not so?"

Mother Wei held the bowl up. "You must eat with me."

Elizabeth looked at the rice and her mouth began to water. She shook her head quickly.

"No, I'm not hungry," she said. "The food is for you."

Mother Wei shoveled rice in her mouth with her fingers. "I never had a daughter," she said. "It is too pitiable."

"Do you have sons?"

"Only one. He's now dead."

"I'm so sorry."

Mother Wei looked at her. "How old are you, girl-child?"

"Twenty-eight."

"You should find a man and marry. Soon you will be too old."

Elizabeth laughed. "In America, women marry much later than twenty-eight."

"What's life like in the Golden Country?"

Elizabeth smiled at the image the Chinese had of the U.S. In Chinese, the word "America" translated as "beautiful country." God, how she wished she could take Mother Wei with her so she could see for herself.

"It's wonderful," she said. "I always knew it was, but like most people who live there, I didn't know how wonderful until I lost it."

"Is it true what they say, that everyone in America is rich?"

"Rich is a relative term," Elizabeth said. "I'd have to say the poorest person in America has it better than we do here. Even homeless people can go where they choose."

Mother Wei finished her food and curled up on the floor. With a full stomach, she soon fell into a deep sleep. Elizabeth leaned into a corner, closed her eyes, and listened to her stomach growling. She knew she needed to sleep, but she wasn't sure what would happen at midnight and wanted to be awake when it did. Despite herself, she drifted into an intermittent sleep.

A low snore from Mother Wei woke her. Elizabeth reached for her watch, then remembered it was gone. She looked at the angle of the moonlight coming into her cell and tried to guess the time. Probably somewhere between ten o'clock and midnight. Mother Wei was sleeping peacefully, breathing strongly. The old woman already seemed stronger now that she'd had some real food.

Elizabeth glanced around the cell. It was impossible to imagine that in two hours or less, she'd be leaving this place. It couldn't happen soon enough, although conditions in the camp had improved dramatically for her in just the last twenty-four hours. No struggle sessions. No beatings. No being awakened in the middle of the night with someone screaming in her face to confess. Those were all welcome changes, but the most important change of all was having Mother Wei with her, ending the terrible isolation.

It did pay to stand up for what she knew was right, no matter what the consequences. Her political views had always placed her at odds with her conservative father, but it was one of her core beliefs: the strong had an obligation to help the weak. Her father had teased her about her "liberal guilt." It was true, she did feel guilty about having so much when others had so little, but her charitable efforts weren't entirely altruistic. Wei Ling was a case in point. If she hadn't stood up for a sick old woman, she'd still be alone in her cell.

It was remarkable how close they'd become in such a short time. She'd talked with Mother Wei into the night about everything. Marriage, family, childbearing, all her hopes and dreams, confided things she'd never told her own mother. God, how could she leave her behind after all this? What kind of monster was she? She leaned her head against the wall. The sound of the woman's breathing soothed her into nodding off again.

The click of a key against her cell door brought her instantly awake. She heard the lock give and saw a hand pushing the door in. Charlie's earnest face peered around the door. He put his finger to his lips and motioned for her to come.

This was it, the moment of decision. She scrambled across the floor.

"Mother Wei. Wake up."

Charlie shook his head violently. "No," he mouthed.

"I can't leave her," Elizabeth whispered. "I thought I could, but I can't."

Charlie closed the cell door and took her by the shoulders. "Don't wake her up, for God's sake."

Mother Wei's eyes opened. "What is it, daughter?"

"Come," Elizabeth said, "we're leaving."

"Are we taking our buckets to the fields?"

"We're leaving the island. You're coming with us."

Mother Wei looked bewildered. She looked at Elizabeth and Charlie, then at the cell door slightly ajar.

"An escape?"

"Yes, hurry."

"No, I'll only cause you trouble. Let me die here."

"You're not going to die, Mother Wei, you're coming with us."

Charlie threw up his hands. "All right, all right. But hurry."

Elizabeth helped Wei Ling to her feet and followed Charlie out the door and down the hall. They stopped at a small wooden door in the side of the corridor. She'd passed the door many times on her way to the struggle sessions, but she'd never seen it open. Charlie produced a key from somewhere and unlocked it. She crouched and followed him through the door, looking over her shoulder. She was glad she'd gotten the extra food for Mother Wei, who seemed able to walk much better now. Thank goodness. Elizabeth felt so weak from sharing her rations that she doubted she could support her for long, and Charlie didn't seem eager to help.

They wound their way down a small tunnel that opened onto a storage room, then crept past bags of rice, whole hams, cases of rice wine, the bottles individually wrapped in straw. The prisoners would never see any of that. No wonder Four Finger Tang was so fat. The storage room opened onto the kitchen. They crept around the blackened stoves and ovens, to a back door. Charlie opened the door a crack and peeked out, then motioned for them to follow him. They scurried down a narrow path into the cover of brush.

Crouching in the dim light, they skirted the fields and headed north. Elizabeth looked up at the sliver of moon, partially obscured by dark clouds, and saw a sprinkling of stars in the western sky. *The launch*. She'd almost forgotten about it. It was scheduled for June 21st. Today was the 13th. There'd still be time to stop it, if she was really getting out of here.

Raindrops began to spatter around her. Heavy clouds scudded across the moon, leaving them in the dark. Oblivious to the rain, Elizabeth heard waves crash against the rocky shore and caught a whiff of the sea, a clean, organic smell. Her mind swirled with excitement, unable to grasp that this was really happening. Who would be there to meet them? What kind of boat would they have? Where would they go?

They came to a knoll that began the descent to the beach. Charlie stopped, held up his hand, and turned to Elizabeth.

"Go down to the edge of the beach and wait for me, there's something I have to do. No matter what, don't stop, keep going."

Elizabeth started toward the knoll with Mother Wei behind her. She heard a gurgling sound. She spun around and saw Charlie with his arm around the old woman's neck.

Elizabeth gasped, a shriek caught in her throat. Tears shot out of her eyes.

"You're insane!" she shouted.

Charlie grimaced and tightened his grip around Mother Wei's neck, twisting her head to the side.

Elizabeth's blood felt like ice in her veins. One more minute and Wei Ling would be dead. "Stop it, you're killing her, she's an old woman!" She looked around frantically and picked up a boulder that must have weighed twenty pounds. Amazed by her sudden strength, she raised it over her head and started toward Charlie, intent on smashing his brains out. She brought the boulder down in a sweeping arc aimed at his head.

Charlie jumped to the side, dodging the boulder. He gripped Mother Wei's neck tighter and clenched his teeth.

"Not me, you idiot. Her!"

Mother Wei reached over her shoulder and grabbed Charlie by the neck. Pulling herself inward, she flipped him over her head. He landed in a jumbled heap in a juniper bush. Morphing into a karate stance, she advanced on him, hissing like a viper. She kicked him in the ribs three times so fast Elizabeth could barely see her foot move.

A flash of lightning illuminated the scene. Elizabeth looked at Mother Wei, unable to believe what her eyes were telling her.

Charlie rolled out of reach and came to his feet, clutching his side. He went into a combat stance. He threw a quick glance at Elizabeth.

"Get down to the beach and wait for the contact."

Elizabeth saw fear in his eyes. Her feet wouldn't move. She stared at the two, crouching, circling, each looking for an opening. Charlie spun around with his right foot, aiming for Mother Wei's head. She stepped back, dodging the blow easily, then retaliated with a kick that connected under his chin, staggering him. Elizabeth held her head in her hands, still reeling at the instantaneous transformation from sick old woman to killing machine. They fought back and forth for what seemed like an hour. Elizabeth looked toward the beach. What if the contact was there and didn't see them? What if they heard the commotion and thought something had gone wrong? What if they left?

She watched the deadly fight, terrified and frustrated, not knowing what to do. It was becoming clear that Charlie was outmatched. She had to do something. She'd gotten him into this mess. She looked around and saw a dead branch about three feet long. She picked it up and maneuvered into position behind the woman, not knowing if she could do this. Aiming at the base of her skull, she closed her eyes and swung as hard as she could. She felt the branch connect.

The woman staggered. It was the break Charlie needed. He hit her hard and fast, spun her around, and got a choke hold on her. Straining with everything he had, he twisted her neck to the side. Elizabeth heard a snap, and the woman went limp. Charlie dropped her in the wet dirt and fell to his knees beside her, gasping for breath.

Elizabeth stood in shock, horrified by what she'd just done.

Charlie scrabbled around in the dirt, panting, searching for something. He picked up a knife. The grip was wrapped with black electrical tape. The blade was long and thin, like a knife for filleting fish. Still struggling to breathe, he held it up for Elizabeth to see.

"You almost got your throat cut."

"I don't believe you."

He rolled the woman over and started tugging her blouse apart.

"What are you doing?"

Charlie ripped her blouse open, buttons flying, exposing a narrow sheath strapped to the woman's left side, under her arm. He slid the knife in. It fit perfectly.

Elizabeth shoved a fist in her mouth.

"She was the fail-safe. You were never supposed to get this far, but if you did, her job was to kill you. That's why they planted her in your cell."

"They didn't plant her, I took her under my wing in the fields. I thought she was going to die."

"They knew you'd fall for that. It's an old trick. 'When weak appear strong, when strong appear weak.' Americans are suckers for the weak."

"But she was an old woman. And she was sick."

"She was no sicker than I am. And she's not old. Mid-forties, maybe. Look at this." He smudged a layer of wrinkles on her forehead. "She was made up to look old."

"My God," Elizabeth said. "Who is she?"

"I don't know, but now you know why I didn't want you to wake her up."

Elizabeth swallowed. And she knew why Charlie had agreed to bring her once she *was* awake—he couldn't leave her behind to blow the whistle. Charlie was right. She was an idiot. She hugged herself to keep from trembling.

"How did you know she had a knife?"

"My grandmother used to say, 'When you see two faces, beware of three knives.' But she didn't need it. She could have killed you with her bare hands." Looking sheepish, he put a hand over his ribs and grimaced. "Damn near killed *me*. Might have, if you hadn't stepped in."

Elizabeth looked at the woman's body sprawled in the dirt and remembered all the things they'd talked about, the special feeling she'd had for "Mother Wei." She felt a wave of nausea grip her insides and spiral up into her throat. She tried to force it back down, but couldn't. She bent over, put her hands on her knees, and vomited.

Charlie laid a hand on her shoulder.

"It's a tough world, little sister."

Elizabeth felt touched by the tenderness in his voice. It didn't help. She felt her stomach convulse again. She retched, then stood gasping. There was nothing more to come up. She wiped her mouth with the back of her hand.

"What a fool I am."

"That recognition is the beginning of wisdom," Charlie said. "The important thing is, her presence here's a sure sign that someone knows what's going on. They obviously thought there was a possibility you might escape." He dragged the woman's body into the brush and covered it with some loose branches. "Let's get out of here. There's a spot down near the beach where we can hide and wait for the Zodiac."

"What if they don't come?"

"Then we're in deep doo-doo, as we used to say in Chicago." He reached in his pocket and tossed something to her.

She caught the object, then opened her hand. A flash of lightning lit a gold and stainless steel Rolex.

"My watch."

"I had to dispose of a fat guy back there with a missing thumb. When they figure out *he's* missing, this island's going to get very busy, very fast. You'd better pray that our ride's on time."

Chapter Ten

Matt stood on the fantail of *CoMar Explorer* in a light rain, nursing a cup of lukewarm coffee. He stared in the direction of Turtle Island, his stomach churning. Sergeant Li's dark form hovered nearby—the guy had been hovering all goddamn day long. He pressed the light button on his watch. Twenty-three-fifty, almost midnight. Li's next call-in was due in ten minutes, precisely when Matt was supposed to rendezvous on the north shore of Turtle Island.

He'd decided that he had no choice but to wait for the sergeant to make his 2400 call before making his move. If he took him after the 2300 call he'd have to wait for the woman until midnight, alerting the Chinese destroyer that something was amiss when the 2400 call didn't come through. He was going to be late for the rendezvous, and there wasn't a damn thing he could do about it. He only hoped the woman and her contact on the island, a man named Charles Shen, would be in a position to wait for him.

He looked up at the sky, a black dome over the earth. An occasional stab of lightning crackled through the heavens, illuminating dark clouds that obscured a sliver of moon. At least the weather was cooperating. With a sky like that, the black inflatable would be hard to spot. He dumped his coffee over the side and walked into the galley. Sergeant Li followed him.

Matt rinsed his cup out in the sink and peered into the adjacent crew's lounge, dark except for the red glow of night lights. The Chinese marines had flaked out, exhausted from their day's work. Corporal Wu and Private First Class Ling had seized the leather couches. One of the young privates was sprawled on the deck, using his backpack for a pillow. They all appeared to be sound asleep.

The remaining marine, the nervous young private named Fong, had drawn guard duty and was sitting on a chair in the corner with his Kalashnikov pointed at the overhead, finger on the trigger, head nodding. It was interesting that the Chinese had posted a guard over themselves. They seemed to understand that with so few men it was they, not Matt's men, who were vulnerable.

"You go to bed now," Sergeant Li said in English.

Matt didn't respond. Ignoring Li made the sergeant nuts. Matt's goal from the beginning had been to wear him down, get him off balance. Sergeant Li had been in a black mood ever since Jason and Scootchy had returned from the freighter with a report—not surprisingly true—that the ship had a tear in the bow that would require some major repairs before it could be moved. Li had insisted on seeing the tear with his own eyes, and Matt, after a subtle yes nod from Jason, had accommodated him. The pull would now have to be delayed until tomorrow night, and the sergeant wasn't happy. Tough. He was going to be a lot less happy in about eight minutes.

Sam and three of his men were in their bunks fully clothed under blankets, waiting. Precisely at midnight they'd each take their assigned marine and package him neatly in duct tape. The sergeant was Matt's responsibility, but first he had to get him away from the others, let him make his call. If Matt went to the bridge, the sergeant, like Mary's little lamb, would follow.

"You go to bed," Sergeant Li said again, this time more insistent.

Matt stretched and yawned. "Soon as I update the log."

He hung his cup on a peg, glanced at his watch, and headed up the ladder to the bridge. To his relief, Sergeant Li followed him. He turned on the small pull-down reading lamp over the bridge chair, picked up the log, and sat down. He twisted in the faded leather chair and clicked his pen. Sergeant Li paced the bridge behind him, muttering something in Mandarin about filthy barbarians who never slept.

Matt opened the book and started writing. This was it. He'd have to move quickly and decisively as soon as the sergeant made his midnight call. There was no margin for error. One of the two inflatable work boats was tied up to the Jacob's ladder from the survey work they'd done earlier in the day, fueled and ready to go. If he and Sam shoved off a few minutes after midnight, there was a chance they could make the pickup and be back aboard before the 0100 report.

The timing would be tight, but it was their only shot. Sergeant

Li's radio was already set to the proper frequency and Matt had memorized the Mandarin words, but he still didn't think he could fake it. Mandarin was a tonal dialect. Each word had a pronunciation that carried one of four basic tones—a high and even tone, a rising tone, a dipping tone, and a falling tone—plus a clear, unstressed tone, and they had to be perfect. Changing the tone changed the meaning of the word. He'd worked hard to get the tones right, but try as he might, he just didn't sound Chinese. Whenever they got back aboard, they'd have no choice but to coerce one of the Chinese marines into making the call.

Earlier in the day, Sam had spotted the same young private, the one named Fong, that Matt had noticed. He had a shrill, reedy voice like Sergeant Li, and he seemed nervous. If they isolated Private Fong from the others, and Sam put the fear in him, they might persuade him to make the call. In any case, Matt would have to be back on time. They couldn't just hand the radio over to the Chinese private if Matt wasn't there to monitor what he was saying. He was the only man in the crew who spoke Chinese.

Sam had proposed taking Fong and the radio with them when they did the pickup, but Matt had argued against it. In the first place there was no guarantee that the young private would actually make the call, and in the second place a belligerent could cause too much trouble, maybe shout out or make a break for it as they approached the island. No, there was no other way. They had to make the pickup and get back aboard before 0100. With luck, they could do it. If they made it, and if they could get Private Fong to say the words, and if he was convincing, that would buy them a few hours to get away, depending on the range of the radio. If not, they'd have to fire up all four engines, shed all the weight they could, and run like hell.

Matt finished the log, stood up, and stretched. He looked out the bridge windows into the semi-darkness. The chain of islands was black except for the island furthest to the west. Dim yellow lights twinkled in the distance, probably floodlights surrounding the prison compound.

He shifted his attention to the direction he'd seen the Chinese destroyer take. He had no idea where *Zhuhai* was now, but the war games were probably somewhere in the vicinity of the islands. At a flank speed of thirty-two knots, it wouldn't take long for her to return. He shoved his hands into his hip pockets and fingered the pistol Gray Wolf had given him. This time he had it cocked and ready to fire. He glanced over his shoulder. The chronometer on the bulkhead read 2359, the second hand ticking slowly. One minute had never seemed so long. At exactly 2400 Sergeant Li switched the radio on in his backpack.

"Aerie, this is Eagle," he said in Mandarin. He sounded tired and irritated. He waited for a confirmation, then said, "The barbarian ship and crew are secure at 2400 hours." He snapped the radio off.

Matt moved into position.

A burst of gunfire echoed from the deck below, bullets ricocheting on steel. The sergeant jumped and reached over his shoulder. Before he could turn the radio on, Matt swung. He connected with the side of Li's head, knocking him back against the bulkhead, then pulled the pistol from his pocket and jammed the muzzle against Li's forehead.

"Don't move," he said.

Sergeant Li froze against the bulkhead.

Matt relieved him of his assault rifle and stepped back two paces. "Place your hands on top of your head and turn around."

Li complied.

Matt returned the pistol to his pocket and leveled the Kalashnikov. The burst of gunfire had him worried. Holding the rifle on the sergeant, he backed up to the bridge telephone console. There was no way he was taking Sergeant Li belowdecks until he knew who was in control of the ship. He pressed the button for the crew's lounge. After the fifth ring, he heard a click.

"Sam."

Matt exhaled. "Everything secure?"

"All set, Skipper."

Matt prodded the sergeant down the ladder and into the lounge. Corporal Wu, Private First Class Ling, and Private Yu were lying face down, hands secured behind their backs with duct tape. Doc Miller stood over them with one of their assault rifles. Sam was putting the finishing touches on Private Fong while Gene Harvey held a rifle on him. The young private was bent over with his hands crossed behind his back.

"What was the shooting about? Everybody okay?"

"Just a slip of the finger," Sam said, spooling a roll of duct tape around Private Fong's wrists. "I guess I startled him."

Matt glanced at Sam's face. Zigzag streaks of green and black camouflage paint made him look like something out of a nightmare.

"Can't imagine why."

Sergeant Li started screeching in Mandarin. "You dog bones have fouled everything up. Listen to me, you miserable whores. Resist these barbarians by all means possible. You are to do nothing they say. Nothing."

Matt resisted the urge to tell Li to shut up. He might have to reveal that he spoke the language at some point, but there was no reason to give up that advantage yet.

"Relieve him of that radio, Doc. Then lock him up somewhere, away from the others."

"Where?"

Matt had been thinking about a place to secure Sergeant Li. The ship had originally been built for the Dutch Navy. It had a two-man brig Matt used for storage. He'd have to press it into service.

"Lock him in the brig."

"You know it's full of stuff."

"Clean it out."

"Where's the key?"

"I don't know. On a ring, hanging on the keyboard on the bridge. Find it."

"What about the others?"

"Lock these three in the bosn's stores locker." Matt nodded toward Private Fong. "Isolate him while we're gone to soften him up. Have him standing by on the quarterdeck, with the radio, when we get back."

"Hold still, Skipper." Sam squeezed a wad of black camouflage makeup out of the tube and smeared Matt's face with it. He stood back and gave him a critical look, then grinned. "Black is beautiful."

Matt checked the magazine on Sergeant Li's Kalashnikov. It was full. He pulled an extra magazine out of the sergeant's flak jacket and shoved it in his belt. He looked at his watch.

"Let's go, Sam. We've got fifty-five minutes to get there and back."

"Just you and me? You sure?"

"Any more men would just get in the way," Matt said. He turned to Jason Tyler. "Weigh the anchor and get the engines started. Retrieve the ground leg lines. Get us free of the freighter, ready to run. We should be back before 0100."

"Aye, aye, Skipper. Good luck."

Matt headed for the quarterdeck with Sam at his heels. The rain had gotten heavier. They clambered down the Jacob's ladder and jumped into the Zodiac. Sam cast off the line, Matt fired up the twin outboard motors and leaned into the tiller, heading west toward Turtle Island. He wasn't sure where the exact pickup point was, but it was on the north beach, somewhere between the two left legs of the turtle. He checked his watch. Seven minutes past midnight. With luck they could be there at 0025. Five minutes for the pickup, twenty minutes back to the ship. If everything went according to plan, they'd be back in good time to convince Private Fong to say the right words for the 0100 call-in.

The wind picked up. Raindrops the size of dimes began to splatter against the rubber boat. The tiny craft labored over swells and dipped down into black troughs, the pitch of the muffled engines rising and falling. Matt looked up at the sky. His forecast of rain based on the northeasterly direction of the wind and the high cirrus clouds had been right. The rain had brought a dense layer of black clouds that obscured the quarter moon. Darkness was good, but the wind was blowing up surf that was slowing him down. Eight minutes had already elapsed and the lights of the island seemed only a little closer.

The dark clouds shifted, intermittently exposing the faint glow of the moon. Sam's massive figure was crouched in the bow, assault rifle cradled in his arms. With slashes of camouflage paint down his face, he'd be a terrifying figure coming out of the night. Matt thought he'd better be the first one ashore—he didn't want to scare the woman to death—then remembered his own blackened face.

A gust of wind blew the top off a wave, drenching him. Raindrops hissed into the sea like bullets. He prayed the woman and her contact would be where they were supposed to be, waiting for him. The quicker he made the pickup, the better. The weather was getting worse, and the added weight in the boat on the return trip would only slow him down more.

Matt blinked the water from his eyes. The yellow lights of the island were clearly in view now, further inland, ringing the prison compound. He thought he could hear a generator humming faintly in the distance. He turned the rudder toward shore. The clouds covering the moon drifted away again and he could see the two dark peninsulas that formed the left legs of the turtle, separated by the relative lightness of the beach.

"See anything, Sam?"

"Negative, Skipper."

Matt felt a flash of irritation at the woman and her contact for not being where they were supposed to be, then reminded himself that he was the one who was late. He strained his eyes. Where the hell were they? Had they given up on him and gone back? Not likely—he wasn't that late. Were they hiding nearby and he just didn't see them? Possible. Or had they been discovered? Very possible, what with his being late. If they'd been captured, the Chinese would have a warm welcome for their rescuers the minute they set foot on the beach.

The boat was now about fifty feet off shore. Decision time. Did he stay or did he go? To hell with it. Without the woman, he had nothing to go back to. If the Chinese were waiting for them, they'd just have to fight their way out.

He spotted a rock formation behind the first peninsula that created a natural cove. It would be tricky to maneuver around the rocks, but they needed some shelter in case anyone opened fire. It made more sense than just running up on an open beach. He steered to port and headed for the cove.

"Good idea, Skipper," Sam said. "That beach is a little too open."

Matt maneuvered around the rocks and got in as close as he could. He idled the muffled outboard motors down to a low purr and listened. Waves crashed through the rocky entry and exploded in a haze of white spray. Raindrops drummed against the inflatable boat. Except for the water and the distant generator hum, there were no other sounds. He cut the motors and lifted the props out of the water. Sam slipped over the side and took up point on the beach, crouching low with his assault rifle. Matt slid into the water behind him and tugged the boat ashore. He wedged a branch of driftwood between two rocks and tied the boat to it.

The cove appeared to be about thirty feet wide with its own private beach. Matt crouched behind a boulder the size of a desk and peered down the beach area that was supposed to be the pickup point, a sweeping panorama about three hundred yards long. At the other end, the beach narrowed down to a few boulders, then petered out. The beach was empty.

"Where the hell are they?" he said.

From behind him, Sam gently put his hand over Matt's mouth. Matt turned. Sam made the shushing motion, his index finger across his lips, then pointed to his left. He'd heard something.

Matt followed Sam's gaze. Across the narrow beach was a stand of twisted brush. He wiped the water from his eyes and studied it. He thought he saw a branch move but couldn't be sure it wasn't just the wind and rain. He couldn't just sit there and wonder what it was—time was running out. He snapped the safety off on the Kalashnikov and motioned for Sam to go left. He would go right.

Crawling across the beach on his stomach, Matt reached the west end of the tangled stand of brush. He came to his feet and saw Sam's dark form rising up on the east end. He leveled the rifle into the brush and cautiously started moving branches aside with the barrel. He saw something move, a glimpse of clothing, and aimed the rifle.

"Come out," he said in English, then quickly repeated the order in Cantonese.

"Don't shoot."

The brush parted and a frail-looking young woman came to her feet, hands raised. Wet, stringy hair fell over her forehead, covering her eyes. Damp leaves and twigs clung to her hair and clothing. She looked like a little girl who'd been caught playing in a pile of leaves in the rain. She pulled the hair away from her eyes and gaped at Matt's blackened face. A breath went out of her that seemed to make her physically smaller.

"Thank God."

Matt stared back. There was little resemblance to the picture he'd seen of Elizabeth Grayson. He'd never seen anyone so fragile-looking in his life. Tall and emaciated, scraggly hair covering a tear-stained face, red eyes. Why was she crying, now that she was leaving? Women were crazy.

"Elizabeth Grayson, I presume?"

"Call me Beth."

"I'm Matt Connor. Where the hell have you been? You were supposed to be on the beach."

"So were you. An hour ago."

Matt looked at his watch. "Forty minutes ago." He looked around. "Are you alone?"

"Charlie hid me here. Charlie Chan. At least, that's what he said his name was."

"Charles Shen," Matt said. "Works under contract for the CIA. Where did he go?"

"There was a routine patrol at twelve-thirty that got too close. Two guards on foot. If you'd been on time, we'd have missed them."

"Did they see you?"

"No. Charlie hid me here and went off to see if he could distract them away from the beach. He thought you might show up any minute."

"Is he armed?"

"No," Beth said. "Well, he has a knife."

"Where did he get a knife?"

"You wouldn't believe me if I told you."

"How long has he been gone?"

"About ten minutes." She was finger-combing her wet hair.

Matt glanced at his watch. "He'd better get his ass back here. We're leaving in about two minutes."

"You can't leave without him. He saved my life." She narrowed her eyes. "You wouldn't leave a fellow CIA agent."

"I'm not CIA," Matt said.

She stopped brushing leaves from her dress and looked at his blackened face. "Then what are you? A marine?" Matt shook his head. "Army, Navy, what?"

"None of the above," Matt said. "I'm a civilian."

"Since when does the U.S. government send civilians out to rescue damsels in distress?" She looked at him with a mixture of curiosity and excitement. "So what *do* you do? Are you a professional hit man, or something?"

"Nothing that interesting," Matt said. "I'm in the salvage business."

"A junkman?"

Matt heard the sound of someone running, crashing through the brush. He placed his hand over Elizabeth's mouth and pulled her down. He gripped her tightly against him, trying to minimize their bulk. He felt her ear against his mouth.

"I'd be glad to go back and let them make other arrangements more to your liking," he said.

"No, no," she said into his fingers. "You're doing fine."

"Then keep quiet."

He glanced around. Where the hell was Sam? The sound of people running, breaking through brush came closer. He motioned for Elizabeth to get back into her hiding place and worked his way forward through the brush along the perimeter of the beach, toward the sound of voices. Twenty feet ahead, he saw a young Asian man in prison garb burst out of the brush, onto the beach. It had to be Charles Shen. The kid ran like a deer. It helps to have someone chasing you. Moving forward as quickly as he could, Matt took up station near where he knew Charlie's pursuers would emerge. Something told him Sam was nearby.

Matt heard the thrashing of brush coming closer. It sounded like two men. He braced himself. He didn't want to kill anyone if he didn't have to. The first guard burst into the open. Matt came to his feet and caught him under the chin with the butt of his Kalashnikov. The man dropped like a sack of wheat. Seconds later, the next guard burst into the open, tripped over the man's body, and went sprawling. Matt hesitated. He didn't want to hit a man when he was down. The guard rolled over and leveled his rifle at Matt. Before he could fire, Sam smashed him in the back of the head.

"First thing you learn at Coronado is never fight fair," Sam said.

Matt looked around. "Tape them up and gag them, then separate them so they can't help each other. Let's get out of here."

With Sam covering his flanks, Matt made his way back to where he'd left Elizabeth Grayson. Charles Shen pulled her out of the tangled brush and stood protectively in front of her with his hands in the air.

"Don't shoot. Charles Shen, CIA."

"Relax, I know who you are," Matt said.

"My friends call me Charlie," he said, extending his hand. "Who are you?"

"This is Matt Connor," Beth said. "Junkman." She smiled at Matt.

Matt looked at her gaunt, Eurasian features in a sliver of moonlight that had broken through the rain clouds. The conventional wisdom was that one could never be too rich or too thin, but he thought Elizabeth Grayson had gone over the line.

Her eyes met his. She seemed to sense what he was thinking.

"I've been on the Turtle Island diet. Works, doesn't it?"

"Don't worry," Matt said, thinking about how Francisco would dote on her. "We'll get you fattened up." He motioned toward Sam. "This is Sam Washington, my first mate."

Charlie nodded toward the inflatable. "First mate of what? I hope it's a little bigger than that."

"A little." Matt glanced at his watch. "Let's get aboard. We're late." He looked down at Beth's bare feet. The coral would cut her to ribbons, and coral infections took forever to heal. He knew he should ask first, but there was no time for formalities. He tossed his rifle to

Charlie and swept her up, expecting her to object. Instead, she looped her left arm around Matt's neck and grinned into his blackened face. Embarrassed, he avoided her eyes. He carried her, all but weightless in his arms, through the surf and dropped her into the boat.

Matt untied the Zodiac and pulled it free while Sam and Charlie backed away from the beach. He held the boat for them, turned it around, and pulled himself over the gunwale. He lowered the props into the surf, started the outboard motors, maneuvered around the rocks until he was free of the cove, and opened the throttles, heading east. He looked over his shoulder. The beach was quiet. With luck, it would take a while for them to discover the guards or to realize the woman had escaped. He wasn't too worried. With the weapons Gray Wolf had given them they could hold their own with any patrol craft the prison would be likely to have available on the island.

The destroyer was another matter. He looked at his watch. 0050. Ten minutes until one. He was going to be late. They'd have to get Private Fong to make a plausible excuse.

"Oh, God," Beth Grayson said.

Through the rain, Matt saw the red and green running lights of a ship moving in their direction. Was it the *Zhuhai*? He wiped the water out of his eyes and recognized the dark superstructure of *CoMar Explorer*. The ship was heading west, coming for him. Jason Tyler had realized that they were never going to make it back in time, so he was bringing the ship to them. Matt wanted to kiss the guy. In the dim light, Jason would never be able to see the inflatable. Matt used a small penlight to blink out a message.

"Going-my-way?"

Matt held his breath, hoping Jason saw his light. After a few minutes, he heard the engines slow. Leaning into the rudder, he cut across the bow of the ship and made for the Jacob's ladder hanging from the starboard side near the quarterdeck. He glanced at Beth, who looked terrified.

"Don't worry, they're the good guys."

"Just in time, too," Sam said, looking at his watch. "It's almost one."

"What's magic about one?" Beth said.

"You might say we have a one o'clock curfew," Matt said. He looked at Charles Shen. The CIA agent had to speak the language. "We've got to fake a radio call to a Chinese destroyer in about two minutes. How's your Mandarin?"

"Passable," Charlie said, "but I've got a Chicago accent."

Obviously American-born, Charlie didn't sound like Sergeant Li or any of his men. Back to Plan A: Private Fong. Matt maneuvered up to the Jacob's ladder as *CoMar Explorer* slowed. Sam tied the boat up and helped Elizabeth get started up the ladder, then Charlie. Matt cut the motors and started up the ladder as two divers jumped into the water to sling the boat for recovery. He stepped onto the quarterdeck and saw Doc Miller holding a rifle on Private Fong. His hands were taped behind him and he looked scared to death. The radio sat before him on the deck. Matt checked his watch and handed the earpiece and lapel microphone to the young private.

"Listen to me carefully," he said in Mandarin. "You will report in exactly as Sergeant Li did. If they ask, you will say you have the watch and Sergeant Li has gone to bed. If you say the wrong words, I will turn you over to the black giant." He nodded toward Sam.

The private's eyes shot back and forth. He shook his head. "Sergeant Li would kill me," he said in Mandarin.

Sam stepped forward and grabbed Private Fong by the throat. He didn't speak Chinese but he understood a shake of the head. His great black hand nearly encircled the marine's neck. He glared into his eyes with the fiercest look he could muster.

"Tell him I'll kill him if he doesn't do it."

"The black giant says he will cook you and eat you for breakfast," Matt said.

Private Fong closed his eyes and shook his head again.

"I cannot."

Sam pulled a K-Bar combat knife from a sheath on his right ankle and held it against the private's throat. "Tell him I'll eat him for breakfast."

"I already told him that," Matt said.

"Gee, thanks," Sam said.

Matt stared at the marine. "The black giant says you have until the count of five and then you will die."

The marine shook his head.

Matt began to count in Mandarin. When he got to five, he saw the Chinese marine tense up and steel himself for the knife thrust.

"I would rather die now than lose face for an eternity. Kill me."

"Damn it," Matt said. He looked at his watch. It was 0102. He had to do something. He picked up the radio.

"Wait," Elizabeth said. "You'll never get away with it. Let me try."

"You speak Mandarin?"

"My Cantonese is better than my Mandarin, but I think I can do it. Just tell me the words."

"Okay," Matt said. "Say 'Aerie, this is Eagle,' then wait for the confirmation. Then say, 'The barbarian ship and crew are secure at 0100 hours.' Got that?"

Elizabeth nodded. She rehearsed the words twice, switched the radio on, took a deep breath, and spoke into the microphone.

"Aerie, this is Eagle."

Matt held his breath. There was a delay. They were questioning her.

"Fong," Elizabeth said. "Sergeant Li is indisposed. The barbarian food is inedible, is it not so?"

If he'd closed his eyes, Matt could have been convinced that it was Private Fong himself. He heard a hawking laugh come through the earpiece. Elizabeth finished her routine and signed off.

Matt snapped the radio off and looked at her. There was more to this girl than met the eye.

"Was that okay?" Elizabeth said.

"Better than okay. Sounds like they bought it," Matt said, walking toward the bridge. "In which case we've got an hour to put as much distance between us and them as we can."

"And if they didn't?"

Matt hesitated. He didn't want to frighten her, but she had a right to know what they were up against.

"If they didn't," he said, "you might wish you'd stayed on that island."

Chapter Eleven

James Lao flinched at the sound of the curtain sliding back on his sleeping compartment and blinked into the morning light. The golden young flight attendant called Lulu smiled in at him.

"Please forgive this intrusion, Senior Colonel. We'll be landing in Beijing soon. May I trouble you to take your seat and fasten your seat belt?"

He sat up and looked at his watch. Almost 0600. In two hours he'd appear before the Central Military Commission, a body chaired by the president of China, and he'd had almost no sleep. He'd hoped to sleep on the plane but had spent most of the night fine-tuning his presentation, trying to anticipate every conceivable question the dithering old cadres on the commission could raise. He'd drifted off once or twice during the three-hour flight from Guangzhou, but it was no use. He should have known better. He'd never been able to sleep on a plane, even one as luxurious as this. He rubbed his eyes.

"Bring me some coffee, a *latte*."

"I'm sorry, sir. The espresso machine is secured for the landing."

"Some tea, then. Strong and black."

"At once, Senior Colonel."

He took a seat in the forward passenger compartment and pulled his seat belt tightly around him. Head lowered in deference, Lulu appeared with a small basket. Using a pair of bamboo tongs, she held out a steaming white towel.

"Your tea will be ready in just a minute, sir."

James wiped his face and the back of his neck with the hot towel. The warm moisture began to revive him. Waiting for his tea, he leaned his head against the cool window of the Boeing 737. The lights of Capital International Airport blinked into view. To the west, he could make out the Forbidden City and Tiananmen Square. A bit further to the west lay his final destination, the rectangular, 250-acre compound known as Zhongnanhai.

His stomach tightened. Behind the high vermilion walls lay the manicured grounds and buildings where China's aging leaders lived and worked. He knew the place well, had grown up in the luxurious compound as the privileged son of a national hero, though he hadn't been back in years. He'd enjoyed his childhood there, but it was the last place on earth he wanted to be now.

Lulu appeared with a steaming teacup filled with a brew the color of ink. Head lowered, she offered it with two hands in the old way.

"Six Tranquilities Black. Very strong."

With all the Western influences in China, it was unusual for a young person to know the old customs. His eyes lingered over her. Hair black and glossy, eyes the color of olives, skin a pale gold. He felt something stir in his loins, then reminded himself where he was. With Beijing's strait-laced Puritanism—imposed by the philandering Mao, but still in effect—he had to watch every step while in the city. Dallying with prostitutes was one thing, but deflowering China's youth was another. Men had been toppled for less, and there were eyes everywhere. Once Phase II of his plan had borne fruit, and he was living in Europe as one of the world's richest men, he'd have a thousand like her. For now, one thought must occupy his mind. He forced his eyes back to the window.

"Thank you. That's all."

The plane began its descent through the permanent yellow haze that hung over Beijing. It touched down on Runway No. 1 with a chirp, reversed its engines, and rumbled to a stop. With the CAT logo on its tail signifying state ownership, the plane was directed to a government hangar on the edge of the field. Through the fogged window James saw that a state limousine stood waiting for him, the driver standing in front of the car.

The door of the plane cracked opened. A blast of humid air flooded in. He gathered up his briefcase and duffel bag and walked down the ramp to the waiting car. The driver, a stooped old man wearing a gray Mao suit, started toward him, walking slowly. He reached for James's bag.

"Welcome home, Senior Colonel," the man said in a raspy voice. "I trust you had a pleasant flight."

"Yes, thank you," James said.

The old man gave him a toothless grin. "You don't remember me, do you? It's Old Wang, I used to chase you around the compound when you were a young puppy."

James flushed, embarrassed that he hadn't recognized the man. Wang Li had been his father's number-one servant for as long as he could remember. Old Wang had always looked out for James. As a child growing up unsupervised in Zhongnanhai, he'd gotten him out of trouble many a time. James had thought Wang was old then. Now he looked ancient. He broke into a smile and gripped the old man by his frail shoulders.

"Of course I remember you. How are you, Wang?"

"Eh, I'm just a pile of bones. But as long as I can move, I'll serve your father."

"How is the general?"

"He's well, but he works too hard." Old Wang leaned in and said in a conspiratorial whisper, "Everyone else in Zhongnanhai works for themselves, but your father works for China. A great man, is it not so?"

"It is truly so."

"And you, the young master, just like him. He speaks of you often, always so proud."

James felt a sickening urge to laugh. What would his father say if he knew about the plan he'd just implemented? He shrugged it off. At eighty-three the general wouldn't be around much longer, and he had his own future to think about.

Wang opened the rear door, and James settled back in the cracked leather seat. The old man piloted the black Soviet-made limousine out of the airport and headed in the direction of Zhongnanhai. James cracked the window. Smells of charcoal and raw sewage drifted in, triggering memories of his youth.

The limousine moved silently through narrow streets. He looked out, uneasy at being so far from where he needed to be. At L minus seven he should have been aboard the command and control ship, overseeing the launch preparations, not placating the old men of the party in Beijing. The ship was due to sail from Guangzhou for the launch site tomorrow morning. If the meeting wrapped up quickly he could still make it. He leaned back into the seat and told himself to relax. He'd have to be at his most composed for this presentation.

Old Wang turned onto Chang'an Avenue, drove past the gate to Tiananmen Square, and pulled up to Xinhuamen, also known as the China Gate, the beautifully preserved main entrance to Zhongnanhai.

The exterior, mainly for the benefit of tourists, was still much as James remembered it. Two white-gloved PLA guards with rifles stood at attention by vermilion colonnades. The red flag of the People's Republic hung limply from a flagpole in the humid morning air.

Just past the guards, inside the main entrance, stood the famous red screen bearing a slogan in Chairman Mao's gold calligraphy: "Serve the People." The screen wall was visible to anyone passing by on Chang'an Avenue, but the people knew what the words really meant: "Keep out, restricted access." Mao had set up camp in Zhongnanhai in 1949 rather than settle in the Forbidden City, but the leadership compound was even more forbidden. Named for the two lakes that dominated the compound, Zhonghai, the Central Sea, and Nanhai, the Southern Sea, Zhongnanhai was also called the "Sea Palaces" by the Chinese. The Western media had a less poetic name for it: "China's Kremlin."

As the limousine cleared the gates he looked up, tempted to smile for the camera. He knew from one of his *chen diyu* working in America that the compound was monitored continually by U.S. satellites. His naturalized-citizen agent worked for the NGA, a government agency even more secret than the NSA, where she had access to all the secrets of the earth.

James had made it a point to drive by the heavily guarded, red brick complex in a suburb of Bethesda, Maryland that housed the National Geospatial-Intelligence Agency on his last trip to Washington. The NGA was new, having evolved from the old NPIC, the National Photographic Interpretation Center, where the Americans had monitored the goings-on in China, Iran, Iraq, Russia, Libya, North Korea, Pakistan, and every other country of interest to them for decades. It was there that the Americans had learned about Chernobyl, and failed crops in North Korea, and Iraq's use of biochemical weapons against the Kurds, and troop movements against Kuwait, long before the rest of the world knew.

The new agency was even more intrusive, using electromagnetic wavelengths to peer inside airplane hangars, and analyze the chemicals in factory smokestacks. Once the high-resolution photos and data were analyzed and the reports completed, they were submitted electronically to various agencies in Washington, D.C., and Langley, West Virginia. After analyses at those sites, the reports would be forwarded to the heads of the various intelligence agencies, and if considered interesting enough would be included in the president's daily brief.

James received all the highlights worth noting before the American president did, but they held little interest for him now. Since launching Phase II of his plan, his sole focus was on the reports emanating from the special group that was devoted to watching China.

His *chen diyu* had managed to penetrate the group and according to her latest report, the Americans hadn't yet seen any components of Raptor, neither the command and control ship, nor the launch platform, nor the satellite itself. That was positive news, but it embarrassed James to know that they'd seen virtually everything else.

His agent had reported that the NGA even knew about the secret underground tunnels in the basement of each residence and office in Zhongnanhai. James had played in the tunnels as a child and knew the escape route well. The tunnels, sealed by steel doors that could be barred from the inside, led to elevators that descended to a secret railroad. The train was manned twenty-four hours a day and was prepared to get under way instantly. It was an escape route designed not to protect the leaders from foreign invaders but from their own people.

The Americans reportedly found this escape route amusing. Let the fools laugh. Very soon now their satellite screens would go dead, and when they came on again, the not-so-amused analysts would be looking at a very different world.

The limousine skirted the lake known as the Southern Sea and drove past the ornamental island known as Yingtai, the Ocean Terrace. It was here that the Empress Dowager Cixi had imprisoned the ill-fated

Guangxu emperor in 1898 after his failed attempt to carry out reform. Today, it was little more than a scenic spot for certain privileged tourists. Bureaucrats under Mao had razed most of the buildings of the Imperial era. Yingtai, and the lakes, and a few dynastic-era buildings were all that was left.

Old Wang pulled up to one of those buildings, the Huairentang, a palace from the late-Qing Dynasty, located on the west side of the lake. The Palace Steeped in Compassion had been preserved and refurbished for meetings of the Chinese Communist Party. It was here that Deng had met with James's father and the other military commanders who'd crushed the protest at Tiananmen Square, just a half-mile to the east. Huairentang was the building where many of the most infamous decisions of the Chinese Communist Party had been made. Careers were made and broken in this building, and it was here that James and his plan would come under intense scrutiny in less than an hour.

The old man shuffled out and opened the door. James recoiled at the smell. As one of Mao's milder acts of insanity, he'd ordered the lake stocked with tens of thousands of carp. Protected from the people, the number had risen exponentially. The accrued excrement from the fish had turned the lake a dun color and created a smell that pervaded the entire compound. James covered his nose and looked around. The majestic landscaping he remembered from his childhood was gone, ruined by the building of roads and parking lots for the limousines that ferried the aging cadres back and forth. Nothing he saw was as grand as he remembered.

He walked into the main hall, the first to arrive. The once-elegant interior of the building had also been refurbished. Clumsy-looking Soviet-era furniture and cheap light fixtures set the tone. He glanced up at the ornate ceiling. The ever-present surveillance equipment completed the sense of desperate old socialists—his father included—clinging to power.

White-coated servants scurried to set up trays of food along the perimeter of the hall. In the center of the room, three long tables had been arranged in a U. A dais covered with a green cloth trimmed in gold had been placed at the open end. In the center of the dais was a high-backed upholstered chair, before it a place card for Xiang Shankun, the most powerful man in China. In theory, the CCP and the government of the People's Republic were separate entities, but in reality the Communist Party had its fingers in every government function. Xiang held the three top jobs in the country: president, Communist Party general secretary, and chairman of the Central Military Commission.

The old man derived his power not from the weak state presidency but from his post as Communist Party general secretary, the most influential position in China. He further cemented his power by chairing the Central Military Commission. It was this chairmanship—and the accompanying title of commander-in-chief—that gave the old men of the party control over the military, control that was vital to their survival.

To the president's right would sit James's father, General First Class Lao Jianxing, as vice-chair. And to the vice-chairman's right was a guest place card on blue paper that read, "Senior Colonel Lao Jintao, chairman and managing director, China Aerospace and Technology."

On the opposite side of the table, to the president's left, were two more place cards on the blue paper that indicated they too were guests. The first was for Yang Deguan, the minister of national defense. The next one he couldn't make out. Curious, he stepped closer until the name, Han Jinhua, CSIS, came into focus. A chill went through him. If President Xiang was the most powerful man in China, Han Jinhua, the head of the Chinese Secret Intelligence Service, was the most feared.

Why was he there? Like the defense minister, Han wasn't a member of the commission, but he had the power to invite himself to any meeting anywhere. His presence was not good news. Han despised the educated youth of China, especially those like James who'd been educated in the West. In Han's view, their education, a privilege Han had never had, should have made them grateful to the state. Instead, it had turned them against the state. Han had been one of the hard-liners on the event that was now whispered throughout China as the "Six-Four," the ruthless crushing of the young pro-democracy demonstrators at Tiananmen Square on June 4, 1989. The old man rightly feared the youth of China, and it was that fear that made him dangerous. Han would be watching James closely.

Commission members began drifting in. The original members were easy to spot. James watched them discreetly, shocked at their appearance. Unlike James's father, who still stood tall and erect at eighty-three, many were stooped and trembling with age. At thirty-two James felt a bit out of place in their midst, though the newest members were closer to his age. The commission had recently been expanded from its original nine members to a maximum of twenty-four and now included representatives from all seven of China's PLA military zones, as well as commanders from what the PLA thought of as special forces—navy, air force, and missile groups.

James's father entered the hall carrying a worn leather briefcase. He nodded to James but said nothing. As they all took their seats and waited for the president to arrive, James watched Han Jinhua shuffle in and take his place. The head of the Chinese Secret Intelligence Service was in his late seventies but looked much older. Born of peasant parents, it was said that he'd learned the 5,000 characters needed to read and write through sheer determination. It was this diligence that had propelled him into the hierarchy of the Chinese government and had kept him there. Han controlled China's *laogai*, and it was well known that the camps were full of the old man's enemies.

A private door behind the dais opened and President Xiang entered the hall, accompanied by two staff members. With a great shuffling of chairs, the assembly came to its feet and stood while the chairman was seated. Lowering his hands, Xiang motioned for the members and invited guests to be seated.

"Greetings, comrades," he said. "Welcome to this special meeting of the Central Military Commission. I now decree that the commission is in session."

A hush fell over the hall. Xiang slipped on a pair of horn-rimmed spectacles and opened a folder.

"At my request, the general political department of the People's Liberation Army has developed a position paper on the Taiwan issue. I will now read an excerpt from that paper, code-named Document

Sixty-five:

'The Taiwan issue has long since become a trump card to be played by the anti-China forces and has deteriorated into a malicious tumor that hinders the development of our motherland. Playing the Taiwan card and using it to contain China is a manifestation of the old Cold War thinking in the new international arena and an important means of opposing China by a handful of politicians in the U.S. Congress who cling desperately to the Cold War thinking. In terms of social systems, it is expressed as anti-Communist thinking; in terms of outlook, it is revealed as naked racial discrimination. In view of this situation, to resolve the Taiwan issue and achieve the reunification as soon as possible not only involves our national sovereignty and national dignity, but also directly relates to our country's development and is an important strategy in opposing world hegemonism.'"

James glanced at the faces of the commission members. He'd already seen an advance copy of the paper known as Document 65. The phrases "anti-China forces" and "world hegemonism" were a direct reference to the United States, without saying so. What the paper also didn't say was that once Taiwan was taken, U.S. hegemonism would be replaced by Chinese hegemonism in Asia.

President Xiang took a sip of water. "The document goes on to state, 'Taking into account the possible intervention by the U.S. and based on the development strategy of our country, it is better to fight now than in the future—the earlier, the better. The reason being that if worse comes to worst, we will gain control of Taiwan before full deployment of U.S. troops. In this case, the only thing the U.S. can do is fight a war of retaliation.'"

Xiang closed the folder. "In summary, comrades, the document concludes that it is a most important task of the Communist Party of China to reunify Taiwan with the motherland, and that this should be done as soon as possible. This has now been adopted as official policy. In support of this policy, we will move to implement our 'two-island chain strategy.' Concurrent with the taking of Taiwan, we will take the Spratley Islands and the Xinsha Islands, what the West calls the Paracels, to confirm our rightful ownership of the South China Sea, one of the world's most important strategic waterways.

"Once the region is secured, we will be in a position to control all shipping through it. Tankers from the Middle East must pass through the South China Sea to bring oil into the region. Conversely, goods bound for Europe and the Middle East must pass through the South China Sea in the opposite direction. An autonomous Taiwan gives the Americans a base from which to keep this waterway open, the primary reason America wants Taiwan to remain independent. By taking Taiwan and both island chains concurrently, the United States will be effectively removed from the area and China will emerge as the preeminent power in the Pacific."

Xiang removed his glasses. "You will recall my New Year's address to this body in which I forcefully requested that the military come up with what I euphemistically called 'assassin's mace,' a surprise weapon that would give China a decisive victory over the United States in such an encounter. I have been assured by the prime minister that such a weapon now exists." His eyes swept around the U-shaped tables, making eye contact with every member of the commission.

"Comrades, we are standing on the eve of momentous changes for the People's Republic. A misstep could have disastrous consequences. The purpose of this meeting is to determine that all of China's forces are prepared to go forward."

Han Jinhua rapped the table. "Please permit this lesser man to speak, Comrade President. As I understand it, the cornerstone of this strategy is the launching of this so-called assassin's mace, an anti-satelllte weapon that will disable the U.S. ability to respond. Everything depends upon it. The readiness of China's forces, if you will permit me to say so, is irrelevant without an assurance that the satellite will launch on schedule and perform as expected. Can this be assured?"

James felt the muscles in his neck tense.

"Thank you, Director Han," President Xiang said. "As always, the esteemed head of the CSIS raises a valid point." He looked to his right. "We are fortunate to have with us today Senior Colonel Lao Jintao, the honorable chairman of China Aerospace and Technology. Chairman Lao is scheduled to make a presentation to the committee later, but in view of the question, perhaps he will be kind enough to brief us now."

James nodded at the president. Han Jinhua sat smirking in the background behind him—the old man's smile didn't quite reach his eyes. The skin across his face was stretched so tightly he appeared to be wearing a mask. Not even President Xiang would cross the meddling old fool, who knew all the weaknesses and peccadilloes of every man in the room. James came to his feet.

"It would be my honor, Chairman Xiang. Thank you for the opportunity to appear before this esteemed committee. I'm pleased to report that the satellite launch is absolutely on schedule—"

"All well and good," Han Jinhua said, "but how do we know it will work once in orbit?"

"The satellite has been thoroughly tested and retested," James said. "Only recently it was demonstrated for the prime minister and several others, including the minister of national defense, the honorable Yang Deguan, who is with us today."

"It's true," Yang said. "It was a most impressive demonstration in which the satellite performed admirably."

"That may be so," Han Jinhua said, "but with all respect, I must question why one so young and inexperienced has been entrusted with this program, upon which everything depends. For example, the decision has been made to launch this satellite at sea, an unproven science. Why not launch it at one of our sites on land, under more controlled conditions?"

James took a calming breath, then forced a smile.

"The technology for launching at sea is actually well established and well proven. A launch there is no more risky than a conventional launch. Moreover, the advantages of a launch at sea are significant. First, it's highly efficient. A launch on the equator directly into equatorial orbit is not only highly accurate but ensures significant fuel savings—"

"I've heard that the satellite is powered by fuel cells," Han said. "If that's true, why is fuel economy an issue?"

James began to feel more confident. If Han wanted to debate him on technical issues, he could make the old man look like a fool.

"The savings on fuel will allow us to launch a heavier payload into orbit at the higher altitude required to avoid detection by enemy reconnaissance satellites. Once there, it will also give the satellite longer life, by providing a backup of fuel for maneuvering to correct the orbit, if necessary."

Han grunted. "All this technical talk obscures the important issues. What about the launch site? I've heard that the rocket will be launched over the sovereign territory of another land. Where precisely will this launch take place?"

"The launch platform will be positioned on the equator at 106 degrees east longitude, approximately midway between Sumatra and Borneo. The launch will be to the east, in the direction of the earth's rotation."

"Then it is so. In other words, you'll be launching over land, Borneo to be precise. Has the government of Borneo given permission for this?"

James had learned from an American attorney never to ask a question unless you knew what the answer would be. He smiled.

"Let's say that government officials have been . . . persuaded to allow the launch over their territory."

The hall broke out in subdued laughter.

Han fell silent.

James looked at the old man. Time to finish him off.

"But equally important as the technical issues are the security issues. As the esteemed head of the CSIS surely knows, American satellites watch every aspect of our country. From the lowest deserts to the highest mountain ranges, the Americans photograph things as mundane as tire tracks around military installations, newly moved earth near industrial plants, and who is walking with whom around the lakes here at Zhongnanhai. I've seen these high-resolution photographs, and I can tell you that they reveal everything, right down to the ranks on shoulder epaulets. A launch at the Wuzhai Missile and Space Center, or any other site in China, would therefore be ill-advised, to say the least. The Americans monitor these sites constantly, and a computer-enhanced photograph of Raptor would reveal that it is no ordinary satellite."

"What makes you think their satellites won't see a launch at sea?" Han said.

"Let them look," James said. "The command and control ship in the Pearl River Basin has been disguised to look like any of a thousand merchant ships moving around China. The launch platform moving toward the launch site on the equator has been configured to look like any of a thousand oil-drilling rigs moving around the world."

"But how can you be sure they haven't seen it?" Han said.

"I receive daily confirmation from my agents in America that those objects have not appeared on the screens in Washington."

"I'm glad to see you take security issues so seriously," Han said. "But satellite reconnaissance is only one way for the Americans to discover what you are doing." He looked at the door as if he were expecting someone. "You've allowed an American scientist into your laboratory in Guangzhou—your half-Chinese American cousin, to be exact. She has seen this satellite and has threatened to expose it. I understand that she has been 'detained' as a result. How can you guarantee that she will remain secure?"

James steadied himself against the table. Han was in charge of all the *laogai* in China. Did he know something James didn't?

"The fact that the woman is, as you put it, my 'half-Chinese American cousin' means nothing. She is secure and will remain so until after the launch. After that she will be of no further consequence."

Han glanced at the door. "Are you certain of this?"

"I am absolutely certain of this."

The door opened. A young officer wearing the uniform of a PLA major tiptoed in. Glancing around, the officer spotted Han sitting at the dais and walked toward him. He handed Han a piece of paper and whispered something in his ear. Han looked at the note, then up at James. James held his breath.

"You say you are absolutely certain of this. Are we to believe the other things you say with equal certainty?" Han paused. "I regret to inform the commission that the American woman has escaped from the reform prison on Turtle Island. A warden and a female martial arts instructor have been murdered. Two other wardens have been brutally assaulted and are in critical condition. Five members of the PLAN marine corps, including a noncommissioned officer, are missing and presumed dead."

James froze. His father stared at him. The president of China stared at him. Even though he wasn't responsible for the *laogai*, he was responsible for the security of his cousin. It had been his idea to put her in what he thought was an escape-proof prison that was at the same time minimum-security, to avoid criticism by the Americans. Son of a bitch. A contingent of marines placed aboard the American ship had failed, and his fail-safe on the island had failed. He glared at Han. Being blamed for the woman's escape was the least of his problems. He'd just implemented Phase II of his plan. If the launch was delayed now, he'd be a dead man.

James's father spoke up. "I feel that under the circumstances, it would be prudent to delay this operation until—"

"No," James heard himself say. "I beg the indulgence of the committee. I have my own intelligence sources. Private sources. Give me twelve hours. I feel confident that I can recover the woman before any contact is made."

James's father looked directly at him. "Don't promise what you cannot deliver."

"I feel confident that I can."

"In that case," Han said, grinning, "I think we should give the young comrade a chance."

President Xiang looked back and forth between the two men. "There is too much at stake here for uncertainty and petty rivalries. I will meet with Senior Colonel Lao, General Lao, and Director Han in my private quarters." He slammed down his gavel. "This committee is adjourned until one o'clock."

James stood apart amidst the sound of scraping chairs, his humiliation overwhelmed by his abject fear. Han came to his feet, smirking. The others gathered their things and walked out, none of them looking at him. If he couldn't recover his cousin, and do it quickly, he was as good as dead. *Think*. He knew things Han didn't know. It had to be the American ship captain. Connor was his name. Beth was on that damn ship somewhere. They couldn't have gotten far—the escape had just been discovered.

He needed to contact the captain of the destroyer *Zhuhai*, Chen. He'd diverted him from playing war games near the island to prevent this very thing from happening. His ship would still be nearby. Chen knew the American ship, had even led a boarding party of marines aboard on James's orders. Marines that were now missing and presumed dead. With state-of-the-art radar, Chen's high-speed destroyer would be able to locate the American salvage ship quickly and blow it out of the water. Contacting Chen by cell phone would take time. James watched President Xiang, his father, and now Han walking toward the president's private chamber.

The meeting would have to wait. The only way to defeat Han was to keep the launch on schedule, and the only way to do that was to capture or kill his cousin as quickly as possible, by deploying assets Han didn't know he had. He walked toward the door of the building, turned on his cell phone, and dialed Captain Chen on the *Zhuhai*.

Chapter Twelve

"**M**iss, you 'wake?"

In a distant corner of her mind, Elizabeth Grayson heard a high-pitched voice and the rattle of a door. Expecting Four Finger Tang to come barging into her cell, she crossed her arms over her chest. Her hands touched warm flesh. She was naked. With a shudder, she opened her eyes. Steel beams and electrical cables came into focus. A beam of sunlight swept across her face. She was aboard a ship. She'd stripped off her prison uniform, showered, and washed her only set of underclothes before drifting off into a coma-like sleep. She sat bolt upright, scrambling to cover herself with the blanket.

"Who is it?"

"It only me, Francisco."

The door opened and the funny little man who'd given her a cup of soup last night walked in. He had an armload of clothing in one hand, a stack of towels and a ditty bag in the other. He laid the clothes on the foot of the bunk, then stepped back and dipped his head.

"I buy for daughter. Here, miss, you take."

Elizabeth looked at the clothes, a pair of stonewashed jeans embroidered with a colorful butterfly design, a yellow sweatshirt, and a pair of white canvas sneakers. She'd grown up with a closet full of designer clothing, but she couldn't remember any as beautiful as these.

"Oh, they're gorgeous. I couldn't."

"No, no. You take. Daughter have too many clothes."

Clutching the blanket around her neck, Elizabeth looked at her tattered prison uniform lying in a heap on the floor. Her eyes went back to the pile of new clothing. She reached out and touched the sweatshirt and jeans hesitantly, as though they might vanish.

"Are you sure?"

"Francisco sure." He held out the ditty bag and a stack of towels. "Shampoo. Soap. Fresh towels. You get clean up, I bring you food."

Elizabeth felt like leaping out of bed and hugging the man, but she didn't want to scare him to death. She smiled at him.

"That's so kind of you."

Francisco colored slightly and looked down. Not wanting to embarrass him, she looked away and saw the room for the first time.

"Where am I? It was dark when they put me in here last night."

Francisco looked around as though he'd never seen the compartment before either.

"Captain stateroom, miss."

She felt a warm glow. She had to admit, the captain had taken her breath away when he swept her up in his arms last night. Even with the blackened face, his good looks were obvious. Tall and lean, with an edge to his voice and an easy manner, he'd reminded her of a young Harrison Ford. He was the last thing she'd thought about before drifting off to sleep. She looked down. The thought that she was sleeping in his bed, naked, sent a shiver through her.

"I'm sorry to put him out of his bed."

"Oh, Boss-man never use. Too far from bridge. He sleep in sea cabin."

"Boss-man?"

Francisco flashed a grin. "No one else call him that but me. No one else get away with it."

Elizabeth grinned back, joining in the conspiracy. "Why does he let you do it?"

"He like my food."

"You're the cook?"

"No cook. Chef. You get clean up, I bring you good food."

"I can't wait."

As soon as Francisco pulled the door closed behind him she got out of bed, stretched, and walked over to a porthole. Green and white waves rolled out from the ship in a V-shape. She moved closer and saw crewmen working on deck. She felt a twinge of arousal, looking at men while she was completely naked.

She stepped into the tiny bathroom and emptied the ditty bag on the counter by the sink. A comb, a pair of scissors, a cake of castile soap in a white wrapper, a little bottle of hotel shampoo, a packet of tissues, a small blow dryer, a new toothbrush, and a partly used tube of toothpaste. Even a disposable razor and a tube of shaving cream.

Francisco had thought of everything but makeup. That was too much to expect on a ship with an all-male crew, but at least there was a blow dryer. Her hair was a mess, but with a dryer she might be able to do something with it.

She twisted the cap off the shampoo and stepped into the small stainless steel shower. She'd showered before going to bed, but she didn't think she'd ever feel clean again after three months in the labor camp. She adjusted the temperature to as hot as she could stand it, drenched her hair, and lathered up furiously. She had to repeat the process three times before her hair felt clean.

She lathered up with the soap, luxuriating in the hot water, getting reacquainted with her body. Her neck felt long and thin, her bones much too well-defined. Her breasts seemed smaller than ever but well-shaped and firm. Her abdomen was concave, her navel so tiny it looked almost invisible. God, she must look like a scarecrow.

Her thoughts drifted back to the captain. She could still feel his arms beneath her, strong and gentle at the same time. She still felt the heat of him on her face, still remembered what he smelled like. In the emotion of getting rescued, she'd wanted to bury her face in his neck and let him do whatever the hell he wanted, but hadn't been able to take her eyes off his. Running her hands over her lean body, she felt her nipples harden. In the three months she'd endured as a prisoner, she couldn't remember having had a single sexual thought. Now her sexuality came back with a vengeance. Because of the captain?

Knock it off. She had some serious stuff to get stopped, and she'd need this guy's help, whoever he was. Any physical attraction would only get in the way.

She buffed herself dry, wrapped a towel around her head, and brushed her teeth. She checked on her underclothes, strung over a towel rack like dead fish drying in the sun. They were clean, but so stiff and disgusting she hated to put them on. She decided to go without the bra but pulled the cotton underpants on. Standing before the mirror braless, she waved the blow dryer around her hair. After three months without shampooing, her hair blossomed under the heat. Even though it was short it now looked soft and shiny, with the natural wave she'd inherited from her father.

She picked up the scissors and comb, evened up the ragged edges, and looked at her face. It was the first time in three months she'd seen herself in a mirror. She still had a few bruises and cuts from her struggle sessions. A nice young guy everyone called Doc had dabbed some antiseptic on them last night and taped the largest cut above her left eyebrow. He'd thought the smaller ones were better left exposed to the air to heal naturally. She pulled the tape off and studied her face. The ruddy glow of her complexion partially masked the bruises. Even with the dings on her face and no makeup she thought she could pass muster.

She unzipped the jeans and pulled them on. Francisco's daughter must be tiny. The jeans fit fine in the waist and hips but were too short by about six inches. She stood in front of a full-length mirror and appraised herself. Even though the jeans were too short, they looked good, like pedal pushers. Her calves had developed nicely from duck-walking down the rows of pepper plants and were nicely tanned. She pulled the sweatshirt over her head and shook out her hair. The sleeves were also too short, but she pushed them up and thought they looked okay. Thank God the sweatshirt was cut full. With no bra on, she'd have looked like a boy. The canvas sneakers were a bit tight, but they'd stretch with use. She squeezed into them and laced them up. She checked out her new look: well-scrubbed, no makeup, tight jeans, loose sweatshirt, decent hair. Not bad, except she was way too thin.

She heard a rap on the door, and before she could answer, Francisco walked in carrying a tray. It was obvious they weren't used to having a woman aboard. He set the tray down on the table by the bunk and stared at her. A wide grin overtook his round face.

"You look beautiful. Like daughter, only tall."

Elizabeth felt her face flush.

"You're very kind."

"You eat now, miss. Not too much. Just enough."

Francisco held her chair. Elizabeth sat down, and he scurried around and lifted the cover on the dish. A cloud of steam wafted upward, releasing the fragrance of tarragon and thyme. A plain omelet with a sprinkling of herbs sat glistening before her. Shredded carrots and zucchini sautéed in what smelled like real butter made a colorful side dish. Her salivary glands ached with anticipation.

"Plain food more better for you."

Elizabeth resisted the temptation to bolt the food, rolling each bite over her tongue, savoring every morsel. Having grown up in a wealthy Washington family she knew good food, and this was amazing. Like the lentil soup he'd given her last night, the omelet melted in her mouth, triggering olfactory and taste senses she'd forgotten she had. She glanced up at Francisco with a new look of respect. It wasn't just because she was starving. The man truly was a gifted chef. What on earth was he doing aboard a beat-up salvage ship?

"This is just wonderful."

Francisco grinned like a schoolboy in love and poured steaming liquid into her cup. "Green tea fix you right up."

Elizabeth sipped the tea and looked at her watch. She'd tried to talk to the captain about Raptor after she'd come aboard, but he'd brushed her off, insisted that she get some sleep. She'd been too exhausted to argue, but today was the 14th. Time was running out. She needed to notify the U.S. authorities as quickly as possible. She heard a knock at the door. Was it the captain? She ran a hand through her hair.

"Come in."

The door opened, and Sam's smiling face peered in. "Good morning, miss." He blinked and looked at her with raised eyebrows. "Well. You look much better."

The expression on his face was all the confirmation she needed before she saw the captain. She smiled.

"We have Francisco to thank for that."

"Skipper would like to talk to you when you're up to it."

"Of course. Where is he?"

"In the chart room on the bridge. But only if you're up to it."

"I'm ready."

"Don't you want to finish your meal first?"

"It doesn't take much to fill me up these days. Could you take me to him?"

"Yes, ma'am. Right this way."

"Excuse me just a minute, will you, Charlie?"

Matt squinted over the CIA agent's shoulder. Through the window of the chart room he noticed a dark, cumulonimbus cloud in the eastern sky. An anvil-shaped thunderhead morphed out on top, indicating the squall line of a cold front. A cloud formation like that almost always brought thunder and lightning, rain, high wind, and heavy seas. Things that could kill you at sea. He opened the door to the pilothouse a crack.

"You watching those storm clouds, Jason?"

"Got 'em, Skipper. They're far enough east that we should miss them if we stay on our course for Kaohsiung."

"Let's hope."

He glanced again at the clouds and did a double take. His bear-like first mate was ambling toward the bridge with a woman in tow. A beautiful woman. Wearing blue jeans, a yellow sweatshirt, and white sneakers, Elizabeth Grayson looked transformed. *This* was the same woman he'd picked up from the island eight hours ago? It wasn't just him. The crewmen working on deck had stopped what they were doing and were staring at her.

The door to the chart room opened and she stepped in, followed by Sam. Matt caught himself staring at her face. Exotic brown eyes, sculptured cheekbones, windblown complexion, auburn hair that looked alive. In spite of her too-thin body and some slight bruises on her face, she looked great. Better than great. He dipped his head in a mock bow.

"Good morning, Ms. Grayson."

She smiled, showing those white, even teeth. "Please call me Beth."

"Beth it is. Please call me Matt."

"I think I'll call you Boss-man."

"I see you've been talking to Francisco. Bad influence."

"He's my new best friend. He gives me food and clothing."

Matt motioned toward Charles Shen, wearing a borrowed blue

chambray shirt and a pair of faded khakis.

"I think you remember Charlie Shen. He was a little easier to outfit."

Beth smiled. "You said your name was Charlie Chan."

"That's what everyone called me at Princeton." He grinned. "I thought it might be easier to remember."

"I wouldn't have forgotten your name, believe me."

Everyone laughed.

"I've been talking with Charlie about the reasons for your imprisonment," Matt said. "He seems to think it was for reasons other than those stated by the Chinese."

"That's what I was trying to tell you last night," Beth said. "We have a problem."

"Who's *we?*"

"The United States of America, maybe the free world, not to put too fine a point on it."

"That sounds dramatic."

"Let me give you a little background," Beth said. "About ten years ago, the Chinese developed a piece of military hardware called the ZM-87 neodymium laser blinder. Not many people ever heard of it."

Matt nodded. "It was a laser device used against ground troops. Supposed to blind them in the field."

Beth gave him a curious look. No doubt she was wondering how the captain of an ocean-salvage ship would know about such an esoteric weapons system.

"That's right. The Chinese government offered it for sale at defense exhibits in Manila and Abu Dhabi about seven years ago."

Matt shrugged. "As I recall, it was full of bugs. A few countries tried it, but it never really got off the ground."

"Right again," Beth said. "But the Chinese made some breakthroughs in the system and as soon as they realized what they had, they stopped selling it. They've come a long way since then. The second generation had improved range and antisensor capabilities. The third generation incorporated automatic targeting and countermeasure resistance. That system evolved into shipboard laser weapons for air defense. Along the way, the Chinese developed a first-rate electro-optical industry that gave them the ability to create advanced optical systems. Those systems in turn gave them improved target acquisition and pointing and tracking. They've had the ability to target enemy satellites for years. All they were missing was a way to increase the power and intensity of the laser beam to a level that would destroy them."

"Let's hope they never get it," Charlie said.

"That's the problem," Beth said. "They've got it."

Matt was quiet for a long moment. Finally he said, "Are you telling me the Chinese have the capability to track and destroy U.S. satellites?"

"I'm saying they have a space-based, laser anti-satellite system, code-named Raptor, that can track and destroy anybody's satellites, in any orbit, at any altitude, and destroy them almost concurrently."

"Jesus," Matt said. "How did that happen?"

"You don't want to know."

"I think the CIA will want to know," Charlie said.

"It's not important," Beth said. "The important thing is, they have it."

Matt looked into her eyes. "That was your specialty at MIT, wasn't it? Laser technology?"

"Microlaser technology."

"And you were in Guangzhou for the last two years doing laser research?" Charlie said.

"To study ways to kill cancer cells."

The three men stared at her.

"All right, all right. I screwed up, okay? I told them more than I should have."

"Like what?" Charlie said.

Beth sighed. "Liquid lasers can fire a continuous beam but need huge cooling systems. Solid state laser beams are a lot more intense but have to be fired in pulses to keep them from overheating. My ego got in the way. . . . I showed them a way to combine the high-energy density of a solid state laser with the thermal management of a liquid laser. The result was an increase in the emission of radiation into a beam of ten-thousand kilowatts, higher intensity laser beams than the world had ever seen before. It was an idiotic thing to do, but of course I had no idea what they'd do with the knowledge. I can't believe I was so—"

"Ease up on yourself," Matt said. "It'll give them a temporary bargaining chip at the table, but it's not the end of the world. It won't take long for the U.S. to develop a counter satellite. If you showed the Chinese how, you can show the U.S. how. We'll come back with one that negates theirs, one that's bigger and better."

"It gets worse," Beth said. "They're going to use Raptor."

"What do you mean?" Matt said.

"They're planning an assault on Taiwan. First they're going to knock out every U.S. satellite in the sky to negate the U.S. forces in the Strait."

"*Every* U.S. satellite?" Charlie said.

"That's right. They don't want even cell phones to be available for use."

"Are you serious?" Matt said. "That would bring down everything, not just the military. The whole U.S. economy is dependent on satellites." He squinted at her. "What makes you think they're going to use it?"

"It'll be put into use almost immediately after it goes into orbit."

"How do you know?"

"Trust me, I know." Beth sighed. "I got suspicious and hid in the test facility. What I saw horrified me. I didn't go there as a spy, but I had to turn into one to try and undo what I'd done. I know their whole plan."

"They wouldn't—"

"Wouldn't they? Remember the failure of the Galaxy IV satellite back in '98? It shut down eighty percent of the pagers in the U.S. Within days of that malfunction, the state-run Xinhua News Agency said in an editorial something like, 'For countries that could never win a war using tanks and planes, attacking the U.S. space system may be an irresistible target.' Believe me, they've been working on this for years.

President Xiang's New Year's exhortation to the CMC to develop what he called an 'assassin's mace' weapon added the emphasis. I provided the missing link."

Assassin's Mace. That was the term Gray Wolf had used. Here it comes. The great conspiracy theory. Even if it were true, someone else would have to fight that battle. All he wanted to do was get Beth back and collect the reward money.

"Putting a satellite like that in orbit is one thing," Matt said, "actually using it is another. That would be an act of war."

"Call it what you like," Beth said. "All I know is, they're going to use it as soon as it's in orbit."

"And when will that be?"

"The launch is scheduled for June twenty-first."

Matt looked at the date on his watch. June 14th. "And you're just now telling us?"

"I tried to tell you last night, but you wouldn't let me."

"Everyone take a deep breath," Charlie said. "I'm just a contract player, but I know the CIA has satellites that monitor every missile launch site the Chinese have. Continuously. China can't just launch something like this without the U.S. knowing about it. I can assure you that someone at CIA knows. And if the CIA knows, the president knows."

Beth said, "Do you think the Chinese don't *know* that every missile site in China is being monitored? They're not launching in China."

"Then where?" Matt said.

"I'll show you where," Beth said. "Have you got a map of Sumatra?"

Matt nodded to Sam, who went to the board and pulled down a nautical chart of southeast Asia.

Beth wet her lips and squinted at the chart.

"It's right here," she said, pressing her finger on a spot east of Sumatra. "The launch site is exactly on the equator at 106 degrees east longitude, roughly midway between Sumatra and Borneo."

Matt exchanged glances with Sam and Charlie.

"There's nothing out there but water."

"Nothing escapes you, does it? Of course there's nothing out there but water. It's a launch at sea. There's a platform heading for that area as we speak."

"What kind of platform?"

"It's a converted deep-sea oil-drilling rig. Retrofitted at a shipyard in Indonesia. Named *Zephyr*."

"An oil-drilling rig? And it's got a rocket on it big enough to put a satellite in orbit?"

"No, that's on the CCS, the command and control ship. They call it *Zenith*."

"How do you know all this?"

"I told you, when I found out what they were doing, I spied on them. It's a consortium between Chinese, Russian, Swedish, and Lithuanian companies. The first and third stages of the rocket were built in Russia, the second stage was built in Lithuania, and the payload fairing and satellite were built in China at the CAT laboratory on the Pearl River. The command and control ship was built in Sweden, it has a Russian captain and crew. It's docked there at the CAT lab, waiting to bring it all together."

"Cat lab?" Matt said.

"China Aerospace and Technology. That's where I worked for two years. They own a forty-percent interest in the consortium. All the components will be assembled on the command and control ship on the way to the launch site."

"And our satellites wouldn't see this?" Charlie said.

"There's nothing to see. The command and control ship looks like a merchant ship. The deck is loaded with phony containers, made out of plywood and painted gray. From above, it looks like any of a thousand merchant ships coming and going through the Pearl River delta. The satellite they're loading aboard looks like crated cargo. Once aboard, there's an environmentally controlled hangar belowdecks where the payload gets mated up with the booster rocket on the way to the launch site." Beth stabbed her finger on the map. "And the launch platform looks like an oil-drilling rig headed for the oil-rich area between

Sumatra and Borneo. None of those things would get a second look."

Matt rubbed his chin. It all sounded like something out of a James Bond movie. He'd heard of small communication satellites for radio and television being launched at sea but doubted that the technology was advanced enough to put a large killer satellite in the higher orbit it would have to attain. The truth was, he didn't want to believe her. All he wanted to do was get her back to the states, pick up a check from her parents, and be rid of her. She'd just spent three months in a Chinese prison. She'd been knocked around. Matt looked at her head injury.

"We can talk more later. I think it might be a good idea if you lie down for a while, get some rest, and then—"

"You think I'm hallucinating from a bump on the head?" she said. "You think I'm *making this up*?"

"Of course not."

"At least let me radio it in, get word to my father."

"We don't have a radio," Matt said.

"Of course you have a radio. Every ship has a radio."

"Ours doesn't work."

"You're just stalling because you don't believe me."

"That's not it," Matt said. "Our radio really doesn't work. We had a Chinese boarding party that saw to it."

"Doesn't that tell you something? What are we going to do without a radio? Where are we going?"

"Back to Kaohsiung."

"And then?"

"Then I'm going to put you on a plane and deliver you to your parents. But maybe there'll be a way—"

"My parents?" Beth stared at Matt. "I'm beginning to see what's going on here. I'm beginning to see my father's fingerprints all over this. That's why you're a civilian. You're a mercenary. He hired you to get me out of there, and there's money in it, isn't there? Knowing my father, it's a lot. How much? How much is he paying you to bring me back? A million dollars? Ten million?"

"That's between your father and me. But whatever it is, I'm taking you back."

"Like hell you are. Look, it can't wait that long. By the time we get back to Taiwan it'll be too late. We can't be that far off the coast. You've got to take me back to the mainland, up the Pearl River to Guangzhou. I've got friends there. I can contact the U.S. authorities from there and get this stopped."

"Back to the mainland? Are you nuts?"

"All right, then take me to Hong Kong. I've got an uncle there who owns half the island. He'll help me."

"Guangzhou or Hong Kong, it won't make any difference. Half of China will be looking for you. Use your head, damn it. If we fall into Chinese hands, none of us will ever see the light of day again."

"If you're worried about getting caught, just drop me off and keep on going."

"It's not as simple as that."

"Oh, that's right. You want to get paid. COD."

Matt felt the heat at the back of his neck. "Now, look—"

Jason Tyler rapped on the window and stuck his head in the door of the chart room.

"Helicopter headed this way at high speed, Skipper. Sounds like the Chinese bird that buzzed us before."

Matt felt a surge of adrenaline go through him. If it was the same Z-8 helicopter, they wouldn't be coming to drop someone in his path. This time they'd be coming to sink him and kill everyone on board.

"Jason, sound all hands, emergency stations. Sam, you and Charlie take Beth below and bring up a couple of Stingers from the engine room."

"Aye, aye, Skipper."

"I'm staying right here," Beth said. "If the Chinese are trying to kill us, that's proof of what I'm telling you."

Sam stood frozen, his eyes darting between Beth and Matt.

Matt glared at Beth. "Bring up the weapons, Sam."

"Aye, aye, Skipper. Sam nodded toward Charlie, and they sprinted out the door.

"Get below," Matt said. Beth didn't move. "When you're aboard

187

my ship you'll obey my orders."

"Don't want the merchandise bruised?"

"I don't have time to argue with you, but when this is over, I'll put you in the brig if you don't obey my orders."

"Suit yourself, but I'm staying."

Matt held up his hand. In the distance, the familiar thump of helicopter rotors pounded the air. He walked out on the bridge wing, adjusted his binoculars, and looked aft. A tiny speck came into focus. Moving fast. He turned and looked to the east, toward the dark storm clouds on the horizon. At a cruising speed of 250 kilometers per hour, the helicopter would be over them in a matter of minutes. No chance for cover. He moved into the pilothouse. Beth hovered behind him.

"I'll take the conn, Jason."

"Captain has the conn."

Matt took the helm and glanced at Beth. "If that helicopter fires on us, the first target will be the bridge. I don't want them to see you. Now get below, damn it."

"You're not going below."

"I've got to fight the ship. You don't. Now, for the last time, get below."

"I'm staying with you."

"Jason, take cover below and take her with you, by force if necessary."

"Aye, aye, Captain." Jason looked helplessly at Beth. "You heard the captain, miss."

Beth folded her arms and shook her head. "No chance."

The sound of three turboshafts roared overhead, drowning them out. Machine gun fire tore through the overhead, ripping through chart tables, shattering windows. Matt grabbed Beth and pulled her down along the steel bulkhead, shielding her with his body.

"They're trying to kill us," Beth said. "Now do you believe me?"

Matt looked up. Jason Tyler lay face down on the deck, a pool of dark red blood spreading out around him. "Jason!" He scrambled across the deck and rolled him over. Jason's eyes were glassy, staring. Matt felt the side of his neck. He was still alive, but every beat of his heart was pumping blood out of him. He sprang to his feet and pressed the button on the PA system.

"Doc Miller to the bridge, on the double."

"Oh, my God," Beth said. "I'm so sorry, I'm so sorry."

Matt ripped his sweatshirt off, threw it down on Jason's chest and grabbed the ship's wheel. "See if you can stuff that in the wound, get the bleeding stopped." He looked out the shattered bridge window and saw the helicopter veer off to the north, fly in a straight line, and begin a sharp U-turn back toward the ship, coming at it broadside. *Torpedo.*

The Z-8 carried only one torpedo, usually an American Mark 46. They were designed to take out subs, not surface ships. Shipboard torpedoes had to be armed, but he wasn't sure about a torpedo launched from a helicopter. If it did require arming, they'd have to set it shallow and arm it early. There was only one thing he could do. Wait until it was in the water, then turn *CoMar Explorer* hard aport and head straight for it at flank speed. If he could catch it before it was armed, it would glance harmlessly off the hull of the ship. If he couldn't catch it before it was armed, at least he'd reduce the size of the target. With a little skillful ship handling and a lot of luck, they might at least minimize the damage.

The torpedo fell from the helicopter in a wavering line and hit the water. Matt spun the wheel hard to port, lining up the bow with the white wake. He rang up All Ahead Flank on the engine-order telegraph, picked up the bridge telephone, and pressed the button for the engine room.

"All ahead flank. Scootchy, give me everything you can pull out of those diesels."

"What the hell kind of mess you got us in now?"

"Just do it." Matt slammed down the phone and felt a surge of power. He held down the button on the ship's loudspeaker system. "Torpedo in the water. Torpedo in the water. Stand away from bulkheads and brace yourselves."

The gap closed between the torpedo and ship. He spun the wheel hard to starboard, held it as long as he could without exposing the stern of the ship, then spun back to port. He could see by the wake that the torpedo would miss the bow but would brush by the port side of the ship. He prayed that it wasn't yet armed.

"I can't stop the bleeding," Beth said, looking up at Matt with anguished eyes.

Doc Miller burst through the door with a medic kit and dropped down beside her. "Let me have a look."

"Brace yourselves," Matt said. The torpedo passed by the bow and rattled down the port side of the ship. For an instant he thought it wasn't armed, then he felt the explosion. The stern of *CoMar Explorer* lifted out of the sea in a spray of white water, knocking him off his feet. He found himself on the deck, scrambling through a pile of arms and legs trying to get up, slipping in Jason's blood. He pulled himself to his feet and rang up All Stop on the engine-order telegraph. He looked out the window. The helicopter had turned. Having expended its only torpedo, it was coming back for a strafing run. He could see the door gunners hanging from straps through the open doors on both sides, machine guns at the ready.

"Where's Sam with that Stinger?"

"Right here, Skipper," Sam said, coming in the door behind him.

"How does it look aft?"

"Looks like the port screw might have been hit. They're shoring up aft. We can probably keep her afloat if they don't hit us with another torpedo."

A burst of machine gun fire rattled through the bridge. Everyone dived for cover.

"Where's the Stinger?"

"Right here, Skipper. Two parts. A reusable launcher and the missile. We only got one launcher but we got three missiles."

"Is it loaded?"

"Armed and ready."

Matt took the hand-held missile out on the bridge wing and positioned himself behind the bulwark. He glanced at the side of the launcher. FIM-92A PROPERTY US ARMY. Stingers weren't available for export, but he wasn't surprised that Gray Wolf had them. Sam came up behind him and crouched down to wait.

The Z-8 banked in a sharp turn and headed back in the direction of *CoMar Explorer*. Secured by their safety straps, the door gunners looked relaxed, prepared to pound away at an unarmed ship until it caught fire and sank. Crouching behind the bulwark, Matt hoisted the 35-pound missile to his shoulder and tightened his fingers around the gripstock.

"Okay, Sam, how does this thing work?"

"Sight through the scope till you see the bird. It's got a passive infrared seeker that picks up the heat from the exhaust. You'll hear it lock on. Then just pull the trigger. There's a small launch rocket that'll get the missile clear of you before the main engine ignites. It's fire-and-forget. You can't miss."

He lined the helicopter up in the scope. As soon as he heard the infrared seeker lock on, he pulled the trigger. The concussion knocked his shoulder back. The launch rocket fell away and the main solid rocket engine ignited. He watched the white trail of the missile spiral upward in a steady line toward the helicopter. He could see the door gunners drop their weapons and scramble to get out of the way. The pilot jerked the helicopter wildly upward to avoid the Stinger, but it was too late. The seeker head of the missile slid into the turboshaft exhaust tubes in slow motion, igniting the explosives behind. The helicopter erupted in a ball of orange flame. The rotors separated from the helicopter and spiraled upward, then began their descent to the sea in a cloud of debris and body parts. He heard cheers go up throughout the ship.

"Way to go, Skipper."

Matt handed the launcher off to Sam and stepped back into the bridge. Doc, Beth, and Charlie were kneeling around Jason.

"That was amazing," Beth said, looking up at him with wide eyes.

"How is he?" Matt bent down on one knee and looked into Jason's face. It was the color of parchment. "You know everyone's blood type, Doc. Can we do a transfusion?"

Doc shook his head. "Scootchy's the only guy with the same blood type as Jason. We couldn't get enough."

"What type is it?" Beth asked.

"O positive."

"That's mine. Take mine. Please take mine."

Doc looked at her thin body. "Even that wouldn't be enough," he said. "The wound's just too massive. All we can do is make him comfortable."

Jason coughed. A thin trickle of blood appeared in the corner of his mouth. He looked at Matt and appeared to try to say something, then his head rolled to the side.

Doc felt for a pulse. After a moment, he laid Jason's arm gently over his chest. "He's gone." Doc looked up at Matt. "I'm sorry, Skipper. What he needed was way beyond what I could give him."

"It's all my fault," Beth said. "If I'd gone below when you asked me to, he might still be alive."

Matt came to his feet, fighting back tears. He'd known Jason Tyler for five years.

"You're finally right about something."

"I'm so sorry."

"Sorry doesn't cut it," Matt said.

"I promise I'll never disobey another order."

Matt stepped over to the PA system and keyed the microphone. "Damage report to the bridge on the double."

The bridge telephone rang. Matt picked it up. Scootchy Carter's strident voice screeched through the wire.

"You happy now? Goddamn port screw's twisted out of shape and we're wallowing around out here like sitting ducks."

"Calm down, Scootchy. Can we get under way?"

"I don't know. I think so. We're shoring up the after steering compartment. Starboard shaft looks okay. If it is, we can compensate and get under way, but at a reduced speed."

"Do the best you can, Scootch. We need to get under way as soon as possible." Matt hung up the phone.

"What are we going to do, Skipper?" Doc Miller said.

"The only thing we can do. Try to hide in that storm and repair the damage."

"We don't need to hide," Doc said. "Let 'em come. With those Stingers we can give the bastards a run for their money."

"No," Matt said. "Shooting down a helicopter with a Stinger missile isn't that hard, especially if they weren't expecting it, but a destroyer is another matter. We wouldn't stand a chance against the *Zhuhai*, and she can't be far behind."

Chapter Thirteen

James Lao paced across the room with his hands behind his back, struggling to conceal his fury with Han Jinhua. The head of the Chinese Secret Intelligence Service had deliberately waited to drop the bombshell about his cousin's escape until the full meeting of the Central Military Commission had been convened.

He looked at his watch. Almost 11:00. The three men had been waiting in President Xiang's anteroom for over two hours, his father sitting stoically, James pacing, Han smirking. As much as he hated to be in the same room with the vindictive peasant, he was grateful for the delay. It had given him time to make contact with the captain of the destroyer *Zhuhai*. Captain Chen had assured him that he'd pinpointed the location of the American salvage ship not far from the island, heading in the direction of Taiwan. He'd invoked his father's name and ordered Chen to dispatch a helicopter to sink the ship and dispose of everyone aboard.

He thought about the summers he'd spent with his cousin on Martha's Vineyard. One summer in particular. Beth was so damn beautiful it made him ache. Physically ache. The thought of killing her made him sick, but it had to be done.

He checked his watch again. It was no doubt done by now. Information was power. Let Han spout off in this meeting. James would wait for the opportune time and drop his own bombshell.

The door opened and Xiang's senior aide, a cadaverous-looking man with white hair, stepped into the room.

"President Xiang will see you now, comrades."

As the junior man present, James waited for his father and Han Jinhua to go first, then followed them into the room. The president sat behind a large oak desk, writing with a fountain pen. Without looking up, Xiang nodded toward the three red leather chairs placed in front of his desk.

James's father and Han took the outside chairs, leaving the center seat for James. The hot seat. Even his father was distancing himself from him. James understood. The wily old general wasn't going to go down for the sins of the son. That was how he'd managed to stay in power and survive to the ripe old age of 83. His father was convinced that China needed him, and he'd sacrifice anything, including his only son, to maintain his position. The old man would do what he could, but if James had made a serious error in judgment, he'd be on his own.

President Xiang closed the folder before him and leveled his gaze at James.

"It was upon your insistence that the American woman employed in your laboratory was placed in a minimum security facility. That decision was approved because of your assertion that an escape from that facility would be impossible. How could this happen?"

"Very simple," Han Jinhua said before James could answer. "All the signs were ignored. We know now that Senior Colonel Lao had ample indications of American intervention, indications that were not passed on to the proper authorities and that were not acted upon."

"Those are serious accusations," General Lao said. "I'll trouble you to explain."

Han twisted his face into something resembling a smile. "Perhaps the senior colonel would care to explain."

James envisioned his hands around Han's scrawny neck, squeezing until that smirk disappeared. He nodded politely.

"I assume that Director Han refers to the American ship salvaging a U.S. flag freighter that was run aground on an island adjacent to the *laogai*. It's true that we were the first to take notice of this ship, but it's inaccurate to say that we did nothing, or didn't pass along this information to the proper authorities. On the contrary, as soon as I became aware of the situation, I took it upon myself to notify the PLA Navy. I requested a destroyer operating in the area to intercept the ship and place a contingent of marines aboard to supervise the salvage operation."

"I assume that Senior Colonel Lao refers to the five marines who have gone missing and are now presumed dead," Han said, his voice dripping with sarcasm. James went right on, as if he hadn't spoken.

"In addition, I took the unprecedented step of assigning a female sergeant in the PLA, a martial arts instructor, to pose as a prisoner and watch the American woman. Her orders were to terminate the woman in the event of an escape attempt."

"I assume that Senior Colonel Lao refers to the martial arts instructor who was found dead," Han said. "And don't forget the agent placed aboard the ship in another amateurish bit of theatrics. He is also missing and presumed dead. Then there is the little matter of one of my wardens, brutally murdered by the barbarians."

James said nothing, waiting for Han to fire his last volley.

Han turned to President Xiang. "In view of the death toll alone, it's obvious that this operation has been bungled from the beginning. In light of the serious breach of security that has occurred, I recommend the operation be delayed until the woman is captured or it can be confirmed that no contact with the West has been made."

"That's hardly necessary," James said. "I've taken personal charge of the recovery operation, and the situation is well under control. I've been in close contact with the captain of the destroyer *Zhuhai*. We have the American ship pinpointed. I spoke with Captain Chen not two hours ago. A helicopter is on the way to torpedo the ship."

Han's eyes darted around. "All well and good, but who's to say the Americans have not already made contact?"

"Impossible," James said. "On my orders, the captain of the *Zhuhai* ordered the ship's radio destroyed upon first boarding it."

"That means nothing. It's obviously a spy ship. They could have had a dozen radios secreted aboard that ship."

"Again, not possible. The ship was thoroughly searched. A few weapons—small arms—were found and confiscated. No other radios were found."

"Surely the marines who boarded carried a radio. What about that?"

"The range on that radio is only a few miles. So you see, Director Han, it isn't possible that the American ship has made contact with anyone. Further, the captain of the *Zhuhai* has assured me that the ship has been sighted and will be intercepted shortly."

President Xiang leaned back in his chair. "Perhaps we've

overreacted. It's beginning to appear that the situation is under control." He nodded to James. "Our apologies, Senior Colonel."

Out of the corner of his eye, James could see Han seething. Smiling graciously, he returned Xiang's nod. "No apology is necessary, Chairman Xiang."

James heard a soft rap on the door behind him. It opened to admit the cadaverous aide.

"Please forgive this intrusion, Comrade President. There's a call for Senior Colonel Lao. The captain of the destroyer *Zhuhai*. Most urgent."

"I'll take it outside," James said.

"No need," President Xiang said. "You can transfer the call in here."

James watched the button on the president's console light up and tried to keep his breathing steady. He'd had trouble making contact with the destroyer on his cell phone and had given Captain Chen the aide's number as a backup, but he didn't want the captain's call transferred into the president's office. He wanted to be in a position to screen out any bad news. President Xiang pressed the blinking yellow button, and James reached for the handset.

"The call obviously relates to the subject at hand," Han said. "Surely the senior colonel will not mind if we hear the destroyer captain's report?"

President Xiang looked at James, his finger poised over the speakerphone button.

"An excellent suggestion," James said.

The speakerphone rumbled with the ghostly sounds of a ship at sea. James leaned forward in his chair.

"This is Senior Colonel Lao speaking."

"Senior Colonel, this is Captain Chen," came the response. "I am afraid I have—"

"Captain Chen, as a courtesy to you, you should know that with me is the honorable Xiang Zemin, president of China and chairman of the Central Military Commission. Also present are General First Class Lao Jianxing, vice chairman of the Commission, and the honorable Han

Jinhua, director of the Chinese Secret Intelligence Service. You are on a speakerphone."

"I'm honored to be in the presence of such greatness," Captain Chen said, "but I fear it makes my report all the more difficult. I regret to inform you and the other esteemed comrades that the helicopter dispatched to intercept the American ship has not reported in and cannot be contacted. I'm afraid it's missing."

James could feel Han's eyes boring into the side of his head. "No doubt it was an accident," he said, too quickly. "Most unfortunate, but accidents happen at sea."

"I fear it was no accident," Captain Chen said. "The pilot was heard to shout the word 'missile' seconds before radio contact ceased."

James felt his voice tremble slightly. "A missile? From where? It had to have come from another ship."

"Radar reports no other ships in the vicinity," Captain Chen said.

"But you assured me that your men had searched the ship and confiscated all weapons."

"I assure you, they went over the ship thoroughly. It's a mystery."

"A *mystery*? That's the best you can do?"

Han reached over and pressed a scrawny finger on the mute button as Captain Chen went on justifying the search. They could still hear the destroyer captain, but he couldn't hear them.

"Missiles?" Han said. "You assured us that all weapons had been confiscated. Now we learn that the Americans have sophisticated missiles aboard. One would assume it would be difficult to conceal something as large as a missile. Where were they hidden? In the pantry? Are we to believe all your other assertions? If a missile was concealed on the ship, surely a radio could have been. How can we now be sure there is no radio and contact has not been made with the outside world?"

James removed Han's finger from the mute button and leaned closer to the speakerphone.

"Where's the ship now?"

"Traveling in an easterly direction, toward a storm. The captain apparently intends to hide his ship in it. That will do him no good—we'll seek him out and find him. What are your orders when we overtake the ship?"

"Same as before," James said. "Sink the filthy thing and kill them all."

"No," General Lao said. "Director Han is right. We don't know whether contact has been made with the West. The Americans must be taken alive so we can find out who, if anyone, has been contacted."

"Just so," Han said. "My sources tell me there were three men involved. One from the inside, a Chinese traitor posing as a prisoner, and two from the outside, a black man and a barbarian with a blackened face who is the captain of the American ship."

"How can you possibly know that?" James said.

"Very simple," Han said. "One of the wardens who narrowly escaped with his life overheard the black man refer to the foreign ghost as 'Captain.'"

James told himself to calm down and think. He could tell by the body language of the three men that he was losing ground. He leaned into the speakerphone.

"General Lao is correct. Seize the American woman and the three men who participated in her escape. As soon as you recover them, bring them to me."

"No," General Lao said again, this time more forcefully. "They must be questioned immediately. The best place to do that is on board *Zhuhai*." He leaned toward the speakerphone. "Captain Chen, this is General Lao. These are your orders, which supersede all previous orders. Hunt down the ship. Arrest the woman and the three men. Interrogate them independently aboard your ship en route to the PLA naval base at Macau, where they will undergo further interrogation. Use any means necessary to discern the truth. Report what you find immediately to . . ."

He glanced up. James stared at him, unable to hide the look of utter humiliation at being stripped of all authority in front of the president of China and his nemesis, Han Jinhua.

His father's face softened. "Report what you find to Senior

Colonel Lao."

"I understand, General. What about the ship? Shall we take it into custody and tow it to the base at Macau?"

"No. Search it top to bottom to determine the presence of a radio. Bring back any you find. Then open the seacocks and scuttle the barbarian ship. Make it appear that it went down in the storm."

"Yes, General. What about the remaining crew?"

James watched his father and President Xiang exchange looks.

"Most unfortunate," his father said. "In spite of the heroic efforts of the PLA Navy, the entire crew was lost with the ship."

Chen Dian stood in the combat information center of *Zhuhai* and watched the black hand of the surface radar sweep around the scope. He pointed to a fuzzy white area at the top of the screen.

"Is that the storm they're hiding in?"

"Yes, Captain," the radarman said. "Last contact was at twenty-two degrees relative."

"They can run, but they can't hide," Chen said, parroting a phrase he'd heard in America. The truth was they'd been hiding successfully for more than twenty-four hours, and Chen was frustrated. "Stay focused on that area. Notify me at once when contact is reestablished."

"Consider it done, Captain."

The CIC fax machine beeped. A sheet of paper rolled out, black ink still glistening. It was what he'd been waiting for, a page out of his Naval Academy yearbook. He picked it up and scanned the black and white photographs. A page of confident-looking first classmen gazed back at him, admirals of the future. The west-ocean ghosts all looked alike, but one of the faces stood out from the rest. He read the words beneath the picture: "Connor, Matthew Baines. Brigade Commander."

As a lowly plebe, Chen would have had no contact with the number-one-ranked midshipman officer, but he'd had the academy chain of command drilled into him, both names and faces, and he knew he'd recognized him. His mind flashed on the naval officer's sword with the odd inscription he'd taken from the barbarian ship, embarrassed now that he hadn't made the connection. But he couldn't be blamed.

He'd asked Matthew Connor where he'd seen him before, had asked him to his face, one officer to another, and he'd lied like the graceless *kwai lo* he was. No matter how exalted they were, the filthy barbarians could never be trusted.

Chen's eyes dropped down to Matthew Connor's biography. Written by his classmates, it went on longer than the others. He'd been a superstar, a leader involved in everything, admired by everyone. When Chen was a plebe, fighting to maintain his dignity, Matthew Baines Connor had been sitting at the top of the mountain, looking down on him. How could he have fallen to such a low state?

The fax machine beeped again and another sheet of paper rolled out. Chen picked it up, wet ink curling the page. It contained two newspaper articles from *The New York Times*. The first one was six years old. It covered a fire aboard the USS *Phoenix*, a Los Angeles-class nuclear-powered submarine. A man had been killed, and the boat had nearly been lost. The captain and the executive officer, one Lieutenant Commander Matthew B. Connor, had been relieved of command. He read the second, smaller, article at the bottom of the page, dated a few months later. After a court of inquiry, the captain had been fired and the executive officer had resigned in disgrace.

Not likely. The U.S. wouldn't sacrifice on officer so valuable over one accidental death. Connor was probably a senior naval officer posing as the captain of an ocean-salvage ship, a cover for the CIA. Chen ground his teeth. Armed with only a derelict salvage ship, he'd brought down one of Chen's most advanced helicopters. The *yang gwei* had probably hidden a shoulder-fired missile aboard, perhaps an American Stinger. How could his men have overlooked it?

He cursed Matthew Connor's ancestors. To have to admit to the loss of a helicopter and crew was bad enough. Admitting it before the leadership of China was a loss of face that would haunt him forever. Not only was the highest-ranking officer in the PLA present, General First Class Lao Jianxing, but so was the president of China himself. Even worse, Han Jinhua was in the room.

General Lao and President Xiang could destroy his naval career, but the head of the Chinese Secret Intelligence Service could destroy his life. Han Jinhua was the most feared man in China, and with good reason. Anyone who displeased him could find himself sentenced to a *laogai* indefinitely, and on his orders alone.

Fornicate all gods. He should have known better than to follow the orders of a Red Prince like Lao Jintao. Lao's appointment to senior colonel had been pure politics—the man knew nothing about military tactics. It made no sense to risk sending a lone helicopter against a ship, even if it had been searched. No one could search a ship and know absolutely that everything aboard had been found. If it had been up to Chen, he'd simply have waited until *Zhuhai* caught up with the American ship. Then there would have been no contest, no matter what weapons they had hidden aboard.

Chen had followed the orders of the son because he feared the wrath of the father, but he'd heard the father countermand the son's orders with his own ears. Now that he knew the father and son were not together, he wouldn't be so quick to accept the son's orders the next time. He dropped the fax into the document shredder and watched Matthew Connor's face disappear into the steel blades. Dealing with the bogus "senior colonel" was another issue. For now, his number one goal was to erase the stain Matthew Connor had inflicted on his record.

The radarman raised his hand. Chen hurried back to the surface radar station.

"A sighting?"

"Yes, Captain, briefly," the man said. "We caught a glimpse of the ship at the western edge of the storm, then it disappeared."

"Can you estimate the speed of the ship?"

"It's difficult because it keeps falling off the scope, but the ship appears to be making around eight knots, sir."

Chen removed his glasses and rubbed the bridge of his nose. A small steel-hulled ship with four diesel engines should be able to make at least fifteen knots. The storm would slow it down to some extent, but not that much. So. The helicopter pilot's report of torpedo damage to the stern of the ship on the port side had been accurate. Possibly the port screw. Compensating for that and running on the starboard screw would cut their speed by half, perhaps more. As soon as the storm lifted, *Zhuhai* would overtake them easily.

"What's the forecast?"

"Storm's moving eastward at approximately ten knots, Captain. It should lift by tomorrow morning."

"Stay on it. Call me as soon as you make contact."

"Yes, sir."

Chen walked back to the bridge. He was grateful that General Lao had countermanded Senior Colonel Lao's orders to dispose of everyone aboard. He cared nothing for the others one way or the other, but killing Matthew Connor from the deck of a destroyer would be too easy. He looked forward to a face-to-face meeting with his former classmate. He had specialists aboard *Zhuhai* who were skilled in the art of extracting information from their enemies. Chen would enjoy watching the American be humiliated as he had been. He picked up his binoculars and looked east, to the dark storm clouds on the horizon that hid the barbarian ship and its troublesome captain. It was only a matter of time before he had him in his sights.

Chapter Fourteen

Matt gripped the wheel of *CoMar Explorer* and blinked into the black haze, still fighting the reality of Jason's death. Salt water burst into the pilothouse through the shattered window, searing his face and hands. He forced his eyes open and faced the punishing force of nature head-on. Pain offered the only relief for the guilt he felt. It had been his need for quick money that had gotten them into this mess. If he'd resisted, waited for a real job to come along, Jason would still be alive.

And to top that one off, he'd done it all for nothing. There wasn't going to be any reward money. Jason's death proved what Gray Wolf and now Beth had been telling him. There really was a Chinese conspiracy to cripple the U.S. All he could do now was try to find a way to survive long enough to get the launch of that damned satellite stopped. What happened after that didn't much matter.

"I hate to say it, but doesn't what's happened prove what I was saying?" Beth said. She stood next to him, gripping an overhead I-beam, her thin figure swaying with the roll of the ship.

Matt held his concentration on the pattern of the swells and braced himself for the next roll. She was right, but he was too damned angry to admit it.

"You're an escaped prisoner. Why wouldn't they fire on us?"

"Fire on us? They tried to sink us with a torpedo. You think they'd be trying to kill more than a dozen Americans if I were just an escaped prisoner?"

"Life is cheap to the Chinese."

"You ever meet a stereotype you didn't like?"

"All stereotypes have some basis in fact. I guess you've never heard of Mousy Dung."

"Yes, I've heard of Mao Tse-tung. I know his insane policies caused the deaths of millions of people. But he was an anomaly. The Chinese aren't like that."

"Aren't they?

"I'm half-Chinese, you bastard. Open your eyes and look at me."

Matt looked up, startled. Beth was staring at him with a world of hurt in her eyes. "Sorry."

She sighed. "That reward my father is paying you must be something for you to rationalize like that. Do you think Beijing would risk an international incident over something as simple as one American prisoner escaping? Everyone on this ship has been contaminated with what I know. That's the reason they're trying to kill us. All of us."

"You're making my point," Matt said. "They'd even kill their own men."

She frowned. "What do you mean, their own men?"

CoMar Explorer labored up a swell and hung on the crest of the wave as though suspended, her one good propeller spinning out of the water. Matt spun the wheel to starboard in a futile attempt to regain control of the ship before she plunged into a black trough. He leaned forward and braced himself against the wheel. Tons of white water exploded from the bow, covering the pilothouse in a stinging spray. Water shot in through the open window, blinding him. He shook the water from his face.

"We've got five men from the *Zhuhai* aboard. PLA marines."

Beth blinked water out of her eyes. "Five? I only saw one. Where are they?"

"Locked in the brig and a forward compartment—"

"What if we get hit with another torpedo?" Beth said. "What if the ship goes down in the storm?"

That was a definite possibility. Matt was beginning to question his strategy of hiding in the storm. Even if he was successful in eluding *Zhuhai*, the storm was turning out to be more than he'd bargained for. The deeper he got into it, the worse it became.

"They're not my biggest problem right now."

"I agree, but you can't keep anyone locked up in a situation like this. Another torpedo could come out of nowhere. There wouldn't be time—"

"In case you haven't noticed, we're a little busy right now. If I let them out, I'd have to assign men to watch them. I don't have anyone to spare."

"I'll watch them," Beth said. "I speak the language. I'll talk to them, get them to promise to behave in exchange for their release."

Matt looked at her standing next to him, an aristocratic beauty with wet, stringy hair and an exposed navel, clinging to the I-beam with both hands, wearing too-short jeans and a soaked yellow sweatshirt. Her doe-eyed naïveté made something inside him crumble.

"Don't you do-gooders ever take a day off?"

"Do-gooders?"

"An earnest but naïve humanitarian."

"I know what it means. It's cruel to leave them there, that's all. They must be terrified. It'd be better to put them off in a boat."

"In a storm? What a great idea."

"At least they'd have a fighting chance."

The door to the pilothouse opened. Sam burst in through a blast of spray and leaned into the door to dog it closed. In his glossy black slicker, he looked like a walrus emerging from the sea.

"Any luck, Sam?"

"Yeah, all bad." He shook out his slicker and wiped his face. "Those Chinese marines did a real number on the surface radar. Murph's pretty good with that stuff, and he says there's no way to fix it."

Matt shook his head, too frustrated to respond. Surface radar wouldn't do them much good in the storm, but once the storm lifted they'd be flying blind without it. Just as they were now, they'd be the hunted with no way to track the hunter.

"What about the radio?"

"Same story. Both Murph and Andy went over it. Smashed with rifle butts, including some circuit boards and diodes, critical stuff. Hopeless."

"Son of a bitch," Matt said. "They wrecked every piece of navigation and communication equipment we had."

"Kinda funny," Sam said. "Now they need it as much as we do. Serve 'em right if the ship goes down."

"I don't care what they did," Beth said. "You can't just leave them locked up in weather like this."

"Watch me."

Charles Shen blew into the pilothouse with a plate of food covered with plastic wrap. Traveller darted in behind him.

"Here you go, Matt."

"What is it?"

"The only thing I know how to cook. White rice and pinto beans. I made enough for the whole crew. If you douche it down with hot sauce, it's not too bad."

"How's Francisco?"

"Sick as a dog. Strapped in his rack, keeps begging for somebody to shoot him."

Matt laughed. It sounded out of place. He was running on pure adrenaline, the exhilaration of combat. Other than target practice he'd never fired a shot during his naval career, but it had been combat nevertheless. He missed it. It was a feeling he thought he'd never have again.

"If that destroyer catches up with us, he just might get his wish." Traveller sniffed Matt's legs, shook himself off, and settled down in the corner. "How about Trav? He had anything to eat?"

"I gave him some dry stuff I found in the galley," Charlie said, "but he didn't eat much."

"He never does when it's rough."

"He's got a lot of company there," Charlie said.

Sam walked over. "Let me take the helm while you eat, Skipper."

"I'm okay," Matt said.

"You sure? You've been on your feet all day."

"It's not as bad as it was. I finally got the hang of compensating for that port screw."

Sam looked out the window. "Weather isn't getting any better."

"That's the bad news," Matt said. "The good news is, it'll be tougher to find us in this stuff."

"Let's hope."

They cruised without talking for a few minutes, each compensating for the roll of the ship in his own way. The distant crack of naval gunfire split the air, a whistling, thundering sound, coming closer. A shell exploded into the side of a wave thirty yards off the starboard bow. Matt's stomach knotted.

"That's got to be the *Zhuhai*. All hands, emergency stations. Take the helm, Sam." He picked up a pair of binoculars and looked in the direction the shell had come from. He adjusted the focus. A signal light blinked on the horizon, a faint glimmer through the black haze.

"See anything?" Sam said, fighting the wheel.

"Just a light, but they can see us."

"What kind of light?"

"They're sending us a message."

"What is it?"

"Heave-to-or-I-will-fire," Matt said. "I don't get it. Last time they wanted to sink us. Now it looks like they want to board us."

"Maybe the helicopter pilot got his orders wrong," Sam said.

"Maybe."

"Maybe that Stinger missile's holding them back," Charlie said. "Maybe they don't want to get close enough to sink us."

"They're not worried about any weapons we might have," Matt said. "They could sink us with one of their missiles from where they stand and we wouldn't even know what hit us."

"So what changed?" Beth said.

Matt didn't answer. The only reason they'd want to board is to take prisoners. He watched the *Zhuhai* emerge from the black wall on the horizon, signal light flashing. Crashing through the waves at flank speed, she repeated the message: "Heave-to-or-I-will-fire."

They stood in silence and watched the ship approach. Matt saw a flash of light and heard the clap of naval gunfire. Another whistling sound crackled across the bow. The shell exploded harmlessly twenty yards off. Closer now. It was Captain Chen's way of telling him he could put the next one anywhere he wanted. The Naval Academy had taught him well. Matt cranked the engine-order telegraph to All Stop.

"What are you doing?" Beth said as if coming out of a trance.

"The only thing we can do," Matt said.

The engine room phone rang. Matt picked it up. "What is it,

Scootchy?"

"What the hell's going on up there?"

"We just took a shot across the bow. What do you think?" Matt slammed the phone back into its bracket. He picked up the binoculars and watched the Chinese destroyer cut its engines and drift into position. It stood off about four hundred yards, heaving violently, guns trained on the bridge. The signal light began blinking a new message.

"What are they saying?" Beth said.

"Maintain-radio-silence. Follow-me. Use-maximum-speed."

"Follow them? Why?"

"It's too rough to board. Too dangerous. They want to take us into calmer waters."

"How do they know where that is?"

"They've got weather experts tracking the storm. They'll know the direction it's moving, where the edge is. Probably not too far from here."

Matt rang up All Ahead Full and spun the wheel to starboard. He picked up the hand-held signal light and flashed, "Port-screw-damaged. Max-speed-8-knots. I-will-follow-you." Then he heaved a sigh and faced the others.

"Listen to me. We've got a few hours to think this through. If anybody's got any ideas, now's the time."

"Can't you radio for help?" Beth said.

Matt shook his head. "I put out a Mayday call on channel twenty-one on Sergeant Li's radio right after we took that helicopter out and got no response. It's got a limited range, I doubt if anyone heard it."

"How about we make a run for it," Charlie said. "Try to hide in the storm again. What's the worst that can happen?"

"They sink us, and we all go down," Matt said.

"We got Kalashnikovs and Stinger missiles and RPG's," Sam said.

"Against a destroyer?" Matt said.

"We can go down fighting."

"Going down won't prove anything," Matt said. "You can't fight when you're dead."

"What kind of fighting did you have in mind?"

"I don't know," Matt said. "All I do know is that Beth has something important to say, and we've got to be around to help her say it."

Beth stared at Matt. "When did you come to that conclusion?"

"The minute that helicopter opened fire."

"Why, you . . . Why did you put me through all that?"

"Not easy to say you're wrong, especially when you want to be right."

The door opened and Scootchy burst into the pilothouse. He pointed to Beth. "She's the one they want. Let 'em have her. Give her up."

"Nobody's giving anybody up," Matt said.

"He's right," Beth said. "Send them a message, see if they'll settle for me. If they will, they'll probably let the rest of you go."

"Not a chance."

"She's talking sense," Scootchy said. "See if they'll take her, let the rest of us go. I ain't looking to spend the rest of my days sitting in prison with a bunch of gooks."

"You might like it," Charlie said. "Might improve your intellect."

"Knock it off," Matt said. "That's not an option. For me or the Chinese."

"Why not?" Scootchy said.

"In the first place, I wouldn't do it. In the second place, the Chinese have to assume everyone on this ship knows what Beth knows. They aren't about to let anybody go."

"Jesus Christ," Scootchy said. "You mean you're just going to let 'em take us?"

"We don't have a choice. Now get back down in the engine room and do your job."

Matt keyed the microphone on the ship's PA system and briefed the crew on what was happening. One by one, crew members drifted up on the bridge to peer at the Chinese destroyer plowing through the sea ahead of them and commiserate with each other. Matt made it a point to apologize to each member of the crew for getting them into this. With the exception of Scootchy, they all said they were okay with it, they'd signed on for whatever, but it didn't help.

As exhausted as he was, Matt stayed at the helm. Beth, Sam, and Charlie stayed on the bridge with him. They moved in grim silence, following in *Zhuhai*'s wake, her aft 37-millimeter guns trained on the bridge. Where were they being taken? Why? Clearly they didn't intend to kill them, at least not yet. Captain Chen could have done that without their ever knowing what hit them. Whatever the reason for the reprieve, it could only be good for Matt and his crew. Every hour they were alive was a chance to get away, try to find a way to stop this madness.

His mind raced for a way out. All he could do was try to drag things out for as long as he could. Maybe he could feign engine trouble. Or simply reduce his speed and say it was the best he could do in this weather. If he could hold them at bay until it was dark, he might be able to make a break for it. . . .

Forget it. With the destroyer's advanced radar and fire control system, it was dumb to even think about it. One shell into his tired old ship and *CoMar Explorer* would sink like a tin can.

After four hours the weather began to clear. The seas were still choppy, but not enough to prevent a boarding. He looked at his watch. It was almost dark. If they were going to board, it would have to be soon. The *Zhuhai* slowed and drifted to a stop. Matt rang up All Stop, and *CoMar Explorer* drifted to within three hundred yards of the destroyer. A signal light from the bridge began to blink a new message.

"Stand-by-to-be-boarded. Do-not-resist-or-I-will-fire."

Long boats filled with dull green helmets were lowered away, rifles bristling above the gunwales. The boarding party was larger than the last time, at least twenty men. Bigger fish now—a largely all-American crew bound for a Chinese prison. There had to be something he could do.

"Secure the bridge, Sam, and get all hands on deck," Matt said. "I'll meet the rest of you on the quarterdeck." He bolted from the bridge and ran down the ladder to his sea cabin. The pistol Gray Wolf had given him was in the top drawer of the nightstand. After his little set-to with the escaped prisoner and his encounter with Captain Chen, he'd changed his mind about throwing a gun that couldn't be detected by metal detectors over the side. He checked the clip and shoved the pistol into his briefs. He'd surely be patted down, but knowing how the Chinese detested foreigners, they weren't likely to touch him there.

By the time he got to the quarterdeck, Beth, Sam, and Charlie were waiting for him. Beth was kneeling, holding Traveller by the collar. The first boat from the *Zhuhai* came up to the Jacob's ladder and reversed its engine. A young sailor stood in the stern with a machine gun trained on the quarterdeck. The second boat eased in alongside the first. There was no room in the first boat for passengers, and only room in the second boat for a few. Matt assumed that the crew of *CoMar Explorer* would remain aboard under guard, and the ship would be taken under tow. Captain Chen was nowhere to be seen. A young officer in the bow of the first boat was the first man on deck.

"Captain Connor, please," he said in English.

"I'm Captain Connor."

"I'm Lieutenant Tan, PLA Navy. Captain Chen sends his compliments. He promises humane treatment if you give your word to cooperate."

"You have it," Matt said.

"I must warn you, however. If you've harmed Sergeant Li and his men, you'll be severely punished."

"They're alive and well." Matt nodded to Sam. "Let them out."

Lieutenant Tan nodded to four marines standing near him, who fell in behind Sam. "Please order your entire crew on deck," he said.

"They're here," Matt said, counting noses. "All of them."

"Bind these stinking foreigners," Lieutenant Tan said in Mandarin, nodding to the rest of the crew. "Hands behind their backs."

Sam emerged on deck with Sergeant Li and his men, surrounded by the four armed marines. A sailor coming from the direction of the bridge met them with an armload of assault rifles. He handed a rifle to Sergeant Li. The look of humiliation on his face couldn't be missed. Sergeant Li's men took their rifles and joined the others, heads lowered in embarrassment.

"Now bind the captain, the mongrel whore, the black savage, and this murderous traitor," Lieutenant Tan said in Mandarin, staring at Charles Shen. "Hands front."

A young marine stepped forward and began taping Sam's hands in front of him.

"What's going on?" Matt said, looking at Sam's hands. "Why are we being treated differently?"

"You must remain silent," Lieutenant Tan said in English.

A young marine grabbed Matt by the left wrist and looped a roll of tape around it. Traveller bared his fangs and lunged.

"No!" Beth screamed at the same time Matt yelled "Trav!"

At the same instant, the crack of a rifle shot broke the air. The old dog crumpled at Matt's feet, a swirl of red spreading around him. Matt looked up. Sergeant Li smirked at him, a wisp of smoke emerging from the muzzle of his rifle. Matt lunged at him.

"You son of a bitch!"

Three marines grabbed him and held him while a fourth looped the tape around his right wrist and bound his hands in front of him.

"Most regrettable," Lieutenant Tan said in English. Switching to Mandarin, he said, "Load these four in the longboat. Lock the remainder of the crew in a compartment belowdecks and open the seacocks. Let the sea take this filthy hulk and the lice in it."

Matt stared at him, too stunned to speak. That was why their hands were being bound in front, so they could climb the Jacob's ladder. The others were going to be killed.

"What do you think you're doing?" he said.

"We're placing your crew belowdecks for safety, Captain. Another ship will be along later to tow your ship to Macau. You four will go with us."

"No," Matt said. "I want to stay with my ship."

"You'll be much more comfortable as Captain Chen's guest," Lieutenant Tan said.

Matt stared at Lieutenant Tan, desperate to do something. He couldn't just stand by and watch his entire crew die. He swallowed.

"Don't do this. Please. I'm asking you as a man. One officer to another. Don't do this."

"You'll be reunited with your men in Macau," Lieutenant Tan said, smiling.

"No!" Matt lunged. Even with his wrists bound he was able to open his hands enough to lock his fingers around Lieutenant Tan's neck in a death grip. He wouldn't let go even if they killed him. His death wouldn't matter as long as he took this monster with him. He felt a thud at the base of his skull, then nothing.

The ringing in his ears brought him awake, the sound of a thousand angry bees. He felt the rib of a keel in his back, felt cool water splash against his legs. He was lying on his back, in the bilge of a boat. He opened his eyes. The black sky was laced with streaks of white. Beth was seated above him, looking down with tears staining her face.

"How are you?" she mouthed.

Matt shook his head. "Dizzy." Sam reached down and helped him to sit up. He rubbed his face in his hands. He felt the boat slow and bump against the fender of the destroyer, felt Sam's hands beneath his armpits pulling him to his feet. Weaving, he reached out for a rung of the Jacob's ladder and pulled himself up. With Sam helping from below, he made it to the top and fell over the rail onto the deck. He opened his eyes and saw a pair of black shoes a few inches from his face.

"Captain Connor," he heard a voice say. "We meet again."

Matt rolled over and came to a sitting position. With Sam's help, he got to his feet. Captain Chen stood before him, resplendent in a fresh uniform. He must have been planning this moment for a long time. Matt felt the vibration of the destroyer's engines in his feet. The ship was rapidly gaining speed. Standing in the gathering haze of nightfall, he watched *CoMar Explorer* fade into the distance and tried to imagine the horror his crew was feeling. He never wanted to forget it. The ship had already begun to list a few degrees to the stern.

"This is monstrous."

"A terrible storm," Captain Chen said.

"You miserable son of a bitch," Matt said. "You're a disgrace to the uniform of a sea captain."

Captain Chen turned to Lieutenant Tan. "Please send the following dispatch to headquarters, South Sea Fleet Command, Zhanjiang, Guangdong Province:

"At 18:30 hours today, June 16, PLA Navy destroyer *Zhuhai* responded to an international Mayday call and went to the aid of a Panamanian flag salvage vessel, *CoMar Explorer*, foundering in a storm west of Macau in the South China Sea. Due to the severity of the storm, the ship went down with all hands before rescue measures could be effected.

"Also copy the Xinhua news agency. Mark it for immediate release to the international press."

Lieutenant Tan looked up from his notebook. He glanced at Matt, Beth, Sam, and Charlie.

"Permit me, Captain. Did you say all hands?"

"You heard me correctly," Captain Chen said, looking into Matt's eyes. "There were no survivors."

Chapter Fifteen

Matt stood staring at *CoMar Explorer*, oblivious to everything but the sight of his ship and crew dying on the horizon. The old ship was fading out of his sight, her list to the stern now pronounced. Numb with the terrible pain God reserved for ship captains who lose their ships and their crews, he felt himself being pushed toward an open hatch on the afterdeck of *Zhuhai*. Unable to take his eyes off his ship, he felt hands tugging him through the hatchway, pulling him down into the belly of the beast.

Still dazed from the blow to his head, he struggled to find the rungs of the ladder with his feet while hands pulled at him from below. With his wrists bound, he gripped each rung as best he could. Sergeant Li came down above him, trampling his fingers with his combat boots. Matt lost his grip and stumbled down to the steel deck below.

Sergeant Li pulled him up and shoved him in the direction of a narrow passageway. At the opposite end of the corridor, two young sailors started toward him. Li barked an order to stand clear. They gawked at Matt, then scurried back out of the way. The sergeant was back on his turf now, and he was intent on regaining the stature he'd lost.

The others came up behind Matt. Beth and Charlie each had their own guard, while Sam had two, one on either side of him. Sergeant Li's men. Why had Li and his men been given the assignment of guarding them after their humiliating defeat? Captain Chen wouldn't have given them a chance to redeem themselves. It was probably a face-saving gesture for Chen himself. Whatever the reason, the grim look on their faces told him it was about to be payback time.

Midway down the passageway, they came to a steel door. A hand on his shoulder signaled him to stop. Sergeant Li spun him around, facing the door. The others were prodded around and told to face the bulkhead. Matt braced himself, expecting Sergeant Li and his men to vent their rage on their bound prisoners.

Bristling with restraint, Li stepped back and ordered his men to search the barbarians. There was no way he'd lay his hands on a filthy foreigner. Matt drew Fong, the nervous young private he'd tried without success to get to radio in to *Zhuhai*. Fong's small paws whisked over him, barely touching him. He held his breath, fearful that Fong would discover the pistol he'd hidden in his briefs. The Chinese marine didn't go anywhere near that area. He finished up by sweeping him with a metal detecting wand instead.

Matt glanced at the characters on the brass nameplate on the door while he was being searched. Before he could decipher what they said, Private Fong scampered around and opened the door. Out of the corner of his eye, he saw Sergeant Li move into position behind him. Something slammed against the back of his head. He pitched forward with a blinding pain, felt his shins scrape across the coaming, then blackness.

A sea of faces flashed before him. Francisco, Doc, Murphy, Scootchy, Andy, Kuntz, the man who'd died in the fire aboard the sub. No one spoke. They just stared at him with haunted eyes.

"I'm sorry. God, I'm so sorry," Matt heard himself say.

"Skipper, it's okay," a distant voice said.

Drifting into consciousness, he felt the cold steel of the deck against his cheek, heard the sounds of people moving and talking above him. He felt hands roll him over, saw blurry figures hovering above him. He blinked and brought them into focus. Beth was kneeling on his right, weeping. Sam knelt on his left, looking as if he were trying not to and losing the battle.

"Thank God," Beth said. "We thought you were dead."

Matt closed his eyes. "You'd be better off."

"Hey, now, that's enough of that kind of talk," Sam said. "You're the captain. We need you to help us get out of this."

"Like I got them out of it?"

"Now don't go writing them off," Sam said. "There's some good men there. They'll figure something out."

"Sure they will," Charlie said.

Beth touched his forehead. Her palm felt cool and soft. "How do you feel?"

He rubbed his face in his hands and tried to sit up, then fell back.

"Whoa," Sam said. "Just lay still and take it easy. You had a couple good knocks to the head."

Matt closed his eyes, trying to get his equilibrium. He had to snap out of it. He was still alive and he still had people he was responsible for. People who were looking to him for a goddamn miracle. He took a deep breath and let it out slowly.

"Help me up, Sam."

"You better lay still—"

"Help me up."

Sam pulled him into a sitting position against the bulkhead. He leaned back against the cool steel and tried to clear his head. As his alertness increased, his mind filled with white noise to block out the pain of what he'd just seen. The death of his ship and crew. He swallowed hard. The ship was nothing, but his crew was his family—the only one he had. Once again, people had died because of him. In spite of Sam and Charlie's hopeful words, he knew—they all knew—that there was no hope. If his crew wasn't dead by now, they would be in a matter of minutes, hours at the most, the victims of his blindness and greed.

He'd heard the theory from Gray Wolf and refused to believe it, and he'd heard the reality from Beth in excruciating detail and still hadn't wanted to believe it. Now he knew beyond doubt. The only way the Chinese would do something as horrendous as killing his ship and crew was if the conspiracy Beth had told him about was true.

Somehow, some way, he had to get the launch stopped—but how? The press release that had gone out to the world had the four of them dead, gone down with the ship along with the rest of his crew. The Chinese could do anything they wanted with them now and no one would ever know. He had no doubt they'd keep them alive for a while—long enough to get what they wanted—then kill them.

The burning question was, what did they want? Why had only the four of them been spared? What did they have in common? There was only one thing. All four had been involved in Beth's rescue. Captain Chen had to be acting on orders. There could be only one reason why he'd kept the four of them alive—to find out if they'd made any contact with the outside world.

What would the Chinese do if they had. Or hadn't?

If the Chinese thought they hadn't made contact with the U.S., they'd kill them as soon as they were convinced of that, dump their bodies over the side, and proceed as planned.

But what if the Chinese thought they had? It would be unwelcome news to whoever was behind Raptor. They wouldn't want to believe it, would have to keep them alive for as long as it took to confirm it. The more doubt he could raise in Captain Chen's mind, the longer they'd stay alive.

Staying alive was good, but there'd be an even bigger benefit in raising doubt in Chen's mind. If the Chinese government thought there was any possibility that the U.S. had learned about the launch, they'd have to order an escort of the command and control ship to the launch site to protect it. A highly visible naval escort.

What ships would be available to escort a vessel that was going to sail from Guangzhou? The *Zhuhai*, for one. But there had to be at least one other ship in the neighborhood playing war games off Macau. The *Zhuhai* wouldn't have been alone—it took more than one ship to play war games. The more PLA Navy ships escorting the command and control ship to the launch site, the higher the profile on the radar screen or satellite screen and the more chance that the U.S. would pick up on it.

Matt rubbed his eyes. The only thing he could do was try and convince the Chinese that the U.S. knew about the launch. But how? They'd never believe what the barbarians told them voluntarily. They'd have to get the answers using their own methods. That would be the plan. In order to be convincing he'd deny it first, then let the Chinese torture him into admitting it.

He glanced around. It was obvious why the four of them had been put in the same room together. The compartment appeared to be a hastily rigged holding cell, probably within earshot of the place that would be used to extract the information the Chinese wanted. Nothing was more persuasive than hearing the agonized screams of a comrade-in-arms, knowing you were next.

Matt wasn't worried about Sam and Charlie handling the torture. They'd been trained to cope with abuse at the hands of an enemy, Sam in his SEAL training and Charlie by the CIA. He wasn't worried about himself, either. He hadn't been trained to handle torture, but he felt dead. No amount of physical pain could overshadow the emotional pain he felt.

Beth was another matter. He couldn't let that happen. He'd have to find a way to manipulate the Chinese into interrogating him first, then be so convincing in his "confession," they'd never get to her.

There was probably another reason they'd been thrown in the same room together. He was sure the room was bugged. If he was right, they could turn it to their advantage. He motioned for Charlie and Beth to talk loudly—about anything—then motioned Sam down to his level. He cupped his hand and whispered in his ear.

"Okay, Sam. Here's the drill. The only way we can slow them down is to convince them that we've contacted CINCPAC about the launch, and the game is up. The problem is, they won't believe a word we tell them voluntarily, only what they extract by their own methods. I'm hoping this place is bugged. We'll let it slip here first—that'll get their attention—then deny it during interrogation. After they torture us an appropriate amount of time, we'll break down and confess that the U.S. knows everything."

Sam nodded and motioned to Charlie that Matt wanted to talk to him. Sam and Beth talked loudly about being hungry while Matt briefed Charlie, then Sam and Charlie picked up the conversation while Beth got the same whispered briefing. They all nodded, faces grim.

Matt said, "I can't believe you're thinking about food. You don't think we're going to get out of this alive, do you?"

"Probably not," Sam said. "But I'm hungry."

"They wouldn't dare harm us," Beth said.

"What makes you think so?" Charlie said.

"Because the cavalry is on its way," Beth said.

Sam laughed, a loud booming sarcastic laugh. "You think just because the captain got a message off to CINCPAC, that's gonna help us? Fat chance."

"Why?"

"Because all the Navy's gonna be worrying about is stopping the launch of that satellite. The press release has already gone out about the ship going down with all hands. The Navy thinks we're all dead."

"Uh-uh, they won't buy it," Beth said. "After getting the captain's message, they won't believe that press release. They'll come looking for us."

"I think she's right," Charlie said. "If the fleet's on its way to intercept the command and control ship before it gets to the launch site, they've got to be close to our neck of the woods. They come across this ship, they might just pull it over and search it."

"You guys are dreaming," Matt said. "But at least we were able to get the word out."

"Yeah," Charlie said. "They'll probably kill us, but at least they won't get that satellite launched."

Matt winced at Charlie's stilted dialogue and changed the subject back to food. He looked at his watch. Time would tell if the bluff had worked.

He didn't have long to wait. Within minutes he heard the lock being opened and the door swung wide. Sergeant Li stepped in and stood with his hands on his hips, glaring down at Matt, sitting on the deck, head propped against the bulkhead.

"You," he said, pointing.

Matt started to get up, then slumped back, feeling faint. Sam stepped between them.

"Cap'n's not feeling so good. Take me. You can talk to him later."

"No, take me," Beth said, stepping forward. "These guys don't know anything."

Sergeant Li swept Beth out of the way and tried to shove Sam aside, but it was like pushing against a concrete pillar. Two marines started toward him.

"It's okay, Sam. I can make it." Matt motioned for Charlie to help him up. He came to his feet, weaving. "What do you want, Li?"

Sergeant Li glowered at the familiarity of being called by his family name. He jerked his head toward the door.

"Come."

Matt followed him through the door, feeling groggy, trying to keep his balance with the roll of the destroyer. With two marines behind him, he leaned against the bulkhead to steady himself and trailed Sergeant Li down the passageway a few yards to another steel door. He'd been right about where the house of pain was located. The compartment was right next door, within earshot of Beth, Sam, and Charlie. He clenched his teeth, determined not to make a sound, no matter what they did to him. Li opened the door and shoved him inside, then closed the door behind him as a pair of brawny sailors caught him.

Wearing white pants, T-shirts, and rubber aprons, they looked the part of "information specialists." With shaved heads that glistened under the floodlights, all they lacked was the black hoods. In the seconds before they spun him around, Matt caught a glimpse of what looked like an operating table with tie-down straps. An array of stainless-steel instruments lay on a table beside it. The two men stood facing the door, holding him upright, neither speaking.

After a few minutes, the door opened and Captain Chen stepped in. The door clanged shut behind him and the two sailors stood at attention, still holding Matt between them.

Captain Chen leaned back against the door and stood with his arms folded, saying nothing.

Matt glared at him. "I strongly protest the sinking of my ship and the inhuman murder of my crew."

"You're hardly in a position to protest anything, Commander. Or is it Captain by now?"

"Captain," Matt said. "Captain of *CoMar Explorer*, a Panamanian flag salvage vessel, which you ordered scuttled in the South China Sea with all hands locked belowdecks."

"Captain of that piece of flotsam?" Captain Chen shook his head. "I don't think so. I'm sure the U.S. can find a better use for one of its most promising naval officers."

"You've been misinformed," Matt said. "I'm a civilian. A private U.S. citizen."

Captain Chen smiled. "I hardly think a former brigade

commander at the U.S. Naval Academy and former executive officer of a nuclear-powered submarine would be stripped of his position over an accidental death. Particularly one who's related to the U.S. Chief of Naval Operations."

"It works a little differently in the U.S.," Matt said. "We care about human life. Anyone who treats it carelessly, as I did, will be relieved of command. Anyone who takes it deliberately, as you did, will be charged with murder."

"Murder? You're a professional warrior. You, more than anyone, should know that killing during wartime is not murder."

"Since when are the U.S. and China at war?"

"Wars are not always declared," Chen said with a shrug. "Now, tell me, what did the crazed half-Chinese woman tell you?"

"I refuse to speak to a murderer."

"Oh, I think you'll talk to me. You'll pray for death before my men are through with you." He nodded to the two sailors.

They picked him up and threw him across the table, onto a thick, hard rubber mat. One of the men produced a knife and cut the tape binding Matt's wrists. The taste of freedom was fleeting. They strapped his wrists down to the table, then pulled his boots and socks off and strapped his ankles down. The larger of the two men attached electrodes to his wrists, ankles, and the top of his head.

"I'd advise you to cooperate," Captain Chen said. He nodded to the larger of the two sailors. "This is Information Specialist Bing. He and his assistant, Ren, are highly skilled in both the old and the new ways of extracting information."

"Good for them."

"Our intelligence sources report that the half-Chinese American woman has been spreading lies about her visit to China," Captain Chen said. "What has she told you?"

"That she wants to go home."

Chen nodded to the younger sailor.

Matt braced himself. A surge of electricity shot through him. The pain enveloped him, intense beyond any he'd ever felt. The blood in his veins felt as if it were boiling. Grinding his teeth, determined not to shout out, he smelled burning flesh and hair where the electrodes were attached. After what seemed an eternity, it stopped. He lay gasping for air, shaking violently.

"If I were you I'd speak up," Captain Chen said. "Depending on the strength of the individual, these shocks are sometimes fatal."

"*Cao ni*," Matt said through clenched teeth.

"Ah, so it's true," Chen said. "Sergeant Li reported that you speak some Chinese." He nodded to Ren.

Matt felt another jolt of electricity surge through him, rattling his teeth. An involuntary moan rose from him.

"*Cao ni ma.*" Go screw your mother.

"You disappoint me, Captain. Your language skills appear to be limited to waterfront profanities. I would have expected more proficiency from one so exalted." Chen moved closer. "Do yourself a favor and tell me what I want to know, Captain. I don't think you're good for many more of these before your heart stops."

Matt steeled himself and shook his head violently. He felt his body rise off the table. With each surge of electricity his tolerance for the punishment seemed to decrease. His tongue felt swollen to twice its size. He lay gasping for air.

"I don't. . . know what you're. . . talking about."

Another jolt shot through him. The pain from the spots where the electrodes were attached seared his brain. He nodded.

"Okay. . .No more." He waited a long moment until his breathing was more normal. "She told us a wild story about a satellite launch," he said finally, "but I don't care about that stuff. I'm no longer a naval officer. I'm a simple mercenary, paid to pick her up and bring her back. I did it for the money. Nothing more."

"Who have you told about this imagined satellite launch?"

"No one."

"Liar."

Another surge, this time longer, more intense. Chen was right. He wasn't good for much more.

"Speak to me, Captain," Chen said. "Who have you contacted?"

Matt lifted his head off the table. "How could we. . .contact anyone? You destroyed our radio." He could barely hear his voice.

"So far you've had it easy, Captain. For more serious cases, we attach electrodes to the genitals of the offender. Specialist Bing here finds it distasteful to touch the genitalia of foreigners but will do so if I order it. The procedure usually results in electronic castration, the irreversible cessation of manhood."

Matt's eyes darted back and forth between the two men. Chen had to be bluffing. No man would do that to another.

"I told you, no one."

Chen turned to Bing. "*Zuo ta nu ren.*" Make him a woman.

Bing snapped his head forward in a nod and pulled on a pair of white surgical gloves. He gathered up loose material in Matt's left pant leg and made an opening cut with a pair of scissors.

The game was over. Whether they were bluffing or not, Matt couldn't risk the discovery of the pistol hidden in his briefs. It was all he had. He raised his head.

"All right, all right. You win."

"Once again you disappoint me, Captain. That was too easy." Captain Chen bent down over Matt's face and spoke softly. "We'll talk now, but you won't be given another opportunity to be truthful. At the first instance I sense you're not being completely candid, I will order Specialist Bing to proceed, leave the room, and there will be no turning back, no stopping it, no matter what you say. Do you understand?"

"I understand," Matt said. He sighed. "Let me up. I'll tell you everything you want to know."

"Very well." He motioned to Bing to release him.

Matt rubbed his face in his hands and tried to sit up, then fell back on the table, disoriented. Bing and his assistant helped him to sit up. He sat on the edge of the table, rubbing his wrists, rolling his head around, trying to focus his mind.

"Let's begin at the beginning," Captain Chen said. "You are currently a U.S. naval officer working undercover."

Matt hesitated. It wasn't a question, it was a statement. Captain Chen would never believe him if he denied it. He had to guess what Chen wanted to hear and give it to him, whether it was true or not. One miscalculation and he'd be back on the table. He nodded.

"And your grade?"

Matt ran the numbers. If the fire hadn't happened he'd probably have been a full commander by now, on track for captain.

"Commander, United States Navy."

"I thought as much," Chen said. "Who do you work for, Commander?"

"The CIA," Matt said. "I've been doing intelligence work off the coast of China under the cover of operating a marine salvage business in Taiwan."

"Very clever," Chen said. "And you report to the Chief of Naval Operations, Admiral Jacobs, a member of your family."

Captain Chen's intelligence was impressive, if a bit out of date. He told himself to go slow. It was another statement, not a question. He didn't dare deny it, but he had to make the danger to them sound more immediate, more pressing.

"Only indirectly," he said. "For this mission I report directly to CINCPAC, Commander in Chief of the Pacific Forces."

"More specific."

"Admiral Vern Taylor."

"And what have you told Admiral Taylor?"

"Everything the woman told us," Matt said, determined to negate any need for Chen to interrogate Beth. He couldn't stand the thought of her being in this room, under the control of the Bobbsey Twins. "We made a full report."

"I want you to make that exact report to me right now," Captain Chen said. "Verbatim. I want to know precisely what you told Admiral Taylor."

"Well, I may not be able to remember the exact words, but I told him about the capability of the killer satellite code-named Raptor. How it will destroy every American satellite, both military and commercial. I told him about the launch methodology, about the launch site on the equator at 106 degrees east longitude, approximately midway between Sumatra and Borneo. I told him about the launch date of June 21st. And I told him about the plan to deploy and use it as soon as it's in orbit.

Everything."

Matt sensed that Chen, working hard to keep his expression steady, was hearing most of this for the first time. To show that he was out of the loop on something so important would be a huge loss of face.

"Yes, yes," he said, waving his hand. "We know all about this. Now, when did you communicate this information to Admiral Taylor?"

"Within twenty minutes after she—the woman—came aboard. Right after she was picked up from the island, almost three days ago, it would have been the early morning hours of the fourteenth."

"And precisely how was this information communicated?"

"By satellite phone."

"Liar. We searched your ship for communication devices and found nothing." Captain Chen nodded to Bing and started to walk away.

"Wait," Matt said. "You also searched my ship for weapons and didn't find the Stinger missile I used to shoot down one of your helicopters."

Chen hesitated, then turned back, glaring.

"And you made contact directly with CINCPAC in Hawaii?"

"No, it was out of range because of the storm. We couldn't get through. We made contact with the USS *Observation Island*. It's an intelligence-gathering ship, code-named Cobra Judy. It operates in waters off China somewhere. I don't know where."

Chen nodded as though this made sense. Matt felt a tingle of relief. The ship had been parked off the coast of China for years. He assumed it was still there. Chen's eyes told him it was.

"What did you do with the satellite phone?"

"We threw it over the side just before you came aboard."

Captain Chen took a couple of steps back, turned, and began pacing. After a full minute, he said, "I think you're lying. We were monitoring all communications. We heard nothing from your ship."

"Do you seriously think we'd be sent on a mission like this without a safe way to communicate?" Matt said.

"I still think you're lying. It's up to you to convince me that what you say is true."

"You don't believe me when I tell you I didn't tell anyone, now you don't believe me when I tell you I did. You have to believe one or the other. Which is it?"

Matt could see him agonizing over the decision. If he reported that the barbarians hadn't made contact, and it turned out they had, his head would be on the block. On the other hand, if he reported that they had made contact, his head would be on the block for letting Beth get away from the island. Either way he'd be in serious trouble, but the only prudent choice to make was to assume that Matt had made the contact.

"Even if what you say is true, what of it? The U.S. can do nothing, short of attacking first, and that would be a declaration of unprovoked war. The world community would be outraged."

"With all respect, Captain, I know I'm a dead man, but you have to know the game is up. Do you think the U.S. is just going to stand by and watch you launch a satellite that will cripple the country, both militarily and economically? Believe me, they have a way to solve this without the rest of the world knowing anything about it."

That got his attention. Matt could see him thinking. If Chen could come up with some counterintelligence, some information that would help safeguard the launch, he might regain the points he'd lost for letting Beth get away and divulge what she knew to the U.S.

"You're a senior naval officer with high connections," Chen said. "You're related to the Chief of Naval Operations, his brother-in-law. You know what the plan will be. You tell me. What will they do?"

"I can tell you exactly what they'll do," Matt said. "And I will— in exchange for one thing."

Chen smiled. "You're in no position to be making bargains, Commander."

Matt shrugged. "Kill me, then. I'm dead anyway."

"There are many things worse than death, Commander. Bing, here, knows what they are. But tell me what it is you want, just out of curiosity."

"We all know we're going to die. We all accept this, it goes with the territory of being a spy. I just don't want what's left of my crew, or the woman, to go through what I went through." He nodded toward Bing. "All I'm asking for is a simple bullet in the back of the head for each of us when the time comes. Give me your word of honor that my people won't be harmed in any way until then and I'll tell you the full plan of attack."

"Very noble." Chen studied Matt's face. He stroked his chin. After a moment, he nodded. "Very well. You'd tell me anyway, I assure you, but in the interest of saving time I'll grant your request."

"All right," Matt said. "The U.S. basically has two options. One, they can file a diplomatic protest over something that hasn't happened yet, or two, they can take military action to preempt the launch."

"That is rather obvious," Chen said.

"The stakes are too high for a diplomatic protest," Matt said, "so they'll choose the second option. Military action. Under that option, they have two choices. Direct and indirect."

"Get to the point."

"Well, the direct approach would be to intercept the command and control ship—basically an unprotected merchant ship—when it's at sea. They could either seize the satellite or just sink the ship."

"Either deed would be an act of war," Chen said.

"Sure," Matt said. "But they might be willing to risk that because of the high stakes. You can't rule it out."

"So far you've told me exactly nothing," Chen said.

"But the indirect approach is probably the one they'll use."

"Which is?"

"The indirect approach would be to simply send out a couple of specialized attack boats, nuclear-powered submarines that operate so quietly they're undetectable. They'll be waiting for you when the command and control ship gets to the launch site on the equator. You won't even know they're there. They can stay submerged indefinitely. They'll just sit there until you mount the satellite on the launch platform, wait for the countdown, then quietly put a torpedo in it. There'll be a huge explosion, they'll disappear, and that'll be the end of it."

"That would also be an act of war."

"Nonsense. It'll be a tragic accident. Happens all the time in rocket launches."

"And you know this how?"

"I'm a submarine officer," Matt said. "That's the recommendation I made. Of course, I have no way of knowing what the president's decision will be. But if I were you, I'd be prepared for either scenario."

Chen stared at him.

"Now I've met my end of the bargain," Matt said. "As a man of honor, I expect you to hold up yours."

Matt could see Chen's face turning red.

"You've told me nothing but a lot of nonsense," Chen said. He turned to Bing. "Get this fool out of here and send in the others, one by one, beginning with the woman."

Chapter Sixteen

C aptain Chen stepped into his stateroom and locked the door behind him. He pulled the black leather chair out from his desk and slumped into it. So that was what the bogus senior colonel was up to. He was about to start a war. Impossible to believe. He closed his eyes and rubbed the lids. It had long been a PLA doctrine that war with America was inevitable, but he couldn't believe it was about to happen.

He retrieved a bottle of Chivas Regal from the bottom drawer of his desk, poured himself a shot, and downed it with a grimace. Twirling the empty shot glass in his hand, he stared at the light refracting through it from his desk lamp and pondered the implications of what he'd just learned.

He couldn't imagine anything more devastating to the U.S. than the destruction of its communications satellites. Even a nuclear attack on America's major cities wouldn't have the impact of such an attack. He'd not only studied in America, he'd studied America itself and he knew how dependent the country was on technology. The loss of every satellite would not only disable the American military, it would cripple the American economy, causing worldwide chaos and ruin.

He hadn't believed Commander Connor at first. The American spy had confessed too easily, had seemed almost eager to reveal everything he knew. Chen had considered it all disinformation until Connor had mentioned the launch date of June 21. That date coincided exactly with an important date entered on Chen's calendar. *Zhuhai* had been placed on alert almost four months ago. Chen had been given sealed orders and told to expect a radio-transmitted cryptogram that would authorize the opening of those orders on or about June 21st. It couldn't be a coincidence.

He would never open sealed orders without authorization—such an act was unthinkable—but prudence compelled him to verify that they were still there, still intact. He spun the combination to his safe, opened it, and retrieved a manila envelope. A bright red band across it contained the inscription "Most Secret" repeated in yellow letters. The envelope had been in his safe for so long he'd put it out of his mind. He looked at the flap, sealed with a splash of red sealing wax bearing the South Sea Fleet Command insignia. He picked the envelope up. It weighed almost nothing. It couldn't contain more than a single sheet of paper. He found himself staring at the inscription stamped diagonally across it in red ink:

Eyes Only Commanding Officer Luda III-class Destroyer Zhuhai (166)

He placed the envelope on his desk and rubbed the palms of his hands against the legs of his trousers. He told himself to put it away and wait for the authorizing code. The opening of sealed orders without authorization would mean death, if discovered. He returned the envelope to the safe and closed the door, then hesitated before locking it. He looked at his watch. Just after midnight. It was now June 17th. The 21st was only four days away. With the date so close, the risk of discovery would be low. He shook his head. *Damn the American spy.* He had to know.

He checked the lock on his stateroom door, took a razor blade from his desk, and carefully slit the bottom edge of the envelope. He blew the edges apart and slid the single page out, letting it fall on the desk before him, not daring even to touch it. He leaned forward in his chair.

Commanding Officer, Luda III-class Destroyer Zhuhai *(166)*

Effective immediately, a state of war exists between The People's Republic of China and the following nations and provinces:

The Republic of China (Province of Taiwan)

The United States of America

All allies of The Republic of China (Province of Taiwan) and the USA

Following are your orders:

1. Proceed with all dispatch to the southern tip of Chilung Island, coordinates 25 N 10, 121 E 48.

2. Rendezvous with the destroyer Harbin *(112), and the frigates* Huaibei *(541) and* Huainan *(540), to form Task Force 34 under the command of PLA Major General Jin Kuan-lun.*

3. As directed by General Jin, commence missile bombardment of the city of Taipei, specifically targeting the Taiwanese presidential palace and defense ministry for total destruction.

4. Provide overall support for the invasion of the island of Taiwan, as directed.

5. Engage and destroy all USA, Taiwanese, and allied naval and military forces encountered.

Chen leaned back in his chair, trembling. It was true. The war games he'd been engaged in with the *Harbin, Huaibei,* and *Huainan* off Turtle Island now made sense. China and the U.S. would soon be at war. No. The world would be at war.

He accepted war with the U.S.—he'd trained for it his entire professional life—but in every war plan he'd ever seen, it was always assumed that China would have the advantage of surprise. If what the American commander had told him was true, the launch of the satellite would not be the surprise the leadership thought it would be. If Commander Connor was telling the truth, and Chen now believed he was, the Americans already knew about the launch and China's plans for a preemptive strike immediately thereafter.

He poured himself another shot of Scotch and sipped it. The American spy was not only right about the launch, he was right about something else. Now that they knew, the Americans would not allow such a thing to happen. He had to notify the leadership—but who? He was under orders from General Lao to report what he found directly to Senior Colonel Lao, his ineffectual son. But could a Red Prince be trusted with something so important?

Chen had his doubts. Something this big should be reported directly to President Xiang, but how could he defy General Lao's direct orders? Still, he was an officer in the PLA Navy. He had to do the right thing for China. He threw back the remainder of the whiskey and made his decision: he'd call General Lao directly, with the excuse that he'd been unable to get through to his son. If the general was unavailable, he'd call President Xiang.

He gingerly placed the orders back in the envelope, locked it away in his safe, and walked quickly to the combat information center.

In the darkened compartment, he spotted the silhouette of his executive officer near the communication console.

"Tan. Arrange for a secure line to Zhongnanhai. General Lao."

"Ah, Captain," Lieutenant Tan said. "I was just going to call you. You have an incoming call from Beijing."

No doubt the impatient Red Prince. Chen shook his head.

"Yes, one moment please," Lieutenant Tan said into the handset. He put his hand over the mouthpiece and whispered, "Director Han Jinhua."

Han. The head of the Chinese Secret Intelligence Service was the last person on earth Chen wanted to talk to. He didn't even want Han to know his name. He hesitated, but he didn't dare refuse the call. He took the handset.

"This is Captain Chen."

"Have you interrogated the American prisoners yet?"

No introduction, no greeting. That was consistent with what Chen had heard about Han. The arrogant director of the CSIS had such power he'd never seen the need for manners.

"We're in the process of interrogation as we speak, Director Han."

"What have you discovered?"

Chen hesitated. Han knew as well as he did that he was under orders from General Lao to report his findings directly to his son. Still, he couldn't directly refuse to answer the head of the CSIS.

"The interrogation is not yet completed."

"Surely you've completed the interrogation of at least some of them."

Chen cleared his throat, buying a nanosecond to think. With the time that had elapsed, he couldn't deny that he had.

"Yes, Director, we have."

"Well? What have you learned? Who have you talked to?"

"So far, only the captain of the vessel."

"And what did he say?"

Chen didn't know who to fear most, General Lao or Han Jinhua. Either could ruin him. He took a deep breath—and a risk.

"With all respect, Director Han. You heard the orders from General Lao. I am to report the results of the interrogation directly to Senior Colonel Lao."

"Yes, I heard those orders, but there's something you have not heard," Han said. "You have not heard about the latest purge taking place in Beijing. There is great concern among the leadership about those in the party who have studied abroad. Concern about their trustworthiness. Senior Colonel Lao studied in America. There are many who believe he cannot be trusted."

Chen said nothing. He'd heard of no such purge, but if Han wanted one, there'd be one. And on his orders alone. He heard pages being flipped in the background.

"According to your records," Han said, "you also studied in America. Annapolis, was it?"

Chen felt his blood run cold.

"I assure you, Director Han, I'm a dedicated Communist, loyal to the party."

"Everyone who has studied in America says this, but can it be believed? You would be amazed what is revealed under interrogation."

Chen's mouth went dry. If Han ordered him to Beijing for interrogation, his relief would discover the opened orders in his safe and he'd be finished. He ran his tongue over dry lips.

"Of course I want to cooperate fully, Director Han, but you know how untrustworthy the barbarians are. How they lie. I simply did not want to provide a person at your high level with partial information that may be inconclusive."

"You will let me be the judge of that."

"Of course, Director. We just concluded our interrogation of the captain of the ship, only minutes ago. Under coercion, he admitted everything. He's an American national, one Matthew B. Connor, posing as the captain of an ocean-salvage vessel. He admitted that he is in actuality a U.S. naval officer with the grade of commander, and that the ship was a cover for espionage. For more than five years, he's been working undercover from a base in Taiwan, gathering intelligence about China."

"Yes, yes, we all know the filthy American spies are everywhere. Get to the point. What has the American woman told him and what contacts has he made?"

"After prolonged electric shock treatment, he admitted that the woman told him about an ASAT-satellite, code-named Raptor, that will be deployed to destroy every American satellite in orbit, both military and commercial."

"What else?"

"She further revealed to him the launch methodology, how the satellite would be launched at sea from a platform on the equator at 106 degrees east longitude, midway between Sumatra and Borneo."

"What about the date? Did he mention any dates?"

"Yes. She told him the launch date would be June 21."

There was a pause.

"What else?"

"She told him the satellite would be used immediately once in orbit."

"Now listen carefully," Han said. "It's critically important to know who, if anyone, the Americans have contacted with this information."

"I agree, Director. At first the American spy denied that any contact had been made. Of course I would not accept this. Under threat of emasculation he admitted that contact had been made with the U.S. Navy. Specifically, Admiral Vern Taylor, Commander in Chief of the Pacific Forces."

Another pause.

"When was this contact made?"

"In the early morning hours of June fourteenth, immediately after the woman escaped from the *laogai* on Turtle Island."

"How was it made?"

"By satellite phone."

"And you believe this?"

Chen started to say the date of June 21 confirmed it, then thought better of it. The less he knew of China's war plans, the better.

"There can be no mistake."

The line went quiet. Chen waited, listening to the faint crackle in the background.

"All right," Han said. "Here's what I want you to do. You say the American spy is a U.S. naval officer. Using any means necessary, I want you to extract every shred of information he knows about American plans to counter this threat."

"We've already done that, Director. The American officer revealed the plan under severe torture. He admitted that the U.S. will either sink the command and control ship en route to the launch site, or have ultra-quiet undetectable submarines in the area, waiting to torpedo the launch pad."

"Which is it?"

"He doesn't appear to know. He says it will be a decision of the U.S. president."

"Knowing the Americans," Han said, "they will avoid a direct confrontation. They will more likely take the second approach."

"Very clever of you to discern this, Director. The American said that is indeed the scenario he recommended. After the rocket is transferred to the launch pad, they'll quietly fire a torpedo into it and disappear. To the world it will look like an accidental explosion."

"And you believe this?"

"Yes, Director, I do. As I said, the information was extracted under threat of emasculation."

"But how would he know this?"

"He's a submarine officer. He'd know about such tactics."

"He may know tactics, but that doesn't mean he'd be privy to such a high-level plan."

"That would normally be true, Director Han, but in this case the spy is well connected. He's a relative of the American Chief of Naval Operations."

The line went quiet again.

"Very well," Han said after a moment. "You've done well, Captain . . . Chen, is it?"

"Yes, Director."

"Listen to me carefully, Chen. You are to tell no one of this conversation. Is that understood?"

"But my orders are to report the information to Senior Colonel Lao."

"You have new orders. Orders from me. Orders that supersede all others. Are they understood?"

"Yes, of course, Director Han, but you heard General Lao's orders. How can I not make a report to Senior Colonel Lao?"

"That's no longer your concern," Han said. "I will notify the necessary authorities."

"Welcome home," Old Wang said, opening the door of the limousine. He swept his arm toward James's boyhood home. "Does it look the same?"

James looked up at the ornate entrance to his father's house, a palatial estate overlooking Nanhai, the southern lake. It hadn't changed much in the years since he'd last seen it, other than looking a bit smaller, a bit more run down, like everything at Zhongnanhai. He stifled a yawn. Exhausted from working nonstop since he'd gotten there, he'd let Old Wang talk him into catching a few hours of sleep before flying out. He dutifully glanced at the grandiloquent Chinese architecture, the manicured grounds, the moon shimmering across the lake. He nodded.

"It's beautiful."

"Yes, the general loves it here."

James glanced across the lake at an equally palatial estate a half-mile away. The home of Han Jinhua dominated a hilltop overlooking the opposite corner of Nanhai. He couldn't fathom the depth of hatred the old man seemed to have for him. Without the general behind him, Han would eat him alive. He noticed a light on in a corner of the house. Unlike his father, Han maintained his office in his home. The scrawny old peasant was probably working into the night, trying to see who else he could ruin. James shuddered. Hopefully, he'd never see the man again.

"Where is the general?"

Old Wang smiled proudly. "Still hard at work in his office—he's seldom in before one. I prepare him a warm bath and a light snack before bed and he's up by five or six, back at it."

James looked at his watch. Twelve-fifteen a.m. He'd be asleep by the time his father got home.

Wang picked up his bag. "What time does the plane leave?

James smiled at the old man. "Whenever I say."

"Good. Then you can sleep as long as you like."

"I wish," James said, looking at the date on his watch. With the passing of midnight, it was now June 17th. The launch was only four days away. He'd been stuck in Zhongnanhai for more than two days, working out of a guest house, dealing with Han Jinhua's troublemaking. With so much at stake, he felt he had to be present during the assembly of the rocket and the mating of the payload on the way to the launch site. Even if that weren't necessary, he'd still want to be there to witness the launch. Because of Han's meddling he'd already missed the sailing of the CCS, but he could still catch the ship. First, a few hours' sleep, then a three-hour flight to Guangzhou, where he'd be flown to the *Zenith* by helicopter.

"Wake me no later than three."

"It shall be done," Old Wang said. He pushed the door inward, then stood back. "The general feels that locked doors are an insult to our neighbors."

James sighed. The residents of Zhongnanhai could afford to be magnanimous. The paranoid Mao had installed his own security system when he moved into the compound in 1949. He called it *waisong neijin*: outwardly relaxed, inwardly tight. It was designed to convince his enemies that he was so loved he didn't need a security system. It was impossible for the untrained eye to see, but it was there and it was highly effective. To even be caught on the grounds would mean death to an intruder.

James led the way down a long hallway to his old room with Wang breathing heavily behind him, struggling with his duffel bag. He felt guilty. In many ways, Wang had been more of a father to him than the general. He would have preferred to carry the bag himself, but that would be an unforgivable insult to the old man.

Wang dropped the bag and scurried around to open the door before James reached it. The old man's face lit up.

"You'll see that your room has been kept exactly as it was. The general wouldn't allow it to be used for anything else."

James glanced around the room, filled with mementos of his childhood. School awards, photographs of him with his friends, posters of his favorite American and European rock bands. He couldn't believe his father had saved all this junk. He pressed his hand against the mattress and nodded. The room was nothing like his villa in Hong Kong, but it was a step up from the guest house and he'd at least be able to get some sleep.

"Are you hungry?" Old Wang said.

"Thank you, no, Wang. Just a short whiskey, no ice."

While James laid out his things, Old Wang slipped out and reappeared with a small lacquered tray holding a tall glass containing two inches of brown liquid. James motioned for him to set it down on his nightstand. A bit of whiskey would help him unwind and get a few hours of sleep.

He checked his cell phone for messages. Nothing. He looked at his watch again. Twelve-thirty. Where was that fool Chen? The captain of *Zhuhai* had called hours ago with word that the Americans had been successfully captured and were being interrogated. What was taking so long?

He told himself to relax. He was in the driver's seat, no matter what came out of the Americans' mouths. His father had ordered that the results of the interrogations be reported directly to him. That had been the only good thing to come out of the humiliating meeting with President Xiang and Han Jinhua. He could still see the look on Han's face when his father gave the order.

Thank God he had. The launch couldn't be delayed, no matter what had transpired, no matter who or what had been told. Because of his father's orders, James was in a position to screen out any bad news. He'd relax for a minute over his drink and then call Captain Chen. If the news was good, he'd let Chen trumpet it to the skies. If it was bad, he'd invoke his father's name and order his silence.

"Good night, young master," Wang said. "Sleep well." The old man slipped out of the room and closed the door behind him.

James stretched out on the bed with one hand behind his head and sipped the whiskey. It went down easily. He'd never seen his father touch liquor, but he stocked the best for his guests. He finished his drink and closed his eyes. He'd rest for a moment before placing his call. Weariness seeped through him like a sponge. He felt himself drifting off. . . .

He heard a soft rap at the door. He shook the sleep from his eyes, not sure how long he'd been asleep. Perhaps his father was home.

"Come in."

Old Wang quickly stepped in and closed the door behind him. He tiptoed over to James's bed and stood over him. He looked frightened.

"Forgive this intrusion, young master."

"What is it? Why are you whispering?"

"Han Jinhua is here."

"To see my father?"

"The general isn't here. He wants to see you."

"I don't. . . How does he know I'm here?"

"He knows everything."

The old man was trembling. It occurred to James that Wang had lived through all the purges, including the Cultural Revolution, and knew what could happen to even ordinary people when one lunatic like Han gave an order. Because of General Lao's status as a national hero, there weren't many people in Zhongnanhai he feared, but clearly he was terrified of Han.

"Calm down, Wang. Where is he?"

"I showed him into the general's study. I offered him a drink, but he refused. Most impolite."

James stepped into his shoes. "I'll take care of it." He ran a hand through his hair, straightened his tie, then walked into his father's study. Han stood peering at a wall of awards, his hands behind his back.

"Director Han. What brings you out at such a late hour?"

"The people's business goes on twenty-four hours a day."

"So true," James said. "But what brings you here?"

"A meeting. You're invited. Your father's on his way. When he arrives, we'll awaken President Xiang for an emergency conference call."

"Really?

"Yes. I want your father to see what kind of son he's raised, and I want President Xiang to see the rotten fruit our education policies have borne."

James felt a cold wave of nausea sweep through him. What the hell was he up to?

"I hope your statements will make more sense to them than they do to me."

"Oh, I think you know precisely what I mean."

"I'm afraid you'll have to tell me."

"All in good time. Your father will be here shortly. I want to see his face—and yours—when I tell him."

James had to find out what Han knew, or thought he knew, before his father got there. It was a risk to provoke the old man, but it was a risk he'd have to take. He forced a laugh.

"Just as I thought. Your words are as empty as your head."

Han's eyes flashed. "My head is empty, is it? We'll see about that."

"You have nothing to say that would be of interest to anyone, old man. Certainly not my father."

Han looked at him with outright glee. "I think the vice chairman of the Central Military Commission will be interested to know that the security for this launch upon which everything depends has been compromised."

"What nonsense are you jabbering?"

"Nonsense, is it? Jabbering, am I? I have it on excellent authority that the Americans have notified the U.S. commander of the Pacific Fleet about the launch, right down to the precise date and launch site."

"Ridiculous. Where did you get such a notion?"

"Directly from the mouths of the participants. Captain Chen has interrogated the American ship captain—"

"Chen's a fool, easily duped into believing anything. The barbarians have tricked him. Besides, Chen went to Annapolis. For all we know, his loyalties lie with America."

That last statement seemed to throw Han, but only for a moment. "You too went to school in America," he said. "Perhaps your loyalties lie with America."

"You see?" James said. "You're making no sense. I don't think the president will appreciate being awakened to hear your irrational gibberish."

"You can be as insulting as you like, but the security has been breached and the launch must be stopped."

"That's not possible."

"As soon as your father gets here, I'll show you how possible it is."

"General Lao will think you're as mad as I do. I advise you to leave before he gets here. I'll overlook your irrational behavior."

"So clever you think you are," Han said. "But your cleverness has caught up with you. I wondered why this launch was so important to you, why it was so critical that it not be delayed. Now I know."

"You know nothing."

"I know that you've recently made hundreds of millions of dollars' worth of short sales of American securities. Short sales made quietly through your uncle's trading companies in Hong Kong, and London, and New York. Your billionaire uncle arranged both the brokerage service and the loans."

"What of it?"

"The loans were secured by hundreds of millions of dollars in corporate guarantees. What corporation would be so foolish as to make such guarantees against such wild speculation? Yours, of course. China Aerospace and Technology."

James felt as if he'd been kicked in the stomach. If his father and President Xiang found out about Phase II. . .

"You're insane, you know."

"Insane, am I?" Han waved a sheaf of papers before James's face.

"What does this look like? Copies of each stock transaction. Copies of the guarantees. Even a copy of your plan."

"Where did you get—"

"From your pig of an uncle in Hong Kong. He agreed to cooperate when we confronted him with our suspicions and a little evidence. We can be highly persuasive." Han's eyes narrowed. "You had it all figured out, didn't you? You're a student of American history. Those who had the insight to sell short before the crash on Wall Street in 1929 not only kept their wealth, they made fortunes on the way down. Once the bottom was reached, they had massive amounts of capital to invest, buying up controlling interests in railroads, hotel chains, steel mills, for pennies on the dollar. Those were the men who became titans of industry."

"You don't know what you're talking about."

"You thought you were going to do the same thing. While a student in America you developed a sophisticated plan—Phase II, you called it—that involved selling massive amounts of stock short, stocks of leading U.S. corporations like Microsoft, and Exxon, and General Electric. After the launch of Raptor, when the U.S. economy had been crippled, you'd ride those stocks down to nothing, then buy them back for pennies. Like your filthy uncle, you'd become one of the world's richest men."

"You're crazy."

"There's only one problem," Han said. "The launch isn't going to happen. You're going to lose hundreds of millions of dollars you can't repay. Those notes are going to be called in, China Aerospace and Technology will have no choice but to cover them. Do you know the penalty for embezzlement of funds from a state-owned enterprise?"

James glared at him, eyes burning with rage. He started toward him.

Han's smirk vanished. He backed up until his legs came up against General Lao's desk. He tried to shrink back.

"Your father will be here any minute," he said. "He—"

James lunged for the old man's throat. Han's papers flew into the air. He croaked a protest. Blind with rage, James spun him around and forced him down across the desk. He twisted Han's head to the side and smashed it against the edge of the desk. Han went limp and slid to the floor. James stood back, breathing hard. The director lay still, not moving. The smell of the old man's excrement filled the room.

James dropped to his knees, lifted Han's head, then let it drop against the hardwood floor. He looked at his hands, disbelieving. What had he done?

Panicked, he came to his feet and locked the door to the study. *Prioritize.* First, he had to destroy Han's evidence. He scooped it up, located his father's shredder, and fed the documents in.

What next? *Think.* He had to verify what Han had said about the Americans knowing about the launch. He turned to the general's communication console, a huge board sitting at a right angle to his desk. The console was state-of-the-art with direct lines to every PLA ship and installation in the world, an exact duplicate of the one he had in his office. The boards were designed to control a war from either place. A call coming from those lines wouldn't be questioned. He picked up the handset and dialed the captain of *Zhuhai*.

"Captain Chen, this is Senior Colonel Lao. I've just spoken with Director Han Jinhua of the CSIS. He tells me that security has been breached. Is this true?"

"I'm afraid it is, Senior Colonel. I apologize for not—"

"Save your apologies. Tell me exactly what the Americans said, word for word."

James listened with mounting horror as Captain Chen related the details of what the American ship captain, a spy named Matthew Connor, had confessed to. His cousin Beth had indeed spied, had learned everything, and the Americans now knew it all. If anyone else talked to the prisoners, the launch would be delayed and he'd be finished.

"I don't believe a word of this," he said. "Send them to me for further interrogation."

"But General Lao's orders are to transfer them to Macau for further interro—"

"I just spoke with the general. His orders have changed. Bring them to me."

"To Beijing?"

"No, you fool. The command and control ship, the merchant vessel *Zenith*. You can't be far from her. She sailed from Guangzhou yesterday morning on a course to the launch site. You already know the location, 106 degrees east longitude on the equator. Chart a course to intercept the CCS. Fly them to the ship by helicopter. I'll get at the truth."

"It shall be done as you request."

"This isn't a request, damn you. It's an order from General First Class Lao Jianxing, vice-chairman of the Central Military Commission. Do you understand me?"

"Yes, Senior Colonel. I understand."

"Now listen carefully, Captain. You are to isolate the four spies. They are to have no further contact with anyone. No one is to speak to them under any circumstances, on your ship or during the transfer to the CCS."

"It shall be done."

"One more thing, Captain. You are never to speak of this matter to anyone. Do you understand?"

"I understand."

James hung up the phone. Two big problems had been solved, but a major one remained. Now that the Americans knew about the launch, he had to order protection for the command and control ship and the launch platform, and he had to do it quickly. He glanced at his watch. Twelve-fifty. His father would be home any minute.

He ran his finger down the list of military commands his father had taped to the communication console and found the code for the South Sea Fleet Command headquarters in Zhanjiang. He picked up the handset and punched in the code.

"This is General First Class Lao Jianxing, vice-chairman of the Central Military Commission."

"Yes, General." James could almost hear the snap to attention.

"I want an immediate naval escort for a highly sensitive shipment aboard the merchant vessel *Zenith*. The ship is sailing from Guangzhou to an area midway between Sumatra and Borneo. The coordinates are zero degrees latitude and 106 degrees east longitude. I want sufficient ships to screen the vessel, and I want them immediately."

"Yes, General. There's a task force of four ships in that immediate area conducting naval exercises. The destroyers *Zhuhai* and *Harbin*, and the frigates *Huainan* and *Huaibei*."

"Very well," James said. "I also want a submarine escort to cover any threat of foreign submarines."

"Yes, General. There are two Romeo-class diesel-electric submarines operating with the task force. One has had mechanical problems but was operational at last report."

"See to it immediately," James said.

"It shall be as you order, General."

James hung up the phone. Now for the fourth problem. He looked at Han's crumpled form, then unlocked the door to the study. He pressed the servant's button on his father's desk. Within seconds, Old Wang appeared in the door.

"Come in, Wang. There's been a dreadful accident."

The old man looked at Han's corpse sprawled on the floor. His mouth fell open.

"What has happened?"

"The poor man tripped on the rug and struck his head on the edge of the desk while he was waiting for the general. It happened just now."

Old Wang stood still, only his eyes moving back and forth between Han's body and James.

"Go, young master. Go now," he said. "The general and I won't be here forever. You must be the one to carry on. For China. The keys are in the limousine. Drive yourself to the airport."

James put his hand on the old man's shoulder. "Thank you, my old friend."

Wang's eyes almost smiled.

"Hurry now, before your father arrives. I'll take care of this. You were never here."

Chapter Seventeen

"W hat have they done to you?" Matt said.

Beth lay flat on the steel deck, dazed, trembling. He looked at her wrists. They'd been tightly bound with nylon cord right over the burns where the electrodes had been attached, just as his had been. Grimacing from the pain, he twisted his own wrists apart and placed a hand on her forehead.

"Careful," Beth said. "I think I'm radioactive."

"Those bastards. I'm so sorry you had to go through that."

"It was nothing compared to what the others. . ."

A pain shot through Matt. While the torture was going on, he'd repressed the memory of losing his ship. Now that it was over, the image of his ship and crew dying on the horizon came flooding back. Tears welled up in his eyes.

Beth looked up into his face. "I'm sorry. I didn't mean to remind you."

Matt tried to swallow. "I just can't believe they're gone."

"Was the ship insured?"

Matt smiled through his tears. Beth's little non sequitur was her way of getting his mind off his crew and suggesting that this was all a temporary situation that would come right in the end. Insurance. Jesus. Not that it mattered now, but the premiums on a ship that old would have broken him. It had taken all he had to buy provisions and fuel for this trip. Even if some miracle got them out of here and he claimed the reward money, the amount was about what he owed Gray Wolf. Any way you cut it, he was finished.

"Insurance is for pessimists."

He remembered the listening device and moved close to her ear. "I'm sorry, Beth. I should have listened to you."

She feebly shook her head. "You did what anyone would do. No one would believe it."

"You're not going to let me off that easy. I didn't *want* to believe it. I was in it for the money, just like you said. All I wanted to do was take you home and pick up a check."

She worked at a smile, still shaking.

"You take me home, and I'll see that you get it."

"If we get out of here, this one's on the house."

Who was he kidding? There was no way out of this. Charlie Shen lay unconscious on the deck a few feet away. Bing and his friend had been particularly brutal to a Chinese they saw as a traitor, even though he'd been born in the U.S. He looked at the bulkhead that separated the two compartments. Sam was in with them now. Matt had heard all the Chinese epithets for black people. He could only imagine what they'd do to a black man, someone they thought of as not quite human. He hadn't heard a sound coming through the bulkhead and didn't expect to. Sam was the strongest man he'd ever known, but he hoped he wouldn't try to be a hero. They'd all agreed they'd take just enough to make spilling their guts convincing.

He rubbed his face. There was no way out, but at least he had reason to hope there'd now be a naval escort of the command and control ship on its way to the launch site. Hopefully, someone would see it. The only thing he could do now was reinforce what they'd all said.

"Sorry it's turned out this way," he said in a normal voice.

"I still think the U.S. Navy will rescue us," Beth said, picking up on it.

"Nice thought," Matt said, "but they think we're dead. The truth is we've had it. This mission's been a total failure. I'm ashamed to admit, I cracked. I told them everything."

"Me too," Beth said. "I sang like a bird. I just couldn't take it."

"Poor Charlie," Matt said. "I wonder if he did any better."

"I doubt it," Beth said. "Not from the looks of him, anyway."

"Sam's a strong guy," Matt said. "He'll never give in."

After a few minutes, the grating sound of a chain rattled through the latch. The door opened and Sam came careening over the coaming. Wrists bound, he slammed against the opposite bulkhead, fell back, and collapsed on the deck. The door clanged shut behind him. He lay still, not moving. Matt hurried over to him.

"Sam. Sam! Are you okay?"

Sam's eyes opened. He winked at Matt.

"Sorry, Skipper. The little bastards were too much for me. I spilled my guts."

Matt let out the breath he'd been holding. "Don't worry about it, Sam. The rest of us didn't do any better."

A soft moan rose from Charlie. Matt and Sam went over to him.

Charlie's eyes fluttered, then opened. He started, not sure where he was. He looked at Matt, then at Sam.

"Anyone get the number of that truck?"

"It was in Chinese," Sam said.

"How do you feel?" Matt said.

"Rough." Charlie stuck out his swollen tongue and moved it around, as if to see if it still worked. "Any water in here? I think they boiled it all out of me."

"No," Matt said. "I tried to get some for Beth when they brought her back."

Charlie swallowed and tried to moisten his cracked lips.

"What time is it?"

"I don't know," Matt said. "They took my watch when they put on the electrodes. I think it's close to dawn."

"What do we do now?" Charlie said.

Matt hesitated. Now that Captain Chen had the information he wanted, that question answered itself. As soon as their monitors heard enough to be convinced of their confession, it would be the agreed upon bullet in the back of the head and a short trip off the fantail of the destroyer. He could see their weighted bodies drifting down into the depths of the South China Sea, bubbles billowing out of their mouths, hair shimmering in the light until all light was gone. It was the same picture he'd had of the man they'd picked up off the raft, the one who'd tried to kill him. He couldn't get it out of his mind.

"I don't know. Everybody just get some rest, try to restore yourselves. Sleep if you can."

He maneuvered his way back to where Beth lay. He wasn't sure why; he just wanted to be near her. There wasn't much time left. After a while he heard the sound of Charlie's heavy breathing and Sam's snoring.

"I don't get it," Beth said in a whisper, staring up at the overhead.

"Get what?" Matt whispered back.

"Where my cousin is, where my uncles are."

"I got a briefing on your family from the CIA. Your cousin heads up the largest tech company in China. One uncle's a billionaire in Hong Kong, another's a top general—"

"Not just *a* general. *The* general. He's vice chairman of the Central Military Commission, the top-ranked military officer in the country. He reports directly to the president of China. One word from him and this ship we're on would be doing somersaults to get us back."

"Why do you think he's been so quiet?"

"I don't know, but there'll be hell to pay when he finds out what these goons have done. Sinking your ship, killing everyone, torturing us."

"How can he not know? Did it ever occur to you that your relatives may be in on it?"

"Don't be ridiculous."

"Think about it. Your cousin's neck is on the line to get that thing launched. If they're going to use it to win a war, the general has to have it. I don't know what connection the money uncle could have, but there may be one. They can't have you blowing the whistle. Maybe it was your cousin who planted those documents."

"That's absurd. My family worships the ground I walk on, especially my cousin. He'd never allow me to be thrown in jail and tortured."

"The stakes are pretty high. You may be expendable."

Beth's trembling resumed. She rolled away from him. "That's a terrible thing to say."

Matt placed his hand on her thin upper arm. It was the only comfort he could offer. Gradually, her shaking subsided. She fell into a fitful sleep, breathing softly, trembling intermittently. He told himself to get some rest and try to pull himself together. He had no idea what he'd do when they came for them, but he'd have to think of something. He closed his eyes and drifted off into a tortured sleep.

The rattle of a chain through the door woke him. He had no idea how long he'd been asleep. The door swung open, and Sergeant Li stepped over the coaming.

"Up. Everyone up," he said, motioning with his assault rifle.

Matt helped Beth to her feet. She couldn't have slept long, but she looked better. Sam helped Charlie up. Corporal Wu took up station behind them, and Sergeant Li led the way out. Matt heard the faint whine of helicopter turboshafts warming up in the distance. They climbed the ladder to the main deck and blinked into the early morning light. The sun was just coming up, a thin red line on the horizon. A helicopter sat idling on the fantail of the destroyer, side door open, rotors spinning. It was another Z-8, identical to the one he'd shot down with the Stinger. Sergeant Li motioned them toward it.

So. Captain Chen had reneged on his promise not to torture Beth and the others, and now it looked like he was going to renege on the bullet in the back of the head they'd agreed on. They were going to fly them out over the horizon, and once they were out of sight of the destroyer, they'd push them out the door. If their captors were in a generous mood, they'd be shot first.

Matt elbowed Sam. "When I give you the nod, create a diversion, anything."

The four pulled themselves into the helicopter as best they could with their wrists bound and took seats on the bench, facing forward. Corporal Wu got in and sat facing them on the opposite bench, rifle cradled in his arms. Sergeant Li closed the door and waved the pilot off.

The helicopter lifted off and flew straight ahead, on the same course as the ship. Matt looked behind him. *Zhuhai* was slicing through green water at what appeared to be flank speed, white waves peeling out from the bow. He moved his hands closer to his belt. Once the helicopter was out of sight of the ship, Sam would create a diversion and Matt would retrieve the pistol. With Corporal Wu subdued and Matt's pistol to the head of the pilot, they might at least have a chance. It was a long shot. The pilot was talking into his helmet. He could alert the ship instantly and *Zhuhai* could blow them out of the sky with a missile. But it was the only chance they had.

Within minutes, the ship was out of sight and the helicopter was flying over open water. Matt braced himself, his muscles as tense as a steel spring waiting to recoil. Corporal Wu sat looking past them, blinking into the bright light, playing with a mole on his cheek. What was he waiting for? It made no sense to do something this risky until Wu made a move. Matt looked at Sam and shook his head almost imperceptibly. *Wait.*

What seemed like an hour went by with not so much as a glance from Corporal Wu. Where were they taking them? Based on the position of the sun they were flying toward the coast of China, in the direction of Macau or Guangzhou.

Matt shifted in his seat. More time passed, he couldn't tell how much. The helicopter began to slow. He tensed. This was it. The pilot would go into a hovering position while Corporal Wu did his work. He wasn't sure why they'd waited this long, but it was probably good. Any helicopter that flew over water would have a life raft. By now they'd be out of range of *Zhuhai*, and they were that much closer to land.

Not taking his eyes off Corporal Wu, Matt inched his fingers under his belt. Beth pressed her elbow into his ribs and nodded downward. He followed her gaze. The white wake of a large ship spread out across the sea. The curved wakes of smaller ships flowed out around it. From the air, it appeared to be a battle group. The little armada was on a southerly course, steaming directly toward them.

Matt motioned for Sam to look down. The helicopter began its descent toward the larger ship. Closer now, the vessel looked like a container ship. It had to be the CCS Beth had told him about. As they descended, the ships surrounding it came into focus. Two PLA Navy frigates and a destroyer, riding shotgun. Closer now, the hull number of the ship on the port side came into view. Five-forty-one. The ship on the starboard side bore the hull number 540. He knew them. *Huaibei* and *Huainan*, both Jiang Wei-class frigates.

The destroyer bringing up the rear looked familiar too. The bow came out of the water and he saw the number 112. She was the *Harbin*, a Luhu-class destroyer. He knew her, too. He'd played hide and seek with them all, just as he had *Zhuhai*. Based on the course *Zhuhai* was on, she was probably on her way to take up the forward position, completing the screen. With the destroyer traveling at flank speed, the two should intercept shortly.

His bluff had worked about the naval escort, but he had no idea why they were being taken to the command and control ship. It made no sense, but he was grateful for the reprieve.

"I told you," Beth said. "It's my cousin, James. I knew he'd come through."

Matt stared down, transfixed. There was no more beautiful sight than a formation of ships at sea. The sky was a bright, incandescent blue. Low-flying cumulus clouds billowed out like cauliflower against the sky. The morning sun cast a path of diamonds across a clear blue ocean. A band of seagulls floated behind the armada, sunshine glistening off white wings. The stunning sight, combined with the realization that they weren't going to die, choked him up.

The pilot circled around the armada, approached from the rear, and began his descent over the command and control ship. Matt stared down, awed by the size of it. The ship had to be 700 feet long with a displacement of 40,000 tons or more, the size of an Iowa-class battleship. The name painted on the fantail came into view. *Zenith,* just as Beth had said. The Z-8 lowered itself over the white circle painted on the after deck and settled down with a sigh. The engine throttled down, and the door slid open. Corporal Wu motioned them out with his rifle.

Matt came out first. He ducked his head and caught a glimpse of a feather, the slight wake of a periscope, trailing *Huaibei* on the port side. A diesel-electric boat. The Chinese had a few nuclear-powered subs, but a nuke would be running deeper than that. There was probably another sub trailing *Huainan* on the starboard side. Good. The more the better. It would be hard for the U.S. Navy to miss that much activity.

A middle-aged Chinese man wearing a business suit met them at the helipad. A security badge dangled from a chain around his neck.

"I'm Wong, aide-de-camp to Senior Colonel Lao Jintao."

Beth almost mobbed the man. "Jimmy? I mean James? James Lao of CAT? He's here?"

Wong didn't appear to approve of Beth Anglicizing his boss's name. He dipped his head in a curt nod.

"Thank God," Beth said. "Now we'll get some things straightened out."

Wong motioned for them to follow as if he wanted to get them out of sight quickly. He led the way down a narrow passageway between rows of deck containers, toward the superstructure of the ship. The containers were phony, made of plywood and painted gray to look like steel, just as Beth had said. Corporal Wu brought up the rear, rifle at the ready. A handful of crewmen on deck stopped what they were doing and stared at the group of prisoners, then quickly looked away.

Wong stepped into the superstructure and motioned for them to stop. A young Chinese security guard gave them a hurried pat-down with a disgusted look on his face, then motioned for them to walk through the frame of a metal detector. Matt let the others go through first. This would be the first test of just how undetectable the pistol hidden in his briefs was. The alarm beeped. Before the security guard could reach him, Matt pointed to his belt buckle. Grimacing from the pain of his bindings, he awkwardly pulled the belt off. He walked through the second time without incident. The guard stepped back, looking relieved that he wouldn't have to touch him. He snorted and waved his hand.

"They stink, but they're clean," he said in Mandarin.

Wong didn't smile. "Please follow me. I must ask you to speak to no one."

With Corporal Wu bringing up the rear, Wong led them up two levels into the superstructure of the ship, then down a passageway with offices on both sides. He herded them through a wooden door into a small room and left them alone with Corporal Wu.

"Allow them to speak to no one," Wong said in Mandarin. He pulled the door closed behind him.

Matt glanced around, trying to get his bearings. They were on the second deck of the superstructure, on the starboard side of the ship. The room they were in appeared to be a small anteroom adjacent to an office. Through the porthole, he could see the frigate *Huainan* cutting through the water alongside the ship, throwing up spray. Beth seemed nervous and excited. The door to the adjacent office was open a crack.

He backed up a step and opened it another inch with the heel of his boot. Leaning back, he caught a glimpse of a tall, slender Chinese man in a business suit standing behind a dark wooden desk. He looked to be in his early thirties or so and had the bearing of someone used to being in charge. He was engaged in an animated discussion in English with someone Matt could hear but couldn't see. From the man's accent and tone of authority, it might be the Russian captain Beth had spoken of. While she fidgeted and Corporal Wu stared at the *Huainan* racing alongside the ship, Matt inched backward, closer to the door.

". . . and now here's another one," the man with the Russian accent was saying. "First you, not an hour ago, and now these people. I don't like unscheduled helicopter landings on my ship."

"That's not your concern, Captain."

"The bloody hell it's not. With the rocket fuel we're carrying and a deck load of wooden containers, all it takes is one mishap."

"You forget your place, Captain. I'm in charge here."

"No, Senior Colonel, you're not. You're only in charge of the launch. I'm responsible for the safe operation of the ship. Which brings me to another point. Why the sudden naval escort? We're supposed to be launching a simple communications satellite, not going to war."

"Normal precautions. The area we're sailing through around Singapore is well known for pirates."

"Pirates? You can't be serious. A ship this size has nothing to fear from a handful of pirates in an inflatable boat. And even if we did, don't you think two frigates, two destroyers, and two submarines are a bit much?"

"Again, that's not your concern, Captain."

"It *is* my concern. If the ship's in any danger, I have a right to know."

"The ship's in no danger, I assure you."

There was a pause.

"All right. You can have your naval escort if it makes you happy, but I don't like the way these people are being treated. Herded off the helicopter like convicts. Who are they?"

"They're my guests."

"With their hands tied, and a gun at their back? From what I saw, they don't appear to be enjoying your hospitality."

"As you said, your concern is with the operation of the ship."

"The safe operation of the ship. I won't have people being herded around at gunpoint on a ship loaded with kerosene and liquid oxygen. One stray bullet and the whole thing could go up."

"You've made your point, Captain."

"You can easily restrict them from sensitive areas, that's up to you. Without the proper security badges and uniform they can't go anywhere, but they're to be untied and given food and water and a decent place to sleep. There are no prisoners on my ship unless I say so."

"Very well, Captain. But there's one thing I want to make absolutely clear. No one other than myself and my aide is to speak to them. Under any circumstances. That includes you."

Matt's brain went into overdrive. This was the third time he'd heard that in the five minutes he'd been aboard. Why so adamant about keeping them quiet? There could only be one reason. Lao was the only one outside of Captain Chen who knew what they'd "confessed" to and didn't want anyone else to know. Beth was in for a big letdown. Her cousin hadn't brought them there to save them. He'd brought them there to verify for himself who Matt had told and to keep them from talking to anyone else until the launch was over. Once it was, he'd have them killed.

"Suit yourself," the captain said, his voice trailing off, "but I want them released and that soldier, or whatever he is, disarmed at once." Matt heard a door slam.

"Take care of it, then bring in the man named Connor," he heard the senior colonel say to someone he couldn't see.

Matt stepped away from the door just as Wong opened it.

"Release them," Wong said in Mandarin. "Remove the clip from that rifle and unload it."

"It's about time," Beth said, holding out her hands. "When can I see James?"

Wong didn't answer her. He waited for Corporal Wu to remove Matt's bindings. "Mr. Connor? This way, please." He nodded toward the office door.

"Hey, what about me?" Beth said.

Wong ignored her and ushered Matt toward the door. Matt walked into the office ahead of him, rubbing his wrists. Wong closed the door and positioned him in front of the desk. Matt glanced around for the captain, but he was gone.

"May I present Senior Colonel Lao Jintao, chairman and managing director of China Aerospace and Technology."

Matt studied him. A senior colonel in the PLA was the equivalent of a brigadier general in the U.S., and chairman and managing director made him CEO of the largest aerospace company in China. Even wearing the corporate uniform—navy pin-striped suit, white shirt, and silk tie—he looked too young to be either. A security badge hung from a bead chain around his neck. The badge was trimmed with a green border, unlike the one Wong wore, which was orange. Given the senior colonel's status, green must mean unlimited access.

"Commander Connor, I presume," James Lao said.

"That's me."

"You've been busy."

Matt shrugged. "Idle hands . . ."

Lao flashed a Jimmy Carter smile. "And how are you enjoying your time with my cousin Beth?"

Matt thought he looked a little jealous. "She's delightful. Beautiful. Intelligent. Caring. Hard to imagine she's related to you."

Lao's smile slipped a rung. "Beth has always had an overactive imagination. I understand from Captain Chen that she's told you some wild tale right out of Star Wars."

Matt raised his eyebrows and waved a hand to indicate the command ship and the escorts. "So far it seems to be checking out."

"He also said you've passed this nonsense along to . . ."

"CINCPAC. Commander in Chief, Pacific."

Lao sighed. "The arrogance of the U.S. never ceases to amaze me. 'Commander in Chief, Pacific.' As though America owns the Pacific Ocean."

"We do," Matt said, "I assure you."

Lao's face began searching for an expression. A smile caught, but it didn't hold.

"And exactly when, where, and how did you make this contact?"

"Is that why you brought us here?"

"Answer my question."

"In the early morning hours of the fourteenth, by satellite phone to the USS *Observation Island*, an intelligence-gathering ship off the coast of China. From there it went to Admiral Vern Taylor, from there to the president."

Lao studied Matt's face. He shook his head. "I can tell by your eyes that you're lying. You may have fooled Captain Chen, but you haven't fooled me. I don't believe your story for a minute."

He'd brought them there to interrogate them, but his mind was already made up. What was up with this guy? He seemed to have everything. Why was he so intent on starting a war with America?

"I can see you don't," Matt said. "That must be why you ordered this screen of warships."

"Merely a precautionary measure."

Matt bristled. "Did you also give the order to sink my ship and kill my crew?"

"Get over yourself, Commander. In a war, people die."

"Yes, they do, and you'll be next."

"Not likely. Even on the outside chance that you did make contact, I doubt you'd be taken seriously. And even if you were, America isn't about to make a preemptive strike."

"That's what Saddam thought."

"And even if they did, nothing will get by this screen."

"You mean these obsolete frigates and destroyers? The U.S. Navy wouldn't waste a shell on them. They'll just send out a nuclear-powered attack boat and wait for you to set up the rocket on the launch pad. One torpedo and it's all over. It's probably there now, waiting for you."

"We have submarines too, Commander. I'm not worried."

"I would be. Time is running out."

"Yes, time is running out. For you.

"The door burst opened and Beth flew into the office, Corporal Wu tugging at her from behind. "James, what the hell is going on here?" She struggled with Wu, who was trying to pull her back through the door. "Let go of me, you asshole."

Lao nodded to Wu. "Release her."

Beth shook herself free and stood glaring at Lao. "What's up with this? You're not going to see me?"

"Hello, Beth. You've lost weight."

"No shit. Do you have any idea what I've been through the last three months?"

"Sorry, but it couldn't be helped."

"What the hell does that mean? You could have gotten me out of there with one phone call. Your father sure as hell could have."

"That wasn't possible."

Beth stared at the security badge hanging from Lao's neck as though seeing it for the first time. "What are you doing here?"

"Senior Colonel Lao is in charge of the launch," Matt said.

Beth looked at Matt, then back to James.

"Is that true?"

"Some projects are too important to be delegated."

Beth stared at him with a stricken look. She pressed the heels of her hands against her forehead. "What are you saying? Was it you? Did you plant those documents? Did you put me in there?"

"For all the good it did." He threw an angry glance at Matt, then turned to Wong. "Take them below and assign them staterooms. One for the three men and a separate one for Ms. Grayson. Put them in the Russian crew section. The filthy Russians are too stupid to speak another language. Post armed guards outside their door. They're not to leave their rooms under any circumstances."

"James, what in the hell are you doing? It's me, Beth."

"Then get back here," James said to Wong. "We have work to do."

Wong gathered them up over Beth's shouts of protest and escorted them to an elevator that went down four levels. Corporal Wu followed. They stepped off into an area marked "Crew's Quarters" in Russian, Chinese, and English. Beth had told him that half the technicians aboard the CCS were Chinese. It looked to Matt like the support staff was exclusively Chinese. Wong motioned for an old woman pushing a cleaning cart to follow him. She scurried along behind, fumbling with a ring of keys in her apron. He found two adjacent staterooms that appeared to be unoccupied.

"Put them here and here," he said in Mandarin. "Get them food, towels, blankets, and whatever else they need. Is it understood?"

"Yes, master," the old woman said.

He turned to Corporal Wu. "I'll send down more guards in a few minutes. They're not to leave their rooms. No one is to speak to them. Do you understand?"

"*Wo dong*," Corporal Wu said. I understand.

Wong turned on his heel and left as quickly as they'd come. Corporal Wu took up station opposite the two staterooms. He slumped down on the deck with his back against the bulkhead, his empty rifle across his lap. The old woman pointed to the three men and motioned them toward the first stateroom.

"Thank you, elder sister," Beth said in Mandarin.

"*Bu yong xie.*" No need to thank.

"As you can see, I'm not well. Surely you wouldn't separate a wife from her husband at such a time?"

Matt stared at her.

The old housekeeper smiled a toothless grin and wagged her finger. "*Xiao cong ban doufu, yi qing er bai.*" Like scallions on tofu, it's green and white.

Matt's Mandarin teacher had battered him with that old saw every time he'd been stumped. It was the Chinese way of saying, "It's as plain as the nose on your face."

"I can never be fooled about such things," the old woman said.

"The minute I looked at you two, I said to myself, 'Those two are one.'"

"*Ni zheng congming.*" You're so smart. Beth smiled at Matt. "Come along, dear." Leaving Sam and Charlie smiling, she opened the door with one hand and pulled Matt in with the other.

Matt closed the door behind him and leaned against it with his arms folded.

"So we're married?"

"Don't get any ideas, buster."

"I'm fresh out of ideas."

Beth started to pace. "That rotten son of a bitch. He used me. He knows I'm a pacifist. I hate the military, hate the thought of war, especially between China and the U.S., the two countries I love most in the world. He lured me over on false pretenses, then expropriated my work for military purposes. When I figured out what was going on, I went to him and raised hell. I thought he was as innocent as I was about the whole thing, how they were planning to use the satellite. Now I can see—he was heading it up all along. He had those documents planted in my room to shut me up, get me out of the way. He sent me to prison, for God's sake. His own cousin."

"He could have had you killed."

"He wouldn't go that far." Beth stifled a sob. "The bastard. I don't know what's happened to him. He told me he loved me when we were kids. I trusted him."

"Let's find a way to screw up his plans," Matt said.

"That's why you're here." Her face brightened. "I've got a plan and I'll need you to pull it off."

"What is it?"

"I'm still working on it."

Matt locked the door behind him. "In the meantime, there's something I've got to do." He reached into his briefs and pulled out the pistol. "This thing's been killing me."

Beth actually laughed. "Well, you're just full of surprises. What else have you got in there?" Her face instantly colored. "I'm sorry, I didn't mean . . ."

Matt chuckled. "I know you didn't."

There was a soft rap on the door behind him. He slid the pistol into his hip pocket and opened it a crack. Two of the ship's security guards had been posted by the door, along with Corporal Wu. The old woman bustled past them with two small cardboard boxes and a stack of towels.

"It's just a box lunch left over from the night crew. What the Russians eat." She reached into her apron pocket and came out with a tube of something. "Tiger Balm ointment. For your wounds."

"*Ni dui women tai hao le,*" Beth said. You've been too good to us.

The old woman's face lit up. "Here are clean towels. I'll bring more food later, but I won't disturb you two. I'll just leave it outside the door."

The woman left and Matt and Beth stood looking awkwardly at each other.

"Look," Beth said. "This is embarrassing, but I've got to get cleaned up."

"Go ahead." Matt picked up the boxes. "I'll fix dinner."

While Beth showered, Matt laid out the contents of the boxes on the small table. Sandwiches made out of some kind of processed meat on coarse Russian rye bread, a container of plain yogurt, an apple, a wedge of chocolate cake wrapped in clear cellophane, and a bottle of Russian beer. He laid out the white napkins as place mats, arranged the food as attractively as he could, and poured the warm beer into plastic cups. Beth emerged from the bathroom wearing a terrycloth robe. Framed by the collar, her face seemed more beautiful than ever. Matt tried not to look at her.

"I know, I know. I look terrible, but at least I'm clean."

"You look terrific." Matt spread his hands. "And dinner's ready."

"It looks wonderful, but I'll wait for you. There's another robe behind the door." Beth smiled at him. "One size fits none."

Matt took a quick shower, washing out his underclothes at the same time. He hung them over the shower curtain rod next to Beth's and pulled on the robe. He could tell by the tie around his waist that he'd lost weight. He ran a hand through his wet hair and stepped out into the room.

"Let's eat." He picked up his plastic cup and waited for Beth to pick up hers. They touched the rims together. "To life."

"To life," Beth said. "I thought it was all over when we got on that helicopter."

"So did I." Matt took a bite of the sandwich. The bread was as dry as sawdust, but it tasted delicious.

"Then I thought we were saved, my cousin had finally come to the rescue. Now we're in deeper than ever."

"He brought us here to satisfy himself that we haven't made contact with the outside world. Funny thing. I got the sense that his mind was already made up on that score. It was like no matter what I said, the launch has to come off, come hell or high water."

"No one's ever had much luck telling James anything he didn't want to hear."

"The other reason he had us brought here—maybe the main one—is to keep us quiet. We'll probably be okay until the launch is over. After that. . . ."

"James wouldn't do that. He's a rat, but he's no killer."

"Someone ordered my crew killed."

"Captain Chen."

"On his own? No chance. He had to have orders from Beijing."

Beth didn't answer. They ate the rest of the meal in silence. Matt cleared the table away.

"Now, what about this plan of yours?"

"We wait until everyone's asleep. Then we sneak out, find the satellite, and sabotage it."

"Wow, what a great plan. Why didn't I think of that?"

"Listen, I helped design that thing. All we have to do is find a way to get to it. I can disable it in such a way that they'll never know. They'll get it into orbit and it won't work. It'll be just another piece of space junk floating around out there."

"Sounds like a piece of cake. All we have to do is get past two— or is it three—guards outside the door, then prowl around the ship for an hour or so to find it, then get into a highly restricted area, then roll up our sleeves and get to work on that baby. I'm sure no one will notice."

"I haven't quite worked out all the details yet, but . . ."

"Let me know when you do." Matt picked up the tube of medicine. "Let's have a look at those burns."

He squeezed a drop of ointment onto the tip of his index finger and moved his chair closer to Beth's. He leaned in toward her and tenderly rubbed ointment on the burns around her wrists.

"What are those from?" Beth said, looking at his chest.

Matt glanced down at the burn scars on the left side of his chest and shrugged the robe closed.

"Wounds from another life."

"On the submarine?"

Matt glanced up at her.

"It wasn't exactly a secret that you were a submarine officer."

"I'm sure you disapprove."

"I disapprove of everything military," Beth said. "The world would be a better place if none of it existed."

"Including guns? Then maybe I'd better get rid of that pistol."

"Not just yet."

Matt smiled. "Therein lies the problem. If the good people give up their guns, the bad people will still have theirs."

"I've heard all those arguments before," Beth said. "You're not going to change my mind." She peered at Matt's chest again. "What happened?"

"Fire. My old nemesis. It was only a matter of time before it caught up with me."

"How?"

Matt looked at her. He'd never talked about it before with anyone, but for reasons he couldn't explain, he wanted to tell Beth. Maybe it was because there wasn't much time left.

"It happened one Christmas Eve. I was twelve. My little brother, Eric, was ten. I woke up in the middle of the night, smelled smoke. His room was at the other end of the hall. My dad was at sea and I was the man of the house, but there I stood, frozen with fear, doing absolutely nothing. I can still see his face melting into the flames."

"You were twelve."

"Been afraid of fire ever since. Faked it all through the academy. In firefighter's school I was a wreck, but I got through it. I worried about it for years, what would I do if there were ever a fire on the sub, and then it happened."

"How did it start?"

"In the galley, that's where most fires start. But the point is I froze up, just like I did back then. I hesitated. That's all it took. By the time I got in there, a man had died."

"But the point is, you went in."

Matt shook his head. "The worst part, after the fire was out, I freaked, went completely nuts. A severe and instant case of claustrophobia. I couldn't stand it down there. Sam was a master chief, leading a SEAL team aboard for a special assignment we were on. He saw it right away. I don't remember what I was doing, but he hit me so hard he knocked me cold. He half carried me into my stateroom, got the chief corpsman to shoot me with something they reserve for nut cases, kept me doped up and in my room until we got to the nearest port. The word was that I'd been injured in the fire. Only Sam and the skipper and the chief knew what was really going on." He gave her a wretched look. "Can you imagine? The executive officer of the boat falling apart like that. You don't know how much I've hated myself."

"I want to see them."

Matt pulled the robe closer. "No, you don't."

Beth hesitantly opened the top of his robe. Matt didn't stop her. She gently traced the scars on his chest with her fingertips.

"They're not so bad."

Matt looked into her eyes. He'd never seen a look of caring like that from anyone before, certainly not from Barbara. He came to his feet and pulled her to him.

She fell into his arms and let her head rest on his chest for a few seconds, then pulled away.

"No, Matt," she said. "We can't. Maybe if we ever get out of here, but not now."

He held both her hands in his and gazed at her with a sad little smile.

"You're right," he said.

"Get some sleep," she said. "We've got a lot of work to do tonight."

"Oh, we're back to that again, are we?"

Beth nodded. "Don't worry. I can be real creative."

Chapter Eighteen

"Matt, wake up."

Matt felt long thin fingers pressing into his back, raking him awake. He rolled over and squinted into the light coming from the bathroom. Beth was hovering over him, kneeling on the edge of his bed, bouncing up and down like a little kid, smiling from ear to ear.

"What is it?"

"Wake up, sleepyhead. We've got work to do."

He blinked. She was wearing a blue jumpsuit with some kind of logo above the breast pocket. A security badge dangled from a bead chain around her neck.

"Where did you get that?"

Grinning, Beth jingled a ring of keys between her thumb and forefinger.

"I went exploring while you were asleep. The old Chinese housekeeper snores like a train."

"Are you crazy?"

"Probably."

"Where was Wu? Where were the others?"

"Fast asleep, poor guys. The housekeeper left a pot of tea for us. I dumped in two boxes of Dramamine tablets and took it out to the guys. They scolded me for being out of my room but took the tea. I guess they thought it would help them stay awake."

"Where'd you get Dramamine?"

"The medicine chest. Every room has some."

Matt rubbed his eyes and looked around.

"What time is it?"

Beth retrieved a small watch with a metal band from the front pocket of the jumpsuit and peered at it in the dim light.

"According to Alena's watch, it's 0200. That's two a.m. to you."

"Who's Alena?"

She pointed a thumb toward the picture on her security badge. "Alena Petrov, payload specialist. She's a sound sleeper too, but she

271

has good taste in underwear. Come on. You've been asleep for hours."

Matt looked at the green border on the badge, then at the logo on her jumpsuit, a springing tiger superimposed over a rocket at lift-off, the initials C.A.T. embroidered in red above it. He sat up.

"What have you done?"

"What women do. Men are hunters, we're gatherers."

She went to her bed and picked up a folded blue jumpsuit with a stack of clean white underwear on top. She tossed the clothes to Matt and draped a security badge trimmed in green around his neck.

"Matt Connor, meet Danya Baklanov, another payload specialist. Also a heavy sleeper, and like all men, he has no taste in underwear. Come on, get up. Let's go."

"And do what?"

"You're a junkman, you should know how to make junk."

"I know how to salvage it, not make it."

Beth put her face close to his. "We can fix this. I figured everything out while you were asleep. Just help me get close to that satellite."

Matt looked at her. "You're crazy, you know."

"Look, I've thought it through. It's the only thing we can do."

"What if these people whose ID's and clothing you've stolen wake up?"

"Stolen is such a nasty word. I like filched better. They won't. They won't be needed until later." She shrugged. "At least, I don't think so."

"You don't think so."

"I'm pretty sure. They're assembling the rocket as we speak, in an environmentally controlled hangar somewhere. Then they'll mate it with the payload. That's when Alena, and Danya, and whoever else, get involved."

Matt took her by the arms. He'd never seen her so hyperactive. "Beth, calm down and listen to me. Do you know what you're saying? It's a bullet in the back of the head if we get caught. There won't be any reprieve for this one."

Beth sighed. "I've thought about that, too. Look. Let's be honest.

We're never going to be any older than we are right now. We're not getting out of this, my cousin will see to that. If he ordered your entire crew killed, he won't hesitate to kill us. Either way, we're dead, so let's get this thing stopped."

Matt looked at her. He was seeing someone he hadn't seen before.

"I wish I'd met you a long time ago," he said.

"You wouldn't have been interested. Geek city."

"Beth . . ."

"Come on, Matt. We can do it. What's the worst that can happen?"

Matt sighed. "I don't want to see you get hurt. Ever."

Beth smiled, her eyes sparkling.

"Oh, really?"

Matt brushed a wisp of hair from her forehead. "Really."

"Well, that gives me just that much more incentive to survive. Let's go."

"No." He swung out of bed. "*I'll* do it. Tell me where it is."

"I'm . . . not exactly sure. I know the satellite has to be stored close to the payload unit of the rocket. I just don't know exactly where. Anyway, you wouldn't have a clue what to do to disable it, once you found it."

"I'll think of something." Matt picked up the pistol lying on his nightstand. "If nothing else, I'll put a bullet in it."

"Oh, that's so damn typical. Men always have to shoot something. Then someone shoots you. Can't you think of any solutions that aren't violent?"

"Oh that's right. You're a pacifist."

"You say that as if there's something wrong with it."

"Sometimes you have to use violence to stop bad people from doing bad things."

"Well, not in this case." Beth looked into his eyes. "Help me find it. I can disable it in such a way that they'll never know. They'll get it into orbit and it won't work. We can stop this whole thing without anyone getting hurt."

Her intensity was like a physical force. Finally he nodded. "All right. Let's go see what we can find. Only this time together."

"Now you're talking."

Matt pulled on the clean T-shirt. He checked the safety on the pistol and shoved it down inside his briefs.

Beth watched with an amused look on her face. "I think you're beginning to like that."

"If we're caught, I can't let them find it. It's our only ace in the hole."

"Just make sure it doesn't go off. That could change our whole relationship."

Matt stepped into the cotton overalls and pulled the zipper up. The blue jumpsuit was similar to the poopy suits U.S. submariners wore as under-way uniforms. The legs were a little short, but other than that, not a bad fit. He looked at the black and white picture on the security badge. The plump face of Danya Baklanov, payload specialist, stared back at him. The Russian appeared to be in his mid-fifties and was as bald as an egg.

"I don't look a thing like this guy."

"There are over two hundred and fifty people aboard this ship, all nationalities," Beth said. "Chinese, Russians, Swedes, Lithuanians. Most of them working together for the first time. So long as no one looks at our pictures real close, we'll be okay."

"How do they get around the language thing?"

"It's only a problem in launch control, an area of the ship that looks like mission control in Houston. Teams of technicians sitting in front of consoles, TV monitors overhead, the whole thing. They have two launch teams, one Chinese-speaking and one Russian-speaking. There's a two-way translation service that keeps them on the same page."

Matt pulled the pant legs down on his jumpsuit. He felt awkward, but he thought Beth looked the part.

He glanced at the picture on her badge. Alena Petrov was a hard-looking character. If they were discovered, he thought he'd rather face a brigade of marines. He looked back and forth between the picture and Beth's face, then smiled.

"No contest."

"I think you're biased."

Matt looked into her eyes, unnerved at the thought of any harm coming to her. He forced himself to focus on the business at hand.

"Okay, where do we go?"

"Logically, the assembly hangar should be on the first deck below the main deck."

"Why?"

"Because the rocket has to be tilted up to transfer it to the launch pad."

"What about the satellite?"

"That has to be located near the rocket, and it has to be stored in a separate compartment, in an environmentally controlled clean room. Logically, the compartment has to be near the nose cone. We'll know it when we see it."

"What makes you think these badges will get us in?"

"Alena and Danya are payload specialists. They have to have access to the satellite."

They were also green, the same color Beth's cousin was wearing. With the senior colonel's ego, green had to mean unlimited access. He nodded.

"All right. Peek out and see where the boys are."

Beth opened the door a crack. "Exactly where they were before. They haven't moved."

Matt stepped over the boxed meals left by the old Chinese housekeeper and pulled the door closed behind him. He steered Beth toward the exit, walking as softly as he could. Corporal Wu sat sleeping on the deck a few feet away from the two snoring security guards with his rifle across his lap. The clip had been removed, but it wouldn't take the marine long to reload it if he woke up.

Closer now, Matt could see that there was little chance of that. Corporal Wu looked dead to the world, with his head leaning into the corner and his mouth ajar. Beth's Dramamine-laced tea, combined with the gentle rolling of the ship, had lulled him into a deep unconscious state.

"Okay, where do we go from here?" he said when they were safely outside the crew's quarters.

"We need to go up three levels," Beth said. "Let's find the elevator."

"That looks like a road map ahead." Matt walked up to a brass engraving mounted on the bulkhead. "Here we are. Emergency exits. There's an elevator."

Matt lowered his head as they walked toward the elevator, but the people he passed along the way didn't seem any more eager than he was to make eye contact at two in the morning. He stepped up and pressed the elevator button, hoping they'd have the car to themselves. The door opened and two men and a woman drifted out, going in different directions. Matt stepped in and touched the button with the close arrows. Before the door closed all the way, a hand slid in between the gaskets. The door bucked open and a man wearing a blue jumpsuit stepped in. He nodded to Matt and said something that sounded like Russian.

Matt could tell by the tone that it was just friendly conversation, but he didn't have a clue what the man had said. He smiled and nodded.

The elevator door opened. Hanging back, Matt steered Beth in the same direction the man had walked. They followed him toward a set of swinging double doors with people in blue jumpsuits going in and coming out. A plump Chinese security guard stood at the door, checking badges. He gave theirs a cursory look and motioned them through.

Matt walked through the door and looked around in wonder. The assembly hangar looked like a floating aerospace factory, with a shop floor the length of a football field. Gantry cranes moved overhead on tracks, flashing red and white lights, sounding monotonous beeps. Technicians in blue jumpsuits clustered around the assembly points, joining the three stages of the rocket. The engines of the first stage flared out before him. He craned his neck to see the opposite end of the hangar.

Feeling conspicuous, he picked up a clipboard from a metal shop desk. Nothing gave you authority like a clipboard. He motioned toward the other end of the hangar and spoke in a normal voice, not concerned about being overheard in the din of the hangar.

"Think it's up there?"

Beth nodded. "It has to be."

Walking along the perimeter of the shop floor, skirting small work groups, Matt couldn't help stealing glances at the gray and white rocket laid out alongside him. There seemed to be no end to it. He counted his footsteps. The first stage had to be well over a hundred feet long.

The second stage was somewhere in the neighborhood of forty feet long. The third stage appeared to be about half that. The first and second stages were already joined together. The bulk of the activity seemed to be centered around joining the third stage with the second.

Approaching the payload unit, Matt could see that it added another forty feet or so to the overall length of the rocket. He couldn't get over the size of the thing. It had to be at least fifteen feet wide at the widest point, and well over two hundred feet long.

He came to a stop by the nose cone, amazed they'd gotten this far without being challenged. He held the pencil to the clipboard as though discussing something on it with Beth.

"Okay, Sherlock, where's the satellite? If it's already inside, we're screwed."

"It wouldn't be mated yet. It has to be around here somewhere." Beth pointed to an imaginary item on the clipboard and glanced around.

Matt followed her eyes to a large door off to the side. Looking up, he could see a gantry crane track that ran on a curved path from the payload unit to the door Beth was looking at, like a railroad spur. Next to the large door was a smaller door with a Chinese security guard posted by it. They glanced at each other and started for the door.

The guard saw them coming and pulled himself upright. He handed Beth a clipboard with a sign-in sheet. Matt glanced down and felt his insides go cold. The signatures on the sheet were in Russian or Chinese. There was no way he could fake either. To his amazement, Beth scribbled a name in what looked like Russian and without hesitating signed another name on the line below. She marked the time on both lines with a flourish and handed it back.

"*Ni zai gan shenme?*" What are you doing? The guard pointed to Matt, then to the sign-in sheet.

Beth jerked her head toward Matt and said in Mandarin, "He thinks he's too important to sign his own name."

The guard looked at Matt with dull eyes. "Who is he, this big-shot friend of yours?"

"He's no friend of mine," Beth said. "He's my boss."

The guard looked at the signatures. Matt could tell by the look on his face that he couldn't read them, but it would be a loss of face to admit it. The guard shrugged.

"All bosses are the same." He waved them through.

Matt closed the door and slumped against it, relieved to be inside, amazed to see that they had the compartment to themselves.

"I didn't know you knew Russian."

"I don't. Those signatures are gibberish."

Matt nodded toward the door. "Should we lock it?"

"No, that would set off all kinds of alarms. If someone comes in, we'll just have to fake it."

Matt felt a chill go through him. He chalked it up to the cold artificial air of the clean room.

"Let's get it done and get out of here. Where is it?"

"Right in front of you."

Matt looked up. A black sphere the size of a small car sat on a stainless steel dolly, connected by cables to several pieces of monitoring equipment and a power supply. A movable scaffold with steps leading up to a work platform stood next to the satellite.

"What do we do?"

"I don't know."

"What the hell do you mean, you don't know?"

"Calm down, I need to think."

"Jesus Christ," Matt said. "You said you knew how to disable it."

"I do, sort of."

"Sort of?"

"Shut up. I need to figure this out." Beth started pacing. "If we can disconnect the onboard computer that controls the thermal management system . . . ." She looked up. "That panel up there, the one that looks like a triangle with rounded corners?"

"I see it."

"I think the control panel's behind that."

"You *think*?"

"It has to be. They have to have access to the control panel. It has to be in there."

"You'd better be right."

"We've got to get it off."

"It's held on with torque screws. You need an air gun to get them out."

"Too noisy. We'll have to do it by hand."

"Okay, but you'd better be right."

Matt found a small kit on a workbench with a ratchet screwdriver and every size of torque bit he was likely to need. Beth had maneuvered the platform into position and was waiting for him on the work station, looking at the panel. He mounted the steps and tried three bit sizes before he found the right one, a T-20. He slipped the bit into the screwdriver and started backing out a screw. It took all the strength he had to break the seal and get it started, but once he had, it turned easily.

"What do we do once we get this thing off?" he said, spinning the ratchet.

"We'll disconnect the on-board computer that controls the thermal management system of the laser, the part I designed. There should be six wires. Disconnect the green one. It won't work, but it won't show up in their diagnostics. At least it shouldn't."

Matt worked in silence for several minutes, breaking seals, backing out screw after screw.

"This is taking too long," he said, glancing over his shoulder at the door. "There are a million screws in this thing, each one an inch long and with fine threads. Can't we use the air gun?"

"Too much noise. They'd hear it outside the compartment." Beth started down the ladder. "I'll see if I can find another screwdriver.

Maybe if you can get them started, I can back them out."

To relieve the tedium, Matt made it a little contest to see how many screws he could get out before she got back. He got caught up in the process and lost track of how long she'd been gone. He had the procedure down now, and it was going faster. He removed the last screw and lifted the panel off. He poked his head inside. A stainless-steel panel with multi-colored wires connected to it lay before him.

"Did you say the green wire?"

Beth didn't answer.

Matt pulled back and felt the cold muzzle of a pistol against the back of his head.

"Turn around slowly," he heard a voice say.

He turned around. His stomach turned to ice. One of the Chinese security guards was standing behind Beth with one hand over her mouth and a pistol pressed against her temple. A woman he recognized from the picture on Beth's badge as Alena Petrov was standing by the door in blue jeans and zoris, pointing at Beth, trembling with rage.

"Are you certain the satellite's not harmed?" James said, pacing behind his desk.

"We've gone over it ten times," Wong said.

"Go over it again. And as far as those incompetent guards are concerned—"

"In all fairness," Wong said, "the woman put drugs in their tea—"

"Tea? What the hell were they doing down there, having a party? Stupid, incompetent bastards. They should all be executed."

Captain Ivanov said, "I don't understand why the Americans would want to sabotage a simple communications satellite. What could possibly motivate them to do such a thing?"

"Who knows what motivates Americans?" James said.

"Anyway, they couldn't have done anything," the captain said. "They weren't in there long enough."

"No thanks to you," James said. "You may as well have given them a key to the ship."

"I'd like to remind you, Senior Colonel, that bringing them aboard the ship was your idea, not mine."

"That may be, but believe me when I tell you, they'll never have an opportunity to do it again." He turned to Wong. "Arrange for a transfer back to *Zhuhai*, then get rid of them."

"I forbid it," Captain Ivanov said.

James glared at him. "You? Forbid? This is all your fault. You're in no position to forbid anything."

"I've told you before. There'll be no transfers on or off this ship unless I say so. It's dangerous and unnecessary. I'd also like to remind you that we're running a business here, the purpose of which is to make a profit, not commit murder."

"And I'd like to remind you that China Aerospace and Technology owns a controlling interest in that business."

"No, sir, you do not. CAT is a forty-percent owner. Russia is also a forty-percent owner, and our Swedish and Lithuanian partners own ten percent each."

"The government of China is paying for this launch and I represent the government. I'm the customer here."

"Yes, Senior Colonel, for this launch the Chinese government is the customer, just as we expect to have many more commercial satellite customers in the future. And as the customer that gives you certain rights, but endangering the ship by unnecessarily transferring people around isn't one of them."

"And just what do you propose to do with them?"

"I'll consign them to quarters, under guard."

"Like you did before. Don't you have a brig on this ship?"

"What the bloody hell would we need a brig for? This ship was designed to accommodate professional people."

"I want the four of them confined to a single room, with the door barred from the outside. I want armed guards over them, day and night."

"All right. You can have your barred door and armed guards. When we get to the launch site you can transfer them to one of your bloody warships. What you do with them after that is not my concern."

Captain Ivanov slammed the door behind him.

James slumped down in his chair.

"Check the satellite again, Wong. Make absolutely certain it's in perfect operating condition."

"At once, Senior Colonel," Wong said, backing out of the room.

James rubbed his face in his hands. He'd very nearly been ruined. His cousin had almost succeeded in disabling the satellite in such a way that he'd never have known until it was in orbit. Not even death was a punishment that would fit this crime. It had been a mistake at the start not to kill her, but he couldn't quite bring himself to kill sweet little Beth. This is what he got for being a sentimental, love-sick fool. It was a mistake he was now prepared to correct. He picked up the phone.

"Get me the commanding officer of *Zhuhai*."

After a minute he heard the voice of Captain Chen over the rumbling of the destroyer.

"Yes, Senior Colonel?"

"Listen to me carefully, Captain. These are your new orders. Upon arrival at the launch site, the CCS will moor to the south side of the launch platform to transfer the rocket. You'll follow your standing orders to patrol the perimeter of the launch site along with the others. At L minus four hours propellant chilldown will begin, and loading of fuel will commence at L minus two hours before lift-off. At that time, all launch support personnel will transfer from the launch platform to the command and control ship. You'll moor to the north side of the launch platform and prepare to receive prisoners."

"Prisoners, Senior Colonel?"

"The four Americans. Your incompetent marine guard fell asleep on watch and allowed Commander Connor and the woman to escape. They very nearly succeeded in sabotaging the operation."

"That's a shocking allegation, Senior Colonel."

"It's a shocking fact. Both he and you will be dealt with appropriately when this launch is completed."

There was a pause. "Please accept my apologies for this unfortunate incident, Senior Colonel. I assure you we'll get to the bottom of it."

"Save your apologies. For now you'll send a contingent of marines to effect the transfer of the prisoners from this ship to yours. Any further slip-ups will be duly noted and introduced at your trial."

There was another pause. "May I ask, Senior Colonel, what I'm being charged with?"

"Gross negligence and dereliction of duty. The idea of sending only one guard, and one so incompetent—"

"With all respect, may I remind the senior colonel that we were following his orders when we made the transfer by helicopter, and that there is a limit as to how many guards could fit in the helicopter?"

"No more excuses. I want no more excuses for incompetence."

"Very well, Senior Colonel. We'll retrieve the prisoners as ordered. What are your orders beyond that?"

"After the launch has been completed, I want you to dispose of them."

"Dispose of them, sir?"

"Kill them, you idiot. Kill them and dispose of their bodies at sea. Do you understand me?"

"Yes, Senior Colonel," Captain Chen said. "I understand."

Chapter Nineteen

"What time is it?" Matt asked.

Beth retrieved her Rolex and looked at it in the dim light coming through the porthole.

"Five-thirty a.m."

"June twenty-first," Matt said. "The big day. I wonder what time they'll launch."

"Sometime this morning. They rolled the rocket out and set it up about eight a.m. yesterday. If the countdown started then, at L minus twenty-six hours, they'll be launching about ten a.m."

He looked at Beth curiously. "How do you know the schedule?"

"I told you, I didn't go there as a spy but I had to turn into one after I realized what they were doing. I know the whole routine."

Matt sighed. He'd spent most of the previous day and night brainstorming with Sam, Charlie, and Beth, and nothing they'd come up with had made sense. He shook his head. "I feel so goddamn helpless."

"I know."

"We can't just sit on our asses and let this happen. We've got to think of something."

"Like what?"

"I don't know—talk to me. Do a brain dump, maybe it'll trigger something. What happens between now and launch time?"

"They'll begin propellant chilldown at L minus four hours. They should be starting any time now. Then they'll start loading fuel at L minus two hours."

"What kind of fuel is it?" Matt asked, searching for something, not knowing what.

"A mixture of kerosene and liquid oxygen. Very volatile. As a safety precaution, they'll transfer all launch support personnel from the launch platform to the command ship before they start loading."

"What happens next, after they get the fuel loaded?"

"All they have to do then is lower the erector arm. That's supposed to happen at L minus fifteen minutes. That'll be the signal

285

that everything's go for the launch."

Matt stepped over to the porthole, careful not to wake Sam and Charlie, who were asleep on the deck. He looked out into the near dawn. The command ship was moored to the south side of the launch platform. The rocket stood erect on the platform's west end, gleaming in the early morning light like a giant phallus, ready to penetrate the heavens. He stared, frustrated and angry and awed at the immensity of it.

"How big is this damn thing?"

"The rocket or the platform?"

"Both."

"The launch platform's like a floating city. Five hundred feet long, three hundred feet wide. Ballasted with seawater to its launch depth, it displaces sixty thousand tons. Accommodations for seventy-five crew members and launch personnel. The hangar's environmentally controlled. They could have transported the rocket here on the launch platform itself if they'd wanted to."

"Why didn't they? Seems less complicated than doing a transfer at sea."

"The two ships were coming from different directions. The command ship from Guangzhou, where they picked up the payload, and the launch platform from Indonesia. It made sense to assemble the rocket and mate the payload to it on the command ship on the way here, then do the transfer at the launch site. As you saw yesterday, the transfer's no problem with the on-board crane system they have."

Matt nodded. He'd watched the crane lift the horizontal rocket out of the hangar on the command ship, engines first, and back it into the hangar on the east end of the launch platform, then tilt it up vertically into launch position on the west end of the platform. The transfer had been disgustingly efficient, which had only added to his frustration. His eyes traveled up the glistening surface of the rocket to the white nose cone. Cryogenic vapors swirled around like gossamer, dissipating into the morning air. In a few hours, it would all be over. He had to do something, but what?

With the light growing brighter, he shifted his attention to the north side of the launch platform. He blinked into the dawn, surprised to see that the sub was still there. He'd seen it come alongside yesterday morning and tie up. With the launch platform ballasted down to launch depth, and the ship riding higher with the rocket off-loaded, he could see it a little clearer now. Looking down from the deck they were on, the top edge of the sail was visible. He pressed his forehead against the glass of the porthole to get a better look. He could just make out the tops of numbers painted in white on the black sail. They appeared to be 2-2-9. With a number in that series, it had to be a Romeo-class diesel-electric boat.

Why was it still moored to the launch platform? Probably having mechanical problems. The crew would take advantage of the amenities on the command ship while the sub was being repaired. Hot showers, maybe a movie. A breakdown wouldn't be unusual. The boats were Chinese-built copies of the Soviet Romeo design, one step up from the old German Type-21 U-boats. They were death traps, completely obsolete. The Chinese had built eighty-four units, but the last time Matt had been patrolling in Chinese waters intel had reported they were down to thirty or so. Of those, they could keep only about half running at any given time.

The bar on the door clattered out of its bracket. The dogs creaked open one by one. Sam and Charlie began to stir. The door opened and the old Chinese housekeeper bustled in with a stack of boxes. More of the all-purpose night rations. This time it was breakfast. The Chinese security guard immediately pulled the door closed behind her and barred it. The old woman set the boxes down and shook her finger at Beth.

"I should still be very upset with you for taking my keys," she said in Mandarin.

"Yes, you should be. Can you ever forgive me?"

"I forgive you, my daughter. But if it was clothing you wanted, why didn't you say so?"

"Don't blame her," Matt said. "It was my idea."

"No, it was mine," Beth said. "I'm such a fool."

The old woman smiled at them. "Lovers always are." She

lowered her voice. "They're coming for you. They're going to take you to a warship." She looked at Beth and Matt plaintively. "Is that good or bad?"

Matt and Beth exchanged glances.

"We'll be fine," Beth said to the old woman. "Please don't worry about us."

"You must take care of yourselves," the woman said, scooping up yesterday's boxes. She turned and rapped on the door. It opened slowly and the security guard pulled her through. The door slammed shut behind her, the bar clanking back into place.

Matt stared at the door. So that was the game plan. Looking out the porthole, he could see *Zhuhai* in the distance, steaming toward the north side of the platform. They'd probably be taken off when fueling began, the same time the launch personnel were transferred from the launch platform to the command ship. It didn't take a lot of imagination to figure out what would happen after that. An idea began to form in his mind, so risky it made him tremble.

Sam came to his feet, stretched and yawned. He pressed his hands into the small of his back. "Man, that deck is hard."

"Sorry to put you out of your room," Beth said.

Sam laughed. "It was worth it. I still can't believe you guys did that." He held his thumb and forefinger an inch apart. "You got that close to putting that thing out of commission. Pretty gutsy."

"Amen," Charlie said, rubbing his eyes. "You missed your calling, girl. You should have been a spook."

"Listen up," Matt said. "I've got an idea." He wasn't concerned about bugs. Charlie had gone over the compartment as soon as the four of them were locked inside and had found nothing. "They're going to take us off to another ship just before the launch, and you know what'll happen next. The best case is we'll end up in a Chinese forced labor camp for the rest of our lives." He nodded toward the porthole and the approaching *Zhuhai*. "But the most likely case is a bullet in the back of the head and a short trip off the fantail of that destroyer."

No one spoke.

Beth broke the silence.

"Well, here's *another* fine mess you've gotten me into."

They all laughed, a release of tension.

Matt gazed at her. They were only hours away from death, and she was doing Oliver Hardy, trying to cheer everyone up.

"The thing is," he said, "at this point it's not important what happens to us. The only thing important now is to find a way to get this stopped."

"I hear that, Skipper," Sam said. "But how?"

"There's only one thing I can think of, and it's so far off the wall, I'd give it about a ten percent chance of success. You can veto it if you like. In fact, all four of us would have to agree before we'd do it."

"Doing anything sounds better than doing nothing," Charlie said. "What is it?"

Matt took a deep breath. "There's a sub moored to the launch platform. Probably in for repairs. It's been sitting there since yesterday, probably with a skeleton crew aboard. If we could find a way to get aboard, we might be able to do something."

Beth stared at him. "You want to steal a Chinese submarine? One that's broken? Are you crazy?"

"I know it's a long shot—"

"Long shot? Matt, listen to me. It's nuts. And probably not even necessary. We're finished, sure, but surely the U.S. Navy's seen all this activity. They'll get it stopped, just like you said. They'll send a sub out. There's probably one out there right now, waiting to put a torpedo in the launch platform as soon as the ships pull away."

Matt gave her a tender smile. They'd told that lie so often she'd begun to believe it. Gray Wolf's words flashed through his mind again. He'd been thinking about them all night. *Governments seldom preempt anything. Nations always wait until they've been attacked and then react. Preemptions, throughout history, have always been done by solitary individuals. Like you, Matthew.* Matt hadn't wanted to hear it, but his mentor was right.

"Beth, I've spent a lot of time in the military. You've spent a lot of time in Washington. We both know how it works. The U.S. can't stop another nuclear power from doing anything, to interfere would be an act of war. All they can do is wait until it happens and then react. By then it'll be too late—the damage will be done. We're the only people who can stop it."

"Even assuming we could get aboard, what if the repairs to the sub aren't completed?" Beth said. "If the crew's not going back, that should tell you something."

"That's a chance we'll have to take."

"Sam, tell him. This is crazy."

Sam shook his head, staring at Matt. "I don't think it's crazy. I've been on a submarine with this man before. He could make it do things nobody else could."

"But you haven't been on a sub in years," Beth said, turning back to Matt. "You've probably never even been on one like that before."

"True," Matt said. "It *has* been a long time, and I've never been on a diesel sub before outside of a museum."

Beth threw out her hands as though the conclusion was obvious. "Well?"

"All subs work on the same principle, whether they're diesel-powered or nuclear-powered," Matt said. "Ballast is ballast. A dive plane's a dive plane. A torpedo's a torpedo."

"Charlie, tell him. There are four warships out there. What do you think they're going to be doing when we take off in that sub?"

Matt held up his hand before Charlie could answer. "It's worse than that. In the interest of full disclosure, there's also another sub out there—one that's working."

"There. See what I mean? He's crazy. Tell him."

Charlie said, "All I know is, the U.S. is screwed and we're dead meat if we sit here and do nothing. Not a whole lot to lose, is there?"

"We're all gonna die someday," Sam said. "For me, the real question is how you want to do it. Like an animal, letting somebody else shoot you in the head when it suits 'em, or like a slave, working on a prison farm till you drop, or like a man, doing something important."

Beth gave him a look that said she'd been there. She nodded. "Okay. I guess when you put it that way . . . " She looked at Matt and screwed up her face. "But do you remember our conversation the other night?"

That was the reason she'd been hesitating. She was trying to protect him. With death looking him in the face there was no reason to hide his affliction any longer.

"Beth's referring to a problem Sam already knows about," Matt said, looking at Charlie. "I'm claustrophobic as hell."

Sam looked relieved that he didn't have to be the one to say it.

Charlie looked astonished. He scratched his head. "Well, I guess we'd better scrap *that* idea."

"I think I can overcome it," Matt said. "I don't know for sure, but I think so."

"If it turns out you can't, we're totally screwed," Charlie said. "None of us know how to drive a submarine, much less fight one."

"You don't have to do this," Beth said.

"Yes," Matt said. "I do."

"You sure, Skipper?" Sam said.

Beth sighed. "This goes against everything I believe." She looked up at Matt. "If we do this, people are going to die."

"If we don't, a lot more are going to die," Matt said. "We've tried it your way. Now we're going to try it my way."

He heard the engines start on the command ship, felt the vibration in his body. He stepped over to the porthole. *Zhuhai* eased up to the north side of the launch platform and moored just behind the sub. Two seamen rigged a gangway to the platform and two marines started across, rifles at port arms.

"They'll be coming for us in a few minutes, two marines from *Zhuhai*," Matt said. "Corporal Wu will make a third."

He reached inside his briefs and retrieved the pistol. He pulled the slide back and cocked it.

"Sam, get behind the door. Charlie, you stand on this side of the door. Beth, you get behind that stack of crates in case there's any shooting."

Matt snapped the safety off and slipped the pistol into his belt, in the small of his back. He stood staring at the door, tension building.

"Okay, folks. All we've got going for us is the element of

surprise. This has to happen in the first five seconds or it won't happen. Follow my lead."

After a few minutes, he heard the bar being removed from the door. One by one, the dogs creaked open. The door opened and Sergeant Li stepped in, followed by Private Fong. Corporal Wu brought up the rear with a roll of duct tape, his rifle slung on his shoulder. Matt assumed from the worried look on his face that he was in a lot of trouble for letting them escape. The security guard stayed outside. He pulled the steel door closed behind them and barred it. They were taking no chances.

Before a word was spoken, Sam eased up behind Private Fong and Charlie stepped up behind Corporal Wu. In one fluid movement, Matt gripped the barrel of Sergeant Li's assault rifle with his left hand, pushed it down toward the deck, and raised the muzzle of his pistol to Li's forehead.

"Don't move or I'll kill your leader," Matt said in Mandarin.

He looked into Sergeant Li's eyes and saw Traveller lying on the deck of *CoMar Explorer* in a pool of blood. He wasn't bluffing about killing Li, and everyone seemed to sense it. The two marines froze. Sam and Charlie wrested their rifles away.

"Let go of the gun," Matt said in English.

Sergeant Li released it. Matt held it by the barrel, not taking his eyes off Li's. "Beth, tape their hands behind their backs. Tight. Sergeant Li first."

Beth picked up the roll of duct tape Corporal Wu had dropped. Sam pulled Sergeant Li's arms behind his back, slammed him to the deck. He pulled his hands together and held them tightly while Beth wrapped multiple layers of tape around his wrists. When she was finished Sam took the tape and placed a strip over Li's mouth, circling the back of his head with it.

"Now do Private Fong," Matt said. He pressed his pistol against Corporal Wu's head. "Remove your uniform," he said in Mandarin. He motioned to Charlie. "Swap clothes with him."

With their leader subdued, Private Fong and Corporal Wu did what they were told. When Wu had stripped off his uniform, Matt motioned to Charlie's dungarees. "Put these on."

Wu looked at him, not understanding.

"You've been sentenced to death for letting us escape," Matt said in Mandarin, not really sure it was true. "If you cooperate, you may save your life. Put these on and act like a prisoner."

When the two marines were subdued and the clothing swap was completed, Matt shoved his pistol into his belt behind his back and motioned for Sam to stand by the door. Charlie picked up Wu's rifle and rapped on the door, a signal that they were ready. The door opened and the security guard peered in. He looked at Charlie wearing Corporal Wu's uniform. Before he could say anything, Sam grabbed him by the head and pulled him into the room, slamming him against the opposite bulkhead. Charlie closed the door and dogged it from the inside. Matt covered the guard with his pistol while Sam held him and Beth taped his hands behind his back. Sam covered his mouth with tape and laid him out alongside Sergeant Li and Private Fong.

"Okay, now do us," Matt said. He placed the pistol in his hip pocket and held out his hands. Sam wrapped a single layer of tape around Matt's wrists to give the illusion of being bound, then did the same for Beth. Matt nodded to Charlie, who now looked for all the world like a corporal in the PLA marine corp. "Tape Sam's hands and we'll be ready to roll."

Sam tossed the roll of tape to Charlie. "There's one thing I gotta do first." He picked Sergeant Li up by the seat of his pants and the collar of his shirt. "This is for Traveller." Before Matt could say anything, he slammed Li's head into the bulkhead with a sickening thud of bone against steel. The sergeant went limp and didn't move.

Matt couldn't tell if Li was dead or alive, but he wasn't moving. Sam had figured he wouldn't have approved, so he hadn't asked permission. He'd just done it. Secretly, Matt was glad he hadn't asked. He was also grateful that Sam hadn't said, "This is for the men of *CoMar Explorer*." Like Sam, he wanted to keep a spark of hope alive.

Charlie looped a single layer of tape around Sam's wrists, straightened his uniform, and motioned that he was ready. Matt looked at Corporal Wu, who was staring at Sam with fear in his eyes.

"You saw what the black giant can do," Matt said in Mandarin. "He'll be right behind you. If you say one word or miss one step, he'll snap your neck like a twig."

Wu bobbed his head. "I'm dead if I return. I don't know where you're going, but you'll have no trouble from me."

Matt stepped up to the door. "Okay, folks. Line up. I'll go first, Beth behind me, then Wu, then Sam, then Charlie." He opened the door and peeked out. There was no one in sight. He motioned them out, dogged the door closed, and replaced the bar. With Charlie bringing up the rear holding Corporal Wu's rifle on them, Matt led the way along the passageway to a stairway that would take them down to the third deck. From the porthole of the room they'd been locked in, he'd seen a convenience ladder at that level that connected the ship with the launch platform. Dodging crew members and technicians who seemed too busy to notice the odd little caravan, they reached the door, a huge opening in the side of the ship with people streaming in and out.

Matt started down the ladder, then stopped in his tracks. There, on the port bridge wing of the *Zhuhai*, stood Captain Chen, staring at him through binoculars.

Captain Chen watched the little caravan troop down the ladder of the command ship. Odd. He'd sent two marines to accompany the prisoners. With Corporal Wu, there should have been three. Now there was only one, marching the four Americans at gunpoint. *What is going on here?*

He focused his binoculars on the lone marine and recognized him as the American spy who'd convinced himself that he was no longer Chinese. He could see Corporal Wu trudging along in civilian clothes with his hands bound in front of him, between the black savage and the half-Chinese woman. In front of her, leading the pack, was his old brigade commander, Matthew Baines Connor.

Chen stared at him, astonished. Commander Connor had obviously disposed of Sergeant Li and his man. How had he done it? But the bigger question was why had he done it, only to bring himself and his people back aboard *Zhuhai* like this? What did he think he was going to do? Take over the ship? After hearing about his attempt to sabotage the satellite, Chen had been prepared for one last, desperate move from his former brigade commander, but this?

Chen watched him come, fascinated to see what he'd do. About fifty yards from *Zhuhai*, Connor brought the caravan to a stop. He stood staring up at Captain Chen. What was he doing? With his back to the command ship, Connor was pointing to his left, toward the northwest side of the launch platform. Chen followed his path. He was pointing in the direction of the disabled submarine, moored directly forward of *Zhuhai*. So that was it. Even more foolhardy than he could have imagined. And to top it off, the arrogant bastard had the audacity to tell him what he was going to do!

Chen reached for the telephone, then glanced back. Connor wasn't moving. He was still standing there, pointing. He wasn't telling him. He was *asking* him. Chen stared at him, dumbfounded. He was actually asking his permission to try to commandeer a submarine and sink the launch platform.

He still didn't know how the man had gotten this far, but there could only be one explanation for what he was trying. The U.S. submarine the American spy had talked about with such bravado that would appear to torpedo the launch wasn't going to materialize. There was only one way he could know that it wasn't. It had all been a lie. They'd never told anyone. It would now be up to Commander Connor to fulfill that prophecy. Chen started again to reach for the bridge telephone, then hesitated.

As much as he hated to admit it, Connor was right. No one in China wanted war with America. Only a few at the top, like the bogus senior colonel, for their own reasons. Chen certainly didn't. He'd been educated at Annapolis and knew something of the American military capability. War with America would be disastrous. It was especially ludicrous to go to war over a renegade territory like Taiwan. Hong Kong had been repatriated from the British, and Macau from the Portuguese, without firing a shot. Taiwan would soon follow. Creeping capitalism on the mainland was bringing the two governments inexorably together. It was only a matter of time until they were peaceably united.

Let him go, a small voice said. If Chen hadn't heard the story of the killer satellite and how it would be used, he'd be frantically trying to stop Connor. Now, suddenly, he found himself wanting him to pull it off. Retaking Taiwan had nothing to do with national sovereignty. The old hard-liners were under siege. Ironically, it was the same creeping capitalism that was bringing the two governments inexorably together that was making the Communist leadership irrelevant and pushing them to do such a dangerous thing. Taking the island by force would solidify the party's base, for now, but Chen doubted that the leadership understood the full consequences of what they were doing. President Xiang had ordered the development of an "assassin's mace" weapon that would allow China to take Taiwan, but Chen doubted if he knew that the senior colonel was planning to use it to destroy America. America would come back—eventually—and China would pay the price.

Let him go. It was a tantalizing notion, especially after the senior colonel had threatened to put him on trial. If the launch failed, the *gaogan zidi* would be too busy trying to keep his own neck out of a noose to prosecute Chen.

Still struggling with the decision, Chen turned away. It was all Connor needed. With his little band following behind, he started toward the submarine.

Chen watched him go. It was an insane move, he wasn't even sure the sub was operable, but with luck and the element of surprise, there was a chance he'd be successful. The target was stationary and it was certainly big enough. All he'd have to do was point and shoot. After the shot, successful or not, he'd dive and try to run for the nearest land, the coast of Sumatra.

There was no chance Commander Connor could escape to tell his story. With *Zhuhai* and the other Romeo sub in pursuit, all his skills as a submarine commander wouldn't be enough to keep him alive.

Chen watched Connor approach the submarine. Once he got aboard and sealed the hatches, there'd be no turning back. He had twenty yards to make a decision. Kill him now or let him go?

Chapter Twenty

Fully expecting to feel the impact of a bullet in the back of his head, Matt approached the submarine. Closer now, he dropped his head and assumed the hangdog look of a prisoner. A fresh-faced young sailor stood on the quarterdeck wearing a yellowed white uniform and a side arm. He watched the tattered little group coming toward the sub with a puzzled, repulsed look on his face. Matt started down the gangplank.

The sailor held up his hands. *"Deng yihuir. "Ni zai gan shenme?"* Just a second. What are you doing?

"Don't get your bowels in an uproar, younger born," Charlie said in Mandarin. "I've been ordered to deliver these prisoners."

"To this boat? Why?"

Charlie shrugged. "Who knows what Senior Colonel Lao has in mind?"

"I know nothing about any Colonel Lao and I know nothing about any prisoners."

"There's always someone who doesn't get the word." Charlie prodded Sam with the rifle, herding the prisoners down the gangplank.

Matt tripped and went stumbling across the brow, colliding with the sentry, who recoiled in disgust. Before he could recover, the others were aboard.

Eyes darting between Charlie's ill-fitting uniform and his Americanized face, the young sailor seemed to sense that something wasn't right. He unsnapped the flap of his holster.

"Ni shi shei?" Who are you?

Behind him now, Matt shed the tape on his wrists. He stuck his pistol in the sentry's back, reached around and removed the side arm from its holster.

"Let's go below," he said in Mandarin. "Sam, secure the hatch."

Matt followed the young sailor down the forward escape hatch with the others clambering down behind him. He prodded the sailor aft, in the direction of the control room. The sub reeked of garlic, cigarette smoke, and diesel fuel. He heard Sam close the hatch and felt the air change as it screwed down. They were aboard, sealed off from the world. A wave of panic swept over him. *Forget about where you are. Think about what you're doing.* He shoved the sailor into the control room and spun him around.

"*Ni hui jiang yingyu ma?*" Do you speak English?

The young sailor shook his head. Matt could tell by his eyes that he was terrified. He had to find a way to calm him down.

"*Nin gui xing?*" May I ask your name?

"*Wo xing Wen.*" My name is Wen.

You and half of China. There were only about a hundred surnames in the whole damn country.

"*Ni duo da, xiao Wen?*" How old are you, young Wen?

"*Wo ershiwu sui.*" I'm twenty-five.

Matt would have guessed him at eighteen. "*Ni zuo shenme gongzuo?*" What do you do?

"*Wo shi gongchengshi.*" I'm an engineer.

"All right, young Wen. No harm will come to you, but you must cooperate. Is the captain aboard?"

The sailor shook his head. "Just a skeleton crew."

"Where's the captain and the rest of the crew?"

"On the command ship, watching the launch. We're supposed to take her out one mile. After the launch we're to come back and finish the repairs."

Interesting that the captain wasn't aboard. In the U.S., the responsibility for taking a sub out even a mile would never be delegated to anyone. But the really interesting news was that the sub was operable. At least one of the engines had to be running.

"How many in the skeleton crew?"

"About a dozen, plus some mechanics and engineers."

Matt nodded. The normal complement for a Romeo class was about fifty officers and men. A dozen crewmen would be enough to do what he had in mind.

"Any torpedomen aboard?"

"One or two. Two, I think. Doing maintenance."

"This boat has a complement of fourteen torpedoes," Matt said.

"How many do you have aboard?"

"I don't know. Not that many."

Matt handed Sam the pistol he'd taken from Wen. "These boats have eight torpedo tubes, six in the bow and two in the stern. Sam, you go forward. Charlie, you go aft. Commandeer the torpedomen and whoever else you can find. Get as many torpedoes loaded as you can, at least four in the bow and two in the stern, then come back and give me the count."

"Can't we just ram it?" Charlie said.

"Romeos only displace seventeen hundred tons fully loaded. Hitting a sixty-thousand-ton platform would be like ramming the battleship *Yamato*. They wouldn't even feel it. Now move, goddamn it."

"Yes, sir," they both said, heading in different directions.

"Beth, loan me your watch."

Beth handed him the Rolex. She was reading a brass plaque on the bulkhead. She screwed up her face.

"My God, this thing was built in 1962 in the Guangzhou shipyard."

"They built these from '60 to '84. This has got to be one of the older ones." Matt looked at the watch. Nine-twenty. It would be tight. He looked at Wen. "Any officers aboard?"

"The number two. Plus the engineering officer."

"Who has the keys to the small arms locker?"

"The number two."

"Where's the number two officer?"

"Right here," he heard a voice say behind him. Turning, he saw an officer in a blue jumpsuit step into the control room. He appeared to be about thirty years old and had a short-barreled pump shotgun pointed at the pistol stuck in Matt's belt. From the size of the hole, it looked like a twelve-gauge. Big enough to cut a man in half at close range. "Put the gun down on the deck," he said in perfect English.

Sam eased back into the control room behind the officer. He must have heard him. For a big man, Sam moved like a cat. Matt raised his hands.

In one fluid movement, Sam grabbed the officer around the neck with his right arm and jerked up on the barrel of the shotgun with his left hand. Matt dropped to the deck as the twelve-gauge exploded with a shattering roar, raining debris from the overhead down on him. Ears ringing, he came to his feet and stared up at the damage to the overhead. A few pipes were dented and the insulation on a brace of electrical cables had been peeled back by the blast, exposing bare copper wires.

"Jesus Christ, Sam."

"Sorry, Skipper. He was a little quicker on the trigger than I thought he'd be." Sam handed the shotgun to Matt. "Think we can still get under way?"

Matt was more worried about being able to dive, but there was no going back now. He turned to the officer and held out his hand. "The keys to the small arms locker."

The officer removed a chain from around his neck and handed it to Matt.

Matt tossed the keys to Sam. "Secure it, Sam, then get back up there."

"I will if you stop getting into trouble."

Matt motioned to the number two with his pistol. "Up on the bridge."

"Who are you and what do you want?"

"We're getting under way. Now. Do you understand me?"

"We can't get under way."

"Why? What's the problem?"

"The engines are down."

Matt didn't believe him. One, maybe, but not both. He turned to Wen, who hadn't understood their conversation in English. "Which engine is down?" he asked in Mandarin.

"The port engine. It's not running properly. One piston is faulty."

One engine was enough to get them into position, but two would be better when it came time to run. He remembered a technique he'd heard about from an uncle who'd sailed on diesels in World War II.

"Can you sling it?"

"*Wo bu dong.*" I don't understand.

"Disconnect it from the crankshaft and sling it at the top of its stroke. The engine will still run while you make the repairs."

Wen's eyes opened wider. "*Wo dong.*" I understand.

"Are the batteries charged?"

"About eighty percent."

Matt removed the tape from Corporal Wu's hands and nodded toward Wen. "Go with him. Do what he says. If you want to save your life, help him get those engines running. Now." He racked the shotgun, ejecting the spent shell and loading a new one. "Beth, can you handle this?"

"I've never held a gun in my life."

"Time to learn. Here. Keep an eye on the control room. Make sure nobody touches anything. I'm going to be busy topside." He turned back to the officer. "What's your name?"

"Lien."

"You lied to me about the engines, Lien. Don't do that again."

"Your Mandarin is quite impressive. So's your knowledge of diesel engines."

Matt heard the starboard diesel engine turn over and begin its rattling idle. He pulled the pistol from his belt and motioned to Lien.

"Up to the bridge. You first."

Matt followed him up the ladder, eager to get out of the sub and nervous about what he'd find when he got there. He wasn't worried about resistance from the surface ships—they'd be expecting them to get under way—and he wasn't worried about undue resistance from the number two, simply because he had no idea what Matt intended to do. Yet. The big question was, had Captain Chen blown the whistle? Would he have a contingent of marines waiting for him on the launch platform when he stuck his head above deck?

He emerged onto the bridge and looked around. The launch platform was empty except for a few stragglers walking toward the command ship, and a pair of line handlers standing by the sub. He looked behind him. *Zhuhai* was gone. He could see her a half-mile away, moving fast. There weren't any marines waiting for him. Was Captain Chen going to give him the free shot he'd asked for, or was he just getting into position to sink him when he pulled away from the launch platform?

The two line handlers, obviously seamen from the crew of the boat, stood by the lines, waiting to cast off. They looked at Matt curiously but seemed to accept his presence on the bridge with the number two officer. The command ship and launch platform were full of foreigners doing strange things.

"All right, Lien. You're going to take her out. Station the maneuvering watch."

Lien keyed the microphone on the Chinese version of the 1MC, the boat's communication system, and spoke in Mandarin. "Now station the maneuvering watch. Station the maneuvering watch."

Several seamen emerged on deck and pulled on sound-powered telephones. The one forward plugged the phone into a jack near the number one line and turned to face the bridge, waiting for orders. Behind Matt, a pair of lookouts climbed into the periscope shears with binoculars.

"Take in the number two and number three lines," Lien said. "Single up number one and number four."

Matt watched the seamen work the lines, numbered one at the bow and four at the stern. The excitement of getting a sub under way came flooding back. If this was going to be his last act on earth, it wasn't a bad way to go out.

"Take in the number one and the number four lines," Lien said. "All ahead one third. Right fifteen degrees rudder."

The line handlers on the platform lifted the eye splices off the bollards and tossed the lines into the blue equatorial water. As the boat eased away from the launch platform, the line handlers on the sub covered their ears with their hands, waiting for the blast. Lien sounded three short blasts on the air horn, the international signal to every ship within a mile radius that the submarine was under way.

Matt looked out over the 250-foot sub cutting cleanly through the water. It felt good to have a ship beneath him. The command ship sounded its horn, signaling the last call to leave the platform. He leaned into the wind and watched the deck crew clean up, stowing lines and capstan wrenches. They finished up and went below, dogging down the escape trunk hatch behind them. If they'd been in a crowded port, they'd have stayed on deck a little longer to drop anchor in case steering was lost, but in the open sea there was no need.

He scanned the horizon. *Harbin* and the two frigates were about a mile out, cruising around the platform in a screening perimeter. *Zhuhai* was turning, moving into position—to do what? Take her place in the screen, or blow him out of the water? He looked at Beth's watch. Nine forty. He had to get into position quickly.

"Now that we're under way," Lien said, "I can't imagine what you expect to accomplish with this little stunt of yours."

"Take her out a half-mile," Matt said.

"My orders are to take her out a mile."

"You've got new orders. One half-mile. Then come around facing the launch platform and heave to."

Lien looked at him. "You're a sub commander, aren't you?"

Matt was too busy making plans to make conversation, but he had to keep the guy calm until they got into position.

"Your job," he said. "XO of an attack boat."

"You're too young to have ever sailed on diesels. America hasn't had diesels for decades. You must be a nuclear officer."

"Ex," Matt said.

"What class of boat?"

"Los Angeles." He looked at Beth's watch. Nine forty-five. The erector arm should be coming down soon, signaling the last fifteen minutes of the countdown. The second diesel engine fired up, running with a ragged edge.

"Here we are, that's far enough. Bring her around. I want the bow facing the platform."

Lien complied, then ordered All Stop. The sub hove to, blue water slapping against the black hull, diesel engines idling with their deep-throated murmur. Scattered whitecaps dotted the expanse between the sub and the launch platform. The sun blazed brilliantly in the eastern sky. A perfect shot. All he needed was one good torpedo. Where the hell was Sam?

"Order battle stations, torpedo," Matt said.

Lien stared at him. "You can't be serious."

"Skipper!" Sam yelled up the trunk from the control room. "There's only six fish aboard, four forward and two aft. We got four loaded in the bow, tubes one and two, three and four. Two in the stern, tubes seven and eight. They're old, they got pistol-type detonators, but they're ready to shoot."

Lien's mouth fell open. "You *are* serious."

Matt heard a whistling sound, an incoming shell. It exploded fifty yards off the starboard bow. He looked to the east. *Zhuhai* was turning toward them. The senior colonel must have figured out what he was doing and ordered *Zhuhai* to stop him. That first shot from Captain Chen was a warning. He had to get this done. "Give the order."

"No."

Matt pressed his pistol against Lien's temple. "If I have to give it, you won't hear it."

Lien hit a lever on the bridge. An insistent gonging sound reverberated throughout the ship. He keyed the microphone, glaring at Matt.

"Battle stations, torpedo. Battle stations, torpedo."

"Flood tubes one and two," Matt said.

"What do you think you're doing?"

Matt pressed the muzzle of the pistol deeper into his flesh. "Say it."

"Flood tubes one and two," Lien said into the microphone.

"Open the outer doors on tubes one and two," Matt said.

"This has gone far enough," Lien said.

"Do it."

"Open outer doors. Tubes one and two," Lien said. "This is insane."

Another shell exploded, close enough to lift the bow of the sub up out of the water. It eased back down into position, rocking back and forth. Captain Chen was putting on a good show, but he couldn't stall much longer.

"No need to mark the range or bearing," Matt said. "Fire one.

Fire two."

"I won't do it."

The rocket engines ignited. He looked at Beth's watch. Five minutes till lift-off. They were cutting the countdown short.

"That destroyer's got our range. The next one's going to hit the bridge. I'm not going to dive until we fire. Do it."

Lien looked back and forth between the launch platform and *Zhuhai* bearing down on them. "I can't."

Matt grabbed the microphone and shoved him out of the way. "Sam! Fire one! Fire two!"

Seconds ticked by. Matt held his breath. "Come on, goddamn it, come on."

The number one torpedo spun out of its tube and churned toward the launch platform, followed by the number two. The rocket engines were brighter now, the platform trembling, the air crackling.

"Hurry up, you son of a bitch. Hurry up."

The rocket shuddered and started to lift off. The number one torpedo slammed into the ballast tank beneath it and exploded. The rocket swayed and tilted to the west, engines blazing. The number two torpedo drove into what must have been a fuel storage tank beneath the hangar. The platform lifted up, an orange ball of flame erupting beneath it. The rocket lifted off, tilting further to the west. A fireball erupted around the engines, climbing the length of the first stage, then a massive, shuddering explosion split the air.

Matt instinctively shielded his face from the heat. Through narrowed eyes, he watched the rocket disintegrate and fall burning into the sea. Beth let out a whoop from below.

He stared at the wreckage, mesmerized. Burning fuel on the surface of the launch platform spread to the hangar on the opposite end. Fuel storage tanks ignited, then detonated, throwing flames a hundred feet in the air, igniting the phony wooden containers on the deck of the command ship. The ships that had been screening broke off and headed toward her to fight the fire.

He looked to the east. *Zhuhai* had kicked it into high gear and was steaming toward them at flank speed. He'd had his free shot.

Captain Chen wouldn't miss again—there was no way he could allow Matt to get away to tell his story. He hit the lever for the Klaxon horn twice and shoved Lien toward the hatch.

"Clear the bridge. Dive! Dive!"

A shell exploded on the starboard side of the boat, slamming him against the bulwark. A searing pain shot through his left side. Grimacing from the pain, he made a quick check for damage. There was a large dent in the ballast tanks, but he couldn't see any breaks in the hull. He shoved the lookouts down the trunk behind Lien, then dropped down the ladder behind them and sealed the hatch.

Lien stood at his post as diving officer. He glared at Matt.

"You fool. You've just killed us all."

"Secure diesel engines," Matt said, holding his left side, breathing hard. "Shift to battery power. All ahead full. Take her down to periscope depth."

"Periscope depth? Are you crazy? That's a destroyer. We need to go deep."

Matt pointed the pistol at Lien's head. "Do it."

Lien rang up Battery Power on the motor-order telegraph and repeated the order in Mandarin to the two planesmen. They started their motors and set the planes on a ten-degree dive angle.

Lien stepped over to the hydraulic manifold and opened the tank vents. He closed the main induction valve and looked up at the light board.

"White board."

Matt stared at the white glow of the lights. It was the "Christmas tree" his uncle had told him about. The World War II-era light board consisted of red and green lights that indicated hull integrity. Red meant there was an opening in the boat somewhere, green meant the hull was secure. The Chinese used white instead of green. He looked around, the realization growing that he was sealed inside a tube that was going down. *Don't think about where you are. Concentrate on what you're doing.*

"Rig out the sonar," Matt said.

Without waiting for Lien's approval, the sonar operator switched on some ancient-looking sonar gear and pulled his headphones on. He adjusted the speaker volume and the control room began echoing with active sonar pings. Passive was the norm, despite what people saw in the movies, simply because the active pings were a double-edged sword. They established the target's range and bearing accurately, but they also gave away your position. In this case, it didn't matter—*Zhuhai* knew exactly where they were.

The boat slipped into an eerie silence. Matt glanced around, fighting a sense of panic, looking for leaks where the shotgun blast had dented some pipes. Even a small drip at this depth could be a major problem when they went deep.

Lien stepped over to a bank of valves that controlled compressed air blown to the tanks. He watched the barometer of the high-pressure air manifold. When he was satisfied with the level, he turned and said, "Pressure in the boat." Everyone breathed a sigh of relief.

Matt watched the depth gauge, trying to control his panic. Everything was in meters. One meter was a little over three feet. Periscope depth was about sixty-five feet.

"Make your depth twenty meters."

Lien repeated the order, keeping his eye on the depth gauge. When it approached the target depth, he ordered, "Shut negative flood. Blow negative to the mark."

The auxiliaryman repeated the order. "Permission to vent negative inboard."

"Vent negative inboard," Lien said.

Matt raised the aft periscope. The target was close, and the smaller attack scope would make less of a wake. Gripping the handles, he pressed his right eye against the black rubber eyepiece and turned the scope in a half-circle. The other destroyer and the two frigates were steaming toward the command ship. The flames were higher now. A huge fireball billowed up from the deck. He turned the scope forward and grimaced from the sharp pain in his side.

Zhuhai was steaming directly toward him. If he fought her conventionally, they wouldn't have a chance. The two aft missile launchers on *Zhuhai* were fitted with CY-1 anti-submarine missiles, a system that deployed a Mark 46 torpedo comparable to the American ASROC system. He'd seen them when he was climbing aboard the helicopter. With its built-in sonar, there was no way they could dive deep enough to escape it. The only chance he had was to kill it now, in the first few minutes of engagement, by doing something totally unexpected, the way he'd taken Sergeant Li. Doing what a sub commander would normally do would be a death sentence.

"Hard left rudder," Matt said, gripping his side. "Steady on course zero-three-zero. Flood tubes three and four."

Lien repeated the orders in English, then Mandarin.

"Open outer doors on three and four," Matt said. "Range."

"Eight hundred meters," Lien said.

It would be a close range shot, but he wouldn't have to override the safety interlocks to arm the torpedoes. The old pistol-type detonators would explode on impact, just as they had on the launch platform.

"Range," he said again.

"Five hundred meters," Lien said.

He sounded panicked, but the closer they were to *Zhuhai*, the less able the destroyer was to train her guns on them, and the less apt she was to fire a missile.

"Make the torpedo depth one meter. Bearing. Mark."

"Zero-three-one."

Matt counted the distance in his head, waiting. "Range. Mark."

"Three hundred meters."

He continued tracking the distance based on the size of the destroyer in the periscope lens. He'd never seen a ship take up so much real estate.

Now. "Fire three. Fire four. Emergency deep. Make your depth five-zero meters."

He felt the thump of two torpedoes leaving the boat. He snapped the handles up and lowered the periscope. From the sonar speaker, he could hear the high-pitched sound of the torpedo propellers over the low-pitched screws of *Zhuhai*.

"Stay away from bulkheads. Brace for impact."

Lien keyed the microphone and repeated the orders in English and Mandarin.

Matt stood in the center of the control room, feet apart, bracing himself, watching the depth gauge. The sub dove like a rock. His guess had been right. Like the old German U-boats she was copied from, the Romeo's hydroplanes were low on the hull, allowing for a rapid dive. Lien was staring at him as though he was insane. Matt couldn't blame him. It was an insane move, one you wouldn't find in any book. Shoot at close range, dive, and try to pass directly beneath the destroyer after it had taken two torpedoes. He had no idea if it would work, or if the sub would disintegrate from the proximity of the blast and debris.

An explosion slammed him to the deck. The pain in his side cut through him like a knife. Chen's final shot must have broken a rib. A second, almost concurrent explosion rattled the sub violently. He'd never been in a boat that had been depth-charged before, but his uncle had told him what it felt like. The vibration penetrated his very soul. He heard the sound of debris raining down on the hull of the boat. He held his breath, waiting for the crack to appear that would take them to the bottom. It didn't come.

"Damage report," Matt said, coming to his feet, wincing. "Zero the planes at five-zero meters." He stepped over to the sonar speaker and raised his hand for silence. The sound of high-speed screws had been replaced by the sounds of a ship breaking up, a low steady roar punctuated by the sound of compartments imploding. He looked at Beth to see if she was okay and did a double take. Lien, Beth, Sam, and the rest of the control room crew were smiling at him.

"Damage control reports no discernible damage," Lien said.

"That was brilliant," Beth said.

"We got lucky."

"What about the other ships up there?" Sam said.

"They're busy fighting a fire and taking on passengers. And now picking up survivors. I'm not worried about them, and I don't think they're worried about us. They know we're not going to stick around to do them any harm, but there's another sub out there somewhere."

Lien nodded. "The 225. Another Romeo-class."

"Where is she?"

"Submerged, screening for enemy subs. They won't be able to communicate with her until she surfaces."

"I'm sure she picked up all this ruckus on her sonar. We've got to get out of here." He groaned and gripped his side.

"What is it?" Beth said.

"That third shot knocked me around a little."

"You might have a broken rib."

He walked carefully over to the plotting table.

"Where are we going?" Beth said.

Matt glanced up at the overhead. Due west to the nearest land, if he could control his panic attacks long enough to get there. *Concentrate*. He pointed to the coast of Sumatra.

"We're about a hundred and thirty-five miles from the coast, about eighty miles from the easternmost tip of this island here, Pulau Lingga. That's where we're headed." He nodded to Lien. "Set course two-seven-zero. All ahead full."

He paced the control room, struggling to control his claustrophobia, all but reeling from the pain in his side, while the boat churned westward, running submerged on battery power at her top speed of thirteen knots. After a half-hour, he was so desperate to get out of there he decided to come up for a look. If the coast was clear, they'd surface and run on diesels. They'd be exposed, but at least he'd be able to breathe, and they could run faster.

"Take her up to periscope depth."

He raised the search scope, which had a greater magnification than the smaller attack scope. Plumes of black smoke billowed up on the horizon. The platform was still ablaze. The destroyer *Harbin* was hove to in the debris field where *Zhuhai* had gone down, fishing survivors out of the burning water. Had Captain Chen survived? His unspoken agreement to stop the launch had made them partners in a Faustian bargain. Any time you make a deal with the Devil, his father had told him, you're going to be the junior partner, and it was true. Even though Chen had tried to kill him afterward, which Matt understood was part of the deal, he felt bad about killing him. But whatever empathy he may have felt for his old classmate and the crew of *Zhuhai*, it didn't extend to the Bobbsey Twins or Lieutenant Tan.

He focused on the command ship. The fire had spread into the superstructure and was blazing out of control. The two frigates were standing off, streaming seawater from fire hoses onto the ship, helping passengers in lifeboats clamber aboard. From the look of things, they were going to be busy for a long time. Beth's hotshot cousin would have his hands full. He'd no doubt dispatch the other sub to deal with them, but so far there was no sign of her.

"Prepare to surface," Matt said.

After all the preparations had been made, Lien keyed the microphone and said, "Surface, surface, surface."

The roll of the sub told him that the conning tower hatch had cleared the surface. Matt cracked the hatch, ducking the seawater that poured in, and breathed in a lungful of moist, fresh air. He painfully climbed the ladder to the bridge and stood there, sucking in air, scanning the area with binoculars. There was nothing in sight except the frantic activity on the horizon. *Thank God.*

"Start diesel engines. All ahead full," he shouted down the trunk. "Course two-seven-zero. Line up a battery charge. Lookouts to the bridge."

Lien repeated the order from the control room, and the diesel engines rumbled to life. Matt felt the surge of the screws biting into the water. The two lookouts scrambled up the ladder and took their places in the shears. Beth came up behind them.

"Hey, junkman," Beth said. "Who says you don't know how to make junk?"

Matt nodded toward the horizon. "I think we created some problems for your cousin."

"I'd say he'll be the first one off that thing. Leave the mess for others to clean up." Beth smiled at him. "What happened to that claustrophobia?"

"I was fighting it the whole time. Good thing I was a little busy."

"You were a little brilliant, is what you were," Beth said. "Now I understand what Sam was talking about."

"Where's your shotgun?"

"Gave it to Sam. We won't need it—this crew will follow whoever they think will keep them alive, and right now they think you walk on water."

"If I could, I'd get the hell off this thing."

"How long do you think it'll be before we see some land?"

"We're making about fifteen knots on the surface. Pulau Lingga is maybe eighty miles away. We might see the tip of it in four or five hours."

"What do we do then?"

"I don't know. I didn't think we'd get this far." He winced and gripped his side.

"If that's what I think it is, you'd better take it easy," she said. "You could puncture a lung with a broken rib."

They cruised in silence for an hour, enjoying the view from the bridge. Lien shouted up the trunk from the control room.

"Sonar reports submarine, bearing one-three-five. A Romeo. It has to be the 225."

"Dive! Dive!" Matt hit the lever for the Klaxon horn and shoved Beth toward the hatch. He waved the two lookouts down, swung down the trunk behind them, and sealed it off. At a bearing of one-three-five, the sub must be on their port quarter. He had to bring her around to line up for a stern shot. He'd done the math so many times in "mental gym" in sub school, the number popped into his head. One-three-five plus 180 equaled 315, the reciprocal heading he needed to be on.

"Make your depth five-zero meters. Right full rudder. Steady on three-one-five."

"Depth five-zero meters," Lien said. "Right full rudder. Steady on course three-one-five."

Matt looked at the compass. Two-eight-zero. They were coming around, but not fast enough. "Starboard engine back full."

"Starboard back full," Lien said.

"What's happening?" Beth said.

"She's coming up on our flank for a shot. We've got to make ourselves small and line up for a stern shot at the same time. That's all we've got left." He turned to Lien. "Mark your head every ten degrees."

"Now passing two-nine-zero," Lien said.

"Enemy submarine close aboard," the sonarman shouted in Mandarin. "Torpedo in the water! Torpedo in the water!"

"Flood tubes seven and eight," Matt said. "Open outer doors on seven and eight. What's our heading?"

"Now passing three-zero-zero."

"Turn, you son of a bitch, turn."

"Passing three-one-zero," Lien said.

"Mark range to the Romeo," Matt said.

"Five hundred meters."

"Helm, mark your head."

"Heading, three-one-five."

Now. "Fire seven! Fire eight!"

He felt two thumps, the welcome sound of torpedoes leaving the boat. "All hands forward. Close outer doors on seven and eight. Close all watertight doors aft."

"Both units running hot, straight, and normal," the sonarman said.

Matt held his breath and waited. A torpedo fired by your own boat was called a unit and an incoming was simply called a torpedo. He heard one of the torpedoes scrape along the hull of the sub, just above the ballast tanks on the starboard side. From the sonar speaker, he heard the other one go churning by on the port side, a clean miss.

"I think they both missed," the sonarman said.

In the distance, Matt heard the sound of an explosion.

"The sub is breaking up," the sonarman shouted. He turned the speaker volume up so they could all hear. "You can hear the bulkheads collapsing."

A cheer went up in the control room.

"Ten-degree rise on the planes," Matt said. "Make preparations for periscope depth. We'll take her up and look for survivors."

The cheer died in the sonarman's throat.

"Torpedo in the water! Torpedo in the water! They must have got two more off before they were hit!"

God help us all. There was nothing he could do but hold his course and pray. "Steady on course three-one-five."

He heard the screws of the first torpedo churn by the port side of the sub and trail off into the distance, another miss. He held his breath, listening to the screws of the second torpedo growing louder. Seconds ticked by.

A violent explosion slammed him to the deck.

"Blow all tanks! Emergency surface!"

The crew aft came scrambling forward. The last man into the control room slammed the watertight door that separated it from the engine room and dogged it closed.

"The after battery room is flooding," young Wen said in Mandarin.

Matt looked at them. Wen, Wu, and three crewmen he'd never seen before.

"Charlie. Where's Charlie?"

He peered through the eyeport to the engine room and saw Charlie on one knee, struggling to close the watertight door that separated the after battery room from the engine room. His right leg seemed to be injured. Seawater swirled around him. Diesel fuel from a broken line streamed out onto a motor-generator set. Praying that it wouldn't ignite, Matt undogged the door and started through the engine room. The bow tilted sharply upward, sending him skidding aft. The sub was sliding backward, sinking by the stern. The weight of the water in the after battery room was overwhelming the electric motors, pulling the boat down.

Matt closed the watertight door and dogged it tight. He threw Charlie up on his back, the pain in his side blinding him, and slogged forward through the engine room, now at a twenty-degree up angle.

An electrical control panel exploded, shooting sparks. The fuel from the broken line erupted into a fireball. Looking through the flames, the faces that haunted him danced before his eyes. His little brother, the man who'd died on the sub. *Not this time, by God. Not this time.*

He picked up a fire extinguisher and blasted his way into the

314

flames, his mind terrorized. His shirt ignited, then his hair. He could feel the skin on his hands melt. The pain seared into his brain. He stumbled through the door into the control room and dropped Charlie on the deck. Beth and Sam started beating the fire on his clothes and hair out with their bare hands.

He turned and tried to pull the door closed behind him, but the angle of the sub was now so steep he couldn't budge it. He felt Sam behind him, trying to help, but there wasn't enough room for two people to get a grip on it. If he let go, the door would swing so far open they'd never get it shut. First the fire, then the water would spread. Summoning strength he didn't know he had, he pulled the door into place and held it while Sam dogged it.

He dropped to his knees on the deck of the control room, grimacing from the pain. The stern of the sub eased into the soft floor of the ocean. The bow settled down and the sub came to rest on her keel, slanted upward a few degrees. The emergency lights came on, flickered, and went out. A battle lantern near the control panel came on with a yellow glow. He crawled to it and pulled it from its bracket. He shined it on the depth gauge. Forty meters. More than 130 feet down.

No one spoke. The only sound was the creaking of the sub, shifting its weight, settling. The sub groaned and shifted a few degrees to starboard.

He crawled back to the bulkhead and leaned against it. He looked at the backs of his hands. Blisters were starting to form. He could feel the heat from the fire through the bulkhead behind him. The water would put it out as the sub settled. *The water*. The cold nausea of claustrophobia gripped him. How many tons of water above him? Around him? *Don't think about it*. In the sweat of the control room, he could smell the stench of his own fear. Sam, Beth, and Charlie were staring at him, waiting to see what he'd do. He wasn't afraid of dying— right now he'd welcome it. He was afraid of how he'd die. He didn't want to die a raving lunatic, held down by Sam, staring up with screaming eyes. *Get a grip*. He'd gotten through the fire. He could get through this, too. He bit the inside of his cheek until he tasted blood. *Don't think about where you are. Concentrate on getting out. One step at a time.* He ran his tongue over dry lips.

"Everybody sit down," he said, his voice trembling. "Distribute the weight evenly. Don't move around any more than is necessary. At this depth we must have settled on a shelf. We don't want to jar this thing loose."

"You mean it's deeper than this?" Beth said.

Matt didn't want to think about it. He'd looked at the charts earlier. There were some holes in the area that went down for miles. He couldn't *let* himself think about it. If they were on a shelf, and they stayed on it, and he could pull himself together, they might have a chance.

"Let's not talk any more than we need to," he said. "Every breath we take we breathe out carbon dioxide. Lien, do you have any CO_2 absorbent aboard? Any soda-lime?"

"About a half-dozen cans."

"Move easy, but set out a couple. It'll help keep the air clean for a while."

"Why bother?" Beth said. "We're not going anywhere. We might as well get up and dance, have a party."

"Listen to the skipper, miss," Sam said. "He knows what he's doing."

"Is the escape trunk in the forward torpedo room operable?" Matt asked.

Lien nodded in the dim light. "Yes. We've done drills with it."

"Sam, very gently go forward and find it. See if you can release the emergency buoy. There should be a lever in the overhead."

"Aye, Skipper."

Matt heard several bangs on the hull, followed by the screech of a cable unwinding from a steel spool as the buoy rose to the surface.

"That's the sweetest sound you'll ever hear." He turned to Lien. "Any Steinke hoods aboard?"

"I don't understand."

"Combination breathing apparatus and life jacket. Upgraded version of the old Momsen lung. Any Chinese version of that?"

"Sadly, no."

"If you're thinking what I think you're thinking, you can forget it," Beth said. "There's no way we can do that."

"Sure we can."

"How? You just heard the man. He doesn't have any of those hoods."

"It doesn't matter," Matt said.

Sam tiptoed back into the control room. "It might work, Skipper. I got the buoy off. The trunk's old and rusted and painted over, but it might work. There's a couple life rafts the first two out can send up."

"What do you mean it doesn't matter?" Beth said.

"At this depth we don't need them. We'll do a free ascent."

"Are you crazy? Nobody can hold their breath for that long. You've got to have some kind of breathing apparatus."

"That was the conventional wisdom for decades," Matt said. "Just before World War Two, a naval officer named Swede Momsen developed a device called the Momsen lung. He also developed the first submarine rescue bell. Used it to get every surviving sailor out of *Squalus* alive. He was a real hero, his rescue bell saved a lot of lives, but the sad truth was those lungs of his killed more people than they saved. They made people think it wasn't possible to get out on their own. After the war they looked at the numbers. Of all the subs that went down, the Momsen lung was credited with saving only five of the men who were still alive. That's when they scrapped it and started to teach the free ascent method."

"How can—"

"Sam's locked out and done it a hundred times. Tell her, Sam."

"Skipper's telling you straight, miss. What you do, you fill your lungs with air, let yourself go, and exhale on the way up. What happens is, the air in your lungs expands as the pressure around you decreases. So you never run out of air. You don't have to adjust to high pressure and you don't have to worry about getting the bends. Works great down to about three hundred feet or so."

"Throughout history, the conventional wisdom has almost always been wrong," Matt said. "The best technology is sometimes no technology. But that doesn't mean it's without risk. You've got to know

317

what you're doing. There was a Peruvian diesel boat called the *Pacocha*, it was a former American sub, sank a few years ago in water about as deep as this. There were twenty-two men trapped aboard. They used free ascent and they all got out."

"Alive?"

"Well, no," Matt said. "Two of them died on the way up and the other twenty had decompression problems. But they obviously hadn't been trained in the method."

"Neither have these guys," Beth said with a wave toward the Chinese sailors. "Neither have I."

"That's about to change. All right, listen up. Sam's going to tell us how to make a free ascent through the forward escape trunk. Lien, I want you to translate and tell your men exactly what he says."

"Yes, sir."

"It ain't complicated," Sam said, "but there's certain things you gotta do. The main thing is, you got to *slowly* let air out of your mouth as you go up. That's important. If you keep your mouth closed, you'll rise too fast and get the bends, or if you panic and really hold your breath, your lungs could burst or you could shoot up out of the water like a rocket."

"Good God," Beth said.

"But the other side is, if you let the air out too fast, you'll stop rising and sink back to a level where the pressure in your lungs is the same as the water pressure. And that's where you'll stop. If that happens, don't panic. Here's what you do. Just pull yourself up the buoy cable until the water pressure decreases and then you'll start to rise again. So the trick is, let it out slow and steady. If you do that, you should have a smooth ride up to the surface."

"Any questions?" Matt said.

Silence.

"Okay, Sam. Let's get started. Start sending them up by two's."

Sam pointed to the two Chinese sailors who looked the youngest and motioned them forward. Everybody else stayed put. The sub shifted a few more degrees to starboard. In the deep silence, Matt heard the clank of the inner hatch, then the flooding of the trunk with seawater. He heard the outer hatch open and the life rafts being shoved out, followed by the two sailors. The trunk was drained and the process repeated until the Chinese crew was out of the boat.

"Okay, Skipper," Sam said, coming back into the control room. "Everybody's out. Why don't you and the young lady go next? Charlie and me can go last."

"I can't do it," Beth said.

"Sure you can," Matt said.

"I didn't have a normal childhood. I studied all the time. I never learned how to swim."

"You don't need to swim," Matt said. "All you're doing is floating to the top."

"You go. I can't do it."

"Sam, you and Charlie go next," Matt said. "We'll bring up the rear."

Sam hesitated. "You're coming, ain't you, Skipper?"

"Of course."

"That shelf we're sitting on," Sam said. "It ain't gonna hold forever."

"We'll be right behind you." Matt stood up, pulled Beth to her feet, and followed Sam and Charlie into the forward torpedo room. Beth watched Sam pull Charlie up the ladder inside the escape trunk and close the bottom hatch. She stared at Matt as the sound of rushing water filled the compartment. When Matt heard the outer hatch close, he opened the drain valve. He motioned with his head. "Come on. Why should they have all the fun?"

"I can't. I just can't."

"Sure you can."

"You go without me."

"Beth, if you don't go, I don't go. And if we don't go, the world's going to miss out on some great kids."

Beth stared at him. "Do you mean. . .?"

"We belong together, for Christ's sake, even the old Chinese housekeeper saw that. Now come on."

Beth let out a sigh. "That's an offer I can't refuse."

Matt helped her up into the escape trunk. He felt the sub groan and shift to starboard again, this time about ten degrees. They had to get out of the trunk while it was reasonably level or not at all. Ignoring the pain in his side, he stood at an angle astride the lower hatch and dogged it tight.

"Okay, this is an air bubble flange. All you have to do is stand under it while I flood the compartment." He reached for the flood valve, then said, "It shouldn't be too cold. We're not that deep and we're on the equator." He opened the valve and stood with her under the flange while seawater poured in. He watched the gauge, waiting for the pressure in the trunk to equalize with the pressure outside. In less than a minute, the water was up to Beth's neck. She looked too frightened to speak. He gave her his best, most reassuring smile.

"Okay, take a really deep breath. Here we go."

He opened the outer hatch, took Beth by the waist, and swam her through the opening, up toward the light. As soon as his feet cleared the hatch, the sub rolled to starboard and drifted from sight in a cloud of silt and bubbles. Matt heard the screech of the buoy cable unwinding as the sub drifted lower. When the cable ran out, the sub would pull the buoy down with it if she were still falling. Matt felt a huge relief to be out of the sub, but now they were really in danger. They had to get up quickly.

He put Beth's hands around the buoy cable and motioned her up. Facing her on the other side of the cable, he rose with her in the dim light, hoping she could see the amount of air he was exhaling as a guide. A stream of tiny bubbles emitted from her mouth. She seemed to be picking up on it. They rose together, the cable steady in his hands. Each length of his body was about six feet. He'd climbed what he estimated to be about sixty feet when he felt the cable begin to slip through his hands. The sub was still falling and the cable had run out.

Looking up, he saw the yellow buoy coming down at them. He looped his arm around Beth's waist and tried to pull her away from the cable. He felt a thump and saw a blur of orange go by, knocking Beth from his arms. She went limp and began to fall, bubbles pouring from her mouth, drifting down into the abyss. Matt dived after her and caught her by the hair, the pain in his side excruciating. He put his mouth over hers to stop the air flow from her lungs. Holding her in one arm, he kicked up and they began to rise again. He could feel her lungs expand as they rose. He took his mouth from hers for an instant, allowing her to release some air.

They rose toward the light, repeating the process. Just as Sam had said, the higher they rose the more the water pressure decreased, and the more the air in their lungs expanded. With no cable to measure his progress, he wasn't sure how much further they had to go. He looked up and estimated another seventy or eighty feet. He wasn't sure Beth could make it. A body appeared, suspended in the water like a huge sodden rag doll. Rising past it, he felt a stab of pain. It was young Wen, the first sailor they'd encountered on the sub. A large bubble emerged from his mouth and billowed upward, rising with them. He could see sunlight gleaming on the water and the dark shadows of the life rafts. Rising faster than they should, he broke the surface, gasping.

Holding Beth's head up, he blinked the water out of his eyes and started toward the nearest raft. Sam was in the bow, already paddling toward them. He reached down and pulled Beth up, then helped Matt onto the raft. Matt bent over Beth's motionless body, applying CPR. The Chinese sailors stared in silence.

Working over Beth, Matt saw the ocean in turmoil about three hundred yards off. He held his breath. The black sail of a submarine slowly broke the surface. *Anything but Chinese.* He saw the numbers 7-1-6 on the sail and choked back a sob. It was the *Salt Lake City*, a tiny little piece of America. He stared at it, unable to speak. His strategy had worked. The U.S. *had* come out for a look. As the hull rose out of the water, officers appeared on the bridge and sailors appeared on deck with lines to throw.

Despite the pain in his ribcage, Matt kept up a constant rhythm. "Come on, baby, come on. We're almost there."

He felt a line come across the raft, felt it go taut, hands pulling them toward safety. As the raft drew closer to the black hull of the sub, Sam placed a broad hand on Matt's shoulder, his old friend unable to say what was obvious.

"No." Matt kept up a constant rhythm. "We're not leaving her. I promised I'd bring her back."

The Chinese sailors scrambled aboard the sub. Charlie and Sam stayed with Matt. Sailors from the sub looked solemnly down from the deck above. Sam was looking at him with moist eyes.

"Come on, Skipper. We gotta go."

"I can't leave her, Sam. I can't."

Matt heard a gurgling sound. A little geyser of seawater erupted from Beth's mouth. She rolled to one side, coughing up more water. She opened her eyes and blinked at Matt. She stared at him for what seemed like a full minute without speaking.

"Are we there yet?"

Matt pulled her to him, tears running down his face. He turned her to face the cheering American sailors on the deck of the sub. Holding her too tightly, he pressed his mouth to her ear.

"We are now," he said in a choked whisper. "We're home."

Chapter Twenty-One

"**M**orning, sir," a seaman who looked too young to be away from home said, peering into the wardroom. "We're approaching the outer islands. Captain would like to know if you'd like to join him on the bridge."

Matt had thought he'd sit this one out. Coming home from the sea was usually a joyful occasion, but seeing Kaohsiung would be bittersweet—there was nothing for him to come home to. Still, it was nice of the captain to offer. He nodded.

"Tell him thanks, I'll be right up."

He drank off his coffee and, clutching his taped-up rib cage, squirmed out from behind the table. Walking forward, he could feel the excitement in the boat. The crew seemed animated, everyone talking, making plans. They'd gone out and come back—alive. He remembered the feeling.

He climbed the ladder to the bridge, wincing at the pain in his side. The chief corpsman had diagnosed him with two broken ribs and had taped him up so tightly he could barely breathe. With the burns on his hands bandaged, he felt like a mummy. Being so constricted would have bothered him before, but after his near-death experience on the Romeo, and almost a week of running submerged on the *Salt Lake City*, his claustrophobia had simply disappeared.

"Morning, Captain," he said, blinking into the sun.

"Hey, Matt. How do you feel, buddy?"

"Healing fast." He started to say, "I'd forgotten how good the chow was on these boats," and thought about poor Francisco.

"Kaohsiung will close the loop for us—this is where we came in, but I thought you might like to see the entrance to the harbor from the sea again."

There was no more beautiful sight than coming into port. The sad part was he'd be seeing a stretch of empty dock when he got there.

"I appreciate that."

The captain looked at him and shook his head, his eyes sympathetic. "I can't imagine losing my whole ship and crew. I just can't fathom what that would feel like."

They cruised in silence through the Taiwan Strait. Rounding the northern tip of Chichin Island, the sub eased into Hsitzu Bay, the narrow channel that separates the smaller island from the island of Taiwan. Gradually, the docks of Kaohsiung came into view. A motley array of ships sat lazily in a row, groaning against their lines.

Matt looked at everything except his old dock space. If he didn't see it, he couldn't feel the pain.

Closer, now, he took a grudging glance. There was already a ship moored to it. Bastards hadn't wasted any time filling it up.

Lucky them. The ship was about the same length and displacement as *CoMar Explorer*. Hell, it even had the same lines. He followed the lines from the bow to the stern. He blinked and rubbed his eyes. Without asking permission, he grabbed the captain's binoculars and focused on a damaged area on the port side, near the stern.

My God.

Matt stood on the dock, looking up at the bow of *CoMar Explorer*. Even with rust stains running down her sides and a slight list to port, she was the most beautiful sight he'd ever seen. How in God's name did they . . . ?

"I still can't believe what I'm seeing," Beth said.

"I told you there were some good men there," Sam said.

"Hey!" someone shouted from the main deck. "It's Matt!"

Gene Harvey leaned over the rail. "Skipper! . . . Sam. Where the hell you guys been?"

Matt sprinted up the accommodation ladder and found himself mobbed by his crew. He stood on the quarterdeck grinning like a fool, trying to shake hands with his bandaged mitts, barely able to speak.

"I couldn't believe what I was seeing when we pulled in," he said. "How did you do it?"

"It wasn't by-God easy," Scootchy Carter said.

"Thank God for Scootchy's rat teeth," Doc Miller said. "He gnawed right through that duct tape. Damn near chewed my wrist off."

Scootchy said, "Time we got those seacocks shut, flooding was so bad the pumps were barely able to keep up with it. Like to never got here."

"Yeah," Gene Harvey said. "Thought we'd never see Kaohsiung again."

Matt felt something brush against his ankle. He looked down at a small yellow dog squirming around his feet.

"I find on dock," Francisco said. "We call him Traveller Two, okay Boss-man?"

People were always discarding puppies on the dock. Matt grinned at the little mongrel as it scampered away, and nodded.

"Gray Wolf been around?"

"No have to worry about Gray Wolf," Francisco said. "We got job."

"Yeah," Scootchy said. "That towing bid you submitted a month ago came through."

It was a towing contract with a major offshore drilling company with operations off southern California. It would keep Connor Marine afloat for a while, hopefully long enough to snag a contract that would pay off his debt to Gray Wolf.

"Are we ready to go to sea?"

"We will be in a week," Scootchy said.

"Good," Matt said. "We'll shift our home port to San Diego." He nodded to Sam. "Take her over when she's ready."

"Sure, Skipper. Where you going?"

Matt looked at Beth. "I'm taking Beth home, like I promised. Then I'm going to get that tax lien off the ship. We're going home, boys."

The black SUV with government license plates turned onto West Executive Avenue, then made a hard right into a short drive that led to a guard shack. The entrance to the basement level of the White House was directly ahead, under a canopy. The guard checked the driver's ID, ran his finger down a clipboard, smiled into the back seat, and waved them through.

Matt unbuckled his seat belt and glanced at Beth. "I still don't get this."

She shrugged. "It's no big deal. You've been invited to meet the president, that's all."

"You mean we've been invited."

"No, no. I've known him forever, he was at our house talking to my father before he even ran for president. It's you he wants to meet."

"Why?"

"Well, gee, let me think. You've just averted a major economic catastrophe for the U.S., not to mention a war. Maybe he'd like to say thanks."

Matt glanced down at the new black shoes, white shirt, silk maroon tie, and navy blue suit.

"I feel like an idiot in this getup."

"You look very handsome."

He took her hand and helped her out. In a simple black dress with a short string of pearls and matching earrings, she was a head-turner. Her hair was still short, but it looked glorious. And even if it hadn't, no one would get past those beautiful brown eyes long enough to notice. They'd avoided discussing Matt's last-ditch proposal on the sub, but there seemed to be an unspoken agreement between the two of them to see where it would lead. Matt had ordered *CoMar Explorer*'s home port moved back to San Diego, and Beth had applied for a teaching job at U.C.S.D. With her credentials, Matt was sure she'd get it.

"All right, let's get this over with."

A familiar-looking man in a dark business suit started toward them.

"Beth. How nice to see you again. It's been a long time."

"Hello, John. It has indeed." Beth waved her hand toward Matt. "John, I'd like you to meet Matt Connor. Matt, this is John Bolling, White House chief of staff."

Matt recognized him from the Sunday talk shows, a short, plump man with a florid face who'd once been governor of Colorado. Alexander Forrest had needed a man with Bolling's toughness to help clean up the mess in the White House the previous administration had made. Matt shook hands, surprised that the president's right-hand man would personally come out to greet them.

"It's an honor to meet you."

"The honor's mine—we've been hearing a lot about you lately."

A Secret Service agent wearing a flesh-toned earpiece and a loose-fitting coat handed Matt and Beth passes, then motioned them through a metal detector. Matt followed Beth through without incident and wondered about the pistol that had saved his neck so many times. Where was it now? He'd turned it over to the captain of the *Salt Lake City* right after they'd been fished out of the water off Sumatra.

With Beth trailing behind, looking at the artwork, the chief of staff steered Matt toward the southeast corner of the West Wing, pointing out bits of history along the way. He opened a door directly opposite the Roosevelt Room and ushered them into the Oval Office. Like most Americans, Matt had seen a hundred pictures of the room, but nothing prepared him for this. Sitting behind the desk with a phone to his ear was the president of the United States.

Alexander Forrest shifted the phone to his other side and waved them in with one hand while making notes on a legal pad. Everyone, from the president on down, was dressed appropriately. The women staffers he'd seen on the way in all looked professional, and the men wore coats and ties, even in Washington's summer heat. The blue jeans and pizza crowd had gone out with the previous administration. He was glad he'd let Beth talk him into some new clothes. He stood quietly before the fabled desk made of wood salvaged from HMS *Resolute*, as awed as a child seeing the inside of a cathedral for the first time.

The room wasn't as big as he'd thought it would be. The opaque windows behind the president's chair gave a surreal edge to the White House lawn he could see through them. Probably bullet-resistant. The president's desk looked clean. A few file folders, a schedule of the day's appointments, an intercom, and an ordinary-looking telephone that Matt assumed was anything but ordinary. The president finished his call, dropped the handset into the cradle, and smiled.

"Well," he said, looking back and forth at them. "You two have been busy." He came around the desk and extended his hand. "You must be Matt Connor."

The president was sixty but could pass for someone at least ten years younger. His handshake felt firm, dry, and callused. The hype about him chopping his own firewood and clearing brush on his Colorado ranch might be true. Matt hardly knew what to say.

"Yes, sir," he managed.

"Beth." President Forrest gave her a peck on the cheek. He took both her hands in his and held her at arms length, gazing at her with obvious affection. "You had us pretty worried."

"Sorry to be so much trouble, Mr. President, but I appreciate your looking out for me."

"It seems we picked the right man for the job," President Forrest said, smiling at her, nodding at Matt.

Beth smiled back. "I'd have to agree with that."

"John, I expect you have some preparations to attend to. We'll be along shortly."

Matt hoped that was a royal "we." He wanted to get this over with as quickly as possible with as little ceremony as possible. In the short time he'd been a guest of the Graysons, he'd been exposed to enough Washington-type socializing to know he wasn't good at it.

"Yes, sir," John Bolling said. He nodded to Matt and Beth and eased out of the room.

"Please," the president said. He waved them toward a pale yellow couch upholstered in silk brocade. "We have a few minutes."

There was that "we" again. A few minutes before what? He glanced at Beth. They were both acting as if they knew something he didn't. He and Beth took a seat on the couch, and the president pulled up a chair opposite.

"Matt, Admiral Jacobs has filled me in on everything you did. I don't have to tell you what it means. We had no idea that the capability you destroyed existed, and even if we had, I'm not sure we could have stopped it without causing a war. Thanks to you, its use was prevented, and thanks to Beth, we now know how to counter it in the future. What you did should be on the front page of every newspaper in America, but for obvious reasons, it'll have to be kept quiet."

"That's not a problem for me, Mr. President."

"I didn't think it would be, after talking with Admiral Jacobs and Senator Grayson. They're both people whose opinions I respect, and they're both very high on you."

"That's good to hear, sir."

The president looked at him for a long minute.

"Admiral Jacobs tells me you'd like to have your Navy commission restored."

"I appreciate the thought, Mr. President, but I've been out of the Navy for so long I wouldn't be qualified for much of anything."

"I understand that you'd no longer be qualified to go back on submarine service, but Admiral Jacobs thought you might be the perfect candidate for a Navy intel job we have in mind, for someone whose work takes him all over the world. Someone we could call on from time to time for special assignments."

"You mean a spy, sir?"

The president paused, but only for a couple of seconds. "We think of it as more of a troubleshooting job. The way you handled this one, I think you'd be perfect for it. You'd be a commander in the naval reserve, activated when needed. Would you take the job as a personal favor to me?"

An involuntary grin spread across Matt's face. He glanced at Beth, who was smiling at him.

"I'd be honored to do what I can, sir."

President Forrest slapped his hands on his knees. "Good." He walked around to his desk, opened one of the folders, and signed his name with a flourish. "I've dated your commission effective today." He handed the document to Matt. "Congratulations, Commander."

"Thank you, sir."

The president looked at his watch. "And now we have something to attend to."

He ushered them out the door and into the Roosevelt Room across the hall. Beth seemed to have some idea of what was going on, but she wouldn't look at him.

A small group of people turned toward them and began to applaud. Matt assumed they were applauding the president. He turned to join in and was startled to see President Forrest facing him and applauding along with the others. Matt looked at the people, astonished. They were applauding him. He blinked and the faces came into focus. Admiral Jacobs and his wife, Beth's mother and father, Charlie Shen, Cliff Howard, Susan Elliott, and a half-dozen people he'd never seen before.

President Forrest held up his hands. "Thank you very much for coming. It's a pleasure to welcome you all to the White House.

"As president I've handed out lots of medals and awards, but it's a curious fact that the most significant achievements can never be recognized publicly.

"We're here to celebrate one of those achievements.

"Everyone in this room has played a role in it, and because it can never be made public, I thought it was important to get us all together so that I can thank each and every one of you personally. Thank you. This was a big one.

"But the person we all have to thank is the man whose boots were on the ground, the one who made it happen. I've anguished over a way to thank him, but I don't know how.

"If he'd been in the military, he'd be a candidate for the Congressional Medal of Honor. But he wasn't. He was a civilian. A lone American with a few stalwart companions, struggling to do the right thing against overwhelming odds."

Turning, he said, "I can't give you or your companions any medals, Matt, but as the elected leader of the people of America, what I can give you is the sincere thanks of a grateful nation." He extended his hand.

Matt took the president's hand numbly. The room erupted in applause. He vaguely heard the president say something about thanks for coming and enjoy the reception before he walked away, leaving him standing there. Beth took his arm and smiled at him as Admiral Jacobs approached.

"Why didn't you tell me?" he said out of the corner of his mouth.

"Because you wouldn't have come." She squeezed his arm and walked over to say hello to her parents.

Admiral Jacobs held out a naval officer's sword. "I had a hell of a time getting this thing past security."

Matt grinned at him. "What's this?"

"I hear you lost yours."

Matt pulled the sword out a few inches. "Onward and Upward" was engraved on the blade. He looked at Jake.

"How did you know?"

"Sam told me."

"Thank you." Matt looked down on the sword, sorry his father hadn't lived to see this moment. "Now what's this I hear about an intelligence job?"

"We'll call on you from time to time to do a little troubleshooting. The president thinks you're good at it."

"Come on, Jake. That whole thing was a fluke."

"Try convincing POTUS of that. He thinks you walk on water. Do a couple more assignments for him, the sky's the limit. You'll probably end up as SECNAV, like James Webb."

"Sure."

"No, it's true. You know what they say about cream. By the way, Barbara says to say hello and to wish you the best."

"How is she?"

"Married again. Some three-striper jet jockey she latched onto. The truth is, she's miserable. Wishes now she'd stuck with you."

"That sounds like Barb."

Admiral Jacobs laughed. "It sure as hell as does. Another by-the-way. I've been dying to ask you, who gave you that gun you turned over to the sub driver? The one that's supposed to not be picked up by a metal detector?"

"Gray Wolf."

"Who?"

"Another wise old man, like you. I didn't want the bloody thing at first, but without it, we wouldn't be standing here today. What about it?"

"He *must* be a wise old man."

"Why?"

"The sub commander sent the gun to CINCPAC with a note saying it couldn't be picked up by a metal detector. CINCPAC got nervous about it and sent it to the FBI lab here in Washington. The FBI folks got real nervous until they tested it. They copied me on the report—the gun's worthless. There's no such thing as a weapon that can't be detected and can still shoot. Those cartridges won't show up, but they also can't be fired. He might as well have given you a toy gun."

Matt said, "You're kidding me," but knew he wasn't.

Admiral Jacobs chuckled. "He knew you'd be getting into some tight spots. What he gave you was the confidence that you'd always have a way out." He shook his head. "A magic weapon."

"That son of a—"

"Don't be too hard on him. It worked. The Xinhua news agency just put out a press release about the malfunction and destruction of a sea launch of a Chinese communications satellite. Happened on June twenty-first. The launch platform and the command ship were so badly damaged in the explosion and fire that followed they had to be sunk. No mention of any other damage, but intel reports that a Chinese Luda III-class destroyer and two Romeo-class diesel subs have mysteriously dropped off the radar screen."

"Any word on the destroyer captain?" Matt asked.

"None that I've heard," Admiral Jacobs said. "Why?"

"It's a long story I'll tell you over a beer sometime."

"She might know," Jake said, nodding to Susan Elliott, who came walking up. "Matt wants to know what happened to the skipper of that destroyer that went down."

"Captain Chen?"

"That's him."

She nodded. "Naval Academy grad. We've watched his career for years. He survived the sinking, but got booted out of the PLA Navy for losing his ship."

"Bad luck," Matt said.

"Even worse luck for some people in the party," Susan Elliott said. "We just got a report that General First Class Lao Jianxing has been purged from the CCP. His son, Senior Colonel James Lao, was summarily executed for embezzling what was described as a 'large' amount of company funds to cover his 'gambling losses' in the U.S. stock market. Cold. The PLA sent the old man a bill for six cents for the bullet they used to execute his son."

Matt thought it couldn't happen to nicer guys, but said nothing. He was grateful that Beth was out of earshot. She'd have to know, but Matt thought he could tell her a little more gently than that.

"Well, we've got to be going." Admiral Jacobs extended his hand. "Welcome back, buddy."

Matt took his hand and looked into his mottled face. "Thanks, Jake," was all he could manage to say.

"Don't worry. You'll earn your money."

Beth and her father came over. Senator Grayson held out his hand. "Congratulations, Matt."

"Thank you, sir."

"I just wanted to let you know, I got a call back from the IRS commissioner. He's confirmed that the tax lien on your ship has been removed."

"Thanks for following up," Matt said. "That closes the loop."

"Not quite. There's still the little matter of a reward."

Beth stood watching him with an amused expression. Her whole family had been hammering on him about the damned thing since he'd been back. He glanced at her and smiled.

"I told you, this one's on the house."

"Oh, go on, take it, junkman. Five mil is pocket change for him."

"No, thanks."

"Look, you don't know the senator. It's a point of honor. If he doesn't give it to you, he'll have to give it to someone else, some flaky charity or something."

Matt could see that the Grayson family was going to be unyielding. He'd written Sarah Tyler a letter expressing his condolences over Jason's death, but words alone would be cold comfort.

"All right." He scribbled Sarah's name and address on a slip of paper and handed it to Beth's father. "If you're determined to give it away, send a million of it to this lady. Jason Tyler's widow."

"Shall I tell her who it's from?"

"Tell her it's from the crew of *CoMar Explorer*."

"That leaves four million dollars."

"Okay." Matt wrote out another name and address. "Send it to this man. It'll keep a ship running that employs some good men."

"Gray Wolf?"

Matt smiled. "That's not his real name, but he'll get it, I assure you."

"Any message?"

Matt hesitated, then said, "Tell him he was right. I was wrong."

"About?"

"The Gray Wolf theory of preemption."

Senator Grayson made a note and shrugged. "If you say so. Anything else?"

Matt paused. There was a lot he wanted to say to Gray Wolf. He didn't know whether to thank him or curse him for giving him the loan, the Chinese lessons, the Stinger missiles, and the gun that wouldn't shoot, but he knew what he did have to thank him for. He looked at Beth. Standing in the azure light of the Roosevelt Room, she looked as fresh and new as a spring morning. The whole world felt new, the way it had the day he'd graduated from Annapolis. Gray Wolf hadn't intended it, but the old man had given him another chance at a life he'd thought was over, and a partner he thought he'd never find. He looked into Beth's eyes and smiled.

"Just tell him thanks," Matt said. "Thanks for everything."

Maurice Medland is the bestselling author of Point of Honor. *A graduate of Truman State University, he served in the U.S. Navy before entering a career in business. A former vice-president of a Fortune 500 company, he holds an Executive MBA from Pepperdine University. He is a member of International Thriller Writers and The Authors Guild, and has taught creative writing at The University of California, Irvine. He lives with his wife, Karen, in Southern California.*

Also by Maurice Medland

Point of Honor

www.mauricemedland.com

www.ingramcontent.com/pod-product-compliance
Lightning Source LLC
Chambersburg PA
CBHW020424030726
47495CB00006B/1650